CW01635268

Quiet World

Alan Michael Butler

Garabrecan Books

Cover by Creative Covers

For Naida, with whom anything is possible

Acknowledgements

With thanks to the team of helpers, voluntary and involuntary, that guided me on this endeavour, with especial gratitude for Barry and Sophie, my editors.

Contents

Part One
Empty Road

Chapter One

Quiet Dawn

Monday 29th April 1991

Adam was hot and felt exhausted, like he had been crushed under a heap of sand and was fighting his way to the surface. The light was coming in through the bedroom curtains, but he had no idea what time it was, had no idea what time he had finally collapsed into oblivion and no idea how long he had been asleep. He turned to look at the bedside clock but then it came back to him that he was in the small bedroom and there was no clock. He pushed off the duvet and rolled onto his back. He stared at the ceiling in the half-light, letting the cool air bring his heat down, slow his racing heart. It was very quiet in the house, no sound at all. But slowly he became aware of sounds outside – birds in the cherry tree at the front, a pigeon cooing repetitively across the road, a dog barking somewhere in the distance. It all sounded normal, like early on a summer Sunday morning when everyone is sleeping and all is right with the world.

But it wasn't Sunday morning, it was Monday! The world was too quiet; the heating pipes weren't rattling and gurgling;

Oscar wasn't playing with his cars on his bedroom carpet, there were no happy giggles coming from Sophie in her room; Jo wasn't softly breathing beside him lost in sleep. Jo was in their bed, in their bedroom and Jo was not breathing at all. No there was nothing normal about this, there never would be.

He lay there for a while, trying to summon the courage to get up and face the day. He really did not want to leave the room. If he could just burrow down under the covers, back through his dream, go down deep into the world of sleep and not return, or at least not to this world.

He got out of bed too quickly and cramp seized his left calf. He swore and stretched his leg out against the wall until it eased. The room was cold and though he had gone to bed fully clothed, he must have taken his sweatshirt off in the night and now he scrabbled around on the floor looking for it. He opened the door and went out onto the landing. It was dark – all the bedroom doors were closed. He hurried down the stairs and into the kitchen. Bright morning sunshine flooded in through the blinds and he could see through the patio doors that the little terrace was already bathed in sunlight. He threw open the door, hesitating just for a second before stepping onto the paving outside. The air was fresh, cool but promising warmth later; the sunlight coming through the blossom on the large apple tree was dancing as the branches moved in the slightest of breezes. A blackbird hopped across the lawn, a small bird flashed across the garden onto the seed dispenser, a fat, bedraggled pigeon sat on the fence looking at him. Everywhere there was birdsong but there was nothing else – no cars starting, no bins being put out, no doors slamming, no traffic, no lorries rattling down the main road, no trains rumbling in the distance, no planes. How could these birds just carry on like that? How could they? Didn't they know?!

Adam slumped onto one of the metal patio chairs and sat gazing at the profusion of pinky-white blossom on the apple tree half-way down the garden, and said to himself: "That's where you have to put them." It was obvious really, it was her favourite tree. It clinched the deal on the house. When they came to view three years ago it was early autumn and Jo spotted the tree when they first were shown into the back garden.

"We had an apple tree like that when I was a kid," she said. "It was a bit bigger than that, just small enough for me to get up into and big enough for me to sit in. I can just see Oscar sitting in it now. Adam, this is the house, it's got to be."

He remembered he had muttered something about who was going to pick up all the apples, but Jo had chosen to ignore that. They bought the house – it took an age to go through and they were up against someone else, but Jo was adamant: this was the house for them.

So here they were, three years later, in that house. Just a couple of weeks ago, sitting on these chairs on a Saturday morning in the early spring sunshine, drinking coffee and looking at the garden, Jo planning what she wanted to do with it, and what she wanted Adam to do for her. She had said, "See Adam, some of the buds are starting to open. I can't wait for the blossom to come."

For a brief moment that memory took him away from the now, but it was only a moment. And with that memory a sick feeling rose in his chest and the tears began to well in his eyes; he slumped forward in the chair as great sobs racked his body and he grabbed at his head, pulling at it as if to try and wrest control of this monstrous, nauseous horror that rose up inside him. He leapt up out of the chair waving his hands wildly and a scattering of birds rose from the trees. The cry burst out of him and became a roar

"Jesus! Why? How? Is this really happening? God! You bastard! How could you do this to me? How Could You?!? What am I going to do? What the fuck am I going to do?"

For several minutes he strode erratically around the garden, clutching his head. He wanted to lash out at someone, but there was no-one. He stopped to listen – had anyone heard him? Did anyone call out to see if he was alright, lean out of an upstairs window and tell him to "keep it down a bit!"? Did anyone laugh? Did anyone whisper? Did a door slam? No, there was no reaction, no response. He slumped into a chair and stared at the ground through his fingers, like a child not really wanting to see the monster in front of him and yet having to peep. This monster was formless, indefinable. I don't believe it. I *can't* believe it, he thought.

There was a bark from the next-door neighbour's dog. He must have heard Adam and was whining, somewhere in the house. It brought Adam back to the here and now. The world had stopped, but pets were still alive, yet, like him, were suddenly bereaved, abandoned in a limbo between the human and the natural worlds. Bonzo was a rescue dog, a terrier mongrel who was now very much a part of the neighbours' family. He would get under the fence and into their garden, which Oscar was very happy about indeed as he loved Bonzo. He had been locked up in that house for a day and a half at least and was probably very hungry and very distressed. Everyone loved Bonzo. If there was no-one left in the world at least there would be Bonzo.

Without thinking, Adam strode back into the house, slipped on his trainers and walked out of the front door. At the gate he paused and looked around the close – nothing had changed from yesterday, nothing had moved, the cars were still parked where they had been and everything was in its place. He walked up the path to number 29 and paused at the front door. He really did not want to see what might be inside. He stopped at the door, listening. He could just make out the soft whining of the dog somewhere in the back of the house. He wondered whether Mick might be lying there, or Sarah sitting slumped over the kitchen table. Or one of the grandchildren even?

He tried the handle, but the door was locked. He heard Bonzo give a questioning bark and then, after a pause, another one. Adam did not want to distress the dog further, so he retreated down the path. He stood by the gate and listened again to the strange quiet of this new world. He strained to listen for human sounds – a car engine, machinery whining, a distant train, voices

– there was nothing that emanated from anything made by the hand of man.

Just then the trees began rustling and as the branches of the magnolia tree at the front of number 25 began to sway, he heard his front door slam. He stood for a moment looking at the door, almost accusingly. He hadn't put it on the latch. The only option was to climb over the side gate. He had tried that once before, and it had ended badly. He looked around for something to climb up on but there was nothing at the front of the house. A dustbin? Theirs were behind the side gate. He decided to look for one down the street.

It was a curious experience walking down the close to Woodland Crescent. It was a quiet area at the best of times, so it was not that unusual not to meet anyone on the footpath in the middle of the morning, but this complete absence of people and sound was uncanny. It felt like he was walking through a deserted film set where all the cast and crew had taken the day off. He walked on until he got to Beech Avenue, the main road through the estate. The scene was exactly the same. The birds were singing in the trees, a blackbird flew low across the path in front of him, a tabby cat surveyed him from the front wall of a house. As he passed them, he looked at the houses to see if there was any sign of life. Many of the them had their curtains closed and in the others he could see no sign of any movement.

Adam had no idea what the time was. The sun was already quite high and it had some warmth in it, even though it was still April. He reckoned it must be about nine. Oscar would have been in school by now and Adam would have been in the office for half an hour already. Jo would have taken Sophie to nursery and be walking into her workplace. Children would have all been in school, workers in their offices, shops, factories, cafes or wherever. But they weren't, not one of them. No-one had gone anywhere at all.

He walked on down the avenue to the bottom where it met the main road. He stopped and looked to his right towards the town. Nothing was moving, but a hundred yards down the road he saw a car abandoned at an angle across the road. Further on there was a lorry and another car, stationary, just come to a stop. Adam wondered if the drivers were still inside but he didn't really want to find out. To the left the road was clear, not a vehicle in sight.

He turned round and made his way back up the avenue, checking the houses on the other side of the road, looking for any sign of life or activity, but there was none. Cars sat in the driveways, and on the street, doors and windows were mostly shut, some curtains were closed, others drawn back. Sometimes a cat would meow at him, sometimes he thought he could hear a dog, but other than that there was just the sound of the birds.

At the corner of Woodland Crescent there was a detached house in a large corner plot which he had never stopped to look at before. The garden was quite overgrown with trees and shrubs, and this, along with the lack of a driveway, its high hedge and the original thirties window casements, gave the house an old-fashioned look. He paused at the pedestrian gate to look up at the frontage when a sudden bark made him jump back. A Border Collie was coming down the path towards him, barking loudly. It stopped a yard or two from the gate and looked at Adam uncertainly. "It's ok," Adam said. "I'm not coming in." Surprised and curious, the dog cocked his head to one side, looked intently at Adam and gave a single bark.

"So, old chap, are you on your own too? What happened to your master then? Is he in there?" he said. The dog continued to look at him, remaining rooted to the spot. Adam looked over at the windows and noticed all the curtains were closed, as if the inhabitants were still asleep in bed. Perhaps they had pulled the curtains for the night and never got up again to open them. It must be the same scenario in so many of the houses he had passed. And yet their dog – if it was indeed their dog – was left outside? Maybe they had just left the door open for him... that was more likely. Maybe the dog lived outside in a kennel? He thought about going in to find out whether the door had been left open. The dog was watching him intently, perhaps to see whether he would take that very step.

Adam decided that he didn't really want to know, and he turned away along the pavement. As he did so the dog barked twice and looked at him intently. "Sorry boy" he said, "I've got to go. You'll just have to fend for yourself." He walked away and as he did so he could hear the dog running along with him on the other side of hedge, barking furiously. There was a second gate into the garden from the crescent, a double gate for a vehicle. The dog was waiting there for him, barking intently.

Adam stopped and looked at him and immediately the dog fell quiet.

"OK, I'll tell you what: I'll open the gate and then if you want to go exploring, you can." He lifted the latch and started to open the gate slowly. The dog looked at him uncertainly but did not bark. Adam held his hand out to him and slowly the dog came towards him, growling softly and looking at him intently. Hesitantly he sniffed his hand, moved his tail slowly in what Adam assumed was a wag of approval. Then he took a few steps towards the house, turned back to look at Adam and gave a bark. Adam felt he was being taken to the house. He took a step into the garden and paused. The dog waited for him, watching his every step. Adam walked over the hardstanding and the dog moved towards a side gate. Adam followed and the dog led him through the open gate down to a side-door. Adam stopped and the dog barked once and pawed at the door. Adam tried the handle – it was locked.

"Sorry pal, I can't let you in", and he turned away. The dog barked twice and ran around him and back to the door again. "Look, it's locked, there's nothing I can do about it." And to demonstrate the problem, Adam went back to the door, rattled the handle again and said, "OK?" The dog just barked.

Adam decided to have a look round the back of the house. The blind at what he assumed was the kitchen window was pulled down and the curtains drawn across the French doors which faced onto a small terrace. They were, unsurprisingly, locked as well. Adam pondered for a moment: Should he try and break a pane in the door and see if he could open latch so that the dog could go in and find his owners? Or should he just walk away and leave the dog there to bark, or to follow him home if he so wished? He turned to look at the dog, who was standing by the corner of the house, waiting to see what he would do.

He walked towards him and immediately the dog barked once and went to the back door again, waiting for him. Clearly this animal was not going to let Adam go if he could possibly stop him. "OK, have it your way", he said, and looked around for something to break the pane in one of the French doors. On the rockery he found a pointed stone, long enough to keep his hand clear of the breaking glass but compact enough to wield like a hammer. He took it to the door and smashed it hard into the small pane nearest the doorknob. The sound of the glass shattering seemed incredibly loud, and instinctively and guiltily he looked round to see if anyone had witnessed this act of vandalism. If only there was indeed someone there to see him, he thought. The dog just watched him.

He quickly had the door open and as he did so the dog ran in, scouted the room with his nose in the air, then disappeared through the open door to the hallway. Adam looked into the room which was now half-lit with the light from the open door and he cast his eyes around to see if there was any sign of life, or of life that had recently expired. With relief he saw that the room was empty. He heard a bark from upstairs and then a whine that continued, first questioningly and then more plaintively.

Adam did not need to go any further to guess the scene the dog had found, and he had no desire to follow him upstairs. He stepped back into the daylight and looked around the garden behind the house. There was no sign of a kennel, but near a shed there was a bowl with water in it and a larger bowl which showed signs of having had food in it. Had the dog's owner somehow known what was coming but hoped that the dog would find a way of surviving outside, rather than starving to death inside the house?

Adam began to laugh, a bitter laugh. Maybe that was it? Humans had failed the test and now it was the animals' turn now to see what they could do. Adam had no right to be here in this new world - just what *was* he doing here? He had lost his loved ones, his friends and neighbours. His world was finished, so what was he going to do now, where was *his* place in *this* world? What was he doing here in this strange garden at all? Why wasn't he lying on the bed next to his wife, near his children?

He wasn't sure yet if he could face the tableau in the bedroom, in the children's rooms, but he knew he had to, sooner or later. It was his job to go back to the house and take care of what needed to be done there and then. Only then, could he start to think about what he would do next.

His mind wandered back to that day he and Jo had sat drinking coffee and looking at the apple tree that had won Jo's heart. That was two weeks ago, in the other world. And now, in *this* world, that's where he would bury her body along with the childrens', under the apple tree. Yes, *he* would dig the grave, not anyone else, and he would bury them. He would do it today. And after that he would shut up the house and leave it for ever. He would drive away, but where to? To find his brother... Jo's sister in Salisbury... his friends? Or just to find anyone who might still be alive in this world.

Chapter Two

Chapter 2

Chapter Three

Pip's Diary

Friday 26th April 1991

Serendipity

I don't know what's happening!!! I woke up with a sore throat this morning. I wanted to bunk off school but I needed to get away from the smell of burnt bacon (we only had one guest staying but Thommo managed to burn his breakfast!) and I had to see Nic to talk about her and W!! Got to school 5 mins late and was expecting nit-picker Parsons to collar me, but apparently he was not in today. So we had the Deputy-Head doing rollcall, and he was very strange, like he was half-asleep. Loads of class was off sick, well 5 at least (OK I exaggerated, but...) and everyone was sooo quiet, it was spooky. By lunchtime lots of people were coughing and saying they had sore throats, including the teachers. We had Smithson for English after lunch and he told us that apparently all over the country people were going down with a virus or something. That was scary, but he kept on saying it was just like a cold going round the school and we'd all be alright next week. He didn't look convinced. 2nd period we went to room 14 for Geography and waited and waited... After absolutely years – or about 10 minutes in human time – Miss Collins came in and told us that the school was closing early and we had to get our stuff ready to go home. Those who went on the village bus would have to wait in the assembly hall, but everyone else was to fanny off home. Amazing! That was radical and I was well cool with that and apart from a bit of a headache, I was feeling OK. But some of the group looked like they would not have the energy to crawl into bed, let alone walk home.

Annie Rogers had gone to sick-bay after lunch but got sent back again and she was crying and saying she was really ill and they should phone her Dad. Paula wasn't looking too good either and Rave Dave looked positively grave (ha-ha). It was a bit scary (again) seeing everyone coming out of school half-way through second period and they were all coughing. Some of the first years were in tears. I was going to walk home with Vicky P, but I couldn't see her outside so I decided to get away before I started feeling ill too. It was weird walking down Roberts Road with all these school kids dragging along looking like death and no-one saying much. It was end of school and end of the week, but no-one looked happy about it.

When I got home, Mum said she wasn't well and was going to bed and I had to answer the phone. (She knows how I hate that: "Hello, Serendipity Guest House – can I help you?.... sea-view? No, we don't have any with a sea view ... well, it's because we're not at the front you see ... no, it's only a short walk from the promenade

... oh, you're in a wheelchair..." Hey, I don't get paid to work here and anyway I'm not 16 till June!) Yeah OK, she did ask me how I was, but when I tried to tell her about school and everything, she didn't want to know. Apparently Thommo had gone to Cash & Carry and somewhere else and he should be back by now. Oh yes, and she had had some cancellations for tonight and tomorrow, but Thommo would have to deal with that. Then off she went up to the bedroom. I followed her up and said do you want a cup of tea or something, what about some aspirin? But she just said she'd be better if she had a sleep and you and your dad got your own dinner tonight. I was just getting myself a contraband choccy-biccy out of the larder when the phone rang and it was Nic wanting to know how I was. Her voice was really rough and I couldn't make out what she was saying. She said something about a boy at school dying, and David Moody, the bane of her life, was sent home at lunch time and now was really ill. (I thought YES!! Die, you spotty little toad-slime!!! But now I feel really bad about that because he might be in hospital or something). Then she had to get off the phone cos her mum was waiting for her dad to call, so I said I would call her later.

I took my juice into the sitting room and put the telly on to see if there was anything on there about Weymouth (like "Sea-side town reels under mass outbreak of flu/foot-and-mouth/skivitis "– take your pick) but they were just showing some old black and white movie. ITV was showing cartoons and there was nothing else on. So I went up to my room and thought I would carry on with my picture. So here I am, with you, my trusty companion, thinking what a weird day it's been and wondering what's going on. Back to the drawing....

8 pm

About five, Thommo gets in and he's coming up the stairs, coughing and wheezing, calling out #Angie, Pip lass? Where are you? Are you alright?# So I told him that I was OK, but Mum had gone to bed and all about school and everything. He said it had taken him three hours to get back from the cash and carry and the roads were all blocked and on the radio they were saying that this was happening all over the country. That was really freaky and I started thinking about Nic being ill and she was in another town. So I went down to the kitchen to make Thommo a cuppa and thought I'd have one too. So he comes down, puffing and coughing and says that we need to try and call the other bookings and cancel them, tell them that we'll refund the deposits etc etc and could I do it because I didn't seem too ill and he could barely talk – which was true. Then he put the telly on and it was the same as earlier so he sat in his chair and tried to drink his tea, but he couldn't swallow it, he said. So I got him some water and put some aspirins in it and he managed to get that down alright.

Then I left him and got the bookings register and tried to phone the first people, but the phone was engaged. It was the same with the other two as well. I kept on trying, but I could not get a line. Thommo was going on about how would we cope and what should we do, and I said that if things were as bad as he had heard on the radio, the people probably wouldn't turn up anyway. Then he wanted the radio so he could listen to that and see if there was any news and I gave him the phone so he could keep trying the numbers while I went up to see how Mum was. She was lying in her clothes, half up on the pillows and seemed to be asleep but she kept muttering to herself, then coughed a lot and then shut her eyes for a while, then started mumbling again. I felt her head and it was boiling. I didn't know what to do so I went downstairs to Thommo to tell him he needed to go and see to her. He was shivering and saying he felt cold. He didn't look good but I made him go up and see Mum. I didn't want to be her nursemaid. That sounds selfish, I know, but I know what a limping lily she can be: When she has a headache she thinks she is dying from a brain tumour. Then I thought if she's running a fever Thommo will need to get some of her clothes off and he'll probably need a hand. But I decided to go to my room and wait until one of them called me. First I tried the phone again, but it was just engaged.

10 pm

It looks like I am writing War and Peace here but it's been a really strange day and I really don't know what's going on. I listened to the radio news and they were talking about a major epidemic or something and that everyone should stay home, don't go out, don't go hospital, don't use the phones and so on. They were talking about Australia and Japan, and how the virus had taken hold there, and then India and the Middle-East. I got really scared then and switched the radio off.

Thommo and Mum have stayed in their room all evening. He got her into her nightdress and when I went in about 9.00 she was asleep, but Thommo was still coughing away and he was sweating now and rambling on about something I couldn't understand. I took them up some toast and some more tea. I tried to get them to eat but Thommo wouldn't have anything and I didn't want to wake Mum. So I ended up eating the toast, but then I felt tired and fell asleep on my bed. I woke up about an hour later and heard Thommo coughing away in the bedroom. Then I thought that I had better go downstairs and check that no guests had turned up or anyone else had walked in. (mental note : next time take a pen-knife in case a burglar/rapist/zombie has strayed into the house). So I locked the main door and turned out the lights.

I've just realised, I don't have a sore throat anymore. I woke up with one this morning and when I got to school I thought I had what everyone else had. But this evening it's gone. That's strange. It's as if this virus thing has given me a miss. I wonder if it's because I'm Asian? I hope I don't come down with it in the morning.

Chapter Four

Taking Stock

Monday 29th April, Afternoon

Adam walked over to the French doors. He could hear the dog whining upstairs. "OK boy, I have to go, you're on your own now." The whining stopped for a moment and then started up again. "*We're* on our own." He walked back down to the front gate and set off along the crescent back to his own house. He had a purpose now as he strode briskly up the road. He spotted a dustbin in the garden of a house and remembered what he had come for. He grabbed the bin, which was full and heavy, and dragged it up the road.

By the time he got it back to Mick and Sarah's house he was hot from the effort. He pushed it up against the side gate, dragged a large flowerpot over to the gate and used it to get a leg up onto the bin. From there he managed to climb up and get one leg over the top of the fence just as the bin fell away from him and clattered loudly onto its side.

The noise set Bonzo barking again. Adam hopped down on to the path and walked around the side of the house to the back door. He tried the handle and the door opened. He was thankful that he would not have to force that door. As he opened it, he saw Bonzo flying into the kitchen and was just able to brace himself as the dog launched himself at him, tail wagging and barking excitedly. "Hello Bonzo mate, easy now, easy! Yes, I'm pleased to see you too, oh yes I am!" The dog licked his hand and tried to lick his face and ran around him twice and then rushed into the garden to do his business. He'd been waiting a long time to do that, Adam thought. He could see the dog's food bowl upturned on the kitchen floor and he noticed the water bowl was dry. He went to the sink to fill it up. There was no water in the cold tap. This seemed odd, but he didn't give it any real thought. The kettle did have water in it and he filled up the bowl, and as Bonzo came back into the kitchen he spotted the water and had a very long drink.

"Come on Boy, there's nothing for you here," he said as he made his way out of the door into the garden. The dog looked at him and gave a strange whine and looked back at the door into the hall. He seemed to be in two minds as to what to do, as was Adam about what to do with the dog. Then he said "Well it's up to you pal, you know where I am." And he walked down the garden to where the hole was under the fence. The fence panel was rotting here and it only took him a few sturdy applications of his boot to smash a hole big enough to squeeze through into his own garden.

He walked up to the garden shed and pulled out a garden fork and spade and went over to the apple tree. He looked for a suitable site, near the tree but away from where the roots would be thickest, and when he was happy, he started an exploratory hole. He dug for about five minutes, making a messy heap of soil to the far side, and soon found he was sweating. He pulled off his jumper and carried on for another five minutes and then he had to stop and sit down. He was feeling quite faint. It dawned him then that he had not had anything to eat or drink since last night. This was going to be a long job and would need sustenance to do the physical work that was required.

He went into the kitchen and over to the fridge to get the jug of filtered water they kept there. As he opened the door he could see that the contents were slowly starting to go off in the warming refrigerator. He grabbed the jug and shut the door quickly. The jug had a plastic top so he thought the water would be alright to drink. He put it to his lips and drank deeply. When he had slaked his thirst and almost drained the jug, he found a banana by the fruit bowl on the worktop and set about that hungrily and followed that up with a handful of biscuits. He took an apple and went out into the garden and sat at the little table eating, now a little less urgently. Before anything else, he thought, he would have to go and find some fresh supplies: bottles of water and some more fruit and fresh vegetables, and maybe some bread, while it was still fresh enough to eat. He picked up his car keys and, making sure he had his house key as well, he set off for the main road.

Driving down through the estate was every bit as strange an experience as walking had been earlier. He turned right the main road, towards the town centre, around the car that was slewed across the road and past the lorry. There were a couple of cars abandoned on the road, and he puzzled over why they had been left there. He pulled up alongside one of them and saw the body of a man slumped behind the wheel. Had he been on the way home when he was suddenly too ill to drive any further? He guessed he would find more cars like that as he went along.

A little further on was a filling station with a shop that he and Jo used for odds and ends when they had run out of something. He drove onto the forecourt. It was empty but for one car parked down the side of the shop. He got out and walked up to the door and was surprised to find it opened when he pushed it. He stepped cautiously into the shop. It was strangely gloomy away from the windows, and very quiet. Adam did not have a good sense of smell, a side-effect of his illness last year, but he knew that it was not good in there. The fridges were all full of food and by the freezers there were pools of melt water. The power had gone off and everything was going bad.

Adam retreated rapidly from the shop and took a deep draught of fresh air. If he was going to spend any more time in that place, he would need a facemask. He went back to the car and found a duster in the glove compartment that was just about large enough to make a neckerchief he could pull up over his mouth and nose. With his makeshift mask on, he walked back into the shop, holding his breath. He picked up a basket by the door and made for drinks cabinet, stuffed as many large bottles of water as he could carry in the basket and exited the shop before he needed to draw breath. He put those in the car and returned to the shop. This time he headed for the chilled cabinet where they kept fruit and vegetables. He grabbed what still looked reasonably fresh, then raced back to the door.

Outside he gasped for breath and looked at what he had picked up. The bags were wet but the contents seemed ok. He put them in the car and then stopped to think what else he needed that he could find there. Making several raids into the shop, he picked up biscuits and crackers, some cartons of long-life milk, some chocolate bars and some soft drink cans. There was no bread. Then he went back for toilet tissues, some batteries and grabbed a couple of torches from the display by the till. It was then he noticed the slumped figure of a man behind the counter. He was sitting on the floor, leaning at an angle against the back wall, head lolling to one side, eyes closed. Adam could not see for sure, but the man's skin looked grey and he showed no signs of life. He guessed he probably died a couple of days ago. He could hold his breath no longer and the rancid air he took in made him start to gag. He stumbled out of the shop as quickly as he could, dropping some of the batteries as he went.

Back outside he took a deep draught of air and quelled the churning in his stomach. He walked over to his car and tried to put the image of the man out of his mind. He forced himself to suppress the feeling of helplessness growing within him and to concentrate on the practicalities. In the car he thought about what he had picked up from the shop. In his haste to get in and out, he had selected at random, but he would need to give this a bit more thought. What were the essential things he lacked at the moment? Heat and light. He needed to get himself some lamps, a portable stove and gas bottles, and more batteries. And where would he find such things? His best bet, he decided, was in the camping and caravan shop on the bypass.

He had a drink from one of the bottles of water then drove out of the forecourt and headed towards the ring road. Fortunately the road was pretty much free of abandoned cars. He was going to need petrol, of course, but where would he find that? None of the pumps in the filling stations would work without electricity, so there was no way of filling up there. He looked at the gauge and he could see that he still had half a tank in the car, enough to travel about 150 miles if he was lucky. Maybe he could siphon some fuel from the tanks in other cars. He pulled up by the main entrance of the camping shop. There were vehicles parked in the forecourt, including some camper vans and one or two cars, but the showroom was dark, with no sign of life.

Adam got out of the car, walked up to the double doors and tried the handle. It was firmly locked. He looked around for something he could use to batter down the door, but there was nothing obvious in sight. He decided to walk round the building. Perhaps there might be a back door unlocked, or an open window, but the rear of the property was cut off by a high fence, behind which was a secure compound where several camper vans and larger vehicles were parked. He went back round to the front and tried the other side, but here he met a wall. He looked across the forecourt and spotted a metal open-and-closed sign. Perhaps he could use that to force the door? The sign was set in a concrete base and could not be removed. It was as much as he could do to drag the thing a few yards over the tarmac. He let it go, there was no point in breaking his back with that.

He remembered that there was a wheel brace in the car. He found it under the spare tyre and went back to the doors and took a swing at the right-hand one. The brace bounced off the glass and nearly hit him in the face, without making any impression on the glass at all. He pulled down the sleeves of his sweatshirt to cover his bare forearms and made another attempt, turning his face away as the metal connected with the glass. Again, the brace bounced off and he recoiled with it. He tried twice more, to no avail, then threw it down onto the ground and stood to catch his breath – clearly this was not going to be easy. He tried again, this time with the other door, but it made no impression. This must be very tough glass indeed. What he really needed was something like a crowbar, to lever the doors open, but he did not carry one of those in the car. He threw the brace back in the boot, shut the lid and leant back against the car to think. He was not going to give up on this.

It was then the idea came to him that the best tool at his disposal to break into this place was probably the car itself. Rather than breaking in through the doors maybe he could use it to cave in one of the huge display windows? It was worth a go. He got back into the driving seat. Could he do this? Mash up his lovely Audi? Really? But what the hell was his car to him now? He could find any car he wanted, parked in driveways and forecourts all over the town. He pondered this and then decided to reverse the car. At least that way he would not damage the lights or the radiator. He turned the car round and reversed slowly up to the window to the left of the door. He came at an angle to the centre of the window, on the basis that this might exert the most force at one point. He backed the car slowly and it hit the glass with a heavy thud and then stalled. He pulled forward to reverse again and when he got almost to touching point he put his foot down hard on the accelerator. The engine roared, he felt impact and heard the tyres squealing as they spun on the pavement. He pulled forward and then reversed hard again. There was a sudden loud bang, like a gun-shot, and he saw the whole window cave in as the car lurched back into the showroom and crashed into a caravan, with fragments of glass showering down on the roof. The engine died.

The car was right inside the building now and Adam was looking at the ragged frame of the window in front of him, laced with broken glass and plastic beading. He started the car and pulled forward slowly. There was a grinding, popping noise at the back as it disentangled itself from the caravan and then much crunching and scraping as the vehicle pulled clear of the debris and out into the forecourt. When he was safely clear of the building Adam got out to inspect the damage. The back of the car was a mess indeed: the wrap-around bumper was hanging off, the lights and housing all gone on one side and the boot lid was open and only attached by one hinge.

He picked his way carefully over the glass into the showroom. He had half expected an alarm to go off, but there was no sound. He wandered over to the reception desk. There were papers scattered next to a computer keyboard and a monitor. Nearby was a shop area with displays and shelves of all the accoutrements and gadgets you might need or want when you went on the road with your van, or your tent. Here Adam was able to get most of the things he would need for his travels: cooking implements, some light-weight cutlery and plates, a couple of thermal mugs, some batteries and lanterns which he piled up in the middle of the floor. He also found a small twin burner gas hob and looked for the gas bottles to go with it. When he thought he had found everything he would need he looked around for something to put it all in. A couple of good boxes were what he was really looking for.

He wandered behind the till desk and into the office. This was quite a contrast to the order and cleanliness of the showroom. There were two desks and chairs, some filing cabinets, another computer – everything you would expect – but the desks were covered in files and paper, which had spilled onto the floor. There were half-drunk plastic cups of machine coffee everywhere, some spilt. It was as if the place had been abandoned in a hurry in the middle of a very busy day. But then, he thought, that is just exactly what would have happened: as the staff came down with whatever virus or plague had wiped out the population, they had probably all decided to head off home at the same time. He found some boxes of paper in a store cupboard at the back of the office and emptied one box out on the floor and took that, and another empty box, out into the showroom where his pile was. He loaded up the boxes and picked one up to take out to the car.

As he got to the broken window, he looked at the Audi and the sorry state of its rear end. Did he really want to drive it with the rear bumper and boot lid flapping about? He put down the box and wandered back into the showroom. Here he was, in a place that offered him the complete choice of vehicles for the travelling man and wasn't that just what he was planning to be? An itinerant, a vagabond, a modern-day frontiersman looking for a new home? A camper van was just the vehicle he needed. He could travel where he wanted and be quite self-sufficient. He strolled around the showroom looking at the all the sleek and glossy steel and plastic, polished and gleaming and waiting to catch one's eye. It was like a warehouse of new toys for the man-child explorer, but Adam resisted the temptation to climb inside them and explore the Aladdin's caves within. What he needed was something more than the smell of new upholstery. He needed a vehicle that was small enough to negotiate round country lanes and abandoned vehicles, yet big enough to accommodate him and his supplies. It needed fuel in it and most of all, it needed to have a key to operate it.

He walked back into the office and started looking for the key safe. He guessed it would be securely locked but maybe he could get a tool from his garden shed and smash his way in. He found the key safe at the back of the store cupboard and, amazingly, the key was in the door. They must really have left in a hurry. Inside – bonanza! – sets of keys all tagged with either the registration numbers of the vehicles or the model-name and number. These latter ones must be for the new vehicles, yet to be registered. He picked a few of each and set off to find their respective vehicles. He started with the new ones. He thought it unlikely that they would have much fuel in their tanks, but he would have a look. He found a van that matched his key and turned the ignition on. The lights on the dashboard came on and the fuel gauge moved just off empty – that would not get Adam very far. It was the same with the other new vehicles he located. What he really needed was a demonstration vehicle. They must keep one for test drives, surely.

He went out onto the forecourt to see if he could locate the used vehicles. The first he found was a splendid beast with all that you would need for a family of four or more. But it was really bigger than he needed or wanted. He needed something much more compact and more frugal with the fuel. The next was an almost new VW camper van. It was just the size he was looking for. He opened it up and turned the ignition – the fuel tank was half full, that was good. The third one was an older model, well-used by the look of it. It had virtually no fuel in the tank. He decided to get some more keys from the safe and check out the stock. There were various vehicles on the forecourt and he tried them all, but in the end, he returned to the VW. It was compact but well equipped, with table and chairs, a little kitchenette and a couch that pulled out into a bed.

It was everything he needed, and it was less than a year old. It started at the first turn of the key and the distinctive air-cooled engine chugged smoothly, even though cold. This will do nicely he thought.

He drove it over to where his car was sitting abandoned, opened up the side door and began transferring all the shopping from the back seat where he had thrown it. he was glad he had not put it in the boot with its now bent lid. Then he walked back into the showroom and began bringing out the boxes he had filled. By the time he had loaded everything in he had almost filled the floor space. He would have to sort that later.

He checked over his new vehicle again and started it up. He was just about to pull away when he remembered there were some things in the Audi he might want. He retrieved a tin of boiled sweets and two packets of chewing gum and then went to the boot. There was a lot of stuff in there, some of it just accumulated rubbish. But he grabbed the wheel brace and the fire extinguisher – he hoped he would never need that, but it might be useful. He had a quick look in the back of the car and spotted one of Oscar's toy cars, the red Ferrari that he had been looking for the other day – it was one of his favourites. He held the small red toy in his hand for a moment and felt a strange tightness in his throat. He took a deep breath then popped the car in his pocket. He put all the stuff in the back of the van and then went back to lock the car. Why he was doing that, he didn't know, but somehow it seemed the right thing to do. He had spent a lot of time in it and it was sort of an old friend. He was leaving it with its bashed and battered rear quarters, but he wasn't going to let just anybody get into it.

He drove his new chariot slowly back into town, reluctant to hurry back to the house. Number 27 Juniper Close was where he lived and yet it was no longer a home. It was a house in shadow... somewhere he did not want to be.

Chapter Five

Pip's Diary

Saturday 27th April

It's ten o'clock and I have been up since four. Thommo was calling to me and that woke me up. I didn't know what was going on at first and then I remembered. I went to their room and Thommo was sitting on the floor. I think he fell out of bed. He was crying and looking lost, like a little boy. I had to give him a hug, he looked so sad. Pathetic really. He kept asking me to do something, but I couldn't understand him. I think he might have been talking in Welsh and I don't think I have heard him do that before. I think Mum is dying. She is so pale and I can hardly tell if she is breathing. I don't know what to do. WHAT DO I DO?

And I'm worried sick about Nic cos if she is as ill as these two....I don't want to even think about it. Nic, why did you have to live so far away? And why did we have to come down here to this dump??!!

11.00 am

*I decided to go outside and see what was going on. Oh God, it was **AWFUL**. There was no-one on the street anywhere and no* *traffic. It was really frightening, like a bad dream or a horror movie. I went down to the end of the road but I was scared someone would jump out at me, so I walked in the middle of the road. There were some cars banged up on the main road and some just stopped in the middle of the road with their doors open. I thought I saw someone in one of them. I think they were dead, but I don't know. I couldn't look, it was too* ***HORRIBLE!*** *The corner shop was shut and in a lot of the houses the curtains were closed. I thought about going round to Vicky P's house but I lost my nerve and ran back here. I nearly dropped my key trying to open the door.*

Chapter Six

Farewells

Monday 29th April, Evening

Adam parked the camper van in the driveway and was just getting out when he spotted the border collie he had met in the morning, sitting quietly on the step by the front door, as if he was waiting for him. As Adam walked towards the door the dog watched him with its head to one side and its tail wagging slowly. Adam held out his hand and the dog gave it a lick. "Hello boy," he said, "what are you doing here?" The dog wagged its tail harder and nuzzled its head against Adam's leg.

"You found me then? Well, you're a clever boy aren't you?" and he stroked the dog's head. He opened the door and the dog looked at him uncertainly. Adam collected a box from the car and carried it into the house. "Come on then, you can come in." The dog seemed unsure, so Adam carried on unloading his booty, piling it up on the kitchen floor. For the moment he would leave everything on the floor, in the boxes and bags. Later he would sort through it and start planning what he needed to take on his journey. But right now he was hungry.

The dog had followed him into the hall, where it stopped and gave a low whine. Clearly it sensed something not right. Adam called it into the kitchen and it seemed happier there, though it was still wary of something. Adam got the camping cooker out of its box, connected one of the gas bottles and lit it with a lighter they kept in a drawer for lighting birthday candles. He made a mental note to pick up some more lighters and matches on his travels. He fetched a tin of soup from the larder, opened it and popped it into a saucepan to heat. He found an unopened packet of bread in the fridge which had not gone mouldy yet. It would have been better toasted, but that was no longer an option. He rescued some other items from the fridge – tomatoes, apples, oranges and some carrots that seemed okay. There was also some processed cheese and a tub of spread which were fine to eat. Everything else he fished out and dropped into a rubbish sack, which he tied up quickly and took to the back door.

As he dropped the sack into the rubbish bin at the side of the house he heard a bark from the next-door garden. He looked up and saw Bonzo rush though the newly enlarged gap in the fence and race down the garden to greet him. He licked Adam's hand, tail wagging furiously, and barked excitedly. He charged into the kitchen, as he always did when he got into their garden, rushing into the house to see the children. He came to a sudden halt inside as he met the Collie. His hackles went up and he growled, and then, in a sudden change of mood, he rushed up to the old dog, tail wagging, and barking. The Collie growled softly and held his ground. Bonzo retreated a step and took a more submissive posture, whereupon the two dogs embarked on a more formal introduction, sniffing each other politely and doing their canine how-do-you-dos.

Adam watched the two dogs and smiled. It seemed that he had acquired two new companions, though he was not sure whether that was really what he needed at the moment. He returned to his soup, which was starting to boil, and gave it a stir. He was suddenly very hungry and he took two slices of bread from the packet, put them on a plate and opened the tub of spread. It tasted fine, and the bread was okay, just. His sense of taste had not been good since his illness last year, so he was not as discerning about his food as he once was. He resisted the temptation to take the soup straight from the pan, poured it into a bowl and sat down at the kitchen table to eat his lunch.

Immediately Bonzo was at his side, watching every mouthful go down. He barked and got closer to the chair, licking his chops. Adam paused in his eating. He clearly wasn't the only one who hadn't eaten for a couple of days. "OK Bonzo, I hear you. Come on, let's find you some food." Bonzo seemed to know exactly what had been said and he raced off down the garden to the hole in the fence, waiting for Adam to catch up. Then he ran ahead through the open door into Mick and Sarah's kitchen. Adam quickly found a tin of dog food in their larder, located the can opener and tipped the contents into the dog's bowl. Bonzo fell to his meal ravenously and Adam left him there wolfing it down. Grabbing a handful of dog food tins, of which there seemed to be a good stock, he returned to his own house, where he sat down to finish his now lukewarm soup. The Collie sat there watching him intently.

"You hungry too?" Adam said, "well, you'll just have to wait till I've finished." Adam reheated the remainder of the soup, buttered some more bread and topped it with some cheese and a tomato he had sliced. Having satisfied his appetite for the time being, he opened one of the tins he had brought back and put some dog food in a bowl on the floor for the Collie. The old dog looked at him as if to say, 'May I?' and then sniffed the food cautiously. "Go on, you can have it," said Adam, and the dog began to eat. He ate a few mouthfuls and looked up to check all was OK and then proceeded to finish the rest. He then lay down by the back door and watched Adam intently. Shortly Bonzo reappeared at the door, licking his chops and wagging his tail. He saw the empty bowl on the floor and gave it a good lick round in case there was anything left, then came over and sat by Adam, looking at the Collie as if to say, "This is my place".

Adam boiled some water in another pan and made himself a pot of coffee, black and strong, and sipped at it slowly. It was the first caffeine he had had for three days and he felt the hit. He sat at the table and looked at the two dogs watching him. What am I going to do with these animals, he thought? He did not suppose that he would be able to leave them behind when he went – they belonged him now, it seemed, or him to them.

He started thinking about his journey. There was only one friend he really felt close to, and he lived in Shrewsbury. He had other friends in London and the south-east but they were really only casual acquaintances. Since he and Jo had got together and the children came along, these friends became less important in his life. No, he would seek out his brother first. If Adam was immune to this virus – if that's what it was - because of some configuration in his genes, then there was a possibility that Sam would be too. It was only an *if*. Adam had no idea what had caused the world to fall ill all at once and yet leave him untouched. If it was a virus that had wiped out his family and neighbours, then why hadn't he caught it? And if it wasn't a virus, then what could have caused the sudden extinction of mankind? And how had he escaped it? He had been completely focused on his loved ones and sharing their last few hours and all that time he'd been waiting, expecting to start coming down with the illness. But three days had passed and he was still showing no symptoms. And the fact that the power grid and all communications had failed so suddenly and completely suggested a total wipeout of humankind, at least in this country. All the evidence told him that this was what had happened, and yet... how was this possible? How could anything like this have happened so completely out of the blue and with such cataclysmic speed? And more, how could he be left behind as the sole witness? That was beyond sense or reason.

He tried to concentrate on the task he had set himself. He was about to bury the bodies of the three people he loved most in this world. He needed to do this and put all other thoughts out of his mind. He went out into the garden and looked at the shallow hole he had started before his energy ran out. He would need to do some serious digging to make a decent grave big enough for the three of them. He didn't know what the time was. He guessed it was early afternoon, so he had several hours of daylight left to get this job done. He set to the digging, working systematically in rows. He planned to make the grave four foot by six foot and as deep as he reasonably could, working his way row by row away from the tree. He thought he would lay Jo's head close to her favourite tree; somehow it felt appropriate, and that happened to be the east end of the grave. Was that how people lay in churchyards? He didn't know but it seemed right for her to be nearer to the rising sun, Jo being such a sun lover.

He rested at the end of every row, and it did not take long for him to dig the outline of the grave. But he was only one spit deep and there was a long way to go yet. Bonzo had run around excitedly when he started digging, but now he lay flopped out by the fence. The older dog had sat himself in the sun and was watching him work. After an hour Adam had managed to get down two spits, but he needed a pause. He reckoned he needed to go double that depth, or more if he could. He wanted to make sure that his loved ones were deep in the ground and safe from foxes and other animals.

He got a bottle of water and sat at the little coffee table, quenching his thirst and catching his breath. He knew he had to do this job and at the same time shut out the memories and emotions that were barely suppressed inside him. He needed to concentrate on the practicalities. After ten minutes he set to again, and before long had deepened the hole to about three feet. After a quick breather he set off again, but now the going got harder. He was hitting more and more stones, some of which were quite large and needed levering out of the ground. By the time he had completed that fourth excavation his back was aching and his arms were tiring. He wasn't used to this sort of work. The sun was now much lower and the shadow of the shed had advanced across the lawn to the newly dug grave. It would get dark within an hour or so.

***

Saturday 27th April 12.00 o'Clock

I am really worried now. Yesterday they were saying that everyone will be better in a few days but I don't think they will be. The radio wasn't picking up anything but music, orchestral stuff and when I tried the tv there was only BBC 1 and that just had music and a message about staying indoors. That was <u>not</u> reassuring at all. I had left the radio on just in case was there was an announcement or something but then it switched off. I did not really register at the time because I was upstairs but when I went to put on the light on the stairs, nothing happened. It was the same downstairs – no lights. It was only when I went into the kitchen and looked at the clock on the oven that I realised we had no electricity. AAAGGGHHH! What am I going to do now? If everyone is sick, who is going to be there to look after them? Haven't the hospitals not got electricity either? God I wish I could talk to

Nic. I hope she is going to be OK. I'm not sure Mum is going to make it.

I can't believe I just wrote that, but I don't want to believe it either. I lost one mum and now I might lose the only one I've ever known? No! NO!! I don't want lose her, or Thommo, or Nic.

I don't want to lose any of them, even Jeffery (yes, even Nic's obnoxious, pathetic excuse of a cousin)

Sorry Nic, I didn't mean that. I know you love him. And I love you. Where are you? I want to see you. I need to go upstairs and see my folks now. I want to talk to you but THE PHONES AREN'T WORKING!!!!

***

He had a sit down and another long drink. He could see that the floor of the grave was as much stone as earth and he knew that to get deeper would take a lot of hard digging and a lot more time, and yet it was hardly deep enough to put the bodies below ground. His eyes wandered up the garden and fell on the pile of old paving stones that they had dug up to lay the new patio. What if he was to lay those over the top of the grave and then pile up more stones on top, to make a sort of cairn? That would make the grave harder to disturb and would act as a memorial as well.

He got a wheelbarrow from the shed and took it down to the heap. The pavers were heavy and uneven, some cracked and broken, but they would do the job. He began to wheel them up to the graveside and to build a new heap there, sorting the stones into sizes as he did so. In half an hour he thought he had enough to do what was required. If he needed more, he would get them later. Adam was sweating and starting to really ache now. The digging and stone-moving had been back-breaking work, but the next job would be much harder, in a different way. Before he got to that, however, he needed some strong refreshment.

He went into the kitchen and opened a bottle of beer, took it out to the little table, which was now in the shade, and sat down to think about how he would do the burial. The two dogs came over and sat nearby looking at him. He was bracing himself to go upstairs and get Jo's body. He wasn't sure if he would be able to go through with it. The memory of Jo's last dark hours came back and filled his thoughts:

After she finally left him at dawn, he spent an age just lying on the bed with her in his arms. Finally he got himself up and went down into the kitchen and sat staring at the garden in the half-light, too weary with grief to think any coherent thoughts. After some time, he couldn't have told you how long, he dragged himself back up to the bedroom. The bed was a mess, with bedclothes rumpled and twisted. In Jo's fever her clothes and the bedsheets had become wringing wet and he had removed the bedclothes and her pullover in an attempt to bring down her temperature, but though she was boiling hot, Jo had shivered with her fever. He had managed to take away the bottom sheet once and replace it with a clean one, but that too had been spoiled when Oscar was sick on it.

Adam set about getting Jo presentable - she deserved that decency. He stripped the bed and put a new sheet on by rolling her body to one side and then the other. Then he removed her top clothes, recoiling when he first touched her now cold flesh. He found her favourite dress, which she liked to wear for summer parties. Looking back he didn't know how he had managed, but he got it on her and arranged it neatly, whilst strangling down his sobs. He got a damp flannel to wipe her face, neck and arms, and used her brush to untangle her natural chestnut curls before laying her out straight on the sheet. Her pale face, which had been contorted by pain and sickness and worry these last forty-eight hours or so, now looked peaceful. She looked really quite beautiful, and he felt that he had done her justice.

Next, he went to Oscar's room, where both children lay in the boy's bed, the two small, cold bodies side by side. A shudder convulsed him as he went into the room and the choking sobs rose again in his throat. Jo had got them into their pyjamas when they first got home on Friday. It wasn't difficult to remove these so that he could wash their bodies with a damp flannel. After that, he found some fresh pyjamas to dress them in and laid them in the bed next to each other and pulled the sheet up to their chins. They almost looked as if they were sleeping.

When Adam finished, he kissed them both and left the room, closing the door behind him. He went back and kissed Jo's cold forehead, laid her hands across her chest, and said quietly, "Goodbye my love." He didn't know what else to say. He didn't have the words for this. Then he went out and closed the door. As he stood on the landing, an incredible tiredness overcame him. He took himself into the spare room, threw all the clothes that lay on the bed onto the floor and collapsed onto the bed. He immediately fell into a deep sleep. That was yesterday afternoon and Adam had slept right through to first light this morning.

Now, more than a day later, he opened the bedroom door and hesitated before going in – would everything be as it was when he shut the door yesterday? Then he had worked in the cold morning light. Now the room was bathed in the warmer glow of the setting sun peeping through the cracks in the curtains, but nothing had changed. Jo lay as he left her, under the sheet, eyes closed, at rest. He wondered whether her body might have gone stiff, but then remembered that it was almost a day and a half ago that she had died. He sat on the edge of the bed and looked at her face. The tears welled up in his eyes. "Jo, I have to move you now. I don't want to do this, but ..." The words were stuck in his throat. She looked so beautiful he almost couldn't bear to look at her. For several minutes he sat with her, staring at her face, wanting to imprint it on his memory forever, as if there was a danger he might forget what she looked like.

He pulled up the sheet to cover her face, and then folded it around her body, so that she was wrapped like a mummy. He shuddered again at the coldness of her as he knelt on the side of the mattress and got his arms beneath her. Jo was quite petite, but he knew that lifting her body would not be easy. Even so it surprised him just how much he had to strain to lift her off the bed. He decided it would be easier and safer to put her over his shoulder and once he was upright it was then not too difficult to carry her down the stairs and through the kitchen into the garden. Both dogs had stayed in the kitchen whilst he was upstairs, as if they knew that this was not something they should be part of. They watched him warily, Bonzo whining softly, as he went by, but they did not follow him as he carried Jo's body down the garden. He laid her down gently by the grave side, her head near the apple tree. He startled a robin who had been busy looking for worms in the newly turned soil. He walked round her and stepped down into the grave. From there he tried to ease her into the shallow pit with as much dignity as possible but her feet dragging on the edge of the grave brought a little avalanche of soil onto the winding sheet. He had never in his life had to bear a coffin or lower it into a grave, and now he was clumsily putting the body of his closest companion into the damp earth. He climbed out of the grave, wiping the tears from his eyes with the back of his sleeve, then went back to the house to get the children.

He fetched Oscar first. He slid his sheet from under Sophie's small, frigid body and wrapped him in it as he had done his mother. He carried him down in his arms, sobbing silently, and laid him next to Jo. Finally, he went back for Sophie. The wee mite was a pathetic sight in her little pink pyjamas, her little face so white, her tiny arms so very chill. He found a spare bedsheet, folded it in half and then used it to wrap her. He took her down and laid her close to Oscar. Adam wiped his eyes and stared at the three sheeted bodies huddling together in the small grave. There was something missing. He went back upstairs and found Sophie's favourite pink piggy and in Oscar's room, his action-man toy. Then he went into the main bedroom, to the dresser, where he took the small mahogany box from the drawer. In it was all Jo's jewellery. She didn't need it, he knew, but somehow he would rather it stayed with her than it be found by some stranger, some thief in the night that had miraculously survived this plague, as Adam had. He carried the things down to the grave. He put the children's toys at their feet – was that how the Egyptians did it for the Pharaohs? – and did the same with Jo's jewellery box. Then he broke off a couple of sprigs of Apple blossom and laid it on Jo's chest.

A thought came to him and he turned and walked back into the kitchen. Pinned to the noticeboard on the wall by the door was a photo from their holiday last summer in Devon, the family group kneeling on the sand with the sea in the background. They had asked a passer-by to take it and he and Jo were thrilled when the prints came back from the chemist. It was such a happy picture. Adam thought that maybe he would like to keep that picture for himself as a keepsake, but then he remembered he had a small version of it in his wallet. He wanted the large one to go with Jo and the children. And if anyone should ever disturb the bodies, they would find a picture of the whole family and know that Adam was a part of that family too. They might even deduce that he was the one that had made the grave and somewhere, somehow, was still alive, though that was a fanciful thought that Adam did not really believe for a moment. He tucked the photo under a fold in the sheet on Jo's chest. Then, again, he stood at the foot of the grave. "Goodbye my loves, goodbye..." was all that came out before Adam broke down again.

He knelt for a while at the graveside, sobbing, and then stood up suddenly. He had been delaying this moment as long as he could, but now he had to do it. He reached for the spade and began to cover the bodies with earth. He worked furiously, as if in anger, and in no time, he had completely covered the bodies, moving the whole heap of soil back onto the grave until it rose in a mound above it. He scraped up every last bit of loose soil and worked to pat down the heap as much as he could. He squatted on his haunches for a few minutes, catching his breath, looking at the mound. Then he took the largest stones he had sorted out and placed them around the edge of the grave until he had made one circuit. He worked his way up the mound, using the half slabs next and finally at the top he was down to the broken pieces of rock. He had built a sort of cairn on top of the grave, but it needed capping off.

He searched the rockery where Jo planted her favourite alyssum and aubretia and found one large, almost pyramidal stone. It was the best there was. He remembered carrying that in from the car when they bought it at the garden centre and how he thought his arms would give way before he got it to the garden. It seemed even heavier now as he struggled across the lawn to place it on the top of the pile. Then he fell back onto the grass exhausted and lay stretched out taking in great gasps of air. It was over. It was done. He had sent them off on their last journey together, as a family. He lay there exhausted, staring at the sky while his breathing and heart rate returned to normal. He remembered how, when he was a boy, his father had put him and Sam and their mum on a train to the seaside, and he followed on several days later with the car. Now the family had gone on before him and he would follow on later, to join up with them once again.

***

Saturday 27th April

It's afternoon, I don't know when. I took my watch off earlier when I washed out the flannels that I'd been using for Mum and Thommo, trying to keep their heads cool. Thommo has got into their en-suite and is propped up against the bath. Maybe he was trying to get some water. He's breathing really loudly, like a sort of gurgling, but really slow. Mum woke about an hour ago and said something like "I love you Filipa" She never calls me that. Then she told me to look after Thommo. Something about <you know what he's like>. Then she fell asleep again. Asleep? Unconscious? I don't know. Think she was talking to me like she knows she is dying.

***

It's getting dark outside. I think Mum's gone. I sat with her for hours, just holding her. Sometimes she didn't seem to breathe for ages and then suddenly she would take a breath. She was wheezing when she breathed. She's been very quiet now for a long time. I think she has stopped breathing. Oh, God, this can't be happening. God, what is happening to us???

***

It was some time before he became aware of the cold which had been seeping into his back from the dampening grass. Slowly he hauled himself upright and stretched out his stiffening body. If it was not for the chilling ache in his spine and a sudden shiver which sent a spasm of pain into his leg, he would have stayed there for hours. Nothing really mattered, and yet he knew he knew there were things he had to do.

He forced himself to turn away from the grave and walked towards the house. A sudden pang of hunger focussed his thoughts. It was time to take care of other matters, like making a meal, getting some lights set up, sorting out what he was going to take with him tomorrow. It was not so much the practical things – he knew he could take care of those easily enough – it was more about the personal things. Which items of significance did he want to take with him? What mementoes? What were the things that would help him in the weeks, months and maybe years ahead? For he felt that once he left this place, he would never want to come back.

He busied himself with putting together a simple meal on the camping stove and when it was cooked, he wondered why he had bothered. Ever since his illness last year he had struggled to regain his appetite. He didn't seem to have much sense of smell and that meant nothing had much flavour. Had it not been for Jo trying to tempt him with tasty meals and treats, he probably would not have bothered to eat half the time. Now he had no appetite for food at all and yet his belly told him he needed to make himself eat. He forced the food down and when he had eaten as much as he could, he opened another beer and went back out into the garden.

The dogs followed him out and Bonzo tried to get the older dog to play with him, but the Collie only humoured him for a while and then gave him a warning snarl. Adam watched them getting the measure of each other, and when they had settled down he listened to the birdsong. Without any other sound to compete, it was amazingly loud. He could hear blackbirds – he knew their song – and something more shrill piercing the still evening. A thrush maybe? He wasn't sure. He had never taken a lot of notice of the wildlife in the garden, probably because he was always so busy and maybe too because Oscar frightened every living creature out of the garden when he was playing outside. But now – what else was there? Could there really be no human noise anymore, anywhere?

At that very moment he heard a distant bell strike the hour, how apt! A man-made sound that rang out after man had gone – on a church, where else? Where was this coming from? He puzzled for a while to think of any churches around this part of town but in these huge estates of twentieth-century boxes, there were no churches he knew of that had a bell tower. It must be the Town Hall Clock in the centre of town, the mechanical clock that played the Westminster chimes on the hour, every hour. That was three miles away and he had never heard it out here before, but now he could hear it as clear as if it was just down the road.

Adam went back into the house. There was not a lot of daylight left and he needed to get his stuff together before the house got too dark. He began sorting out what he would need in the way of cooking equipment, going through what he had acquired today and what he already had in the house. He went back and forth to the camper van, filling up the little cupboards in the kitchenette with pots and utensils, gas bottles and water. Then he started on the food. He deliberated over what to put in, then he thought to himself there would be plenty of supplies in the shops. So he threw in enough for two or three days on the road and then turned to bedding and clothes.

He did not want to disturb their bedroom, but he needed to get some of his clothes out of the wardrobe and had to pull the curtains back to let some light in. He filled up a suitcase with some essential clothing and when he thought he had got all he needed he gathered up all the dirty bedding which he had rolled into a ball on the bedroom floor yesterday and threw it into the bath. He could not face looking through Jo's wardrobe but locked the door and put the key in a drawer. Then he took the silk throw from the linen cupboard and draped it over the bed. Satisfied that the room looked neat and tidy, he closed the curtains again and shut the door.

He took the suitcase and the bedding downstairs and as he went out to the van he saw a ginger cat sitting by the open door of the van. “Oh no,” he said, “sorry cat, you’re out of luck, this van’s not taking any more passengers.” The cat watched him putting the clothes on the on the fold-down couch as if eying a potential berth. Adam got out, clapped his hands at the animal, and then decided he should close the van door. He went back into the house. Seeing the cat had got him thinking about his canine travelling companions. He guessed that they would each need a food and water bowl along with the tins of dog food he had taken from Mick and Sarah’s kitchen. And some bedding? He went back through the garden and the gap in the fence to fetch Bonzo’s bed. He had a small dog basket in the kitchen. He tipped out the grubby-looking bedding and gave the basket a good shake in the garden. He knew they had some old blankets upstairs for emergencies and he would fold up a couple of those for the dogs.

Back in the house they were watching him with interest. They sensed something was happening and did not want to miss out. They must be feeling a bit insecure right now, he thought. Adam got the blankets and took them into the kitchen. The old dog could use one of them tonight. He had better find a name for him, he thought, as he was clearly going to be around for a while. And as for the cat, it was too bad. There would be thousands of cats, dogs and other animals looking for food and a home, and it was not pleasant to think how all these creatures would fare without their human carers, but two was enough for him to manage. He dropped the blankets, one in the kitchen and one in the sitting room. Without really thinking through why, Adam locked the van and the front and back doors of the house. Then he made his way wearily up to the spare bedroom, lay down on the bed and fell sound asleep.

***

Saturday 27th April Late

Mum is dead. *I sort of fell asleep on the bed and when I woke it was really dark. I was lying next to her and I could not hear her at all. She felt cold. At first I wasn't sure if she really was dead because I've never seen a dead person before, but now I know she is. Thommo is still wheezing. I want to move him to the bed but he is far too big and heavy. I sort of got him a bit more upright against the bath. I got a pillow behind him and put a blanket round him. He opened his eyes for a moment and started talking to me. He said something like "sorry Pipkin" I tried to say something but I just cried. Maybe he will pull through. I don't want to lose him as well. God I hope he makes it.*

Chapter Seven

Bon Voyage

Tuesday 30th April, Morning

Adam slept heavily for a while, but later in the night was troubled by dreams about Jo and the children, about friends visiting and lying down on the floor to die, about breaking into his workplace and finding no-one there he knew, just strangers. He came to as the light started to come though his window and, like yesterday, he lay for a long time listening to the birdsong. The house was quiet, no sound or movement from the dogs. The street outside was quiet and the world beyond was quiet – nothing had changed.

He and Jo had been in Reading for eight years now. For six years they were happy in their cottage in a village on the north side of Reading, but two years ago they had found a house on the south side of town, a large detached on a newish estate, which gave them the space they needed, a garden and garage and a safe neighbourhood for the children. Plus it was handy for Adam to get on the motorway when he was visiting other branches. Jo was pregnant when they viewed the house in the autumn and Sophie arrived not long after they had moved in.

They had celebrated her second birthday just a few weeks ago. The years in Reading had given them everything they were looking for and together he and Jo had slipped seamlessly into a contented life, a comfortable, professional couple with a young family and so much to enjoy, and more to come. But now, it was very apparent, more was not going to come. There would be no more.

Adam's brief reverie burst apart like a crystal vase smashing onto a tiled floor. Everything before last Friday was suddenly a cruel memory. Now he a was man on his own, waking up on a Tuesday morning to a completely different world. And for all he knew maybe it was just him, only him in this world: a man, two dogs and his memories.

The room was cold and in the night he had pulled the bedclothes right over him. And he was still in the clothes he wore yesterday. He hadn't washed at all, not even his hands. Instinctively he went to the bathroom to relieve himself and added to the urine he had left in the bowl yesterday. There was no water left in the cistern to flush it. He would use some of the bottled water from downstairs maybe. No, better than that, get the watering can and fill it from the water butt by the garage. He would use the bottled water to give himself a wash. The practicalities of the situation temporarily took his mind away from his gloomy reflections. He stripped down in the chilly bathroom with the water he brought from downstairs and washed himself all over. He found himself some clean jeans, sweatshirt, underwear and socks. He might as well start out on his journey feeling clean and presentable, he thought. Feeling the chill in the air he dug out a pullover and put that on as well. Bonzo was now wide awake and followed Adam round the house wagging his tail. He seemed to think that something exciting was about to happen – a long walk maybe? The collie had wandered out from the lounge, where he seemed to have settled for the night, and came over to greet Adam. He too watched Adam closely, sensing something going on.

Adam threw his dirty clothes into the rubbish bin outside. It seemed wrong, but then what was right anymore? The clock said 7.25. He guessed he must have been asleep for ten hours or more last night, something he never normally did. He lit the camping stove to boil water for coffee. He felt hungry but wasn't sure that he wanted to sit around eating breakfast. He wanted to get going, felt he had to get away from the house and away from Reading. He would head west to his brother's house in Wiltshire and no doubt stop somewhere en route.

While the water boiled, he did a last scout around the house for things he might need. There was not much really that he could not find on his travels. But the photos in albums and frames, treasured paintings and objects they had collected on their travels, books they had given each other, Oscar's drawings: He could fill the van with all that alone, but he had to be ruthless. He thought about it while he drank his coffee. He would take one holiday album and their wedding pictures, a few small, framed photos and a mug that Jo had made him in a holiday pottery class. That was all. That was enough for now. He could come back and collect more things another day. If he ever came back.

Then he took two pages from the notepad. On the first he wrote:

"Sam, if you find this note then there is hope after all. I am driving down to Mere now and then I'll go to Salisbury to see if Anna and Pete made it. I'm on my own. I'll leave messages. Hang in there Sam. 30th April 1991."

He slid the note under a glass dish that they kept for special occasions and placed it to the side of the window where the sun would not bleach it. On the second note he wrote: *"Adam Fisher left this house alive on 30th April 1991. The key is in the usual place."*

It was only his brother, who knew that they kept the spare key behind a loose brick at the side of the garage. He placed this one inside an envelope and pinned it to the front door.

He gave the dogs half a bowl of dog food each, which they clearly were not expecting, and while they were eating he went out to the shed. It had come to him that he might need a few basic tools in the van on his journey. He sorted what he thought he might need. The showroom sparkle of the van was now somewhat counterbalanced by the piles of stuff that Adam had thrown into it. He really had no idea what he would need on the road so his packing had been rather random. With two dogs on board and a dirty pan or two, he thought, the place will soon look lived in. When it got too dirty, he would find a replacement. Adam smiled wryly to himself. That's almost funny: a new vehicle every week, a new shirt every day, a different view every morning. There really was nothing he could not do now, if it took his fancy. Nothing was illegal anymore. And yet there was nothing that he really wanted to do without someone to share it with, someone to relate his adventures to. He had no idea what was out there in this quiet world. He could only hope that he would find other survivors and that there would be some reason then to go on living.

He went back into the house and had one last look around. Returning to the back garden he spent a few moments by the burial mound. He was torn between wanting to absorb the sight, as if committing it to memory, and his desire to get moving.

Then he locked the back door, picked up his wallet from the hall table without thinking why, and when the dogs were outside he shut the front door and locked it. The dogs were watching, somehow expectant. "Come on boys, we're going on a trip, in you get." Bonzo jumped into the van, which he had already thoroughly checked out earlier when Adam was packing: he was ready to go. The old dog was not quite so sure and Adam had to coax him in. He sniffed around suspiciously and then made himself comfortable on the blanket that Adam had laid on the sofa seat. Bonzo had climbed over the front seats and taken pole position behind the wheel, so when Adam climbed in he had to move him onto the passenger seat. The dog seemed quite at home in the van and was clearly a seasoned traveller. It was twenty past eight when Adam finally pulled away from the house. He looked in his rear-view mirror as number 27 Juniper Close receded behind him, and as he did so he saw the ginger cat watching him from the road. She'll survive, he thought. Maybe.

On the drive through their estate everything looked as it had yesterday. He didn't expect anything to have changed, but all the time he was alert to any sign of movement, any sign of life. It was a fine, cool April morning and he had his window down. He drove slowly and listened out for sounds. There seemed to be lots of birds everywhere flitting busily from tree to bush. Maybe they had always been around, and he had just never noticed before. Near the junction with Beech Avenue they surprised a cat asleep on the road, most reluctant to move. "OK, so it's your road now is it?" he said, as he steered around it.

When he got to the main road, everything was as it had been previously as far as he could remember. The same cars were abandoned in the road. He drove slowly past the caravan centre and his car was still there on the forecourt, the hole gaping in the showroom windows. He had half expected to see the windows boarded up and some police tape around the building, but everything was as he had left it.

At the roundabout over the motorway the exit to the west-bound carriageway was coned off with a sign saying, "Road Closed". Adam got out of the car and, moved the cones aside and set off down onto the carriageway. He was several miles down the road before he came across the blockage. An articulated lorry was slewed across the carriageway and when Adam pulled up he could see beyond it the remains of a couple of burned-out vehicles and several other cars. He would have to find a way past the accident or else take a long diversion, which he was not keen to do.

He drove slowly around the lorry using the hard shoulder and then negotiated his way between two wrecks, driving slowly over broken glass and other debris. He tried not to look but he could see two figures slumped in the front of a small red car as he squeezed by. Here the road surface was scorched by the fire from what he could now see were three burned-out vehicles. He found a way round the remains of a van, but it was a tight gap between the twisted wreckage and the centre barrier. He heard a scraping of metal down the side of his van as he eased past, but he managed to get through. A little further on he stopped to get out and check the van. There was a long dent and scratch down the passenger side, but nothing serious, and as far as he could see there was no damage to the underside of the vehicle. He got Bonzo back into the front of the van and set off again, travelling slowly at first to make sure everything was alright.

From there on the road was clear, the empty carriageways stretching ahead of him over the Berkshire downs. It seemed that most people had got home on Friday before they succumbed entirely to the virus, or had at least managed to get off the motorway. Most, but not all. Here and there were cars and trucks pulled up on the hard shoulder and in many Adam could see bodies. Poor souls who had not managed to make it back to their loved ones before they were laid low... what a lonely death they must have had. The sun was rising higher in the sky now and Adam could imagine the state that these bodies would be in after three days in the greenhouses which their cars would have become. It was hard to reconcile that picture of putrid decay with the trees greening up in the woods beside the road and animals grazing beyond on the hills in the beautiful spring sunshine. He knew that these scenes must be repeated wherever he went, and as the days went by the sights would become much worse.

After a couple of hours' driving he found himself on the section of road which overlooks Stonehenge, and decided to make a stop there to have some breakfast. He went into the back of the van and set about making coffee. This was the first chance he had had to get know his little kitchen and it took him a while to get the stove connected to the gas bottle, find the coffee and a cup, fill the little kettle, hunt for the matches to light the gas. When he had had something to eat, he took his coffee, wandered across the verge to the fence and looked over at the ancient stone circle.

He noticed then, for the first time, that there were several cars parked down the old road that ran past the site. He peered at the stones and tried to see if he could see any signs of people. This was when he really could do with some binoculars. It seemed that there were figures, some lying on the grass in the middle circle, some on the fallen stones, and others dotted around the site. He looked for a long time to see if there was any sign of movement, but he could see none.

Why were these people here? He supposed that they were new-age pagans who somehow knew that they were dying and chose to spend their last moments on this earth among the ancient stones. It was appropriate that as the world of humans drew to a close, people should head for a monument erected by their forebears five thousand years ago in the early days of human endeavour. Or maybe they had just come together for a weekend gathering, taking advantage of the better weather? He veered towards the first thought, that they wanted their bodies to lie among the great stones which meant so much to them and which had stood from the dawn of civilisation, and would no doubt continue to stand for many thousands of years to come.

He drained his coffee and turned away from the fence. Bonzo was looking up at him expectantly, ears cocked, as if to say "Where are we going now? Are we going for a walk?" The dog made Adam smile; he had always been quite a comical animal which was why the children loved him so much, and his expressions were somehow so human, so child-like. The sun was shining, the birds were singing – it was no place to be so gloomy. "Oh Bonzo" he said, "we'll have a walk later boy, I promise you. But right now I have to go and see if I can find my brother." He went back to the van, swilled his cup out and left it in the little sink. He called the dogs into the back and slid the door closed, then got in behind the wheel and started the engine. Bonzo immediately climbed over into the front seat and climbed up with his paws on the window ledge to see where they were heading. "Next stop, Mere," said Adam, and wondered if he was prepared for what he might find there.

Chapter Eight

Pip's Diary

Sunday 28th April

I fell asleep at my table. This was on the floor – sorry diary. It's daylight so I guess it must be Sunday. My mouth tastes like a dry toilet. God, that's disgusting. I'm going upstairs and I don't know what I'm going to find.

Thommo is still wheezing. He had slipped over again and I got him upright. I wish he was in bed, but maybe he will breathe better if he is not lying down. I touched Mum's hand. It was very cold. I stroked her face and that was stone cold. I could not kiss her. Isn't that awful? I just could not make myself do it. I pulled the bedclothes up over her face; I have covered her up. It did not seem right somehow to leave her just lying there like that. I'm going outside.

*

It is so quiet out there. It's the middle of the day but there is no sound at all, from anywhere. Even the sea gulls seem to have gone away. I don't think people are going to get better, because there is no-one here to help them. There's nobody on the street at all. I went into the kitchen to get some water from the tap but nothing came out. There's NO WATER! There was some lemonade in the fridge but it was slightly flat. I had a glass but I still feel thirsty. Why has our water stopped? Have all the houses lost their water? Oh God.

*

Thommo's breathing has got really slow now, like Mum's was. I'm losing him.

***

Thommo's gone. He went this afternoon. One minute he was breathing these slow gurgly gasps, that's how they sounded. And then I was listening for the next breath but it never came. I was sitting against him, sort of snuggled. I just wanted to be with him. I couldn't stop crying; I just stayed there pouring tears into his old jumper until the room got dark. I could see his face in the light from the hallway. He looked like he was asleep, really peaceful. A great big grizzly bear asleep under a tree. I kissed him on the cheek and his face felt cold but it didn't bother me or freak me out. In the end I had to leave him, even though I didn't want to leave him on his own. I tried to shut the en-suite door. I was pushing his foot back because it was stopping the door closing and then I thought maybe I should leave it so he and Mum could see each other. Then I shut the bedroom door.

Thommo, I have lost Mum and now you have left me on my own. I don't want to be here without you, you lovely, silly old bear!

Chapter Nine

No Sign

Tuesday 30th April, Late Morning

It did not take him long to drive to Mere. The road was empty most of the time and Adam was able to enjoy the views across the greening fields to Salisbury Plain. In the bright spring sunshine this morning the Wiltshire countryside looked very tranquil and alluring, unlike his previous visits to Sam's house when he had driven there in the dark.

It was a while now since he last visited his brother and probably a few weeks since they had spoken on the phone. The last time he had seen him was in February, and that was the first time in over a year. Adam had been on his way to bed after a long day, when the phone rang.

"Adam!"

"Sam?"

"What are you up to this weekend?"

"I'm not sure, nothing planned, I don't think. Why?"

"Excellent. We're going to London, you and me. Pick you up Saturday morning at ten?"

"What are you on about? What's going on?"

"England Wales, at Twickenham. Five Nations. I've got tickets."

"Oh, OK. Wow. I'll have to check with Jo and see what we're up to."

"I've spoken to her and she says it's fine. You're free to go."

"Did she now? When was that?"

"The other day. Don't know about you but I haven't been to Twickers since Dad took us as kids. I've got great seats, front of the stand. Oh, and bring a weekend bag – I've got us a room in this lovely old pub in Richmond."

"Sam, that's great but I need to check the diary and ...

"That's sorted then. Make sure you're ready, I've got a great day planned. See you at ten."

"Sam...?" But the line had gone dead.

That was just so Sam: maddening, unpredictable but lovable. Like it or lump it, he would always be there, his little brother. And as frustrating as he could be, Adam loved him for it, and now he wanted to see him more than ever. Yet, as he kept reminding himself, he mustn't get his hopes up. More than that, he must prepare himself for what he would find inside Sam's cottage, which was in all probability going to be the same desperate scene as in every other household. Adam just hoped he could cope with that when he got there.

He drove slowly down to the main street and turned off into Sam's road. He pulled up in the middle of the road near where he remembered the cottage to be. He shut the dogs in the van, then walked slowly along the terrace of cottages until he found the house. There was no sign of movement in the street or in the house. He could hear the chatter of sparrows above, up behind the eaves, and in the distance what sounded like a distressed cow. Apart from that it was quiet. He rapped on the door, softly at first and then louder. He peered in through the letter box but could neither see nor hear anything from within.

It was as he expected. Part of him wanted to get back in the van and drive away but the other part knew he had to go into the house and give himself certainty. He knew where the spare key was hidden in the back garden and the way to that lay down a lane that ran along the backs of the properties. He looked back at the van. Bonzo had his paws on the dashboard and was watching him intently. He barked when he saw Adam look over. "OK boy, you can come too," he said. He could do with some moral support here. He let the dogs out and set off down the road and then turned left up a narrow lane. The old dog loped along behind him while Bonzo darted here and there finding all sorts of smells.

After fifty yards the lane met a narrow alley which ran along behind the terrace of cottages. There were gates at intervals issuing from the long gardens and Adam tried to remember which was Sam's. He thought it had a red gate, but it might have been brown. He tried three or four gates before he found one that opened and, of course that was Sam's: He was not one to get hung up on locking things. He made his way up the narrow cottage garden. The bottom part was somewhat overgrown with some old fruit trees in need of pruning, but the rest was neatly dug over and he guessed that Sam had done some work in the garden quite recently. In the courtyard at the back of the house was a heavy bench which commanded a view of the length of the garden. Sam liked to sit here, he remembered, surveying his domain, smoking a roll-up, with his lurcher, Robbie, at his feet.

Adam reached behind the bench and found the spare key to the back door. He put it in the lock and opened the door slowly. It was quiet inside and he stepped slowly into the kitchen. All seemed as he remembered it. He walked through into the living room at the front of the cottage. No bad odours assailed him. The room was tidy, but for some letters on the floor under the letterbox in the front door. He picked them up. It looked like the post had been there a few days, probably since Friday last week at least. Was Sam away, he wondered? He made his way up the steep stairs that led out of the living room up to the bedrooms. The bedroom doors were open onto the landing and Adam looked in each to make sure, but both were empty. There were some clothes over the back of the chair in the front bedroom, which is where Sam slept. By his bed there was a clock radio, a bedside light and a magazine. On the chest of drawers there was a photo of a woman that Adam did not know and next to that an old photo of their parents, taken on a holiday back in the early seventies. The room was surprisingly tidy, Adam thought, remembering what a messy lad Sam used to be. The influence of his new woman perhaps?

The back bedroom was as it had been when Adam stayed a couple of years back, a depository for all of Sam's possessions that could not find a space in the rest of the tiny house. Somewhere under the clutter was the spare bed. He went back downstairs and through the kitchen to the bathroom, which was housed in a small extension on the back of the property. Again, all was as expected: a towel over the bath, Sam's dressing gown on the back of the door, assorted toiletries on the window ledge and on the bath. But, Adam noticed, there was no toothbrush in the mug on the shelf above the basin. It was looking likely that Sam had gone away, presumably before the virus struck.

Adam went back to the kitchen and opened the back door, where the two dogs were waiting for him. Bonzo's curiosity took him straight into the kitchen where he went sniffing around the cupboards and walls. He could smell Robbie's scent. Adam left him to explore and went out into the sunny courtyard and sat on the bench. The old dog came over, wagged his tail and sat down at his feet. So, Sam was not here and had not been since some time last week it seemed. Where had he gone, he wondered?

Adam had no way of knowing whether his brother was still alive or where he was or had been. In one way this was a relief: he had not had to encounter Sam's corpse festering in the confines of the tiny cottage and, more importantly, there was still the hope that Sam could be alive somewhere. Yet this left Adam in exactly the same position as when he set off from Reading: not knowing. Now he was unsure what to do next. He sat on the bench and began to wish that he still smoked. It seemed like the right time to draw on a cigarette and fathom out where to go from here.

He only had one cousin in this part of the country, his father's only nephew John, and he lived in Winchester. Adam had his details in his address book, but he had not seen him for years. All the cousins on his mother's side were in the north, and he didn't know their addresses, having lost touch after his parents died. The only family that he and Jo kept in touch with, apart from Sam, was her sister Anna who lived in Salisbury with her husband Pete. They had all met up at New Year but not since. Adam knew that Jo chatted to Anna once a week but it was a while since they had visited her in Salisbury. Adam and she got on quite well, but they had never been close.

All-in-all he was not convinced that there was any compelling reason for him to go to Salisbury, except that he knew that that was what Jo would have expected of him, and it was on his way to Winchester. So he decided that he would drive down to Salisbury and if, as seemed likely, Anna had succumbed to the virus, he would go on to Winchester to see if he could find his cousin John. He was the last person he knew how to find who carried the family genes. If he was dead, where then? Adam had not yet given this any serious thought. He had it in his mind that he needed to find a place with a water supply, fuel for heating and cooking and fertile land where he could, as a complete novice, somehow manage to keep chickens and grow vegetables. His family had enjoyed holidays in a farm in West Dorset when he was a boy and he fancifully thought that somewhere in that part of the world he might find the place he was looking for. He would start with that farm of his childhood, Friarswood. So, after Winchester he would head west into Dorset and, on the way, drive into a few different towns to see if there were any human beings still alive.

Now that he had a sort of plan, he could get moving. First, he went back into the cottage and had a good look around for any indication of where Sam might be. What was his girlfriend's name? He did not know for sure that there was anyone special in his life, but he was sure there was a woman somewhere. Nowhere in the cottage, however, could he find any clue as to her identity or where she lived. He searched through his brother's drawers for a diary or an address book, but could find nothing. He went into the small bedroom and started rummaging through the piles of stuff, turning it all over and rifling through a couple of cardboard boxes, but they just contained old magazines and technical books.

In this tiny house there was no desk, and so few cupboards that there were very few places to store anything. He looked in all the kitchen cupboards, and in the larder, but drew a blank. Where on earth could Sam keep his important documents? They certainly didn't seem to be anywhere in the house. In his car perhaps? At his girlfriend's place? There was really no clue at all. The dogs had followed his rummaging with interest at first but now had gone back out into the garden. Adam was going to join them but then remembered that he was going to write a note to his brother. He found a note pad and a pencil on the kitchen worktop. He tore a page off and wrote:

"Sam, I hoped I would find you here alive but it seems you have gone away. Let's hope you come back to read this message. I am going to Salisbury to see if I can find Anna, then to Winchester to look for John. After that, I am going to head into Dorset. If you are reading this, come and find me at Friarswood Farm, near Friarswood (just north of Charmouth). You should remember it when you get there, though it's probably changed a bit over the years. I will leave a message for you there as to where I am, if I am still on this planet. Take care, little brother, wherever you are. We'll meet up somewhere. Adam."

He placed the note under an upturned bowl with a corner sticking out then locked the back door and put the key back under the bench. "OK boys, you're right. I'm not going to find anything here, am I? Let's go." And he set off down the garden preceded by Bonzo and followed by the old dog, his canine escorts.

Chapter Ten

Pip's Diary

Monday 29th April

I'm writing this in bed. I've been lying here all night and I don't know if I have been asleep. It's daylight outside but I've only opened the curtains a crack so I can see what I'm doing, as the lights have gone out and my radio alarm clock isn't working. I ought to get up but I don't want to. I don't want to go outside cos I don't know what I'm going to find, but I know it's going to be bad. It's Monday morning and all I can hear are sparrows, gulls and, if I listen hard, the sea. That's all I have heard for hours now. There is no other sound.

I can't believe that my parents are dead. I can't believe that in the space of a weekend I have lost my family and, probably, my best friend too. And maybe all my school mates. It doesn't make sense. It can't be really happening. IT DOESN'T MAKE SENSE.

*

EVERYTHING HAS STOPPED!!! There's no sound in the house, it's really weird. I cried and cried for so long eventually there were no tears left and it was just really painful. And then I fell asleep again and I had these horrible, mixed-up dreams which I can't remember but they were so bad I had to wake myself up.

*

And now I am awake, everything is even worse than my dreams.

*

Well actually there is another sound: the grandfather clock downstairs struck eleven. I think it was eleven, I didn't check. All of a sudden I felt strangely removed? Remote? I decided that I had to pull myself together and do something. It was as if I had cried as much as I could and that had not changed anything, so now I had got to go and just.... get on with it?

I went along to the bathroom but when I flushed the loo nothing came out. I had to put the lid down. I checked in the cistern and it was empty. Then I remembered there was NO WATER in the tap last night. I really wanted a shower as I felt all cruddy, but too bad I guess. No one's going to care much about that. I went down to the kitchen to get a drink but I didn't fancy lemonade. Then I had a brainwave – try the hot tap. I remembered that we had a tank in the roof and sure enough there was water. Thommo always said don't swallow that water, so I thought: I could boil it up in the kettle. And then I remembered there's NO ELECTRICITY!!

But I also remembered that Thommo had bought some bottled water a few years back when we had problems with the supply. I remember he put them in the garage. So I got the keys and went out of the back door down the path to the garages. I opened the gate ajar. Peeped out and then jumped back like a right scaredy-cat.

There was a bloke sitting propped up against the big waste bin. He was slumped over on one side against the wall. I watched him for a while but he didn't move. He must be dead. I don't know who he was. Luckily I didn't have to go past him to get to the garage, but I kept my eye on him to make sure he didn't move. There was no light in the garage and I forgot to bring a torch. Luckily the water bottles were near the front under a pile of old blankets and other rubbish – Thommo never throws anything away. I grabbed three big plastic bottles and took them back to the house. I ran back. The bloke did not move.

The water tastes a bit funny, but I think it's ok. I put some squash with it just to make it taste a bit better. Then I started looking for something to eat. I hadn't eaten for two days? Or was it three? There's loads of stuff in the fridges but it's all got warm and some of it a bit whiffy. So I had to sort the food out and get rid of anything that was not going to keep. I filled a big sack full of cold meat, a pot of stew, cheese and loads of stuff, salads – chucked the whole lot in the bin outside. That was pretty full too. The bin-men would have come round today, but that's not going to happen now. It's going to really pong in a day or two. Anyway I made myself a sort of breakfast (dog's breakfast Thommo would have called it) of bananas and yogurt, that was still just OK. Then I had bread and butter and jam – I reckon the butter will keep a few days. I just stuffed my face cos I was so hungry. I took it into the guests' dining room and it was strange sitting in there with no one about. And when I had finished I just sat there, not knowing what to do. I felt a bit sick and I really wanted to go out and get some fresh air, but I was scared because I did not know what was going to be out there. In the end I came back up to the bedroom, and here I am writing all this to you.

Chapter Eleven

No Welcome

Tuesday 30th April, Afternoon

As they were heading away from Mere he was thinking about his brother and wondering if he would ever see him again, alive or dead. Without finding him it was unlikely he would ever know whether his own apparent immunity to this virus was down to genetics or some other reason. He recalled *The Day of the Triffids*, which he had read as a teenager many years ago. Everyone who stayed out to watch the comet that night had gone blind, but the hero was unaffected as he had been in hospital, his head wrapped in bandages after an operation on his eyes. Others who had also not looked at the comet, had not gone blind. But what sort of combination of circumstances could have saved Adam from being struck down like everyone else? There had been nothing unusual in his routines over the days and weeks leading up to last weekend. He went to work, he went to the nursery, he had been shopping, he had been with his family, he had met up with friends: he could think of nothing unusual he had done, no activity that was unique to him among all the thousands of people in Reading and Newbury, Berkshire or Wiltshire, Britain or the world. It could not be possible that he was the only person left alive, it just could not. It was too fantastical to contemplate, the laws of probability and nature would not admit such an aberration; it was just ridiculous to even think it. And yet, and yet – here he was.

And if he could not fathom out the how, then what about the why? Adam did not believe in God, but if there was a supreme being, what possible reason could there be for making him the sole survivor? Was there a woman somewhere waiting for him? Would they have the job of repopulating the earth, of re-starting humanity to set it on a new course? That's not a role he would have volunteered for, he thought.

Adam tried to think about Jo and the children, what should have been going on this week. Oscar was back at school now after the Easter holidays and was already getting in training for Sports Day which came later in the term. Sophie had recently gone into the toddlers' group at the little playschool she attended, and she just loved her teacher and her friends. Jo was doing well in her job and there was the unspoken promise that the next promotion would be to Director level. This coming Saturday they would have been out with their friends Ivor and Sally. And on Wednesday, tomorrow, they had booked a baby-sitter and were going into town for a mid-week treat at their favourite Italian restaurant.

His reflections were brought to an abrupt stop by a fox running out into the road in front of him. Adam braked hard and swerved to avoid it. Bonzo shot forward into the dashboard and yelped. Adam pulled up in the road and checked that he was OK and the old dog too. They seemed none the worse for wear. He had not been driving fast but he was on autopilot and the sudden appearance of the fox had caught him out. He guessed that this was going to be something that would happen more often as animals lost their fear of motor vehicles and no longer felt the need to avoid the roads. He set off again, more slowly now than he would ever normally have driven. He realised that the turn-off to Salisbury was almost upon him and that he probably would have sailed straight on past had he not met the fox.

The lower Wylie Valley was looking very pretty in its new spring colours, but Adam was focussed only on getting to Salisbury without mishap. He was thinking about Jo and her sister. Anna was the first-born and there was quite a gap between them. It was no surprise to anyone who knew her when she decided to go into teacher training. She had found her vocation early and thrived as a teacher in a girl's secondary school. She met Pete, a teacher at a private boys' school, and married him quite soon after. They led the quiet life of serious professionals and filled their large Victorian house in with books instead of babies.

It seemed to Jo that Anna became more elusive after she married Pete. The two sisters did not get the chance to meet up very often and, when they did, Anna seemed reserved, almost guarded, much more like a work colleague than a sister. Jo tried to find out from Anna why she had changed but no amount of subtle probing elicited any answers. And when she asked about her relationship with Pete, her sister just closed shop and made it clear that this was not open for discussion. Adam knew that Jo felt that she was missing her sister; that she was worried whether Pete was somehow making it difficult for Anna to meet up with her. It seemed a pointless exercise but nevertheless Adam felt it his duty to Jo to go to Salisbury and see if her sister was alive.

As they drove into Wilton later, the sun went in and suddenly it looked like it might rain. The darkening sky matched Adam's mood and as he came into the old part of Salisbury and the Cathedral area, where Anna and Pete lived, he was full of foreboding. What was he going to do when he got to their house? Break in, like he had at the old corner house – and then what? It was the middle of the day, but the quietness was like a blanket over the town. He couldn't hear any birds or other animals and when, as he got to the house, raindrops started hitting the van it was almost deafening. Bonzo looked up at him expectantly but did not seem in any hurry to get out of the van. The old dog sat up on his blanket and stretched and gave a quiet, questioning whine.

He got out of the van and stood in the road looking up at the double-fronted house. The curtains upstairs were closed. He walked through the wrought iron gates up the path to the front door. There was a neatly engraved sign by the door with *Dr P and Mrs A Watkins* in gold lettering. Pompous, he used to think, like Pete. He pressed the bellpush but there was no ringing inside. He tapped softly on the quarter light, and when that yielded no response, he banged hard on the door three times. There was nothing. It was as if the whole street had fallen silent and was watching him, waiting to see what he would do next. He walked over to the window to the left of the door, which looked out from their front sitting room. The curtains were closed, as they were on the study windows, to the right of the door.

There was a high side-gate on the right-hand side of the building and Adam could see nothing past it. The gate was bolted on the inside. One good shoulder barge though was all that was needed to open it. To the side of the house was a stained-glass window that led into the small passage off the hall. Be a shame to break that too, he thought, and walked around to the back of the house. The back door was locked, as he expected and again he considered whether to break the glazing. In the end he opted to go for the small window in the "snug", a corner of the kitchen where Anna would curl up in an armchair and read. The light was good there, she said. He found a stone from a nearby rockery and it did not take a moment to take out all the glass from the window. He pulled over a garden bench and used that to get up to window level so he could ease his way through the window frame into the kitchen.

The kitchen looked remarkably tidy, even for Pete and Anna, and there were no signs of any recent activity. It was as if they had tidied it up the way people sometimes do before going away on a long trip. Perhaps they *had* gone away, like Sam. He went through to the hall. The coats were on the rack by the front door, as always, and there were no letters on the floor. He looked into the study, which, with the curtains closed, was in semi-darkness. No-one in there, or in the sitting room opposite, where the daylight filtered weakly through a gap in the curtains. The dining room curtains were open, and it looked as tidy as it always had done, as if awaiting the arrival of a special guest for dinner.

Adam went up the broad staircase just as the sun came out from behind a cloud, lighting up the stained-glass window. He paused on the landing. He could see that all the doors upstairs were closed which he thought was odd. He took a deep breath and climbed on up to the first floor and went across the hallway to the main bedroom. The scene inside was total disorder, in complete contrast to the tidiness downstairs. The bedclothes spewed across the floor, tangled with clothing and towels. The drawers of a tallboy were opened and spilling clothes, the wardrobe doors were wide open with shirts hanging off the hangers and piled on the carpet. He walked round the bed cautiously and when he got to the window he opened the curtains a little. He looked at the other side of the bed, but there was no sign of Anna or Pete there.

He went back onto the landing. He went to the other front bedroom – the guest room – and opened the door. All was as he remembered it when they had stayed for a night some years ago, tidy and sort of bare, like a hotel room. The next door opened into Anna's reading room, where she used to curl up on a vintage chaise longue to do her marking and listen to music, which was something Pete was not fond of, according to Jo. It did not appear to Adam as if anyone had been in there for a while. Next to that was a little box room and that was literally full of boxes, mainly of books it seemed. That left just the door to the room over the sitting room: that must be where he would find their bodies.

He hesitated a moment and then turned the doorknob. The door would not open – it had been locked. Why would they have locked this room? Was there something in there that they did not want anyone to find – jewellery, valuables, papers? But if a burglar broke into the house while they were out or away, as Adam had done very easily, then a locked door was surely an invitation to investigate further? Adam pondered what he should do next. Should he break the door down and find out what there was inside that was so valuable? Or should he just forget about it and leave? After all it was not as if Anna really meant a lot to him and he had no love at all for Pete, so what was the point? He might just as well go.

He turned away and set off down the stairs and then, at the landing, stopped abruptly, turned round and climbed back up the stairs. He stopped at the door, leant back and then stamped his boot hard at the lock. The door flew open as the lock gave way.

The room was very dark, with the window completely obscured behind heavy velvet curtains. The air was thick with the smell of death. As his eyes adjusted to the gloom, he could make out the body of Anna lying on the bed. He went out, took a deep breath and pulled up the collar of his sweatshirt to cover his mouth and nose. Then he went back in, pulled the curtain back and opened the window to let in some air. Anna was laid out as if in a coffin. She lay on her back with her hands together on her chest. The bedclothes were laid across her, as if she were sleeping and someone had tidied up the bed while she slept. But the sheet showed a large stain where it was folded back on the counterpane, and Anna's nightdress was rumpled and dirty. Her eyes were closed but her mouth seemed contorted, as if in pain and her face, though drained of all colour now, showed signs of bruising under the eye. There were dark marks on her white neck. What had happened here. What had Pete done?

Adam could feel himself wanting to heave and could stay in the room no longer. He retreated to the landing, gasping for air. Part of him wanted to know what had happened, how Anna had died. Was this Pete's doing? - he could not be sure. Everything seemed wrong to him. He just had to get out of the house.

Back down in the kitchen, he tried to open the back door, but the key was not in the lock. Typical of Pete, he thought, to remove the key and hide it somewhere. He sat down at the table and thought what to do next. He could cover up Anna's body, but what would be the point? He did not think he had the strength to dig another grave and though he would like to have given Anna the dignity of a burial, she was at least lying in a bed, and one could almost believe that she was at peace. Her suffering was over, that much he knew.

He went into the study and opened the curtains a little so he could see better. He wanted a pen and paper to write a message, and then he noticed that the waste bin was quite empty. Was it just coincidence that it been emptied so recently, or was it that Pete had done it deliberately? Adam went back into the kitchen and opened the fridge door. As he anticipated, inside it was completely empty and looked almost new. The larder was similarly clean and organised.

It seemed to Adam that the way the house had been left so tidy suggested that Pete had made a huge effort to put everything in order before he left. But why would he have done that, and how had he had the energy to do it unless he didn't have the virus? And why did he leave his wife's body and the main bedroom in such a state? Was he planning to see to that later and then, when everything shut down, he realised that it was not just Anna that was sick, it was everyone? Was that when he decided to leave?

There were so many questions. Why had he moved Anna from their bed? Why was she in the other room to start with? In what order had these events unfolded and what were Pete's motives? And what about the marks on Anna's neck and the bruise under her eye? – had they fought, had he forced her in there? Or had he taken her life even, to alleviate her pain and suffering, maybe suffocated her with a pillow? Questions, questions.

Adam felt he couldn't achieve anything more now by staying in the house. He had seen what he had seen and, short of breaking into Pete's desk, he was not going to learn anything else. He sat down at the kitchen table and started to write a note:

"This was the home of Peter and Anna Watkins. Anna died on or about the 27th April 1991 ...." He stopped, pen hovering above the paper. Then he put down the pen, screwed the paper up and fired it into the waste bin. What was the point? Who would read it and would they care? And why was he fretting about what had happened to Anna? Who would know? Were any of her friends or family still alive? As for Pete, he was nothing to him now – he didn't even like the guy. He had done what he had to and he had done it for Jo.

He got up to go but paused, thinking how he should leave things upstairs. He decided to close the door to Anna's bedroom. Then he opened a window in the spare bedroom and another in the bathroom. That way at least there would be some air getting into the house.

Satisfied that he had done all he could, he went back downstairs, unbolted the front door and walked out, letting the door slam shut behind him. Once outside he stood in the front garden and took in some deep breaths of spring air. Without a glance back he returned to the van.

Chapter Twelve

Pip's Diary

Monday 29th April Evening

I fell asleep for a while and then when I woke I was thinking about Thommo and Mum. I can't really believe they have gone like that. How could they just die? Why am I still alive and they aren't? What about Nic, is she dead too? I really could do with her here now so I could just talk to her. And Scott – it would be nice to see him. I woke up crying again. So much for getting on with it. there's no one to get on with it for.

I realised that I had been in the same clothes since I got back from school on Friday. I was getting a bit whiffy, like the fridge. So had a wash in the bathroom. The water was lukewarm, so it was not too bad. I couldn't face doing my hair without hot water though. I changed into some fresh clothes, put a bit of underarm on and brushed my hair. It's going a bit greasy now – too bad. I opened the bedroom window wide to get the air in and then I went to Mum and Thommo's room. I didn't want to go in, but I made myself. The curtains were still closed so I pulled them back and opened their window. I looked at the bed and mum was lying there as I left her, but when I pulled the bedclothes off her face, she looked different. She was very pale and her skin looked like it was made of wax. Thommo was still in the bathroom, but he had fallen over on one side. I guess he must have been leaning on me and when I left him he toppled over. I stared at them for ages, and then I just had to get out of the room and out of the house.

I put my denim jacket on, and my boots and went out on the street. I made sure the back door was locked and I locked the front door behind me. Everything was the same as yesterday, with not a soul about. I walked slowly down our road to King Street and looked up and down. Nothing seemed to have moved, but there were several cats about, some just sunning themselves in the road, though there wasn't any sun showing to speak of. I walked in the middle of the road. I think I was afraid that someone might lurch out of a building like a zombie. It didn't look likely that I was going to meet anybody, but I wondered how it would be if I did. I can't really tell you what I was thinking, but it just seemed really scary, the thought that in every building I passed there were dead people. It was like I was watching myself walking down the road and thinking – this is not happening!

I think I'm starting to take it in a bit more now, but then, at that moment, walking down the middle of a high street on a Monday afternoon with no-one about and no noise except for the rumble of the sea and the calling of the gulls – then it was just unreal. I carried on till I got to the Esplanade, and still no movement or sound. I turned right, along the esplanade past the Royal Hotel. Cars were parked everywhere, as usual, but there were some just abandoned in crazy places. Some had doors and *windows open. There was a red car, a Ford or something, and there was a woman slumped against the passenger window. I thought she was dead and then I saw that her eyes were open and it was like she was watching me. Sh*t I almost jumped!! Then I realised that she really was dead after all. So then I decided to walk on the pavement overlooking the beach. It was low tide, but the sea was not out far. It was grey and a bit choppy. There was a body, lying on the beach – looked like a boy my age. Further on there was another body on the shoreline and I could see some sea-weed on it.*

I carried on until I got to the end of the pier. There was no-one there, thank God. And I just sat on the bench, where Scott and I sit sometimes, looking across the water to the town and I just cried. It sort of all came out in a flood. I think I just let it all out because there was no-one around to hear. I must have gone on for about half-an-hour, I don't really know. I sat there for a long time, until I started getting chilly. I could not face going back to Serendipity so I walked back along the beach, past King Street all the way up to the end of the town. I stopped there and sat down by the water's edge and the sun came out. It was warm in the sun, and so peaceful sitting there. I lay back on the sand and shut my eyes, trying to pretend that nothing had happened and that when I opened my eyes I would hear people, cars on the road, an aircraft flying over, a speed boat in the bay. It didn't work. So I carried on all the way along to Overcombe, walking in bare feet along the water line.

It was nearly four when I got back to the Victoria Clock, so I must have been out for a couple of hours or more. But so what.

Who's counting? On the way back along the beach I had been trying to focus my thoughts on what I was going to do. I thought that maybe I could drive Thommo's car up to Bath and see if Nic is still alive. But I don't know how to drive and what if I crash the car somewhere and I'm in the middle of nowhere? Then I thought how I was going to eat and how I could make hot food. (Note to self – remember to try the gas stove) (Note 2: don't be silly, there won't be any gas either).

** No, there is no gas**

Then I had the idea that I could see if there were any shops with the doors open, collect up all the tins I could find and get them back to the house. So all these ideas, and lots more, were going round in my head, and now I'm sitting here in the sitting room, thinking WHAT'S THE POINT? I'm all alone, no-one else is alive, why do I want to be alive? WHAT AM I DOING HERE?!!!!

Chapter Thirteen

No Hope

Tuesday 30th April, Evening

His route to Winchester took him along the old London road, once a major arterial route. Not since the days of the barrow builders, had this road been this empty. The afternoon sun coming through the new leaves gave the trees a luminescent quality and the fields stretching away either side of the road wore various shades of green and yellow reflecting the different crops that were coming up. These crops would not be harvested this season and would still be rotting away this time next year, Adam thought, and the landscape of England would look very different then. And so the joy of driving through the beautiful English countryside on a spring afternoon on a deserted road was undercut by a looming sadness: this could not last, just as human existence could not last.

Adam tried to focus on the landscape and not let his thoughts wander back to the house in Salisbury he had not long left, or his garden in Reading. But as he came down the hill into Stockbridge and over the river Test, he was brought back to reality by the sight of a police car with its nose in a hedge and as he drove around it he saw a figure in navy blue slumped against the driver's window. The village high street looked quaint as ever and deserted as on an early Sunday morning and Adam did not see any other bodies. They would all be lying in their beds, no doubt.

It wasn't long before Adam was driving into the outskirts of Winchester. He pulled up and checked John's address in the address book he had brought with him. Alder Close was the road and Adam had vague recollections of a white-fronted semi-detached in a small close on the south-west side of the town. But it had been many years since he last visited his cousin. He remembered driving round a large housing estate, but he could not remember much else. He had been looking for half an hour when he came to a road whose name, Linden Avenue, he recalled from his last visit. Linden was his mother's maiden name, and he knew this road took him close to John's place. A few minutes later he came by the small close and drove slowly towards the house.

There were two cars on the drive, a small hatchback, a fairly recent model, and a grey Morris Minor dating from the sixties. He remembered how John had always liked those cars and loved to tinker with the engines and keep their rusting bodywork together, and this one was in A1 condition. As far as he could recall, John lived alone, so Adam guessed that the hatchback was his everyday working car, and the old Morris was only taken out on high days and holidays. Adam stopped in the road and got out of the van. He was careful to ensure that the dogs stayed inside, though neither of them seemed that keen to get out. They had had a busy day already and perhaps Alder Close did not seem so attractive to them. Maybe they could sense Adam's reluctance to do what he knew he would have to do, yet again. He walked round to the side door, noticing that the front room's curtains were closed but that those upstairs were drawn back.

The side door was the original timber and glazed door that looked like it had not been painted since the house was built. John did not earn a lot and Adam remembered him recounting how his wife had cleaned him out in the divorce. He had been living on his own a long time now, he guessed, and Adam imagined that his cousin was probably not the type to worry too much about appearances. Hopefully, he would not mind too much if Adam damaged the door on his way in. He took a step back and then stamped high up the door near the handle. Rather to his surprise the door flew open at first kick with a splintering of wood as the keep was wrenched out of the frame. The door swung back and crashed against a cupboard, toppling a biscuit tin which clattered loudly to the floor. A large tabby cat came screeching out of the door and disappeared up the path.

He walked through the little kitchen to the door leading into the dining room beyond. He did not have to step into the room to be aware of the smell and a quick peek around the door revealed the source: John's body lay on the floor to the side of the table, his feet tangled in the chair he had been sitting on. Books and magazines were scattered over the table and on the floor and a coffee stain spread across the carpet from the cup that was still in his hand. Adam could see by the colour of his skin that John had been dead a while and there was no point in getting any closer to check for vital signs – he had most probably died three days before. Although he hardly knew his cousin, it was still a shock to see him lying there like that, as it had been with Anna. To see any dead body is shocking, but far worse when it is that of someone you know.

He knew that finding John dead had put an effective end to his quest. John had not survived and Adam had no other blood relatives whose whereabouts he knew. He was about to head back out of the door when a thought crossed his mind: He remembered that John had two siblings, his cousins, and he might have their contact details somewhere. It would be good to have their addresses just in case.

Adam was keen to get away from this dismal scene, but he knew he would regret it later if he did not even make an attempt to find some information. He held his breath and had a quick look around the dining room but there did not seem to be any furniture in there in which personal papers might be stored. The obvious place to look for names and numbers was by the phone and he found that straightaway on a little table in the hall. Sure enough next to it was an address book. Adam had a quick look under "F" and found three Fishers there. A Michael, a Susan (now Rogers) and his own name and number. Michael and Susan were John's brother and sister, and they were probably the only people that could be of interest to Adam. Michael only had a phone number by his name, but there was an address for Susan in Wellington. Wellington was near Shrewsbury where his old buddy Gerry lived. If Adam travelled up in that part of the world he could look for both of them. He closed the address book – he had what he needed and he could leave this gloomy house.

He made his way out of the town, headed south towards the coast and then followed the signs towards Bournemouth. The road was clear most of the way and there were only a few occasions when he had to manoeuvre around abandoned vehicles. The sky had cleared completely after the showers in the middle of the day, and as they turned west and headed into the New Forest the lowering sun was in his eyes. He drove steadily with the window open. The rain had only cleared recently from the forest and the sweet smells of damp, fresh grass drying in the evening sun filled the van. Bonzo was standing on his hind legs, sniffing at the breeze coming through the passenger window and the old dog, on his couch in the back of the van, had his ears pricked up. "Well boys, we had better start thinking about where we are going to spend the night," he said. "What do you reckon – hotel or campsite?" He realised how glad he was of the dogs' company. He and Jo had never had a pet and while he liked animals, Adam looked on his pet-loving friends and their endless stories of feline or canine love and fidelity with a detached amusement. But now he began to see how a pet could be a life saver for someone bereaved or left on their own. These two might be the only creatures he would ever have to chat to.

As he drove westwards the trees began to recede as the road climbed towards the open heathland. Just then he remembered that a little while back he had seen the sign for the Rufus Stone, the memorial in the trees marking the spot where King William the Second met his end. He remembered going there as a lad with Dad, on their way down to the West Country, and he had a fancy that he would like to go there again. His memory of the place was a broad, open, grassy sward surrounded by trees. He and Sam had raced around on the grass playing a sort of game of tig where they each had to stop the other from reaching the Rufus Stone. It would make a good camping spot.

He turned round in the road and drove back a mile until he got to the turning. A lane took him a way into the trees and after about a mile there was the old stone monument in a grassy clearing – a perfect level and sheltered spot for a camp. He parked in a sunny corner and got out of the cab and had a stretch. The dogs were eager to get out of the van and ran around exploring the terrain. Adam was feeling tired all of a sudden and could feel the tension in his shoulders. It had been a long day and pretty intense.

He wandered over to the memorial stone, taking in the tranquillity of his surroundings. There was no breeze at all here and no sound except for the birdsong. The two dogs ran around happily as if they too sensed the specialness of this moment. Meanwhile Adam read the text on the stone: *"Here stood the oak tree on which an arrow shot by Walter Tyrell at a stag glanced and struck King William the Second, known as Rufus, on the breast, of which he instantly died on the second day of August Anno 1100."*

Adam remembered his father recounting the story of how this unpopular king was killed, and his body taken by a humble cart to Winchester Cathedral. His father had also told them stories about the King's ghost and a phantom black dog, which was supposed to belong to Tyrell. It was over 800 years since this event took place, ancient history to a child and irrelevant to the hectic "nowness" of modern life. And yet, standing here in the quiet of the evening, with no traffic noise or aircraft to disturb the sounds of nature, it felt as if nothing had changed in this forest, and it could all have happened yesterday.

Adam wandered back to the van and started setting up camp for the night. He put up the foldaway table and found a plate, cutlery and a saucepan. He looked in the supplies box and fished out a tin of frankfurters and a tin of beans. It was hardly cordon bleu, but it would do to satisfy his appetite tonight and Adam suddenly felt very hungry. He found a can of beer, not as cool as he would have liked, but welcome, none the less, and began preparing his rudimentary meal. While the food was heating up he sorted out his bed for the night. The couch folded out into a narrow double bed, the foam just about cushioning the sleeper from the wooden base. He got a couple of lamps ready for later and when the sun dropped behind the high trees, he needed them. Predictably, the dogs smelled the food and came back to the van expectantly. Adam opened up a tin of dog food and shared it between them. He made sure that the old dog got his first as he guessed that Bonzo would bolt his food down and look to finish off the other bowl. He need not have worried. The old dog soon let Bonzo know that his meal was not for sharing.

As the sun set and the stars started to appear in the darkening sky, so the temperature in the clearing dropped. It was going to be a chilly night. He put on a sweater and sat looking out through the open side door. He looked back over the last few days and the thought crossed his mind that he had never in his life been totally alone for so long, having no communication whatsoever with another human being. And yet now, all alone in this still forest under the vast, dark sky, he felt strangely at ease with himself. He was alive, he had survived; most, maybe all, of the rest of the world, had not. A man, on his own in the world with no loved ones, no one depending on him and no responsibilities, other than his own continued existence – and even that was optional. He was tired now and ready for his dreams to take him where they would. Tomorrow was another day.

Chapter Fourteen

Pip's Diary

Tuesday 30th April

I did not want to get up this morning I could not face it. I was really tired cos I really did not sleep properly last night. The whole night I was getting weird, horrible dreams. So horrible I had to force them from my memory. I kept waking up and then I did not want to go back to sleep. So I just lay there and tried to remember good times but then I would just start remembering all the grotty stuff. Like the time last year when that cow Miranda called me a Paki bitch. She says that because she knows full well I was born in India and it winds me up. So I went mad and started pulling her hair and then we were having a full-on fight. I got a week of detention for that and she only got three days. That was not fair. So I stopped thinking about school and thought about holidays we had had, but that just made me really sad. And then I would fall asleep again and I would have another bad dream.

When it started getting light I pulled back the curtains hoping that would keep the dreams away. I listened to the waves on the beach and then the gulls, when they started. I think the sounds must have calmed me cos I slept then, on and off, till 11.00.

Eventually I had to go to the bathroom, so I put a jumper on – it was cold in the house – and then went past Mum & Dad's room and when I did that I thought about them lying there, cold and dead. I didn't like thinking about that, so I got dressed quickly and went downstairs.

I could not face eating, so I made myself some cold black coffee with three sugars (I know! Who cares! And it was still not sweet enough) and I sat in the guest lounge and looked out at the sky. It was sort of sunny, with white clouds and looked like it could be a nice sort of day. And then I thought about everything that had just happened and I wondered how there could ever be a nice day again. I could not face staying in the house so I got my coat and my keys and then – as an afterthought – my rucksack, a bottle of water and a packet of biccies and off I went. I walked for miles, all the way round the bay to the holiday camp and then up to the cliffs and along to the Smuggler's. All the way these random thoughts were whirling around in my head – what am I going to do? Is Nic alive? Shall I try and get to Bath? Are there people alive somewhere else? Is the army going to turn up or a posse of bandits? Have the aliens come down and wiped us out and are they going to find me and take me off to some remote galaxy? No, I wasn't really thinking that, but I might as well have been because any idea or theory I had just seemed crazy. I mean what the hell just happened here?!

***

My watch had stopped so I had no idea what the time was, but by the time I got near to Osmington I was getting really hungry and feeling a bit spaced out. So I sat on a bench there looking out across the bay. It was quite sunny now and I munched my biccies and tried to shut out all this NOISE in my head and just enjoy the view, as if it was any normal day in the hols and I had gone for a walk. Then I thought of that time that I persuaded Thommo to come for a walk with me (with the lure of him having a pint in the pub garden). He was completely knackered by the time we got back home but we had a great day, just me and him. Thinking of him then, and how he was yesterday in the bathroom made me really sad and I just sat on the bench and cried. After an age I made myself get up and I went down to the beach and threw pebbles in the sea. I decided then that I needed to get a grip and sort myself out. So on the way back home I started making all these grand plans about what I was going to do, like:

- *Sort the kitchen out and work out what food I needed (break into the Co-op??)*

- *Look in the tank in the loft and see how much water there is*

- *Get Thommo's car out of the garage and try and teach myself to drive (I know, I'm not sixteen yet but that doesn't mean I can't learn)*

- *Get a barbecue and some charcoal and start cooking outside (The Reader's Digest book of home cooking????)*

- *Adopt a stray dog and train it to be a guard dog (!!!)*

I know, it's not funny but I was trying to think positively but I kept thinking that I should be at school now, going back for first period after lunch doing – what day is it today? – Maths. I hate maths and I don't particularly enjoy school but I would give anything to wake up with Rusty Smith throwing a text book at me or being made to stand on a chair on one leg and explain Pythagoras. Anything to get back to normality.

***

I got back about three, I think, all set on getting myself together, but the first thing I did was make myself a proper "meal". I remember that Mum always said you could not do any serious work on an empty stomach and when you eat it should be a proper meal. So I laid a place in the dining room and my starter comprised crackers with butter, some cheese and a tomato which I sliced up restaurant style, like Thommo had shown me once. My main course was a small bowl of spaghetti hoops (not bad cold, surprisingly) and for pudding I was going to have rice pudding, but I was full, so I decided to save it for later and just enjoy my glass of "wine" (Ribena).

I started to write down my action plan like a checklist, but there was a big something missing from the list: <u>what am I going to do about Mum and Thommo</u>? I can't just leave them there, all cold and stiff upstairs. But how can I move them? I could probably *wrap Mum in a sheet and drag her down the stairs but Thommo? I could never move him. Maybe I should lay them out straight and roll them up in sheets, tie the ends up and find some flowers to strew over them. Do I say a prayer or read from the bible?*

I do not know what to do but I think I should go into their room and at least try and get them "tidy" and then tomorrow I'll get some flowers and give them a proper "send-off" – is that what it's called?

***

I managed to put this off for another hour, faffing about in the kitchen and then trying to get the loft door open and giving up and then eventually I just had to do it. I went into their room and there they were. It was just so horrible seeing them like that, Mum on the bed and Thommo by the bath in the en-suite – like they weren't related. It wasn't them, it was these two ***bodies****. The sun was coming in and the room was really warm. There were flies buzzing around and there was this smell – it was gross! I went straight out and shut the door and went to my room. I lay on my bed and thought I was going to puke. And then I thought, I have got to do* ***something*** *and I have to do it now, or I never will. So I went to the blanket cupboard and found some clean double sheets, four of them. Then I tied a scarf around my head to cover my mouth and nose and I went back into the room. I covered Mum up with two sheets. It seemed kind of respectful and it somehow looked right, her body laid out straight on the bed, wrapped like* *an Egyptian mummy. With Thommo I just had to cover him up where he was, though it looked really strange, this mound of sheets by the bath.*

I was not sure whether to leave the window open or close it, but I decided it would be better to open both windows just a bit to get a draught through. I pulled the curtains across though. I didn't know what to do about flowers but then I remembered the cherry tree across the road was in flower. So I took the kitchen scissors and cut off some of the blossom and took it up and placed it on the bodies. Mum looked like something out of a Hindu funeral I had seen in a book once. I did not say a prayer – it would have sounded odd coming out all muffled through the scarf. Instead I got the bible from the bookcase down the hall and laid it on the bed next to Mum, and put Thommo's favourite book of Dylan Thomas poetry by him. And that was it. I said goodbye and shut the door and locked it.

That was it? That was all I could do? God that's awful. But what else should I do? Mum, Thommo I'm sorry. I love you both so much. I hope you are safe, somewhere.

I'm in bed now. My eyes are watering from writing this by candle light (I couldn't find any spare batteries so I am saving the torch for essential manoeuvres) and my hand is aching so I'm going to try and sleep.

Chapter Fifteen

New Beginning

Wednesday 1st May, Morning

Adam slept heavily and dreamlessly for the first time since the plague struck on Friday, though he was vaguely aware of the dogs moving about in the night. The sunlight coming low through the van's windows woke him out of his stupor. He didn't know what time it was but the birdsong was incredibly loud. His shoulder was aching, so he rolled over onto his back and closed his eyes again. Bonzo had climbed on top of his bed in the night and when he saw Adam stirring the young dog climbed on top of him and began licking his face. Adam pushed him away roughly with a grunt and turned over onto his other side. It took a moment for him to register where he was and why the dog was there, by which time he was properly awake. He turned onto his back again and reached out for his watch. It was seven o'clock and he had been asleep nearly ten hours – no wonder his shoulder was stiff.

He sat up slowly and looked around him. The sun had already cleared the trees and was filling the clearing with the low morning light. It sparkled on the dew in the grass – it must have been a cold night. Bonzo was sitting by his bed looking at him with his head on one side. Adam held out his hand to him and the dog licked it and wagged his tail furiously. Not to be outdone, the old dog got off his bed and came over to say hello as well. "Hello boys," Adam said. "Are we well? It's a fine morning, where are we going to go today?" Bonzo barked and ran over to the side door while the old dog looked at him expectantly. Adam got out of the low bed and moved stiffly to open the door. The dogs ran out onto the grass and Adam followed slowly. When he got down from the van he felt the damp grass on his bare feet. He raised his arms high above his head and stretched himself up to his full height and gently got his limbs moving. That bed was not very comfortable and clearly was not designed for people of his stature, and yet despite that he had slept through the night. The grass was cold and the air still had a chill in it, He shivered and stepped back into the van to find some clothes to put on.

Once dressed, cup of coffee in his hand, he sat down on the door sill and watched the dogs running around the clearing, finding exciting new smells, perhaps of an animal that had passed in the night. He glanced at his watch and saw that the date had a 1 showing . It's the first of the month, he thought. It was May Day. A new day, a new month, a new start. The day seemed full of promise, but Adam had no idea what it was promising.

He drained his coffee cup, climbed back into the van and set about stowing things away for the travelling ahead. The van started first time, which was encouraging. At the junction with the main road he instinctively looked in both directions before pulling out, but the road, of course, was quite empty,. The sun was behind them and still quite low in the sky and as they crossed the high part of the forest Adam could see the folds of the land stretching away to the south towards the coast. He was heading down into Dorset to see if he could find Friarswood Farm, as he told Sam he would do in the note.

Adam glanced at the fuel gauge. It was getting down below a quarter of a tank now and he started doing some calculations: he had driven perhaps two hundred miles yesterday and was going to do another seventy or so today. He would need some fuel soon and he still did not know how easy it would be to find and, more pertinently, how he could get it from wherever into the van. He needed some sort of pump or, failing that, some piping he could use as a syphon. He really needed to get into a garage repair shop and have a hunt there for the right tools. He drove past Ringwood and wondered about turning into the town to hunt for somewhere. But it was quite a small place and maybe he would be better off looking around in Bournemouth or Poole, which were not much further on down the road. He followed the main road to the west, until he got to the outskirts of town, keeping his eyes peeled for a small workshop he might be able to get into. As he got into the built-up area, he noticed that increasingly there were animals wandering onto the road. Mainly it was stray dogs and cats, but also a fox that trotted across in front of him. He kept his speed down and scoured the side roads for any promising-looking buildings. There was nothing to be found on the main road, but he saw a sign for an industrial estate and headed off down there.

The place was closed up and deserted, as if it were a Sunday. There was a car body repair shop but nothing like a mechanic's workshop. There was a big building with several large trucks parked in front and Adam wondered whether there might be a maintenance section somewhere, but all the steel shutters were down and it did not look as if it would be easy to break in there. He drove back to the main road and carried on slowly, passing a supermarket, then a filling station, and a bit further on he come upon a row of small shops. In the middle was a pet shop, which gave Adam an idea: if they sold aquarium supplies, he could get a small hand pump and maybe he could use that for siphoning out petrol.

Leaving the dogs in the van, he walked up to the shop front and did a quick survey. The door was plate glass, like the window. It was going to be thick, but it was not toughened glass. He reckoned it would be easier to get that open than take out the window, but he needed a tool for the job. Remembering that there was the wheel brace somewhere in the back of the van, he opened the tailgate and rummaged under the pile of bags, boxes and stuff that he had slung in the storage area. In the end he had to get most of it out onto the road in order to get to find what he was looking for. Meanwhile Bonzo was wanting to get over the back seat and out of the van but when Adam said "No!" in a no-nonsense voice, the dog responded surprisingly obediently and sat down again.

He went over to the door and took a big swing at the glass with the wheel brace, closing his eyes as he did so and bracing himself for the recoil. A crack appeared across the glass, which was encouraging. Two more heavy blows and the glass shattered and fell into the shop doorway. Adam used the brace to chip off the remaining fragments from the frame and then stepped into the shop. As soon as he set foot inside, he became aware firstly of the excited chittering of small rodents and secondly the rank odour of animals. Even with his muted sense of smell he got the strong reek of urine and faeces. The large glass window let plenty of light in, so he was able to find his way around the shop. Down one side there were cages of small pets: mice, gerbils, some rabbits, and the poor creatures were going wild. He guessed that they had not been fed or watered for perhaps five days now. He could see many of the mice were lying dead and all of the animals were distressed. He hurried on towards the back of the shop, where the accessories would be. The shop stocked fish tanks and bowls, and there must be other items that aquarium owners would need. The light was fairly low here and he had not brought the torch. He went back to the van, avoiding the animal cages by going down another isle.

The dogs had picked up the pets' noises and were showing great interest. He got the torch, making sure that the dogs stayed in the van, and went back into the shop. The noise inside was deafening. He quickly found a hand pump for emptying out fish tanks. Adam reckoned he could adapt that to get petrol out of a car's tank. He picked up a second one and some clear tubing, which he found on the next shelf. He saw some packets of dog biscuits and picked up three of those, plus some dog chews. The dogs deserved a treat, he thought. He threw everything into a carrier bag and took it out to the van. A thought struck him and he went back to the shop. He remembered he had seen an open door at the back of the shop and sure enough, there were stairs going up, Adam guessed, to a flat above. He made his way up the dim staircase and came out on a landing. To the right there was a kitchen and to the left, a short passageway with doors leading off to other rooms. The smell up here was even stronger than in the shop and he was starting to know that smell too well now. He had a quick scan around with his torch and saw what he was looking for – key hooks on the wall and on one of them, a set of car keys. Adam grabbed them and went back down the stairs.

He was heading out of the shop when, as an afterthought, he went back to the pet section. There was not much hope for the inhabitants, but they stood a better chance out in the world than trapped in their cages. One by one he opened them all. Some opened at the front, some at the top and those he tipped gently onto their sides. The rodents were out of the cages like a shot and scuttled round the floor looking for cover while they weighed up their options. The rabbits just sat looking dazed or cowered in the back of their hutches. The cockatoo and the canaries did not wait a moment to launch themselves into the air and then flew wildly round the shop looking for the way out. Adam had to cover his head and duck as he made his way out while the birds crashed about above him. By the time he got outside it was pandemonium in the shop and the two dogs were looking out of the van windows, barking excitedly. He put the bag of gear down on the pavement and then had a look around to see if he could see which car the key might open. The fob was not going to give him any clues – it had Cymru with a red dragon and a picture of Carnarvon Castle. There were two cars parked in the pull-in by the shop, but the keys did not open them. Adam walked round the corner into the side street and tried down there. He got lucky with the third car on the left. He put the key in the ignition and turned it on, so the dials lit up. The needle in the fuel gauge crept slowly up to half a tank – that would be enough, he thought.

He went back round the corner to the van, grabbed the bag and jumped in the front. The dogs were both still glued to the window watching out for small furry animals doing a runner from their prison, and as Adam pulled away they rushed to the back of the van to keep the prey in sight. He pulled up close to the car, leaving just enough room for him to manoeuvre between the two vehicles. Using the pump and some piping he was able to get a stream of petrol into the van's tank. It seemed to take forever for the fuel to run out but eventually the car's tank would not yield any more. He gave a little fist-pump. It was a long time since he had to siphon petrol, and certainly he had never had to steal it, but now he had mastered the art. He smiled at the thought that this could become a regular activity in the future.

The way through the built-up areas at the back of Poole was littered with cars, lorries and buses. Sometimes he would see a body slumped against a car window and from time to time, a body on the pavement. How desperate those people must have been, he thought, to get to their homes before they became too ill to carry on. For the first time he saw dogs sniffing around a car, hunting for food he guessed. They looked up in surprise when they heard the van driving up and shied away at first. But as Adam drove slowly past, one started barking and the next moment there were three dogs running after the van. Bonzo had spotted them and started barking. Adam accelerated and the dogs gave up the chase.

The road took him round the hinterlands of Poole, skirting the north side of the harbour before eventually getting out into the countryside again. He was taking the road to Dorchester, following a route he could remember from childhood trips to Dorset. Increasingly there were animals on the road. Adam drove slowly and generally they moved off when they heard the van, but on a couple of occasions he had to brake sharply or swerve to avoid something that ran out into his path. He was probably the only road user in the whole of Dorset, but it seemed he had to pay more attention to the road now than he would tackling the motorway at rush hour.

To the west of Dorchester the road ran straight as a die for several miles, following the old Roman road across the rolling patchwork of light green wheatfields and dark green copses. He remembered how his father would put his foot down here, dodging oncoming traffic to pass the caravans that they had been sitting behind for many a mile. And then they would bowl along, the summer scented air filling the car from the half-opened windows, the holiday excitement building as they neared their destination – who would be first to see the sea?

A flash of a russet in front of him, a bang and a sickening thud under the car, snapped Adam out of his reverie, as the van lurched across the road. He braked hard and wrestled to steer back on course. He looked in the rear-view mirror and saw a deer thrashing around on the tarmac. He pulled up some yards in front, his heart racing. A memory of a dark moment in his past came over him and momentarily he was unable to move. He turned round slowly and watched the animal lying on its side in the road, its legs kicking wildly. He got out of van but took only a few steps towards the dying animal. The kicks got weaker, and then stopped, the head lolled down on the tarmac and he could see one brown eye looking up at him, accusingly it seemed. The deer lay motionless, quite dead. He was very grateful for that, for the animal's sake and for his. He did not fancy having to administer the coup de grâce to such a large animal.

He walked round to the front of the van and surveyed the damage: the front bumper was hanging off but still attached. The deer seemed to have gone under the van, thankfully not through the windscreen. He tried pulling off the damaged bumper, but it would not come. He guessed he would have to drive on with it like that until it came off by itself. The dogs were both up at the windows, Bonzo barking excitedly. Adam got back in the van, calmed them down and set off again slowly. He could hear the bumper banging about at the front and as he picked up speed he heard it hit the tarmac repeatedly. He decided that he would stop a bit further down the road and assess the damage properly. It would give the dogs a chance to have a run around and he could make himself a coffee. The clock on the dashboard said 10.12: he had been going for two hours and was ready for a break.

Half a mile on he pulled up on an open section of road with no hedgerows and uninterrupted views across the country on either side. He got out to have another look at the damaged front section while the dogs rushed off, keen to explore this new place. He could see that the bumper was now almost completely detached and part of the panel behind was coming away exposing the bottom of the sump. One light was smashed but it did not look as if there was any serious damage to the underside of the vehicle and he still had a front light, should he need it. He decided he should try and get the bumper off, rather than risk it coming away and puncturing a tyre, and after a bit of twisting and pulling he managed to pull it clear of its mountings and detach it completely. Only two days out and the van was already damaged on the front and sides. Oh well.

Back in the van he made himself some coffee and sat down on the door sill with the road map on his knees to see where he needed to go. He could see the route to Friars Wood village would take him less than half an hour. But he remembered that the village was surrounded by a web of small lanes and he hoped he would be able to get through and then, that he could actually find the farm. He stood up and looked around. The dogs had been busy exploring the hedgerows and now had gone under a fence into a nearby field, following some interesting scent. Adam surveyed the green landscape of West Dorset spread out all around him, unremarkable, but with a rural charm somehow quite different to anywhere else that he knew. Could this be somewhere he could make a home, he wondered? Right now he wanted to check out Friarswood and see if that could be the place to eventually settle, or somewhere nearby. And he could leave messages there for Sam, as he said he would. He whistled for the dogs and as soon as he started the engine they jumped into the van.

Chapter Sixteen

Revisiting

Wednesday 1st May, Afternoon

The road to the village of Friarswood was as narrow and twisty as he remembered it, and the tiny village and its church, nestling in the trees, looked unchanged. The farm itself was a little way beyond the village and Adam was not quite sure how to get there by road. He followed the little lane through the village up to a crossroads where a sign pointing to the right indicated Woodbourne St. Lawrence, which, he remembered, was the little village down the hill from the farm where the dairy was. Sure enough, a half a mile down the road, there was the farm entrance. Adam barely recognised it as the place in his memory, with its thatched farmhouse and the old cow houses behind. The farmhouse now had a tiled roof and was an office and behind were large steel sheds. Two cars were parked by the office and beyond the sheds, large farm vehicles and tractors could be seen. It was the sleek modern sign that told him where he was: *Friarswood Farm, Wyld and Sons Dairies Ltd.* Where was the old barn where he and Sam would burn off energy chasing each other over the straw or performing daring leaps from the hay loft into the bales of straw below? There was no sign of that now.

Adam turned off the road into the farm. He pulled up just past the office and got out, making sure the dogs did not follow him. The sound of cows greeted him, lots of them, and the noise was jarring on the ears. It was the sound of distressed animals, crying and wailing, and it was coming from the pastures over to the left. There he could see a herd of cattle pressed up against the fence, their udders bloated with milk. They were trying to get to the milking parlours but today the gate was not opening. Behind him he heard the barking of dogs coming from a kennel near the office. That too was an unhappy sound and Adam did not know if they were guard dogs or sheep dogs and he did not want to try and find out. He looked around him and wondered what to do. All he wanted to do was drive off and away from this place. But this was going to be the rendezvous for Sam, should he ever find the note that Adam had left in his cottage. He could leave another note pinned to the farm office door, but now, he realised, he had no idea what to write. Where was he going to go next? He did not know.

He got back into the van and sat staring ahead at the huge cow sheds. It was going to take some time to find what Adam was looking for: a homestead with access to fresh water and power, somewhere to establish a small-holding and become self-sufficient. What he needed was a temporary base from which he could scout the area. In his mind he had decided on Dorset because, and only because, of Friarswood farm and the holidays they had as children. Dorset was as good as anywhere else, but he did not know now where else he should look. He just knew that this farm was not the place.

While he sat there the dogs were restless. They could hear the cows, and the dogs in the kennel nearby, and they were clearly unsettled by it all. Adam got out the notebook he had found in the pet shop and tore a page out. He wrote: *"Wednesday 1st May. Sam, if you find this, I have gone to look for somewhere to set up home. I am going to go eastward along the coast and find a temporary base to park this camper van."* He paused and then he added: *"This is my home for the moment. I will come back in the next 5 days and leave another note for you. If you have been here in the meantime, please leave me a note saying where you are. Adam."* He looked at the note and wondered if it made sense at all and decided it would do the job for the time being. Sam would know he was around and would be back again by Monday. No, that's too long he thought. By Saturday, would be better and he changed the five to a three and then added *"Missing you brother. Don't disappear on me."* As Adam did not have any envelopes, he folded up the note inside another sheet, on which he wrote SAM. Then he went up to the farm office and looked for somewhere to place the message.

The office entrance was to the side of the old building, in a modern extension. The door was a typical office door, glazed with two large panels. To the right on the wall was a brass plaque inscribed with "Wylde and Sons Dairies Ltd" and "Wishburn Ltd". He peered into the dimly lit office: it looked like the reception area of a firm of accountants and nothing like a farm. There was no clue that this was once the rustic farmhouse of his memory. There was a letter box in the door and Adam tucked his note under the flap so it was secure, but could easily be seen should Sam ever get to Friarswood farm. And that was a very big *if*.

Once back into the van, Adam had to make a decision about where to go next. Head for the coast or go inland? He had a fancy to see the sea before he started his farm search so he decided to head for Seatown, a tiny seaside village not far from the main road. It was a place that the family went to twice when he and Sam were lads, staying in a rented caravan for a week each time. He could remember the little stream running down over the beach and the great yellow cliffs of Golden Cap they looked up at from their little camp on the beach. Sam was very much his little brother then and Adam was quite protective of him. He would patiently show Sam how to skim stones on the water or the best way to build a campfire while Sam would get bored and start messing about. "You'll never learn anything, you won't!" Adam would shout in frustration while Sam poked his tongue at him or mimicked him. And then the next day he would skim his stone further than his dad or his brother and he'd say to his dad, "Adam showed me how to do it." He had that easy way about life while Adam always had to work at it.

It was the same now, it seemed. He hadn't seen or heard from Sam for a long time when their dad died suddenly after a stroke, Adam was down there as soon as his got the call from his mum. He brought her home from the hospital, where she had spent the night, and made her eat some breakfast. She seemed strangely calm and almost unemotional, as if in denial. He then spent the rest of the day on the phone, dealing with all the administration of death while she fussed about hunting through paperwork in his dad's little study. Late in the afternoon Sam turned up, took his mum in his arms and then all her grief poured out. He stroked her head and held her tight until she became calm. "Mum, you're exhausted," he said. "You don't need to be doing this today. Come on, I'm taking you upstairs – you need some rest." And he gently led her upstairs. He came down sometime later and said, "She's sound asleep on the bed. Do you fancy a cup of tea Adam?"

And there it was, his maverick little brother had glided into their lives again and immediately everything seemed easier, more manageable. How did he do that? It was infuriating but how could one ever be cross with him? He was just being Sam. And where was he now and when would he pop up in his life again, he wondered. Anytime would be good now.

He followed the lane down the hill from the farm which eventually got him back to the main road. From there the road to Seatown wound between high hedges and was so narrow that any obstruction would block the way completely. Fortunately there was none, and it did not take long till he reached the end of the road by the pub, which was the last building before the sea. He pulled up at the very end of the road by the shingle beach. The dogs had been alert all the way from when he left the main road, as if they knew that they were near their destination. How do dogs do that, he thought. What signals do they pick up which we cannot sense? As soon as he opened his door, they were out.

There were only two cars in front of the pub. He guessed that few people felt well enough to go out for a drink last Friday evening. The car park by the beach was almost empty too, which he was glad about: The fewer cars there were, the less likely he was to find bodies. He walked onto the shingle beach and down to the water's edge. There was a gentle swell and the waves were breaking onto the shingle bank and then falling back, sucking the water noisily back through the stones. Cloud had come up during the morning and now the sea was as grey as the sky. Adam decided to walk along the beach and the dogs ran ahead of him, rushing hither and thither, sniffing the strange smells of the sea, probably for the first time in their lives.

When they'd all had a good stretch, he turned round and walked back towards the pub. It was getting towards lunch time. He thought how nice it would be to stroll in, get a pint of the local brew and look at a menu. A Wednesday lunchtime – there would be some locals in, and no doubt a few walkers and other visitors. He could sit at the bar and read the paper, listen to the local gossip and wait for his hot pasty to arrive. The happy thought hung in the air for a moment, then disappeared. He'd had nothing to eat today and his stomach was growling at him. He decided to go back to the van and prepare himself some hot lunch. After that he would think about where to go and what to do next.

He needed to make a base somewhere, even if only temporary, so that there was somewhere Sam could find him. That was the short-term goal. And in the meantime he could make recces of the area and look for a long-term home. But did that make any sense? Setting up home meant not travelling, thus reducing his chances of finding someone else alive. What was the point of having a home and no-one to share it with? These thoughts rolled around in his head but no clear plan emerged. For the time being he would take it one day at a time. There would be enough bottled water, tinned and packet food and cooking gas to keep him alive for a good while yet. He could wash in the sea, or a stream and that was all the personal hygiene he needed. Today he would explore the local countryside and either come back and set up camp here tonight or maybe he would find somewhere else. And then tomorrow he would drive into Dorchester and Weymouth, perhaps, have a look for signs of life.

He had looked at the road map and saw that there was a network of lanes running near to the coast on the east side of Bridport and there would probably be plenty of homesteads and farms along there that he could investigate. He could spend some time meandering about there, and then tomorrow he would be that much closer to Weymouth.

He took the lane back to Chideock and a little way out of the village he saw a sign to Catwood Farm and decided to have a look down there. The lane went half a mile and stopped at what seemed to be a large dairy farm. As with Friarswood, the sound of the cows in distress was too much to bear and Adam turned back to the main road. Further along he turned off down a lane and came to a smaller farm. There was one large shed and some smaller units but no sign of any livestock here and he guessed this was an arable farm. It was clean and tidy and in good order, which was promising. The homestead was away from the farm buildings, just off the lane. He stopped the van in the lane, got down from the van and was about to walk down to the house when a pair of large dogs appeared from behind the house and came towards him barking loudly. Bonzo had jumped down from the cab but stopped when he saw the dogs and his hackles went up. Adam thought that a nasty confrontation was developing here and decided to get Bonzo back into the van before it got serious, and he got himself in and shut the door behind him.

He spent the next couple of hours reconnoitring the byways of West Dorset, meandering around the tiny lanes that threaded their way among the hamlets and farms behind the coast. Several times he found the road blocked by abandoned vehicles and had to turn around and take a different route. Twice he encountered cattle in the road and wondered how and why they had got out of their fields. He found two or three farms that looked promising as a long-term home. One had some holiday cottages, which he figured could make comfortable homes without the problems associated with removing deceased residents. He did not stop to explore any of these places closely. At this stage he felt it was enough to make a general assessment of likely spots where there was a good chance of a clean water supply, timber and shelter. He noted the names and locations of these places in his notebook and gave them numbered references on his road atlas. What he really needed to get, he decided, was the Ordnance Survey map for the area.

By late in the afternoon they had had enough of winding around the country lanes. They had been on the road, on and off, since early this morning, and Adam was ready to stop. The sky had cleared to blue and there was the promise of a fine evening and sunset. It made sense to set up camp now and enjoy the evening sunshine. Tomorrow he would head into Weymouth and look for maps, binoculars and other items that had occurred to him during the day. A they crested a hill, a vista opened out on their right and he could see the sea stretching out below. He passed a field gate and pulled up to have a look. The gate was not locked and opened onto a large pasture that had been recently grazed right down, but there were no animals in the field now. The ground looked firm, so Adam decided to take the van in.

As they bumped slowly across the field the land began to drop down and ahead the sea spread out in front of them. At the bottom was a hedge and beyond that the land fell away steeply down towards the shore. He took the van towards the hedge until he found a level spot and then he stopped with the side door opening out to the south and the ocean view. He figured that this was as good a spot as any to rest up and enjoy his supper. He stretched and took in the view. He could see the coast spread out before him for miles in each direction. To the east was the shingle bank of Chesil Beach stretching all the way to Portland and to the west the yellow cliffs of Golden Cap stood up proud from the far coastline, and beyond, in the haze of the afternoon sun, the coast stretched away in a misty line.

Sometime later, after he had given the dogs a good run around, he was sitting on the step of the van with a beer in his hand surveying the view. It took him back to an evening many years ago, before Oscar was born and they were living in London, when he and Jo borrowed a friend's caravan for a few days by the sea. It was early in the season, like now, and one evening after supper they walked down to the cliffs overlooking the rock arch of Durdle Dor, where they sat and watched the sun go down. It had been a very wet day but the rain stopped late in the afternoon and the skies cleared to leave an evening that was too good to be missed. So they climbed down to the beach and threw stones into the sea, then, as the sun was disappearing, they climbed back up the steep path to the top of the cliffs.

Suddenly Adam felt a yearning for his wife that he had not felt since he left Reading. At that moment he longed for her so much; to be sitting next to her, looking at the view, her head on his shoulder perhaps, the scent of her hair wafting in the evening air. For a moment he almost caught her smell, the memory was so strong. And then it was gone, and he felt a terrible ache within him, as if part of him had been ripped out. For the first time since he went on the road, his emotions overpowered him, and the tears flowed. He sat there and just let the grief well up, shaking with the sobs, on and on for what seemed like minutes on end. The old dog came over and put his head on Adam's knee and he stroked the animal's grey head until the sobs subsided. He rubbed the tears from his eyes and looked out across the fields. A flock of gulls was winging its way back towards the coast, perhaps heading somewhere to roost for the night. He shivered; it was getting cool now. Time to get washed up and cleared away before it got dark.

Chapter Seventeen

Pip's Diary

Wednesday 1st May

It's a new month, it's the first of May. May Day. Mayday, Mayday – the world has stopped and I want to get off!! What am I even doing here?? Can I wake up now, I don't like this dream.

*

I am sitting in the dining room cos it's sunny and I don't want to be upstairs anymore. The smell was in the passageway this morning and it's only going to get worse, so I have decided to move down to room 1 – "Selsey". It's the cheap room at the back above the kitchen, but it's as far from the smell as I can get unless I sleep on the sofa. And I might still do that. I found some long-life orange juice and some sterilised milk in the garage when I was looking for the lamp (found that too, hooray) so I had cornflakes and juice for breakfast. I gave the cold coffee a miss. I don't really like coffee, let alone cold.

I looked at my checklist, tore it up and started again. Then I threw the second one away. I know what I need to do:

- *Make an inventory (is that the right word?) of what food I have and list the things I need to get*

- *Check the cold-water tank and see how much is in it*
- *Find somewhere I can break into like a corner shop maybe to look for food*
- *Break into Poulson's for candles and torches and stuff (yeah, and a crow bar for breaking in with)*
- *Try and get the car out of the garage and then have a go at driving*
- *Break into the library and find teach-yourself books on cookery in a power cut, driving for beginners, the basics of woodworking and home maintenance, self-defence, be fluent in Spanish in three weeks, sewing and tailoring yeah, yeah.*

Probably won't need the needlework skills though.

I didn't write any of this down though because even the serious ones just seem so ridiculous. What's the point? And I am pretending this is a great big Joke because underneath I am REALLY SCARED. And I know I like my own company – comes of being an only child I suppose – but I don't want to die here on my own. There must be someone else alive somewhere. Which means that I have to keep myself together and I have to keep on looking. Don't I?

So here's how I got on with my "list":

1. *I checked out all the food in the house and got rid of some more stuff. I know I am going to have to live on tinned*

food (a prospect which does not thrill me!) and I need to have some fruit and vegetables in the diet so to find some tinned stuff petty soon. Otherwise it's soup, beans and tinned tomatoes for the next two weeks.

2. *I could not get into the loft but I know that the water won't last for ever so I need to think about where I can get water for "personal hygiene" as Spindle-legs Watkins would call it.*

3. *I went for a walk and did a recce of the local shops and I reckon I could get into the VG shop, but not the Co-op. The ironmongers would not be so easy. Had a thought:– I bet the hotel front doors are not locked. They must have plenty of stock sitting in their kitchens*

4. *Have not tried the car yet. It's a bit silly, I know, but I don't want to make a mess of Thommo's car. It was the only thing he really looked after. Maybe I can find a car with some keys in the ignition. Tomorrow*

*

I tried the phone this evening, it's really pointless, I know, but I just wanted to check. Nic I wish I could talk to you. I don't know if you are alive but I know that if you were, you would be the only one who could make any sense of all this. I MISS YOU.

I could not face making any food tonight so I ate half a bar of cooking chocolate - I saved half for you - and then felt really sick.

I got all my stuff down from my room, well all that I think I will need, and I have moved into Selsey (good old Selsey William. Not as sturdy as Portland William, but much more refined...ha ha). I found some more candles and I have the lantern in there, so I have some light. I have shut the door to our part of the house and put some parcel tape around the frame. Hopefully that will keep the smell out. God isn't that awful? Your mum and dad die and you have to shut them up in the roof to keep the smell away. I am probably not smelling too good myself. I will attempt to have a cold wash in the bath tomorrow and I am NOT looking forward to that!

Goodnight diary, good night Nic and good night Pip.

Chapter Eighteen

Reconnaissance

Thursday 2nd May

Adam and Jo were outside the flat in London and Jo was getting into a car. The children were in the back seat. She was going out somewhere in the car with the children, but Adam could not go with them. Adam felt angry and sad. She was leaving him, why? They were so happy together, they even had children together. Why did she have to go? They were arguing and Adam was saying: "Why can't I come? Why are you going without me?" Jo was not answering but she made it clear that they had to go without him and Adam was saying, "But that's not our car." Then Jo just turned and looked sad and said: "You *know* why".

Adam woke up then. He was hot and his bedclothes felt damp. The low morning sun was streaming into the van, right into his face. He unzipped the sleeping bag and rolled out onto the floor, out of the sun. He lay there on his back staring at the van's ceiling, just above his head. They had to go, he thought, and now they were gone, for ever. He lay there for several minutes, maybe longer, feeling bereft, empty; he was hollow, as if his soul had been ripped out. There seemed no point in trying to move, no point in being alive.

He could have lain there like that for hours, he thought later, but a cold wet nose was nudging his hand and a low whining noise slowly percolated into his consciousness – it was Bonzo telling him to wake up, that he needed to go out. Adam hauled himself up stiffly from his bed and stretched slowly, tentatively coming back to the world. Bonzo licked his hand and gave a little bark of pleasure, then ran over to the door. When Adam pushed it open the dog jumped out and ran straight over to the hedge to cock his leg. The old dog followed, shaking a leg out behind him stiffly as he eased his old bones into action. Outside it was cool, but the breeze had dropped overnight and the air was still. The sound of the waves breaking on the beach below mingled with the chatter of the birds in the hedgerow and conspired to drag Adam back to the here and now. It was a beautiful May morning, the sky was clear blue and a new day beckoned him out as if to say "Come on Adam, this is your life now. Embrace it."

He boiled up a pan of water and made himself some coffee. He sat on the door sill and looked out at the sea. It was a deep blue streaked with green and looked as cool as the morning. The memory of the dream was still with him, but he pushed it into the background: *Got to keep busy, got to keep moving.* Then another memory cut across: a Sunday morning, children playing happily in Oscar's bedroom, Adam standing by the window looking out on the street and Jo, in bed, saying:

"Come back to bed Adam, the shed can wait. Let's see how long we can hide here until the children come looking for us."

"Well that's a very naughty idea, young lady," he said, "now you've asked for it!" as he jumped back into bed and started kissing and tickling her all over. She was screaming and shrieking with laughter and the next thing they knew the two children were climbing into bed with them, Oscar laughing and wriggling and Sophie crying, "Mummy, what's Daddy doing?"

That was only a month back, but it seemed like a lifetime ago now. He shook the memory out of his mind and set to getting ready for departure. Adam thought that Weymouth would be a good place to find some of the things he might need, like maps, binoculars, a spade and a brush. On the way there he was also going to check out some more farms and homesteads. He drove down the lanes, some twisty, some very narrow and some impassable. Several times he had to reverse and find another route. He got quite lost in the little back roads, but noted the names on the gates of promising properties, and when he got back to a road with road signs to give him his bearings, he worked out where he had been on the road atlas and marked the spot with a number. In all he spent two hours winding round the small hills, at one point finding himself up on the coast road again. By mid-morning he was feeling peckish and started looking for a breakfast stop.

At the top of a steep, winding road there suddenly opened up a view down across the countryside to the sea. It seemed a good place to stop. He let the dogs out and was getting the pan out again to make another coffee when he heard the dogs barking excitedly. Adam got out of the van to see what was going on. The dogs had gone into a field and were terrorising a herd of young steers. The old sheep dog had reverted to instincts and was running around them, herding them towards the old wooden gate where Adam was standing. Meanwhile Bonzo was snapping at their heels and making them panic and buck. Adam did not know a lot about cattle, or dogs, come to that, but he sensed that a dangerous situation was developing. He had already seen a flailing hoof narrowly miss the dog's head and one of those would kill instantly. He was also worried that if the herd was pressing en-masse against this gate, it was unlikely to hold for long.

He called the dogs, whistled at them and shouted to Bonzo at the top of his voice. There was no response and the herd was advancing. He shouted more and more frantically, but the dogs' blood was up and they were not going to be called off. Adam jumped back in the van and drove it right up against the gate. Then he revved the engine and blasted the horn. The bullocks leading the stampede hesitated and slowed. The dogs glanced up and seemed for the first time to see Adam waving and calling them from the van window. He got out and roared in his loudest, sternest voice: "Bonzo, come HERE!!!". Amazingly the terrier responded and came running past the herd to where Adam stood. He slowed as he got near, his tail wagged feebly, then dropped between his legs as Adam roared again: "Get in the van!" The old dog had tired and, seeing his comrade in arms retreating, decided to follow and as he came up past the young cattle he gave a final authoritative snarl of authority at the leading group, before going under the gate and into the van.

Adam could feel his heart pounding. Once he had made it clear to the dogs that he wasn't happy, the old dog settled down on the floor at the back and Bonzo with him. It was a good twenty minutes before the young dog bucked up courage to get over onto the front seat again.

Adam followed the winding lanes back towards the sea and when he got to the coast road he headed east towards Weymouth. As he drew close to the outskirts of the town, he looked across to the isle of Portland stretching out into the sea and wondered whether any of the personnel on the base there had survived the virus. He must check that out later.

He followed the road through the outskirts and into the residential areas at the southern end of the town, keeping an eye out for a hardware shop and somewhere he might pick up some more water – a grocery or a convenience store. He followed the road to the town centre without seeing what he was looking for. He drove along the harbour and eventually out onto the sea front. There was the Victoria Jubilee clock tower he remembered and the esplanade that ran along in front of the elegant hotels and apartments. He would have liked to have got out and walked barefoot on the sandy beach, but that was for later, he thought. He needed to be where the shops were.

He drove along the esplanade, then turned away from the sea. There were lots of small restaurants, guest houses, pubs but not many shops. Did Weymouth even have a real shopping centre, he wondered? He drove slowly round the town, weaving around parked cars and abandoned vans, tooting the horn at lazy cats and wandering dogs, keeping look out for signs of life and promising-looking shops. Eventually he found a street which seemed to be a shopping area and, ignoring the "no vehicles" sign, stopped half-way down. The van was in the shade, so Adam felt happy leaving the dogs there while he went wandering. He took the wheel brace, a scarf to act as a mask, a torch and put them in a small knap sack then set off to explore the shops.

The street was empty of life, and he guessed there was nothing of interest for stray pets here – they were more likely to be found around the hotel kitchens and rubbish bins. In the doorway of one shop was a figure curled up in a sleeping bag and Adam could see the flies swarming around it. How pitiful was that, he thought, dying alone in a shop doorway? At least that person did not have to see his family die first -- they were spared that.

He found a homeware store at the bottom end of the street which he thought might be worth looking into, but hard as he tried to break the glass doors with the wheel brace, his blows hardly made an impression and he was forced to give up. He wondered if the back door might be a better proposition, but he could think about that later. Round the corner was a mini-market and when Adam tried the door it swung open. He wrapped the scarf around his head, covering his mouth and nose, took a deep breath and went in.

It seemed that he was not the only person who had gone into the shop and helped themselves. There was stuff all over the floor and it looked as if a gang of street kids had been on a rampage. The shop felt suffocatingly warm so he wasted no time in hunting the things he needed. He made a couple of forays around the store, grabbed the things he could find and headed outside again as fast as he could. The heat in the shop was overpowering and he felt as if he was literally suffocating in the fetid air.

Once out of the shop he made his way back to the van and parked the trolley there. The dogs barked excitedly and then looked wistfully as he walked off down to the other end of the street. He found a stationer, which he reckoned would be the best place to find local maps and some reading matter for the long days ahead. However, he could make no headway with the door there, or at the pharmacy. What he really needed was a jemmy, he thought. Further on was a newsagent's shop and here the door was not locked. When Adam walked he could almost feel the bad odours emanating from the little office at the back of the shop. He started to heave and he made for the door and, as he did so, he saw a carousel containing local maps and guides. He went outside to fill his lungs with air and then returned, holding his breath while he found the maps he needed, then dashed out of the shop before he needed to take a breath.

It took a while before he could get the smell out of his nose. In that short time it seemed to have permeated his clothes and it made him quite nauseous. How on earth do people work with dead bodies, in morgues and path labs, he wondered. He made his way back to the van and stowed his haul in the back section. He did not think he would find anything else he needed in this area, and he could not face any more stuffy, dark and rancid shops so he headed in the direction of the sea front. At the esplanade he drove along to the beach and pulled up there. Here he could let the dogs have a run without having to worry about cows or other countryside creatures and he needed to get some fresh, clean air into his lungs. He let the dogs out and they ran down onto the sand, Bonzo racing around and barking excitedly. Adam went down by the water and strolled towards the pier keeping a wide berth from a body he could see further up the beach. It was above the high-water mark so had probably been in that spot since last weekend. He could see some herring gulls patrolling the carcase and could imagine what state it might be in by now, and he had no desire to get any closer.

Bonzo had been running in and out of the sea playing tag with the little waves as they broke on the sand, while the old dog trotted along beside Adam as he strode on down the beach. As they got a bit further along, Adam looked back to see where Bonzo was and he saw him standing by the body, growling and barking uncertainly. He called him but the dog did not seem to hear so he started walking back towards him. At that moment he saw a figure up on the esplanade and at the very moment he sighted it, it disappeared behind the café.

His heart almost stopped. Was that...was that a person? Someone alive? He stopped and looked intently at the spot, waiting to see if it would appear again, or perhaps emerge on the other side of the building, but there was no sign of anybody. He walked slowly back up the beach a few yards, keeping his eyes pinned on the place he saw the figure. "I did see someone," he said to himself, "I am sure I did." He wasn't sure, but he had to find out. He jogged back up to the steps and along the pavement past the café building. There was no one. He looked all around and down the road that ran down from the esplanade, but there was no sign of movement anywhere. Maybe he had just imagined it, a trick of the light perhaps, or was it just wishful thinking? No, there definitely was a figure, or something there.

He turned round and went back down to the beach. He called the dogs and they followed him back into the van. He sat behind the wheel, his heart still racing. Was this just wishful thinking that made a shadow look like a figure? What sort of figure it was, man or woman, or maybe a child – it seemed quite small - what they were wearing he couldn't tell. He just felt he had seen someone. Or had he? He got out of the van and walked again to the street where he thought the person might have gone, but there was no sign of anyone down there. He must have imagined this figure. If there was somebody, they surely would have seen him, and the dogs, so why on earth would they hide?

He went back to the van. “Boys, did I see someone or was I just dreaming?” Bonzo looked up and then carried on with cleaning the sand out of his paws. “You don’t think there was anyone there – is that it? Maybe you’re right.”

Not knowing quite what to do next he drove off along the esplanade towards the pier and then round to the harbour front and over the old bridge, back the way he had come not long before. He stopped again a quarter of a mile down the road, two voices having an argument in his head:

You need to go back and drive around all the streets again, just to be sure.

No, it’s pointless. Why would someone see me and run away – that’s just ridiculous!

You need to go back and check. You know you’ll regret it if you don’t.

No, you’re being silly. There never was a figure. You’re just imagining things. Leave it!

He drove on and it wasn’t long before he was on the causeway to the Isle of Portland and he stopped halfway along at a car park. It that gave onto what was the eastern end of Chesil Beach, the stony embankment that stretches for miles along the coast to the west. He took the dogs over the wooden footbridge that crossed the end of the lagoon, and onto the shingle bank. As they crested the rise, the view of the bay opened up in front of them and they caught the full force of the breeze. It was bracing and it was just what Adam needed to clear his lungs. And a good run around on these stones would tire them dogs out nicely for the afternoon, he thought.

An hour later the dogs were flat out in the back of the van and Adam had satisfied a sudden hunger pang with a very rudimentary lunch. He headed back towards the town centre, but this time did not go towards the beach but kept to the west side of the marina and took a road off to the side that looked promising. Some way along there was a parade of shops, and there was just what he was looking for – a hardware shop. He pulled up outside and saw it had an old-fashioned door with two plate glass panes and a lock that did not look especially sophisticated. It did not take him very long to take out the glass and he was in.

The shop was a little treasure trove of tools, hardware, household items, gardening supplies – a paradise for the practical man, which was exactly what Adam needed to be. There was no unpleasant organic smell here. In fact, Adam could smell very little but in his memory, there were the distinctive odours of the hardware shop of his childhood – a mixture of hemp twine, linseed oil, timber, sawdust and bird food. He found a dustpan and brush, a spade, a long crowbar, some rope and some heavy-duty wire-cutters. He reckoned that would do for the moment, but he knew that this was a place he would probably need to revisit before too long. He had managed to find all the items on his list today, plus he had reconnoitred several likely farms and homesteads to the west of the town, so he decided that he would head to the country on the east side and see what else he could find out there and then find a camping spot for the night.

As he set off, a thought crossed his mind: What if it been a child? A child might run away, would be frightened and run back to his home. But a child on its own would be desperate for human company, wouldn't it? It all seemed rather unlikely. He decided, though, he would drive back through the town centre to the beach and have one more scout around for his mystery figure. He went back towards the sea, past the villas, guesthouses and hotels that would have been getting ready for the first holiday weekend of the summer and past little shops full of things that no-one would ever want to buy now.

He drove slowly along the route he had taken this morning, past the café and along to where the body was. The water was almost at the corpse's feet and Adam thought that one good wave and a receding tide would probably take it off the beach. He pulled up where he had stopped before but did not get out. It was starting to rain now and there was not a soul in sight, nor any life down here apart from the sea birds. He drove down the side road and back to the esplanade and saw no-one, then followed a course around the centre of the town eventually coming back to the sea front. He just knew he wasn't going to see that figure again.

The rain was coming down harder now. He had a look at the maps but suddenly he didn't fancy driving around anymore farm lanes. He had it in his mind that he would like to go to Lulworth Cove again, a place he had visited often in the past. He could come back here again tomorrow and have another look, just in case.

He turned around and drove off down the esplanade in the other direction. Half a mile on, the buildings stopped abruptly and then to the left of the road was seemingly open countryside and, on the right, a high seawall. At the end of the wall the road swung away inland and took him to a junction with the old coast road. He followed this for some miles until he reached West Lulworth where he followed the road down through the village to the Cove. The sea was grey and choppy inside the cove, though here there was some shelter from the wind in the lee of the chalk cliffs that formed this natural harbour. He pulled up at the very end of the road above the slipway, switched off the engine, pushed his seat back, leaned back and closed his eyes. The dogs did not stir in the back, as if they too thought that they were better off in the van than outside. He could hear the wavelets lapping on the stones and the breeze was rocking the van gently. That, along with the patter of rain on the windows, was like a lullaby, singing "Close your eyes, drift away, shut it all out." Suddenly he felt weary. The business of searching, exploring, stocking up on supplies – it gave him a purpose and yet really... what was the point? Maybe tonight he would park the planning, the speculation, the memories and just spend the evening with a book and a bottle of wine. Why not?

Chapter Nineteen

Pip's Diary

Thursday 2nd May

Well it was NOT a good night at all. The bed was strange, so big and springy, and not comfortable, like mine. I could not get to sleep and kept thinking of things that I had forgotten to bring from my room, but I was too scared to go and get. I kept hearing animal noises outside and then once I thought I heard voices. But I listened and listened and did not hear them again, so I guess I was dreaming. But when I did sleep my dreams were horrible and two or three times I had to wake myself up. In the end I put the lantern on and when I woke this morning it was barely still giving off any light. I'll have to get some more batteries from somewhere soon. Maybe tonight I'll make do with a candle.

***

I HAVE SEEN SOMEONE! *I was down on the pier this morning (had to get out of the house) and I thought I heard a CAR. The tide was in and the sea was quite choppy, so it was noisy, but*

I was sure I heard it. I didn't know what to do! I was frightened and excited at the same time. I wanted to see if there was a car or something, but I was afraid of being seen. I decided to go back to the Quay where there was more shelter so I could hide if I had to. I got back to the Custom House and I did not hear or see anything. I was ducking behind walls and keeping out of sight and when I was in sight of the esplanade I checked that there was no one about. I was making my way back towards town along the back roads and thinking that I had been dreaming, when I heard it again. It was definitely a car or something driving along the esplanade. And then it stopped and I could not hear the engine at all. So I walked down Gloucester Street towards the sea, keeping close to the buildings like I was a guerrilla or something, and when I got to the front I peeped round the corner really carefully and looked to the right where I had heard the car. And then I saw it! Further down the road, by the beach, was a camper van that was not there before. I watched for ages but I could not see anyone about, so I crossed the road and peeped over the railings and then I saw him! A bloke in bomber jacket walking along the beach away from me and there were two dogs running around with him. I watched them for a while and one of them found the body on the sand and started barking and barking at it. The man walked on past it, but the little dog would not leave the body alone, so the man turned round to call the dog and then he looked up. I ducked back behind the café but I'm sure he must have seen me. But when I peeped round again he was busy with the dog so for some ***STUPID*** *reason I got scared and I ran across the road and back down Bond Street and then* *hid in a side alley. My heart was thumping and I was breathing so hard I'm sure I could be heard a mile away.*

What an IDIOT I am! I was thinking all these stupid things like what am I going to say to him? or what if he is a kidnapper/sex maniac/lunatic/bandit? And then I thought what if he is just a normal guy with a family and kids? And even if he is a maniac that's got to better than being on my own for ever. Isn't it? And he might be a hunk! Oh yeah, as if! I don't know what to do and I'm thinking all these thoughts and then I think what Thommo would say "better not to die wondering". So I walk back to the esplanade, really slowly, cos I am still not quite sure if I am doing the right thing. And then just before I get to the front, I hear the van starting up and as I turn the corner I see it driving off down towards the harbour. So I shout and wave my arms but he is way off and probably can't see me. So then I have a clever plan (no bozo me ya know) and I think he's probably going to go round and come back along Commercial Road so if I run flat out down Bond Street I might get there before him and can flag him down. So I do that and get to the end of Bond Street by the Marina and I hear the van but it does not come down by the marina, I can hear it going off towards Portland. He must have gone across Town Bridge. I've lost him! What a STUPID MORON!!!!

So here I am back sitting on the front doorstep drinking a warm can of Coke listening to the gulls and not hearing an engine anywhere. I walked back to the esplanade several times after he drove off in case he came back but nothing, nada. He's gone, whoever he is. He didn't see me and he is probably never coming back. Aaaaaaggggghhhhh!!!!!!!

***

I heard the van again this afternoon. I ran down to King Street but it seemed to be ahead of me, so I went down Queen Street and it was somewhere behind me, and then it stopped. Every time I tried to go towards the sound it went off somewhere else. Then it disappeared into the distance. He's definitely gone for today. Was he looking for me? If he had seen me he would want to find me wouldn't he? I mean who else is alive in this goddam town???

*

OK, I've calmed down now and I have made a plan. I shall go back to the Esplanade tomorrow at the same time as today – well half an hour before at least. And I will wait there and see if he comes back again, cos that's what I would do if I was him and I had seen someone. I'll give it a few hours (note: take a book, jumper, choccy biccies). And if he does not turn up, I'll try the next day. And maybe I will write a big message in the sand for him like "I am Pip. What's your name?". Or maybe something more intelligent than that, I don't know. That's the plan then. Hardly need to be brain of Britain to work that one out. But what else can I do.? I shall leave a window open tonight so I can listen out for an engine.

***

So eventually I got myself organised. I made a meal – if you can call it that, sorted out the stuff I need from my room and brought it downstairs to Selsey. I had to hold my nose every time I went past their bedroom because of the smell. I keep thinking about maggots, like the ones we saw in biology. Then I found a case in the loft and I have packed it with going away stuff. Why? – in case I have to leave in a hurry, I don't know why. So now I'm sitting in bed and I can't stop thinking about the man and who he is, how old is he, what's he called, why is he here and How Come He's Alive?? And does he have other people with him somewhere and where are they? Or is there just him? Are we the only two people alive? That can't be. Nic, I wish you were here. it would be so much better if you were with me when he comes back. If he comes back'

That's yet another big IF. I'm going to read my book now and hope I fall asleep.....

Chapter Twenty

Rendezvous

Friday 3rd May, Morning

Adam spent the night parked in the grassy carpark at the top of the village. In the morning bright sunshine was streaming in through the front of the van. He remembered nothing of the night, seemingly having slept right through. He slipped his jeans and a sweatshirt on and went outside, stretched and drank in the cool morning air. There were puddles everywhere and everything looked washed and clean. The heavy grey sky had lifted and the sky was clear blue. The van gleamed, the leaves on the branch overhanging it were glossy, the roof slates of the houses back on the road glistened in the sun. He relieved himself in the bushes behind the van and marvelled at the volume of the birdsong in the tree above him, the gulls down in the cove and, somewhere in the distance, the sound of sheep.

It was a perfect morning and Adam felt like stretching his legs, so he took the dogs out of the car park up onto the hill beyond. The path started with broad steps cut in the chalk and then climbed from there up to the crest where the view opened out. Weymouth Bay was twinkling in the low morning rays, yesterday's wind having whipped up the white caps all the way across to Portland. The bright sunshine and the blue vista lifted his mood. However, as he descended the hill he couldn't help thinking how the little village spread out below him so prettily, was at the same time so empty of life.

Back in the van he sat down with a cup of coffee to plan the day ahead but instead he found himself thinking again about what had happened yesterday. He had driven away from Weymouth convinced that what he had seen on the promenade was nothing, a shadow perhaps, a trick of the light. But now a little doubt nagged at him again. Perhaps the figure he thought he'd glimpsed had been on the small side. It could have been a child. A child could have hidden or run away. He had seen something that looked like a figure and maybe it *was* a figure, a person. He would never know for sure but the possibility was enough to warrant another visit, surely? It was highly unlikely that his mystery figure would appear there again, but *if* there had been someone there on the promenade, then wouldn't it be a huge tragedy if he didn't make the effort to look for them again?

He decided that he would go back into Weymouth, reconnoitring some villages en-route. Then he would park on the esplanade where he had stopped yesterday, around the same time, a little before one o'clock. He would wait and if, after a good while no one appeared, he would wander a bit further around that part of the town, maybe go down to the harbourside and along to the pier. The van would be open while he was gone: if anyone wanted to find him, all they had to do was wait there.

And if no one turned up he would go and have a second look at a couple of the houses he had found yesterday, and this time check them out more thoroughly. After that? He would think about that later.

***

Friday 3rd May

I woke up early this morning, as the clock was chiming six. It felt like I hadn't really slept all night, but I probably did. I remember a dream about Nic, and another about being in class, but the class was on the beach. I was trying to tell the teacher (I think it was Nobbo, not sure) about the man on the beach, but he wasn't hearing me and all the class were laughing at me. I was getting so angry!!

I still can't get used to not being in my room. Sleeping in a guest bedroom is like being in another house. But then this place does not really feel like my home anymore, it has become another house and I don't like it. I have slipped through a mirror and I'm in Looking-Glass Land, where everything looks the same but it's ALL WRONG!!! Every morning I wake up hoping that it's last Friday and everything is back to normal, that the last seven days were just a big old bad dream. But no, here I am still.

I could not face going out of the room, so I crawled back under the bedclothes and tried to think of nice things, like me and Nic doing our crazy Moonwalk to Michael Jackson or sitting on the beach with Scott and wondering if he is going to try and snog me again after I pushed him away last time. (it was in the middle of the afternoon and a girl's gotta play a bit hard-to-get, hasn't she?). I'd snog him now, if he was here. If he walked in the door now I would lock him in and never let him out of my sight (that would sure freak him out!). These were the silly thoughts I was having when I fell asleep and when I woke up I was in a real panic cos I didn't know what the time was and I was really frantic in case I had missed my rendezvous with van-man. (Well, it's my rendezvous – not sure if he knows about it) I almost jumped out of bed to go and look at the clock in the hall, then I remembered that I had wound my watch up last night. It was only 9.30 – panic over.

***

Till then he had time on his hands so he thought that this was a good opportunity to have a tidy up and get things straight in the van. Perhaps it was the small possibility of someone else seeing it that made him look at all the stuff packed into it and think that maybe it could be sorted out a bit more efficiently.

He set about tidying the van and arranging all his stuff. Tools, clothes, food, he put away methodically, stowing what he could into cupboards and recesses and the rest into boxes or cases. There was not much available space in the van, but when he had finished it did look a lot tidier and less oppressively cluttered than before. Having spent time and energy on the domestics, Adam felt hungry enough for some breakfast. He still had time to spare after that, and he used it to heat up some water and had a wash and a shave. He spruced himself up and then it seemed only right that he should put on a clean sweatshirt. He smiled to himself as he checked his fresh-shaven visage in the wing mirror – it's a bit like getting ready for an interview, he thought.

***

I've had a good wash in the downstairs cloakroom – that's my bathroom now. I have all my stuff in there. Saves me going upstairs. I put on some roll-on, and a drop of Miss Dior, and cleaned my teeth. That was weird – I don't even do that when I'm meeting Scott. Why?!

.....Scene One: girl (on knees): "Are you here to rescue me and take me to Happyville, where there are lots of living people and there's hot and cold running water and fresh food?"

Vanman: "Well, my brief was to find human survivors and take them to a parallel universe where everything is as it was before. Unfortunately, you have failed the personal-hygiene test so you're staying here."

Girl falls on ground wailing....

I have my bag packed with biccies and a drink, my book (Robinson Crusoe, ha ha) and a magazine, so now I am ready to go. Report back later. Wish me luck.......

***

Later in the morning he was driving slowly along the sea road and coming into Weymouth. When he got to the esplanade, he parked in the spot about where he had stopped yesterday. He got out of the cab and looked around: there was no-one in sight. He let the dogs out and they went towards the beach steps. When they got there, they looked back at Adam as if to say, 'Come on!', but he had stayed put in the van. The dogs were clearly in two minds about whether to go down to the beach or come back to their master. Eventually they drifted back slowly, looking distinctly disappointed and sat on the pavement looking longingly at the sea.

Adam pulled out his book and carried on where he had left off last night, but he couldn't really concentrate on it as he was constantly looking up to see if there was anyone about. He gave up with the novel and got out his notebook and the local one-inch map and looked at his notes from yesterday. He ticked off the farms that he had visited and marked their locations on the new map with a pencil cross. Then he looked more closely at the ones to the east of Weymouth that he had marked as possible sites on the smaller scale map. He could see straightaway that two of them were not farms at all, but one place looked much more promising on the one-inch map and he decided to make that his first call.

He had been sitting in the van for what seemed like at least half an hour and he had had enough now. If the person was going to come back, they would have been here by now, surely? He decided to take a walk along to the pier. He reasoned that if someone was watching him yesterday, they might well be watching him now. If they wanted to be seen – and Adam thought he would certainly want to be seen – then they would reveal themselves sooner or later. He got out of the van and slid the rear door across, leaving a gap of a few inches. Then he set off down onto the beach, walking in the direction of the pier, the dogs tearing happily around on the sand.

From time to time, he glanced back, but could not see anyone and by the time he got to the end of the beach and onto the promontory he began to wonder if maybe no-one would appear. Perhaps his eyes had deceived him yesterday, willing his eyes to see a human, instead of shadows from passing clouds. He walked along the promontory to the end of the ugly concrete building that sat on the short pier beyond. Here he found a bench on the sunny side from where he could look back towards the town and see anyone that might be coming from that direction. The dogs had been running around exploring all the new strange smells that lingered around a harbour – seaweed, fish, bait and so-on – and now they saw that Adam had sat down, they wandered over and sat at his feet, as if awaiting instructions. What obedient and loyal creatures these two had become, Adam thought. Or maybe that was wishful thinking as well.

As if on cue, the old dog suddenly gave a low growl. At the same moment Bonzo jumped up and started off down the pier, barking shrilly. Adam looked up and saw a young girl standing at the end of the building. As Bonzo ran towards her she shrank back against the building.

"Bonzo!" roared Adam, "Come here, now!" The little dog paused. "It's alright," he called out to her, "he'll only lick you to death."

Bonzo started advancing again.

"Bonzo!" Adam shouted again as he walked towards the girl. The dog paused. "Just offer him your hand and he'll be fine. He just wants to be friendly." Adam hoped that this was true. The young girl was older than he first thought, a teenager, rather small for her age, of Asian extraction. She wore jeans and a Parka jacket, which did not quite seem to fit her or suit her.

She held her hand down, rather nervously, and Bonzo trotted up to her, tail wagging, and licked it. She stroked the back of his head cautiously, then squatted down so she could stroke him.

"Hello, I'm Adam," Adam offered in his most welcoming voice.

"I'm Pip," said the girl, addressing the dog.

"Was it you I saw yesterday?"

"Yes," she replied.

"I came to look for you, but you had vanished into thin air."

"Yes," she said, hesitantly. "I wasn't sure. I got scared." And then after a pause, "I haven't seen anyone since my parents died last weekend."

"I'm sorry," Adam said gently. "I lost my family last weekend and I have not seen anyone either. But now...there's you. This is amazing!"

The girl looked up: "Yes, it's..." she faltered, her eyes had filled up. "I'm sorry", she whispered, then, looking down at the ground, "I..."

Adam instinctively squatted down by her, reached out and touched her arm gently. The girl sobbed, sniffed, wiped her nose and laughed all at the same time.

"I'm so silly!" she said. "I told myself I would not do this." And then, "I can't believe it."

"No, nor can I. It's incredible." And it was. "Amazing!" he laughed, "Someone else alive on the planet!"

The dog was still making a fuss of his new friend. "This is Bonzo, by the way." The girl took his paw and shook it.

"Hello Bonzo, pleased to meet you, I'm Pip," and she laughed, the tears still running. "And what's your name?" she said to the old dog, who had now decided to say hello to the newcomer.

"Oh, he doesn't have a name yet. I haven't thought of one."

"Well, hello, whoever you are."

Adam stood up and let the girl pet the dog. "Bonzo is my neighbours' dog. He came round after they had died. The other one, well, he just adopted me."

"Oh," she said, looking up at him for a moment. "So where do you live?"

"I live in Reading, or I used to. Since Tuesday I have been living in a camper van. Did you see it?"

"Yes. I saw you walking with the dogs on the beach."

"So who did you think was going to bite you, the dogs or me?" The girl stood up and smiled shyly but did not answer the question.

"You know what? I could really do with a cup of coffee, do you want to join me?"

"Can you make hot drinks? In that van?"

"Oh yes. And hot dinners too."

"Can you make tea?"

Adam nodded.

"With milk?"

"Yes, I have milk too."

"I've been dreaming of a hot cup of tea," she said.

"Great. Come on boys," Adam said. "It's only long-life milk, I'm afraid."

"Oh, that's OK. Anything would do; I haven't had a hot drink for a week."

They walked off back down the pier, the dogs keeping close to their new companion, she watching them with great interest. It was easier than looking at this stranger maybe, Adam thought.

"So where do you live, Pip? Nearby, I guess."

"Yes. We run a guest house, on a road not far from where you are parked. We've lived here for three years now, but before that we lived in Bournville, in Birmingham."

"Ah, the chocolate factory. Birmingham – that's not a city I know very well. We used to live in London – my wife and I – but when we got together, we moved out to Reading."

"Is it nice there?"

Adam laughed. "Well I suppose it's OK. We're happy enough there. We *were* happy there."

"Have you got, er, did you have children? Sorry, that's..."

Adam smiled, "Yes, we had two children. Like you, I had family, friends, work, a life. Now, I just have two dogs." After a pause, he added, "And do you like living here, or do you miss Birmingham?"

"It's OK here, I suppose. I like the sea, especially in the winter when the visitors have all gone. I don't miss Birmingham particularly, but I do miss my old friends."

"Haven't you made new friends here then?"

"Yes, one or two. But here I'm still the new girl. The darkie with the funny accent. They don't see many people my colour here."

"No, I can imagine. It can't be easy for you."

The conversation seemed to have reached a pause point and they walked on in silence for a while. Adam mused to himself that he had not had any conversation for a week and now he had run out of things to say. It was a bit like the first time you talk with someone you have been dying to meet. When the nervous chatter dries up you desperately think of something to say to get the conversation going. All the while the important things you want to get to, but can't, are banging away in your head.

"Wow, it is so good to find you, to find someone alive," he said at last. "You know, I've been driving around wondering if I was the only person alive in the world. And thinking, why me?"

"Yes, I know. Me too."

"So tell me," Adam said, as they got back to the Esplanade, "what have you been doing since last weekend when it all happened?"

"I'm not sure really," Pip said slowly. "I didn't know what had happened. My folks got ill, the phones stopped, the TV stopped and then the lights went out. I didn't know what to do. I was really scared. I stayed in my room a lot at first and then I started to get myself together, make some food, look after myself, you know." She dried up, but Adam waited for her to carry on. "Is it the same in Reading as well?"

Adam nodded. The girl slowed up and then looked straight at Adam.

"Is everyone dead? All over the country?"

Adam frowned, then shrugged. The expression on the girl's face showed that he had not allayed her worst fears.

"But no, not everyone. I mean, there's us, and there must be others around."

She turned and walked on slowly. After a while she said:

"Have you been to other towns? Is it the same everywhere?"

"Well, I've been in Salisbury, Winchester, Poole; It was the same there." The girl said nothing, so he carried on:

"I went to look for my brother in Wiltshire, but he seemed to have gone away. I don't know if he's alive or not. But my sister-in-law and her husband are dead, and my cousin in Winchester. I've not seen a living soul since Jo died."

"I'm sorry," said the girl, "and your children...?"

"Yes, they died first, on Saturday. Oscar was only seven, and Sophie two. They..." Adam petered out; it was too much to talk about yet.

They walked on in silence and soon they were at the van.

"Well here we are," said Adam as he opened the side door, "welcome to my little house on wheels. Come on in."

He stood back to let the girl go in first, but the dogs beat her to it. "Hey boys, where are your manners? Ladies first, remember!"

The girl smiled. "They know whose home this is. They're so sweet."

"Sweet? They are a couple of tramps, I can tell you." Adam followed her in. "Let's get the kettle on. This is where the magic happens!" he said, waving grandly at the kitchen area. He set to boiling the kettle and got out two mugs, coffee, milk and hunted out a tea bag. "Are you hungry? Have you eaten today?"

"No. I've not been very hungry. But I'd love a biscuit," she said.

"We can do biscuits. And maybe later I can rustle up some lunch. It's lunchtime now, really."

"I have been trying to eat proper meals at the proper time," the girl said, "but mostly I don't know what the time is and I wait till I'm hungry. Things like that don't really seem to matter anymore."

Adam looked at this wee skinny girl and smiled. "Maybe you need to have two biscuits – you look like you need feeding up."

After he said it, he reflected that maybe that was not the cleverest thing to say to a teenage girl, but she seemed to take it well.

"That's the sort of thing that Thommo, I mean, my dad, says. He is always telling me that I'll slip through a crack in the floorboards one day. He says silly things like: I'm a pip without the squeak. He's a big man, like a big old bear." Adam saw her smile at the thought and then her face cloud over. "But Thommo was great."

Adam saw the tears well up again. He felt she wanted to talk. "And your mum?"

"Mum? She wasn't my real mum either. I never knew my parents. Angela brought me up – they never had any children of their own – and she was a good mum, I suppose."

"So you didn't call Thommo, Dad?"

"Thommo's real name was Peter, Peter Thomas. He came from south Wales. His mates all called him Thommo and he talked about himself as Thommo, you know, like he was talking about someone else. He'd say to Mum: 'Thommo's hungry, Mother, are you going to make him some tea?' And she'd say something like "Well Thommo had better ask nicely then'. So I thought she was *Mother* or *Mum* and he was *Thommo* and that's how it stayed."

"They sound like good people," Adam said, unsure quite what to say.

"They were," said Pip quietly and then, with a sigh, "but now they've gone." She put her hands to her face and turned away.

Adam thought that maybe this was a good time to change the conversation.

He turned back to the kettle, which was boiling away furiously now, and set about making the tea. He gave the girl a little time to compose herself again and then asked, "OK, how do you like your tea? Strong, weak? With milk, of course. And sugar?"

"Not too strong, with sugar. Two spoons. Please."

Pip munched her biscuits and hunched over her tea as if it was something precious, something to study. Adam sipped at his coffee. The dogs watched them, their eyes going from one to the other, biscuit to biscuit. Pip spotted them staring wistfully at the last piece of biscuit. "The dogs look hungry - can I give them some biscuit?" she asked.

Adam laughed. "They want you to think that they're starving, but they had some breakfast. I've got some little dog treats you can give them in a minute if you like."

"OK," she said, and then to the dogs, "did you hear that? In a minute you'll get something." Bonzo put his head on side, as if to better understand what this girl was saying to him, and Pip smiled. "Bonzo's a good name. I've never heard that before."

"Haven't you? There was a band, a sort of comedy group, back in the sixties, called The Bonzo Dog Doodah Band. I think Mick, my neighbour, was into them in a big way. He had strange tastes that man. Apparently, the band was named after a cartoon dog that was popular in the twenties – Bonzo the Dog."

"So when are you going to find a name for the other one then?" Pip asked, looking at the old dog, who had by now given up on the biscuit and laid down in the corner.

"Mmm. That's a good question. Maybe you can come up with something."

"We've never had any pets." Pip said. "My parents used to run a café and now we have a guest house and they don't think it's hygienic."

"We never had dogs," Adam told her, "but my mum had a cat. Living in a London flat, I never thought about having a pet. But, you know – these fellas have been good for me since I've been on my own. They give me someone to talk to. I don't suppose you have even had that, have you?"

"No," said Pip, "I haven't. I talk to my friend quite a lot, in my head. I think she is dead."

"Really? Are you sure?"

"No but when she rang me last Friday, she didn't sound well at all. That was just before the lines became engaged all the time... I don't see her very often as she lives in Bath now, but we talk on the phone a lot. Well, we did."

"She might still be alive then," Adam said gently, "you never know."

"I hope so. Do you think it's possible?"

"Well, there are two of us that have managed to bump into each other. There are sixty million people in the UK so there must some others dotted around. I plan to keep on looking." Adam sipped his coffee thoughtfully.

He looked up to see Pip looking at him, as if waiting for him to say something instructive. He wondered where to take the conversation next. "So," he started, hesitantly, "how have you been managing, you know food and everything?"

"I haven't really felt like eating much. There wasn't much left in the house I could eat really. I had thrown out a load of food on the Tuesday. It was such a waste, but it was getting smelly in the fridges. I kept the butter and some cheese, but they're getting a bit off now. So I've been living on spaghetti hoops, and stuff like that. And biscuits."

"But nothing hot I suppose," said Adam

"No. I started to make lists of what was in the house and the things I needed. I sort of put together a plan of what I had to do, you know, like find some food in the hotels, find some more water and... try driving the car so I could go and look for Nic..." She gave a little ironic laugh. "Well it was a load of rubbish really, I don't really have any clue what I'm going to do. And now you've turned up..." She fiddled with her cup for a moment or two and then looked at Adam, "What about you?"

"Well...," Adam paused to think about what he was going to say next. Did he want to talk about this now. He took a breath, then began slowly: "After Jo died, I was so exhausted by it all I just slept, for hours and hours. I didn't want to wake up, I guess. The next day, Monday, I sort of got myself together and decided that I needed to give my family a proper send-off, to bury their bodies in a grave as best I could."

He paused again and decided to move on from the burial. "My next job, I decided, was to go and see if I could find my brother. We've become quite close recently, after not having much contact for a while." He took a slow breath. "He's my only blood family now, not counting a couple of cousins I never see. I figured that the reason I'd survived might be to do with genetics; something in my genes that meant this virus didn't make me ill. If that was the case, then there was a good chance that Sam, my brother, would have survived too. If he hadn't, or if I couldn't find him, then I'd search out my cousin."

Adam had stopped talking, so Pip summoned up the courage to ask: "And did you do all these things? Did you bury your family?"

"Yes."

"That must have been hard."

"It wasn't easy. But I knew I wouldn't forgive myself if I had left them in the house like that. I wanted to, needed to, say goodbye properly, to do the best I could for them in death, I suppose, as I tried to do in life." Adam took a deep breath before he carried on. "I didn't find my brother, but my cousin is dead, so I don't know what the chances are of finding Sam alive."

"You mustn't give up hope, he might be OK, like you," Pip offered, looking as if she was trying hard to sound encouraging, but not convincing herself. "So, what made you come to Weymouth?"

Adam proceeded to explain his idea for the house with a clean water supply, firewood, somewhere to grow crops etc. It did not sound so solid a plan when he relayed it to Pip as it did in his mind. "But as well as that, I was thinking of driving up north to see if I can track down my friend or my cousin, and that gives me the chance to see if there are any other survivors."

"So you won't be staying around here then?"

"Well, I need to go back to Friarswood Farm and see if my brother has been there. I promised to do it within five days – or was it three? Three, I think – so that would mean by tomorrow. But first I wanted to find a base for the longer term. Going north was something I would do after that, maybe. But I haven't thought it through yet."

Pip seemed to be mulling this information over in her head and Adam was waiting for the follow-up question, but she remained silent. He got up and found a couple of doggie treats in the tin and gave them to Pip. "They love these," he said, "but they can only have two a day, or they get spoilt."

Pip laughed. "Do you hear that? Isn't he a meanie?" The dogs immediately moved close to the girl, eyes fixed on the treats. Bonzo pushed in front. She held the biscuits out to them tentatively and winced as Bonzo snatched it from her and wolfed it down. The old dog took his biscuit from her hand gently, but then it was gone in a shot. She laughed nervously. "Do they always eat like that?"

"You don't know dogs, do you?" Adam laughed. "They're not graceful eaters." The dogs were watching the newcomer intently to see if any more presents were forthcoming. "OK boys, no more now. All gone. That's your lot." The dogs looked at Adam, then back at Pip, who was trying to indicate to them that she had no more biscuits. "You'll be friends for life now," Adam said.

Pip wiped her hands on her jeans and looked around the interior of the van. "There's not a lot of space in here – where's the bed?"

"Under that seat," said Adam, smiling at Pip's puzzled expression. "You fold the table and it turns into a bed of sorts, not a very comfy one, mind. It's all very clever how everything fits in here. It's not very spacious, but it does for one. Well one and two dogs at a push."

"So how did you and the family all sleep..? I mean did you have a tent or something as well."

"Oh no." and Adam smiled at the thought of the chaos of camping with the children. "This wasn't our van. I stole it. Well, I requisitioned it, if you know what I mean." He went on to explain about the reconnaissance trip to the camping store and having to leave his beloved Audi behind. "This is my first time camping, and I am quite taken with it. Except for the bed. That really kills my back."

Pip was looking puzzled: "But what do you do when you need to...?"

Adam smiled and saved her finishing the question.

"Well I make do, you know. Bushes and trees."

Pip's frown turned into a smile of understanding.

"I've been wondering how long the water will last. You know, from the tank in the loft."

"It's not going to be easy for you staying in that house. That water *won't* last and it won't be heathy for you to stay there with, you know..."

"Their bodies? You can say it. I know, I don't know what to do about them. But Serendipity is my home – I know, corny name. But ..." she trailed off.

"You could come with me. Help me find a long-term base, come up country with me and see if we can find others. You can't stay here on your own. Well, of course you can if that is what you want. But you know it won't be safe out there. It's going to get wild. I mean literally. There will be a lot of hungry dogs and other animals that will turn feral. It can't stay as it is now."

Pip looked alarmed at this: "Wild animals? I have heard some barking now and again and cats are fighting in the alley behind the house. But I hadn't thought about them becoming dangerous. So how do we survive? What do we do when the food and water run out?"

"Well," Adam said, "we get organised, we plan ahead. There are the resources out there, we just have to use them and make them work for us."

"But even if we could do all that, what would be the point? What if we couldn't, you know, get on? What if we get ill?"

"Well that is why we need to find other survivors."

"And if we don't?... Find anyone?"

Adam smiled – it was the thought that he had pondered himself. He gathered his words together carefully. "You know,

Pip, we *have* to have hope. Without that everything is pointless. We have brains and skills between us." Pip laughed, ironically, but he cut in quickly before she could argue the point.

"Yes, you have, more than you realise, I expect. Look, you and I found each other, and we will find other people, I'm sure of it, and they will have other skills."

"But if there's no electricity, no gas or water, how do we live?"

"I've thought about this. There are cars and trucks out there, they can generate electricity. There won't be gas, except for bottled gas, while it lasts. But there is plenty of firewood to heat a home and cook food. As I say, the resources are all there, it's just a matter of learning how to use them."

Chapter Twenty-One

Two for Tea

Friday 3rd May, Afternoon

They sat and talked for a long time and when the conversation had dried up, Adam stood up and said: "How do you like the sound of curry tonight?"

"Definitely like the sound of that! Can you make it in here?"

"Well, I can make camper van curry – it's a special recipe."

Pip laughed, and then: "Is it going to have meat in it?"

"Hm, that's going to be difficult. I think this one will have to be a vegetable curry. Unless you would like hot-dog sausages in it?"

"No, vegetables are just fine with me. I'm not a big meat eater." Pip said

Not a big anything, Adam thought. But then, he remembered, a girl friend he had at college, a tiny little thing who ate like a horse.

"OK then why don't I start getting that together? I could do with some potatoes – have you got any in your guesthouse?"

"Pip thought for a while... "There are some potatoes and other vegetables in the larder – I don't know if they are still going to be OK. I could go and get them for you. Or you could come back with me if you like and see if there is anything else you need. You can see where I live. If you want to...?"

"That's a good idea," said Adam. "We'll leave the dogs in the van, don't you think? Might be best. So – shall we go?"

Adam locked the van and they set off down George Street. As they walked down the road Pip asked Adam again if the other towns he had been through were like Weymouth, so empty and so quiet. He told her about where he lived in Reading, hearing the town hall clock for the first time. How Salisbury and Winchester were the same.

"I'm sort of getting used to the quiet," said Pip, "I kind of like it in a way. It sounds bad I know, but I guess I'm a bit of a loner really. But then I get scared as well and wish there was someone else around."

"I can understand that," said Adam.

They got to the guesthouse and Pip opened the front door. She seemed to hesitate a moment, as if not quite sure whether to bring Adam into the house or not. Then "Welcome to Serendipity," she said, "for that special sea-side holiday experience." Adam smiled.

He walked into the gloomy hallway and was struck by how dim and dingy the hall and the staircase off it were without any lighting. He looked into the room on the right which seemed to be a dining room. "That's where I eat," Pip said, "and on the other side is a sitting room. Come on through." He followed her down a dark passageway into the kitchen. This had the benefit of a large window that looked out onto a small walled yard and, beyond, a gate, garages and the backs of other tall, Victorian buildings. The sunlight slanted across the yard, but did not reach the window. Pip walked over and unlocked the back door. "Need to get some air in here," she said.

To the side of the kitchen was a large walk-in larder and Pip beckoned Adam to have a look at what was stored there. There were lots of tins and dry goods and on a rack some potatoes, and carrots, some fruit and a couple of cabbages. The leaves were yellowing and they looked as if they needed to be thrown out. Adam was about to ask Pip why she had not done anything with these when he remembered that, of course, she had no means of cooking.

"We can certainly use these." he said pointing to the root vegetables, and the fruit."

Pip found him a large shopping bag and told him to take what he wanted. "I'm not much of a cook," she said. "And there's lots of other stuff here – biscuits, cereal and all that. But I guess you can get what you need anywhere you can break in." She gave a sly smile when she said this, and Adam laughed.

"Yep, food, tools, camper vans – even petrol at a push. Well, a suck actually."

He picked up the bag and made as if to leave: "So are you going to come back with me now or do you want to come over later when supper is ready?"

"No, I'll come with you. If that's ok with you? There is something I might need your help with though..."

"Your parents?"

"Yes. What am I going to do with them? I can't just leave them up there. And I don't like being in the house with them there, thinking about them... you know... Do you think you could help me move them and, I don't know, take them somewhere? I mean digging a grave – that's a lot to ask, but..."

Adam could see the girl's discomfort. There were bodies of the two people she was closest to, her family. They needed to be put to rest somehow, somewhere.

"I think we need to give this some thought, "Adam said slowly. "And you say they are at the top of the house?" Pip nodded. "It won't be easy to move them. Let's go back to the van and think what we can do."

Pip locked up the house and they walked back to the seafront. Adam was thinking of something to take the girl's mind off her dead parents. Then a question came to his mind that he had been meaning to ask:

"So Pip, where does your name come from? Were you christened by your mum and..."

"Thommo?" Pip answered, "sort of. My full name is Filipa Maria Evangelina Thomas. But Fil***i***pa is a bit difficult for most people and I don't like the English *Phil*ippa! Thommo has always called me Pip, or Pipkin, so I tell everyone that my name is Pip."

"Filipa is a nice name," said Adam, "but I can see why Pip is easier."

"When they first found out my real name at the comp – you know, school – they teased me something awful. But they've got over it now. And it's my name, it's what I am called."

"Well Pip, I think it's a very good name; it's short and sweet."

"Like me?" Pip said, smiling. "And it's palindromic"

"It's what?"

"It's a palindrome – reads the same forward and backward."

"Ah, is that what it is?"

"Like *madam, I'm Adam.*"

Adam puzzled that one out for a moment and then, "mmm. I see; clever! I can remember one, I think...*Evil rats on no star live*. Was that it?."

"Yes, that's right."

Back at the van the dogs were very pleased to see them, Pip as well as Adam. They were keen to go and explore so Adam took them down to the beach and Pip followed. They went down to the water and stood looking at the waves while the two dogs ran around, noses up, scenting the breeze. The old dog found a piece of driftwood and brought it over to Adam and dropped it at his feet.

"No, I don't want it." he said to the dog. "Try Pip. See if she wants it." The dog put his head on one side while he tried to compute this, but it was too difficult. So he picked the wood up and took it to Pip instead. She laughed as she picked it up.

"You're a clever dog, aren't you? I suppose you want me to throw it?" She pulled her arm back and threw the stick as far as she could. The dog brought it back to her in a moment.

"Now, who's the clever one here – him or you? You'll have to carry on doing that till feeding time! Here, give it to me." He took the stick from her and hurled it into the sea. Pip looked horrified but the collie ran into the sea and started paddling out to fetch it.

"Don't worry," he said, laughing at the look on her face. "Dogs can swim." The dog soon got to the stick and swam back to the shore with it then, unsure who to take it to, dropped it between them. He then shook himself vigorously and while Adam quickly ducked out of the way, Pip got the full force of the spray. Adam watched her brushing the water off her jacket and jeans and laughed:

"Tell you what, you stay here and keep an eye on the dogs, and I'll go and get supper organised. How about it?" Pip didn't look too sure about that, but Adam was already walking up the beach. "When you have had enough, just come back to the van. They'll follow you."

He left her throwing the stick and the two dogs competing to bring it back. She was still a bit nervous with the animals, but she seemed to be enjoying herself. Back at the van he started getting things organised for cooking. He was glad to get a moment to himself. Everything had happened so quickly and ever since they had first spoken to each other, they had not stopped talking. It was no surprise really, given that for a week neither of them had anyone to talk to. But Adam felt he needed to catch breath and think about what he was going to do now that 'he' had become 'they', for the time being at least. That was assuming that the girl was going to join up with him. He could not imagine that she would want to be left alone here now when he went off in the van. But there again, she had survived five days on her own and not crumbled. She's tougher than she looks, he thought. Unless she insisted on staying on her own, though, he certainly had no intention of leaving her behind.

So now there were two of them, where were they going to go? Searching for a home in Dorset? Up to the Midlands to see if he could find Gerry or his cousins? For them to travel in the van he was going to have to get a tent, a sleeping bag and something to put under it. And there were other issues, like privacy – his and hers. Although he was a father, he had no experience of taking care of teenage girls – how was that going to work out? Maybe he would let her solve those conundrums and leave him to sort the practicalities. Perhaps when they'd had a meal, he could introduce the subject, tell her his plans and see what she had to offer.

He was pondering this whilst chopping vegetables for the curry, occasionally looking over to the beach to keep an eye on Pip and dogs. He became aware of a lot of barking and he tried to see what it was about. Two large dogs had appeared, and one was chasing Bonzo while the other was heading for Pip. He dropped the knife and grabbed the wheel brace from under the driver's seat. As he jumped out of the van he heard Pip scream and saw her trying to fend off the dog. He could hear Bonzo yelping as the other dog rolled him over on the sand, while the old collie was snapping at the first dog. Adam raced down the steps and across the beach towards them shouting as loudly as he could. At this moment the second dog looked up and, in an instant, had turned away from Bonzo and was coming towards him, snarling. Adam stopped, took a deep breath and then ran towards the animal. Just before dog and man collided Adam stopped, swung the wheel brace and caught the onrushing dog full on the muzzle. The dog dropped like a stone, whining pitifully. The first dog had his jaws on Pip's arm and she was screaming and trying to hit the dog, whilst struggling to stay upright. The dog spotted Adam running towards them and let go of Pip's arm. He looked uncertainly at the big man looming towards him roaring and then turned tail and ran away up the beach, with the Collie in pursuit.

Pip was shaking and crying and clutching her left arm. He said, "It's OK. They've gone now. Let's have a look at that arm." He could see her jacket was torn, and the sweater underneath. "Let's get you back to the van and check you out," he said, guiding her gently up the beach.

The first dog was lying on his side, whimpering softly. His head was a mess of blood and Adam guessed that he would not be getting back on his feet again. He thought he should perhaps put an end to the dog's distress, but he could do that later. He called the dogs as he helped Pip up the beach. Bonzo was snarling at the wounded creature and didn't look like he wanted to leave him. The old dog had chased Pip's attacker off up the beach and was trotting back to join them.

As they got to the steps Pip pulled away from Adam and said, “I’m OK. I’ll be alright now”.

Adam let her go on up the steps whilst he stayed to call Bonzo and to make sure the other dog did not come back. Bonzo came trotting over. He was ruffled but it did not look like the big dog had bitten him. Adam caught up with Pip at the van. She was still shaking and looked very white.

“OK sit yourself down. We need to get the jacket off and the jumper and have a look at that wound. Can you move your arm?”

“I think so.” Pip said.

Adam found his medicine box and got out some antiseptic lotion. “What happened? I didn’t notice those dogs before, where did they come from?”

“I don’t know. They just appeared all of a sudden. I thought they wanted to play with your dogs but Bonzo snarled and one of them went for him. Then suddenly the other one jumped up and got hold of my arm.”

Pip was wincing as she removed her arm tentatively from the jacket. Adam helped her, as best he could. He could see blood around the jagged hole in her jumper. “Can’t I just roll the sleeve up?” she said. Adam realised that she was shy about removing her jumper in front of him, understandably. He watched her trying to roll back the sleeve over the wound. “Let me help” he said, “I’ll cut it away.” He got the scissors from his washbag and cut the jumper around the wound.

"Look away now," he said as he quickly, but carefully, peeled the jumper away from her arm. He could see the ring of marks on her arm made by the dog's teeth. They were oozing blood, but he didn't think that the wound was very deep. Pip was looking nervously at it while Adam reached over to grab the big water bottle from the top of the cabinet. "Come over to the door a minute," he said, and offered a hand to support her while he guided her over to the open door. She held her arm out while he washed the wound with the water. He went back and found a clean tea-towel which he used to dry the water from her arm and then he applied the lotion with some cotton-wool and dressed it in a bandage, which he tied off with a knot. He brought her back in and sat her down on the couch.

"Wow," Pip said, "you've got everything here, haven't you?" She looked up at him shyly: "I don't know what I would have done if you weren't here."

Adam threw the tea towel onto the floor, put the first aid stuff away and then sat down on the couch next to her. "I don't know, I really don't know what would have happened. But that was pretty hairy," he said. He suddenly felt exhausted and realised that he was trembling. "You know, I've been expecting something like that to happen before long, but it's a bit of a shock when it does. We are going to have to be more careful from now on."

Adam got the meal together while Pip sat on the sofa bench, both dogs lying at her feet, as if guarding her from another attack. She was very quiet, clearly shaken from what had happened. Adam got busy with preparing the meal and when he next looked over she had curled up on the seat, with her head on her good arm, and looked as if she was sleeping. She looks quite at home, he thought, and smiled to himself.

When the food was ready, he pulled down the table and got out two plates and two forks and served out equal portions of rice and his home-made curry. The smell of the food seemed to rouse Pip from her slumber. "Sorry," she said, "I just came over really tired."

"That's the shock. That's what happens after a trauma; it's a natural reaction.

It was quite traumatic, what happened on the beach. I was shaken up too. You were very brave."

"I don't think I was," she said

"Well, that was a big dog and you were fighting it off. It's really important to show the animal that you are not afraid and that he should be scared of you. You did that well."

Pip laughed: "I think you are just being nice. I was scared out of my wits."

"Exactly, but you didn't roll over and give in. Some people would just freeze, but you fought back. I was scared too, but I didn't let the dog see that."

"You saved my life."

"Well, whatever. But now it is time to eat. You'll have to squeeze up, I'm afraid – we don't have any other chairs in this dining room."

Adam sat down next to the girl and got stuck in hungrily. Pip was a bit more circumspect and dabbed at her food tentatively. Eventually her hunger overcame her inhibitions and she too got stuck into the curry.

"There's more, if you'd like it," said Adam.

Pip nodded eagerly, "Please. It's amazing!"

When they had finished Adam cleared the plates and came back with two small bowls and a larger one.

"It's only fruit salad, but it's got some fresh fruit in it. And I've got some evaporated milk to go with it."

"Mmm," Pip said, "that was Thommo's favourite."

When they had finished, she helped Adam wash the things up and make hot drinks. Adam put the table away and sat down on the floor in the doorway. Pip came over to join him and they sipped their drinks and looked out to the sea. It was quieter now that the tide was going out and the sun was getting lower in the sky.

He turned to the girl, took a deep breath and said, "You know Pip, I've been thinking about what you said earlier, and I don't know whether we are going to be able to get your parents' bodies out from the house." He paused to see Pip's reaction, but she said nothing and was waiting for him to go on. "It won't be possible to move their bodies with any… dignity. To try and carry them down three flights of stairs and then take them somewhere to bury them or whatever. We would have to drag them and… well… that's not going to be very pleasant."

He was going to mention the issue of disease, but thought that a bit insensitive. "I know that you want to do the right thing by them, to give them a funeral, a send-off of some sort, but I just don't see how we can do it, you know?"

Pip was quiet, digesting what he had just said. He was about to go on, but, seeing that, she cut in, "I know. You're right, and I've thought about this a lot over the last few days. I can see that it wouldn't be easy. I just had this idea that it would be good to make a grave for them, or put their bodies in the sea or something, I don't know. But it's not realistic, is it?"

"No, I don't think it is," Adam said softly. "Not really. But let me give it some more thought and maybe I will come up with something. I have no idea what, but there might be a solution."

"I don't know that I want to stay in Serendipity, even if we could bury them. It would be strange. It wouldn't be like home any more without them."

"So why don't you come with me in the van? We can see if Sam has been to Friarswood Farm at all, and we can check out this farmhouse I've got my eye on. Then maybe after that we can head up country, look for your friend, see who else we find. What do you think?"

Pip pondered this for a moment. "It sounds like a sensible plan but... but how can we live in this van? I mean, there's not a lot of room, is there. For two of us and two dogs. There's not much...privacy."

"We can get a tent, and I can sleep in that, or you can, if you prefer. In fact, that might give you more privacy. We can find you a blow-up mattress and a sleeping bag; make it quite cosy. It's coming on for summer now so it won't be too cold. And maybe we look for a larger van, one of those big mobile-home jobs. What do you think?"

"Yeah, OK, I suppose."

"You don't drive, do you?"

Pip shook her head apologetically.

"Have you ever had lessons?"

"No, I'm not old enough yet. But I'd like to learn."

"Why not?" Adam said. "Why not?"

She was quiet for a while, evidently thinking through what he was proposing. "And what do I do about... you know? How do I make... how do I say *goodbye*?"

"Well..." Adam ran his fingers through his hair and looked out at the sea. "I think you have to gather up your things, and when you are ready to move out, you have some time in the house to say your farewells in your own way. Then you lock the door and walk away. It's a new start, a new world. But you'll always have your memories."

Pip sat quietly and stroked the old dog, who had curled up at her feet, almost protectively. "Yes, that's what I've got to do," she said. After a moment or two, she looked at Adam and said, "So, when do you want to go?"

"Well, I need to go to Friarswood tomorrow so we can do that first and then look at that other farm place. After that, come back here and get everything ready for our trip the next day, which is Sunday, I think. You don't go to church, do you?" he said jokingly, immediately regretting it.

"No," she said, "and I don't think anyone else will be going either. But I'd like to go back to Serendipity now and get myself sorted."

"Let me walk you home and then I'll come and pick you up in the morning. But are you going to be OK in the house tonight?"

"I'll be fine. I've been there all week. It is my home, after all." She said that in a way that, to Adam's ear was saying: *I can look after myself* and, at the same time, *but I am leaving my home and my family, and you need to know that.*

"Can we drive there?" she asked. "I don't want to meet that dog again."

"God no! Of course, I'll drive you. But first we need to have a bit of a tidy up. We don't want these curry plates rolling around the floor."

***

So where do I begin to tell you about Adam? He's tall – really tall from my viewpoint, (which admittedly is quite low) He's got curly hair, sort of sandy brown and quite short, quite a small nose and a wide, serious-looking mouth. He looks a bit severe but then when he smiles his eyes, which are grey, twinkle, like he's been having you on about something. Is he a gangster, kidnapper or rapist? I don't think so, but then how would you know? What I do know is, he has a kettle and he made me a hot cup of tea – what more can an abandoned girl ask for?

*

So now I am back here, getting my stuff sorted ready to go with him on Sunday. Well that's the plan, but I'm still not sure about it. Am I ready to spend time travelling round the country with this guy, squeezed into his van with all his stuff and his two dogs? After this afternoon, I've gone off dogs a bit. But that's unfair — these guys are OK. The old one chased off the other dog and Adam tells me that they will always protect me now. Hmmm.

He says we can get a tent and I can sleep in that if I want – for privacy. I need to think about this. And if I go with him, then can I ever come back here? But unless I can do something with mum and Thommo then I really can't stay here anyway. I don't know what to do. I need a cup of tea!! And that's another thing. He's got a stove and gas and can make meals, and he knows how to make stuff and do stuff.

And then I think: what if he tries it on with me? I couldn't just knee him in the lunchbox and make him go away. But I don't think he's that sort of bloke. I mean you never know for sure, but I think he's OK. I mean he's got a wife and kids. Yeah. So you say.

Well - I think he's OK.

+ - + - + - Nic, I wish you were here with me tonight. You would help me think straight. + - + -

OK, I'm going to carry on sorting my stuff now.

***

I've packed up the big case with my stuff but I'm not sure that it's the right stuff. I put some clothes in, undies, pyjamas, washbag and all that. Then I thought about a dressing gown, and then thought, stupid! That's far too big - the bag's already full. And if Adam can get himself food and tools and a camper van, I'm sure I can get myself some new clothes. So maybe if I take out some of the clothes, I can get more books in, but books are heavy and I can get those from a bookshop. So maybe I put a few ornaments in just so I can make the place my own a bit. So I take all the clothes out and make piles all over the floor and start again. Now I have filled the big case and a small case and I'm looking at other stuff I want to take and I think – that van is not very big, so where is it going to go? And then I had a really BIG THOUGHT – where am I going to keep this diary? I don't want anyone looking at this. Maybe I leave it here in the house., hidden somewhere. After all I am leaving my old life behind. Aren't I?

Aaaaggghhh! I don't know what to do!!!!

*

OK, I've got a plan. I'm going to put all the really important things in the big case, so if I can only take one, it's going to be that one. Then less important things in the small case and the rest of the stuff I have put in a big cardboard box. If I can't take them on this trip, then they can stay here for now.

*

So I did that and there's still stuff left over, but that can just stay here in carrier bags until I can collect it. It's 11.00 now and

I'm feeling tired. I had to have a couple of biccies earlier to keep me going. I could have died for a cup of Adam's tea to go with them…

I'm not sure about tomorrow. Adam seems like a nice bloke and his plan sort of makes sense. I mean, there must be other people like us somewhere and it's only right that we should see if we can find some other survivors. And he says we can go into Bath to look for Nic and then go to Bournville, and that's all great, but I would like to have the option of coming back here. But then Adam doesn't think we can do anything for mum and Thommo so if that's the case, I can't really come back here, can I? Maybe he's right – I have to say my farewells and then move on. I'm going to sleep now and in the morning I will know what I have to do.

That's what Thommo always used to say to me.

***

When Adam dropped Pip back at Serendipity it was late afternoon and there was still plenty of the day left. He remembered that when he drove into Weymouth the day before, he had made a mental note to come back and have a look around the naval base. With meeting Pip, he had forgotten all about it, but now he had some time on his hands.

Instead of driving back to the sea front, Adam took the road out of town, across the causeway and onto the island to a military site, which the signs said was a naval air station. He drove up to the main gates which were closed, just as he had expected. There was no sign of life in the sentry post or anywhere inside the base, that he could see. All he heard was the rattling of the flag lines on a pole nearby. It didn't look promising. He gave up on that idea and drove around the small town behind the base and then, finding no sign of life there, he went down the length of the island to the lighthouse at Portland Bill.

It was a place he had never been before but, like so many people, he was drawn to it by the romance of it, the lonely isolation, comfort in the teeth of a storm. When he was a boy, he had read about the life of a lighthouse keeper and he imagined sleeping inside the tower hearing the wind and the waves lashing the building. Now they did not need humans to operate them, but they still retained their enchantment, guardians of headlands and capes. He took a walk around the headland with the dogs and then decided to make his camp there for the night.

Chapter Twenty-Two

A Warm Send-off

Saturday 4th May, Morning

In the morning Adam let the dogs out and joined them outside for a stretch. The sun was low in the sky in the east, rising behind the silhouette of the Isle of Purbeck across the bay. It was only 6.30, so Adam had time to kill before picking up Pip and he used it to scour the map and his earlier notes to find sites to have a closer look at. He had already earmarked the one that he planned to visit to the east of Weymouth and wondered about going to look at it before he collected Pip. On reflection he thought it would be better to do this with the girl today -- it would help take her mind off the situation in Serendipity. He might get an indication of her capabilities and, who knows, she might come up with things he had not thought of.

It would be good if they could look at another place for comparison and he started looking at the farms and houses to the west of Weymouth which they could visit on their way to Friars Wood. He found one promising place, a tiny hamlet nestling in a fold in the hills not too far from the main road to the west. There was a large house near a lake – the manor house, perhaps

– and there were other buildings that might be farms or houses and there was a large wood and streams that seemed to issue from the hills. He ringed it on the map, along with the one he had identified the day before. Visiting those two places would keep them busy this morning, he thought, before they set off for Friars Wood.

By nine o'clock Adam was making his way back down the island towards Weymouth. He took the long way round to Serendipity as he wanted to see if he could find a place that sold camping equipment.

***

Saturday 4th May

It's very early, or maybe it's very late. I've no idea what the time is. I don't know if I have been asleep even, but now I'm wide awake. My arm hurts so I think I must have been lying on it. I hate waking up in the night. The house is cold and I keep on hearing creaks and bangs and I get really spooked. I'm trying not to think about the bedroom upstairs. I thought I heard dogs barking earlier and then I got to thinking about those dogs on the beach. Adam said we're going to see a lot more of that, and that makes me really ***not*** *feel good about being out and about on my own. I think he's right – I've got to go with him and we have got to find other people like us.*

I've been thinking about mum and Thommo and I have decided what to do. I'm going to give them a cremation. I shall get some flowers and strew them around the bodies and then I'm going to make a big pyre and light it. That's what the Hindus do and that's what I'm going to do. I have worked it all out. We've got loads of cardboard and newspapers in the garage and some big cans of cooking oil. I think there might be a can of petrol or paraffin or something in there too. I'll start with the paper, then cardboard and pile some sheets and things on top. Then I'll light it before Adam comes over. Do you think that's a good idea Nic? You always liked a good bonfire.

My torch is getting dim and I'm getting tired so I'm going to sleep now.

***

Eventually I fell asleep and slept really heavily. And, I forgot to set the alarm – major brain lapse there. The clock said 8.45 and Adam was coming at 9.30 which left me ¾ of an hour. I thought about going with him today and coming back home this evening and then I thought: NO! I am going to do what I said I would.

So I went to the garage, got loads of newspaper and some cardboard. I had to walk past that body - ugh. It was covered in flies and think the foxes had been at it. There wasn't any petrol but I found three cans of cooking oil, which I carried in one at a time. Then I remembered the flowers. So I went out the front door and got lots of blossom and some flowers I picked from that garden (well, they're not going to miss them, are they?). I carried them upstairs but when I got to the bedroom door the smell was really bad and I just couldn't face going in. So I just scattered them outside the door instead.

And now the fire: I thought about this and I decided it would be better if I made it on the floor below. But first I opened the windows in the upstairs bathroom to get a good draught and then I built a bonfire at the bottom of the second-floor stairs. It was a pretty good construction, I have to say. That was when I realised that I didn't know where the matches were. And it was twenty past nine. AAAAGGGHHH!! I rummaged all through the kitchen drawers and eventually I found the lighter that mum kept for lighting candles if we had a power cut. So I went upstairs to light the fire. I was going to say a few words, but I didn't know what to say, so I put the lighter to the paper and watched it smoke and smoulder for ages and I wondered if the fire would ever start. I wanted to get it going slowly before Adam came, but not really blazing cos I didn't want him to see it. So I left it smoking while I got my cases and my box of stuff down the stairs and out into the street.

I went back into Selsey to see if I had left anything behind and then I heard this loud Whoomph and I looked out of the bedroom door to see a wall of smoke coming down the corridor towards me. I was still looking for the lucky bangle which you gave me last year which fell down behind the dressing table two nights ago. I could **NOT** *go without that. I managed to move the dressing table and found it in a pile of paper and other rubbish. I put in on my wrist so I wouldn't lose it again. The room was starting to fill up with smoke and in the corridor it was really thick. It was scary how quickly it filled the house. That's when I realised that the door to* *the top floor had banged shut. I couldn't do anything about that now and I was choking with the smoke.*

I ran down the stairs and took some air in at the front door and was about to close the door and then thought, I can't leave my diary here, I just can't. So I went back into the hall, grabbed a scarf from the coat rack (one of mum's – I almost cried when I smelled her perfume), wrapped it round my head, took another deep breath and went up the stairs again. It was getting hard to see through the smoke now and I was barely breathing at all. I almost had to feel my way into the bedroom but when I got down onto my knees, I found the smoke was thinner and I could crawl over to where I'd hidden the diary under the loose floor of the wardrobe. I shoved it inside my waist band, under my jumper and crawled back across the room and out onto the landing. I could feel the heat now and the fire was really roaring somewhere above me. I was coughing and trying not to breathe in the smoke. I couldn't see a thing and I had to feel my way to the top of the stairs.

***

Turning into King's Street he thought he saw smoke coming up from somewhere over on the right, but he could not see where. When he got to the end of Pip's road he saw all too clearly. Halfway down on the left-hand side, smoke was pouring out from a building – it was Serendipity. Adam accelerated down the street and pulled up just short of the guesthouse. Smoke was coming out from an upstairs window and he could see flames through the glass. There were some cases and a box sitting in the road outside. He leapt out of the van and ran towards the front door when a window exploded on the first floor and a jet of flame shot out. He paused briefly, then taking a deep breath, pulled his sweatshirt up over his nose and stepped into the hall.

It was dark in the hallway and smoke was pouring down the stairs and along the corridor like a great grey snake. He pulled down the front of his shirt and shouted up the stairs, "Pip, are you up there?"

He could hear the roaring of the fire somewhere up above him.

"Pip, can you hear me? Pip!"

Just then he heard her, coughing as she stumbled down the stairs and into the light. He grabbed her arm and more or less dragged her out of the door and along to the van.

"What happened?" he cried, "Are you alright?" Tears were streaming from her eyes but she nodded in answer.

"I need to go back." she said. At that moment another window blew out and flames could be seen in the second-floor windows. Smoke was billowing out from the roof. Adam held on to her arm tightly:

"You're not going back in there!" he said. "For God's sake what happened? How did it start?"

Pip did not answer but was shaking, tears streaming and not just from the smoke.

"Did you do this?" he asked. The girl did not answer but carried on sobbing. He held her arm tightly, but she was straining to look at the burning house. An explosion took out another window and debris rained down on the road in front of the house. The smoke was getting thicker now and swirled around the street. The dogs, which had got out of the van, were barking at the fire and whining.

Adam gave her a while and then said, "Come on, we've got to go. You need to get in the van." He steered her towards the passenger door but she struggled against him. "I need my things!" she cried. "My cases!"

"It's OK, I'll get them," he said, "get in the van."

Adam picked up the cases and took them back to the van. He dashed back for the box and as he got there, he could feel a wave of heat from the building. Pip was standing in the road staring at the fire. Adam grabbed the box under one arm and seized her arm with the other hand and forced her round to the passenger door. He put the box down, opened the door and pushed her into the seat. He picked up the box, put it on her lap and shut the door, called the dogs in, then jumped in the driving seat. He turned the van around and he could see that Serendipity was now completely engulfed in smoke and flames and that it would not be long before the fire spread to the adjoining properties.

As he drove off down the street, he saw that Pip was looking back at the burning building. "You did this, didn't you?" he said.

The girl nodded her head, and a new fit of sobbing overcame her. He went down to the seafront, turned left and drove slowly along the esplanade towards the east end of town. He carried on for about half a mile and then stopped the van. He reached over and touched her arm and Pip winced.

"God, sorry, that's your bad arm," said Adam, "Listen, it's OK. It's done now. It's over."

Pip nodded, but her sobs kept coming. She turned away from him and looked out of the window.

Adam was going to try again, but decided to leave her alone for a while. He drove on down to the end of the seafront where the road turned inland. At Osmington he turned right at the road junction and took the road east, away from the coast.

Pip had stopped crying and after a while she said, "Where are we going?"

"We're going to check out a farm I found on the map. It's a place called Holmwood. I think it could be a possible long-term base and I thought that it would be good to have a second opinion."

"OK." Pip said, but offered nothing else.

"It might not be suitable for what I'm looking for, but it will give me an idea of what might work or not work. Then later we can look at another place I have spotted on the other side of Weymouth. Does that make sense?"

Pip nodded, but said nothing.

The place he had identified on the map was down a long farm lane which led off the road up a low incline, named on the map as Hangman's Hill. At the top of the hill the ground levelled off and. Adam pulled up and turned off the engine. He sat quietly for a moment and then looked at Pip.

"Do you want to talk about it?" he asked.

After a while she said, "I just felt I had to do something for them." Adam waited for her to continue.

"I couldn't just leave them like that, in the house." She spoke slowly, hesitantly. "They should have had a proper funeral, but that wasn't possible." She sighed and took a breath. "So, I thought I would do what they do in the country I was born in: what the Hindus do."

Adam nodded in understanding.

"I put some flowers from the garden down the road and laid them by their bedroom door. I wrote them a letter..."

Adam waited for her to go on.

"I just wanted to give them a good send-off," Pip said.

Adam smiled: "Well, you certainly gave them that."

She looked out across the fields, as if trying to see the fire. "Thommo would have been so angry, but I think Mum would have approved – she never really like Serendipity."

"She wasn't happy there?"

"No, she hated having people in the house"

Pip seemed to smile, almost, at the memory, and then looked away through the window. Adam saw a sob shake her.

"Pip, it's OK. That was a fine thing you did for them."

Pip said nothing and continued to sob silently. Adam started the engine and drove slowly down the hill to the tiny hamlet of Holmwood.

This comprised a large, white rendered house set back from the lane that looked rather like a vicarage or something, and a little way further on, some farm cottages and the farm itself. Adam drove down the drive to the white house, turned the engine off and listened. There was no sound here apart from birdsong and sheep away towards the farm. There were no dogs barking.

"I'm going to have a look – are you coming?" Pip made to open the door. "Don't let the dogs out ..." But Bonzo was out of the door before he could finish. "Oh well" he said.

He let the old dog out and grabbed the wheel brace, just in case. He wandered over to the front of the house. Pip came and stood by him. He felt that they were intruders and that they should knock on the door at least, before they explored any further. He banged the heavy knocker hard on the door, loudly enough to raise the sleepiest of sleeping dogs. But if they were lying in there, they did not stir. He peered in through the front windows and saw a typical sitting room through one and a dining or breakfast room through the other. He walked down the side of the house and then round to the back. He wondered how many bodies there might be inside, slowly decomposing. The house faced down the drive while the back looked down across the fields. There were assorted sheds and garages and a tree-lined lawn. He walked round again, taking in the details of the building. Pip trailed behind him, but she did not seem to be showing much interest in what she saw. Back at the van he studied the map to see the lie of the land, where the spring was, how far from the house. It looks promising, he thought.

He called Pip back to the van and they drove slowly down to the farm, the two dogs chasing along, not wanting to be left behind. The lane ended there and became a rough track. The farm itself was a collection of different buildings: the original stone and brick farmhouse and two other dwellings either side, one converted from stables by the looks of it. There was a small garden running along the front, and on the other side of the farmyard, a collection of agricultural sheds. To the right of the lane was a duck pond, which Adam had noted on the map, and which presumably was fed by the spring, which was about two hundred metres away up the hill. There was a bridleway marked on the map which led up to it. He turned off the engine and listened again. He heard nothing but the sheep in the field behind which, mercifully, the dogs had ignored as they chased after the van. Had there been dogs here, the sound of the van would have aroused them. He got out and looked around cautiously.

Pip stayed in the van while he walked down to the farmyard and looked at the buildings. There was a pen with lots of muck and straw and dung which looked fairly new, but there no animals around. Maybe they were all in the fields now. Maybe they had been sold – he didn't know. Behind it the sheds were silent and he got the impression that they were only used from time to time. He walked across to the farmhouse and cottages. Each would probably make a fine home, he thought, and probably had been much-loved homes until last weekend. He decided not to investigate them any further but crossed the lane to look at the pond. It was surrounded by trees and overgrown with rushes, but the water was clear and not stagnant. A couple of small black waterbirds flitted into the reeds, but there were no ducks about.

According to the map, which Adam was studying, there was a path just beyond the pond which would lead him right up to the spring. The stile had disappeared almost completely into the undergrowth but he forced his way through and then found a rough track leading up the hill through open pasture, pretty well in the direction of the spring but veering north of it. Another track led to the south of it, but in between Adam could see a small copse and he guessed that this was where the spring would be.

He indicated to Pip where he was going and walked across the broad, grassy pasture and around the copse. It was fenced off, presumably to keep the livestock out, but under the trees he could see a dense undergrowth which could well indicate the presence of water. On the far side of the copse, he noticed that the ground was quite soft underfoot and this was at the end of a line of much darker grass running down the slope of the field towards him. He followed this up to its source where a tiny pool of water in the grass betrayed the presence of a spring. Not very impressive as a water supply, he thought. Would it even be there at the end of a dry summer? There were two other springs shown on the map, by a small wood nearby and he decided to investigate these as well. One was at the corner of the wood and as he approached he saw a tank of water for the use of livestock, and he could hear the trickle of water into the tank. Clearly this was being fed by a spring, but again the supply was only a trickle. Still, it was a water supply and that was important.

Adam set off across the field, back to the van. He was thinking about how to engineer a reliable water supply from a spring when a thought dawned on him. How stupid he was! Of course, a farm, or a hamlet, in a remote spot like this would *have to* have a private water supply – there could be no mains water this far from the main road. They would have dug wells originally, but in more recent times they would have tapped into the spring and piped the water down to the houses. He was sure that if he went into any of these houses he would have found water in the taps, and this would be true, surely, in any remote settlement. They did not need to look for springs at all, they only had to look for properties away from the mains and check for water inside the houses. That widened the scope of the search right out again.

***

The strange thing was that it wasn't until we were driving down the road along the front that it really hit me just what I had done. I had been in such a rush this morning to do it before Adam came that I wasn't really thinking about just what I was actually doing. I know it was what I had planned but I'm not sure that I really thought I would do it. But I did. I have cremated my parents and burned down Serendipity. Isn't that... surreal?

I'm sitting in Adam's van by a farm somewhere. I've just dug this out from my bag and I have a bit of time as Adam is off looking for something up the hill. I can't stop thinking about what has happened this morning and I feel really sad when I think about Serendipity in flames. I feel bad about mum and Thommo too, but I know they had already left this world last weekend. I think I've done the right thing, I'm sure I have.

And now – is this is my future? Travelling the roads with a man I didn't know before yesterday, looking for survivors, looking for a home. It's the right thing to do, I know and he's the right sort of person to do it with. Well, I hope he is. And what's the alternative? It's too horrible to even think about but even when I curl up really tight under the bedclothes, those thoughts still come to me. Before last weekend I thought of death as something which just happened to other people, like old aunties, people in car accidents, bad guys in movies, Nic's hamsters. And then I saw my parents die.

***

When he got back to the track he saw Pip had got out of the van and was looking at the farm cottages. "What do you think?" he said as he came over to join her. The girl shrugged and said: "They seem alright. Where did you go?"

"I went to look at the springs. There seems to be a good water supply here."

"Do you think this would make a good place then?" she asked. It was hard to know how interested she would be in his answer, but he carried on as if she was.

"Well, it has water, it has fuel, there are farm vehicles and a tank, probably with diesel in. And it's not a bad spot, is it?"

"Mm, I suppose," she said.

"You don't look very convinced!"

Pip did not answer. It was probably hard for her to focus on anything much after what had happened earlier that morning, he thought. "OK, we can talk about it later. And there are other places we can look at. Shall we go?" He walked back to the van and the dogs waited for Pip to follow. They drove back up the lane, past the white house and over Hangman's Hill to the road.

He planned to take this road to Dorchester, rather than go back to Weymouth. It would be a quicker route to Friars Wood, and they could take a small detour on the way to look at the place he had found on the map earlier. However, twenty minutes down the road they found it was completely blocked by a lorry and there was no obvious way round.

"What happened there, do you think?" said Pip

"Who knows. The driver was taken ill. Or maybe he just decided to abandon his vehicle there because he lived nearby. We'll see a lot of that. Well OK then, we'll just have to take the other road."

So it was that a bit later they were coming down a hill when a view of the bay and the town opened up briefly. A column of smoke was rising from the town and drifting high over the houses. Pip spotted it straight away:

"Look! Oh God!"

"I saw it. It looks like you have started something there." He glanced over at Pip: she looked very pale, all of a sudden.

As they drove down the long seafront road towards the town, the smoke loomed larger and larger in front of them.

"What have I done?" Pip gasped.

When they got near the clock tower they could smell the fire and there were bits of ash drifting in the breeze.

"We've got to do something," said Pip desperately

"What can we do? Nothing. It will go out eventually."

"But what if the whole town burns down? Oh God, I was so stupid. Oh God!"

"Well, no-one's going to get hurt," Adam said, trying to sound reassuring. "What will it matter? What's done is done and there's nothing we can do. You weren't to know."

"I never gave it a thought. I didn't think that the fire might spread. I was so silly."

Adam was going to turn into King Street, but the smoke was thick in the road ahead. He decided to carry on, down to the harbour and over the old town bridge. Pip was looking over her shoulder anxiously, trying to see the smoke, but it was soon out of sight behind the buildings. Adam felt that the best thing was to get as far as possible from the reminders of the demise of Serendipity, and he was glad when they had crossed the harbour and were on their way out of town. The road took them away from the coast and up into the rolling hills behind. A few miles on he took the back road up Portesham Hill. They came to a crossroads where a signpost pointed to *Hardy's Monument*, on the right.

"Can we stop here for a minute?" said Pip suddenly. "It's a special place for me."

"Sure," he said, "Why not? We could have a hot drink. What do you say?"

"That would be nice."

Adam reversed and took the small lane which led up to the monument. A little way along, the stone column came into view, reaching up to the sky. He stopped at the little parking area and Pip immediately jumped out and ran up the slope to the building. "OK," said Adam to himself, "if that's what we're doing." He got out of the van, let the dogs out, and followed the small figure who was already at the top of the hill.

"This is one of my favourite places," she said quietly, when Adam reached her. "Thommo loved this view."

And the view across the lush greenery to the bright blue beyond, was very calming. The land fell away in all directions and the coastline could be seen all the way from horizon to horizon. In the distance was the Isle of Portland and next to it Weymouth spread out behind the coast. The smoke from Serendipity was just visible but from this far away it did not seem threatening.

"We quite often came here, just him and me."

Adam walked around the monument and let his fingers trail along the cool, smooth, Portland stone, happy just taking in the view and seeing Pip's mood lift a little. They sat down together on the grass and Adam left her to her thoughts. After a while Adam offered to go and make them both a drink and walked back to the van.

While he heated up the water he watched Pip walking around the hill, from time to time calling the dogs who came running up, quite obediently. She's still a child in some ways, Adam thought. He walked back up to the monument with their drinks and some biscuits and Pip joined him sitting on the grass while the dogs sniffed around.

"You realise that I am now technically homeless, as well as being an orphan." Pip said.

"Hmm. You've certainly burned your bridges. I hope you don't mind a spot of camping for a while."

"I did a guide camp once and I survived that."

Adam laughed. "You'll do just fine then." Pip smiled shyly at him then looked away.

"OK, here is what I propose. Today we drive down to Friarswood Farm and see if my brother has left a message for me, and on the way, we can check out this other place I want us to look at. If there is no message from Sam, then I think we should head for the nearest large town and see if we can get ourselves a tent and some more bedding. Then we could drive up to Bath – assuming you still want to see if you can find your friend...?"

"Nic," said Pip, "Yes, I'd like to."

While they finished their drinks, Pip pointed out some of the places she could identify along the coast. Some way off they could still see the smoke spiralling up over Weymouth.

"Do you think it's not quite so thick as before?" Pip asked.

"Yes, maybe." Adam was actually looking out to sea beyond the town where he could see something black in the water. It was very far away and it might just have been the shadow of a cloud, he couldn't tell. He looked over at the town and it was true, the smoke did not look so bad now. When he looked back to the sea he could not find the object he had been looking at. He turned to Pip and saw that she was staring at her feet.

"I'm not sure how I did that," she said quietly, "but I'm glad I did. It's better than a burial – their spirits are released into the sky with the flames"

"Is that what you believe?" Adam said.

Pip shrugged her shoulders and Adam could see a tear in her eye.

"That's a nice way of looking at it. It was a wonderful thing you did for them."

"When I lit the fire and saw it start to spread..." she took a breath, "...I almost wanted to join them." She fiddled with her cup and stared at the ground between her feet. "But I know I couldn't have done that, I'm too much of a coward. I just hope that they are happy together, wherever they are now."

"I'm sure they will be." And Adam wondered if Jo and the children were happy together, wherever they were.

At that moment a skylark rose up from the grass nearby and hovered above them, hanging in the air as if borne up by the breeze. They both turned the heads up to see the creature that was making this enchanting song. For a full five minutes the bird sang its trilling call, a bubbling stream of notes pouring down from above. Even after it had flown off, the two of them remained sitting quietly taking in the scenery spread out before them. Adam became aware of the rustling of the grasses in the wind, the steady panting of the dogs, the sound of cows in a field somewhere below them. In the woods far behind them he faintly made out the chatter of rooks.

There were no human sounds to be heard, though. Not a car, nor a plane, no church bells, no distant buzz of conversation from passing walkers, no children playing around the monument. It seemed that the absence of human sound had never been as palpable as it was at that moment, sitting with this girl at his side. The land without humans was very peaceful, and this was the world they inhabited now. Wherever they travelled they would be intruding on this peace. Yet this was what they had to do: to see what other humans there were still living in this quiet world.

Part Two

The View from Hangman's Hill

Chapter Twenty-Three

Return to Friarswood Farm

Saturday 4th May

As Adam drove away from the monument on the hill, the thought struck him that this was the beginning of another journey. A week ago he had driven away from his house in Juniper Close for the last time, knowing he would never go back again. Now he was setting out again, but this time with Pip, a girl he only met yesterday, travelling up the country to who knows where. But the job at hand was to find his way to the other promising-looking place he had marked on the map yesterday, a settlement that looked as if it might have the potential to be a long-term base. Adam had the map in his lap and was navigating the narrow lane whilst working out their route. A little later they were coming down a steep hill into a small settlement.

They had driven away from the monument and were now coming down a very narrow lane into the bottom of a shallow chalkland valley. They followed what was a private drive and a large old pink-stoned house loomed up ahead of them. Adam slowed while he scanned their surroundings.

"What's this place?" Pip asked

"The village is called Combe Bredy, but I'm not sure if this house has a name. shall we have a closer look?"

The building was a grand manor house dressed in pink stone, castellations topping the elegant façade with its tall windows.

"What do you think?" Adam asked. "Fancy living in a place like that?"

"It's huge." Pip said. "It would be like living in a museum, or a school. Cold and draughty too, I bet."

"You're right, you'd never keep that place warm with a log fire. It has a great view though."

They drove past the front of the house and saw that on the other side there was a lake.

"That's beautiful," said Pip.

"Nice, isn't it? Fancy a swim?"

Pip shook her head. Adam was studying the map. "There are some springs that feed into that, at the other end of the village. Could be a good water source. And there is plenty of timber here. But this place is not practical. Let's drive around and see what else we can find."

Adam followed the driveway round the park until it came back onto the road, then took them back past the farm again and on towards the church. He took a left turn after the churchyard and here there were more houses, large cottages with old-fashioned cottage gardens, just bursting into bloom now with displays of tulips, may blossom and other trees and shrubs which Adam did not know the names of.

"They're lovely," said Pip. "Imagine living here."

"Maybe," said Adam. He was trying to be pragmatic, thinking about what sort of properties might be sustainable in this new world. But he could not deny they were all rather lovely, in a chocolate-box sort of way. They did a thorough drive-round inspection of the village and the outlying properties until they had seen all there was to see.

"What do you think of Combe Bredy then, Pip?"

"I think Miss Marple would be at home here. I guess if you have to live without electricity and gas and telephones, you might as well be living in a place from the past."

"There's a certain logic in that," Adam said. "We'll have to get used to living by candlelight and cooking on an old range and they probably have those here. I'll add it to the shortlist. OK, and now to Friars Wood."

Adam followed the road out of the village and when they eventually came out onto the main coast road, he took the road west. After a while Adam found he was driving down the same bit of road where recently he had the nasty encounter with the deer , and that prompted him to keep his speed down and his eyes on the road ahead. The motion of the van seemed to have lulled Pip to sleep. Adam guessed that she had not slept well last night.

He was thinking about the places they had looked at this morning and figuring out how they would make the facilities work for them. And then he remembered the more immediate issues of getting what they needed for the journey north.

Pip woke up when they got to Bridport. Adam was driving slowly along the high street.

"We need to look out for a camping shop, or somewhere we can get a tent and stuff."

"We could look in Yellow Pages." Pip said. "There's a phone box over there."

"That's a good idea." And he pulled the van over.

Pip woke up when they got to Bridport. Adam was driving slowly along the high street.

"We need to look out for a camping shop, or somewhere we can get a tent and stuff."

"We could look in Yellow Pages." Pip said. "There's a phone box over there."

"That's a good idea." And he pulled the van over.

Pip got out and went over to the phone box and came back with a copy of the thick tome in her hands. She had a flick through and found '*Camping and Camping Equipment*'. "There's a camping shop in Dorchester."

"That's back the other way." Adam said

"Or there's the caravan and camping centre in Charmouth – that's near here, isn't it?"

Adam peered over and looked at the book: "That's just down the road a way. That's handy, we can go there after we've been to Friarswood.

"Shall I put this back?" Pip asked

"I don't think anyone else is going to be needing it, do you? It could be useful for us though."

Before long he was negotiating the back lanes up to the farm, following the route he had taken on Wednesday in reverse. When they got near to the farm Adam noticed some cows wandering down the road, grazing on the verge and hedgerow. Further on he had to manoeuvre the van around the carcass of a cow in the road and when they pulled into the short lane to the farm, he saw two more. A group of magpies were pecking at one carcass and they flapped away, cawing indignantly, as the van came towards them. He saw that the gate to the large field had been trampled down, which explained the loose cows in the road. He could see more cows lying on their sides across the field, their udders bloated.

"What's wrong with them? Are they dead?" said Pip, looking horrified.

"They've not been milked," Adam said.

"And that's killed them? That's awful."

Adam tried to remember what he had learned as a child on this very farm. "Well, I think it can. The cows' udders fill up and that can cause them to become infected, which can then kill them. Some of those cows are not dead yet, but they soon will be. There will be animals waiting for them to die, and others, like foxes, may attack them before they die. That one over there was probably finished off by a fox, or a dog."

"That's really horrible. I don't think I like this place."

"No, Nor do I. Just stay there a mo – I need to check something out." He got out and walked over to the office. As he expected, the envelope with his note was still attached to the door. There was no sign of it having been disturbed, nor any other activity around the building. The dogs in the shed had stopped barking now, he noticed.

When he got back into the van Pip said, "it doesn't smell very good here, does it? and I can't smell much normally."

"It's pretty bad, isn't it? That's modern, intensive farming for you. Let's go. No, hold on – I need to leave another message for Sam, in case he does turn up here." He grabbed a pen from the side pocket of the door and went back again to the office. He wrote as neatly as he could on the note without taking it off the door. *"4th May. Came back to see if you had been. Going up North to look for people and will be back in a week. Will pop by again after that. Adam. PS: I found a survivor, a girl. She's travelling with me."* He got back in the van and turned out onto the lane.

"So, this is the farm you stayed in for holidays when you were little – was it like this then?"

"No it was quite different, a small place. Just the farmhouse and a couple of sheds, that's all. We loved it, Sam and I: There were so many places to play. I used to like watching them milking the cows. Sam refused to believe that this white stuff was the same that we had delivered in bottles to our door. It was so funny to see the look of horror in his eyes when I told him."

They were now slowly following two cows who were wandering along the road. He sounded the horn, but they took no notice. "This would never have happened," he said. "If a cow got out, they would round it up in no time." They got past the cows and made their way back towards the main road. Adam was thinking about Sam and Pip was looking out of the window.

"I'm sorry that Sam hasn't been here. But that doesn't necessarily mean that he's not alive."

"No. I know. But it would have been good to have found a message from him. I'm not feeling hopeful that I'll see him again."

After a pause, she asked, "So where are we going to go, once we have found this camping shop?"

"I was thinking we could go down to the beach and have some lunch. There's a nice little mobile café I know."

"But that won't be open," said Pip, "unless you mean the Vanman's lunch truck."

"Is that what you called me?"

"It seemed like a good name."

"Vanman!" Adam laughed. "White-van man, I suppose?"

"Well," she said with a little smile, "whiter than me."

They had crossed the main road and were driving into the village of Charmouth, when Pip spotted it. There ahead of them was the place they were looking for, *Charmouth Camping and Caravanning Supplies*. Adam stopped the van in front of the shop.

"Looks promising – shall we go and check it out?"

There was a single-story building with display windows at the front and the entrance at the side. There were caravans for sale parked along the roadside and at the back of the shop. Adam sized up the door, which was a simple part-glazed door. He rattled the handle and felt the door shake.

"This should not prove too much of a problem," he said, and with a couple of heavy kicks and a shoulder barge he had the door open.

Pip followed him into the shop, the dogs just behind. With the bright sun outside there was plenty of light for them to see. Adam was scouting for any sign of dead bodies, but his nose, and the dogs, told him that no-one had stayed behind to die here. They looked at the tents and Adam found one that he thought would be large enough for their needs, but not too complicated to erect. Next, they looked at bedding and Pip found an airbed and a sleeping bag with a garish pattern that was not quite to Adam's taste. He found another one, which he could use for himself, either in the van or in the tent. Adam had his mental shopping list, but he thought he would see what Pip would think of.

"Do you need some more gas?" she said, "and water? What about lights?"

"We're OK for gas at the moment. Some more water would be useful, and some spare tent pegs – they never give you enough. These look good and sturdy. Another lamp would be good, and some more batteries."

Pip was exploring the shop, looking at the large frame tents on display. "These are enormous!" she said. "Can I have one? I could have a television in the corner."

"If you can put it up and take it down on your own, of course you can have it."

Pip pulled a face. There was a two-man ridge tent on display. "Is this like the one we've got? It's not very big, is it?"

"We don't have a lot of space in that van, so we'll have to make do with that for the moment. But I'm happy to sleep in the tent. You can have the van," Adam said, "but you'll have to share with the dogs."

Pip thought about this and frowned.

Adam laughed. "Come on, let's get all this together and put it in the van – not sure where, though. By the way, have you got any money? Because I haven't."

"I don't suppose we'll ever need that again." She went round the counter and tried to open the till. "I bet there's a load in here."

"It's probably in a safe somewhere, or gone to the bank."

"I used to think it would be nice to have a great wad of notes, like in a gangster movie."

"It's all just Monopoly money now. No use for anything, except lighting a fire," he said.

They carried their booty out to the van and Adam stashed it in the back.

"We're going to need a bigger van, you know. This is one is not really large enough. Have a look in the yellow pages and see if there is a place that sells camper vans in this part of the world."

"They have caravans here," she said. "Why don't we have a caravan? My friend's dad had a big caravan, it was lovely. We went down to Cornwall in it once. Look at how big that one is."

Adam followed Pip's gaze over to a six-berth luxury van. "A caravan needs a car to tow it, so we'd have to get a car too. With the state of the roads in some places, towing a large van could be a real challenge. No, a camper van is much better."

The dogs were sniffing around the back of the building. Adam put his fingers in his mouth and whistled them in.

"OK boys, you'd better get in, we're going now," Pip said, as Adam shut his door and started the engine. Bonzo jumped into the van, but the old dog was reluctant to leave an interesting smell behind. "Come on you," she said, and as the dog got in the back, "we are going to have to find a name for you, as you can't tell us what you're called. What about *Blackie*? But you're black-and-whitey really. What sort of dog is he?"

"A border collie," Adam said as he turned the van around.

"Hmm. I don't know much about dogs or what people call them. Fido, Rex?"

"Rover, shadow?" Adam offered.

"Shadow, that's a nice name. But he is not black like a shadow, is he?"

"Guardian?"

"Like the newspaper? Thommo bought that sometimes."

Adam laughed. "No, as in he's your guardian. He chased that dog off yesterday."

Pip tried it out, "Guardian, here boy. Guardi."

"Or Guard?"

"Guard? Sounds like you're on a train."

They tried out other names as they drove through the village. Shortly they came to the end of the road, a small car park, a few beach huts and the beach in front of them.

"This should do for a lunch spot, don't you think?"

"What do you think Bonzo?" Pip said to the dog, who had been sitting on her lap with his nose out of the window. "He says: definitely!"

They got out of the van and the dogs immediately ran down over the beach to the sea. It seemed that the novelty of the waves, the salty air and the seaweed had not yet worn off for these two inland canines. Adam breathed in the salt air and felt the sun on his face – he too liked the seaside – didn't everyone? He looked at his watch: it was getting on for three o'clock.

"I expect you're hungry," he said to Pip.

"I'm starving. That cup of tea and the biscuit was all I've had today."

"Well, why don't you go through the cupboard and see what we can have for lunch. Have whatever you fancy. Do you think you can get the stove going, or do you want me to do it?"

"If you show me how to light it, I can do the rest," she replied. Adam showed her how to operate the stove and where to find everything. "What are you going to do?" she asked.

"I'm going to go and have a wash. It's over a week since I last had a shower. I'm surprised you haven't complained."

"I don't have much sense of smell. And anyway, I probably smell as bad."

"Well I'm going to check out the temperature of the water."

"In the sea?" she said, with a look of horror, "You're mad."

"Probably. Listen, stay in the van and if you see any dogs, shut the doors. OK?"

She nodded. "But what about you?"

"I'll take this," he said, brandishing the wheel brace, "and the boys will come with me."

Sure enough they followed him across the shingle and down to the water's edge. They watched him undressing as if waiting to see what he would do next. He stepped gingerly over the stones and dipped a foot tentatively into the water. It felt icy cold on his ankles, but he knew he had to go in. "Last one in's a cissy!" he said to the dogs, and ran forward and plunged into the waves, swimming several strokes underwater and surfacing some way out. He trod water and caught his breath; the water was cold and refreshing and he felt as if, in some way, it was washing away the pains of the last weekend with his family. He pictured Sam swimming up to catch him, floats on his skinny arms, thrashing through water with frantic strokes, as he always did. Perhaps his spirit was in the water with him, letting him know that he was OK, in some other life.

He spent some time swimming along parallel with the shore and then turned and swam back to where his clothes sat in a pile on the beach. When he felt he had had enough he waded back to the beach and stood on the edge drying himself. The air was cool on his wet skin and he towelled vigorously. Bonzo had been waiting for him at the water's edge, barking. The collie sat on the shingle and watched Adam emerge. They both greeted him with excitement, as if he had been away for days. He found a stick and hurled it into the sea and the collie went in after it. Adam put the towel around his waist and then made his way back to the van with his clothes under one arm.

"That looks good," he said, surveying the table, "very nice. Mm, crackers and cheese – haven't had that for a while!" he said, laughing.

"Would you like me to go outside while you dress?" she asked.

"No, you stay here and eat something. I'll grab my things and change over there behind that hut."

Over lunch – it was lunch for Pip, but Adam was not very hungry and made do with an apple and a bit of cheese – they talked about what they would do and where they would go.

"I found a place in Exeter that sells caravans and camper vans and one in Shepton Mallet – that's near Bath, I think."

"That would be more on our route. Does it look like it might have a selection?"

"Says here it's the 'best in the west'."

"It would say that, wouldn't it? Anyway, I'm sure we can find something there. I think we should be thinking about heading off soon. But we could do with some more supplies, so if we see a promising-looking shop, we can go and see what tempts us for supper. And I was thinking just now, after my swim, that we could do with a couple of towels. I don't suppose you brought one with you?"

Pip shook her head.

"Just what have you got in those cases? No, don't answer that. It's none of my business. But if you think of things you think we need, or that you need, just say."

Before they got back to the main road Adam stopped outside the camping shop and after a few minutes he emerged with a couple of large beach towels under his arm.

Back in Bridport, they drove around the town until they found a supermarket at the back of the high street. It looked likely it would have a good range of stock and the main door looked as if Adam might be able to break it down. However, after five minutes of swinging away with the wheel brace and crowbar and working up a good sweat, Adam had to admit defeat. He climbed back into the van, puffing hard, red-faced and looking very cross. "We are going to have to find another technique to get into these places," he said. "Let's see if we can find a small grocery shop somewhere."

Back in the high street there was a small Co-op and Adam was quickly in the door.

"Come on in," he called to Pip, "but hold your nose."

Pip followed him into the shop, pulled a face and walked out again. Adam did a quick recce and found a few things that would make do for supper that night, picked up some beers for himself and a packet of tea bags for Pip, plus a few packets of chocolate biscuits. She would like those. He threw them into a cardboard box and took them out to the van.

"That shop not to your liking?" he said. "Thought you had no sense of smell."

"I can't smell much, but that smell of rotting meat – ugh, made me want to heave."

"Well next time I'll make a mask for you and you'll be fine. I'll just put these in the fridge and then we can go."

When they were out of Bridport and on the road to Crewkerne, Pip said: "I'm sorry about that, you know, back there in the shop. It's just that smell. It reminded me of ... you know?"

"I know. I understand. It can be pretty overpowering. I can't imagine what it would have been like if I had smelled that before last year. I wouldn't have been able to stay in that shop."

"What do you mean, before last year?" Pip asked

"Well, my sense of smell was fine until I had a spell in hospital last year. Since then, I can't smell much at all."

"That sounds like what happened to me." said Pip. "I got this really bad cold or something last summer: coughing, sneezing, shivering. My throat swelled up so I couldn't breathe or swallow. And ever since I can't smell much either."

"That's interesting." Adam said, and he took his foot off the accelerator as if better to concentrate on what she was telling him. "Did they tell you what it was, this illness?"

"I don't think they really knew. They said it was a virus, but not one they had seen before. They tried lots of different drugs before they found something that worked. I was ill for three weeks, but I can't remember much about it. I was really out of it most of the time."

"So how did they sort it in the end? Did it take a long time to clear up?"

"They tried a different drug – I don't know what it was called – and then it cleared up really quickly. But I felt very tired for a couple of months afterwards – kept falling asleep in lessons. And for a long time I couldn't taste or smell anything much at all. They had to force me to eat almost. Thommo was good at that. Kept giving me treats when mum wasn't around."

"But you're OK now?" Adam asked.

"Yes, I think so. My sense of taste and smell came back slowly, but they're still not right. I don't really enjoy food much these days, not like I used to."

"No, I know all about that."

"So what happened to you?" Pip asked.

"Much the same as you really. The cough, the fever, the sweats; I went into a coma for a while, and then they found the right drug and – bingo! I was ok again."

"What did the doctors say to you about what it was?"

"I don't think they knew. They didn't think it was a virus. They thought it might be some sort of auto-immune reaction going on. They kept on sending in different specialists to see me. I was the enigma, a medical wonder. I felt like a freak show some days. I think there might have been someone else in the hospital with the same illness, but I didn't meet them."

"I've been thinking," Pip said slowly, "do you think that there's a connection with that illness and what everyone got last weekend?"

"Well it did cross my mind, when you said something about losing your sense of smell." said Adam, "But I didn't realise you had been that ill. The thing is, it took quite a while for this illness to get a hold on me. I had it for several days and carried on working. Last weekend, the illness came on very quickly; it was all so sudden. The children were absolutely fine in the morning – as was Jo – but by the time I got home that evening they were all really unwell."

"But don't you think it is a bit of a coincidence that we both had a similar illness last year and we have both survived this virus, or whatever it is?"

"Yes, it's possible. It does seem odd ."

They drove for a while in silence. Adam was thinking over what Pip had been saying about them both being very ill last year. But he had got ill in April and by June was back on his feet and fully fit. Pip mentioned the summer. He was going to ask her about the dates when, as they came down the hill into Beaminster, a pair of deer leapt out from the verge and ran right in front of them. Adam swerved and jammed on the brakes, just managing to avoid hitting the second one. Pip screamed, Bonzo flew into the dashboard and the old dog yelped in the back. Adam brought the van to a halt and sat there for a minute his head in his hands, his heart pounding and a cold sweat breaking out on his neck.

Pip was nursing Bonzo and talking to the collie. "Are you OK?" she asked, and Adam looked up to see her looking at him quite concerned."

Yes," he said shakily, "I'm fine. Are you alright?"

"Yes, I'm OK," the girl said. "Poor Bonzo got a bit of a bump. I didn't see them until they were in front of us – where did they come from?"

"From the hedge. That's the second time that's happened in the last few days. Last time I killed one."

"God!" Pip said. "Are you sure you're alright?"

"Yes. I'll be fine in a minute.."

"I'm sorry," she said, "we can stop for a while, if you want."

"No, I'm OK. Let's keep going."

At the bottom of the hill they crossed a little river and came into an elegant old square with a four-legged stone butter cross at the centre.

"This is Beaminster then. It looks like a one-horse town."

"It's quite pretty though," Pip said.

They were driving through the square and Adam noted the mixture of old buildings on the square and the stone cottages on the high street. It looked like the sort of place he and Jo would have pottered about, exploring the little shops and the side streets. But no sooner had they arrived, they were driving out again, following signs for Crewkerne. They followed the road through the rolling Dorset countryside. A little beyond Beaminster the road went into a deep cutting and then a short tunnel.

"I remember this bit of road." Pip said. "I took the bus to Bath once, to see Nic, and it went this way. That was the last time I saw her."

Adam said nothing and they drove along in silence for several miles. Adam went slowly, frequently using his horn to move startled small animals from their path. A couple of times they encountered cows grazing on the verge and sometimes wandering in the road. The early evening sun was slanting across the road, sometimes strobing through trees on the side. Adam was starting to feel weary. He had been on the go since early this morning. They had just gone through the sprawling village of Mosterton and were climbing a hill when a lane appeared on the left and Adam instinctively took the turning. The lane wound up the hillside and at the top a view of the countryside to the north opened up. Adam stopped the van by a gate, behind which a grassy pasture led up to a ridge.

"Where are we?" Pip asked. "Why are we stopping here?"

"I thought this might be a good spot to spend the night." Adam replied. "I think I've had enough for today. I'm quite tired and I'd like to get the tent and van sorted and some food organised. What do you think?"

"I guess so. I'm pretty tired too."

"I'm just going to check out the field. Don't let the dogs out yet." He went over and opened the gate. The field had been grazed fairly recently but there were no livestock around now and the grass was growing back. He jumped back in the van and drove in. The ground seemed firm enough, so he drove slowly up the rise until they got to the hedge line on the crest. He brought the van to a stop so that the side-door opened out onto the view.

"I think this will do, don't you?" he said, and got out and let the dogs follow him. Pip got out and stood there yawning and stretching, taking in the scenery.

"OK," said Adam, "you get the tent out and see if you can work out how to put it up while I sort the food out and think of what I'm going to do for supper."

Pip looked a bit worried when he said that, and more so when he tossed the tent bag out at her and said, "There you go."

An hour later and Pip had managed, with some help and direction from Adam, to erect the tent. The first site she had picked was on a slope so Adam pointed out that a sloping bed was not conducive to a good night's rest, and they had settled on a level piece of ground a few yards from the van. They had eaten the meal that Adam had prepared and now they were sitting on the door sill watching the shadows lengthen over the patchwork landscape of fields, hedges and trees. Below them was the town of Crewkerne and beyond that the countryside stretched away into a misty meeting with the horizon.

"Thank you for dinner," said Pip, "and for everything ... you know. You saved my life. Again."

"No, I didn't do that. But I might possibly have saved you from injury. You know Pip we are going to have to be more careful, both of us. In this new world there are no ambulances and there may be no doctors. We might not find anyone else alive for a long while yet, so we need to take care of each other."

"You're right. I hadn't thought of that. Somehow, I got through last week without really thinking of how I was going to live long term. I wasn't sure that I did want to live. Do you know what I mean?"

Adam nodded: he knew exactly what she meant.

"I vaguely thought about killing myself, though I had no idea how."

"But not now though?"

She shrugged.

"Well you're not going to do it on my watch! I've only just found you and I don't plan to lose you. And I'm never going to leave you either. Those are the rules. OK partner?"

She looked at him and saw the smile in his eyes. "OK," she said.

He gave her shoulders a squeeze. "At a girl!"

She smiled and looked embarrassed.

"Right, he said, getting up stiffly. "I don't know about you but I'm tired so I'm going to get ready to turn in now."

Chapter Twenty-Four

Pip's Diary

Saturday 4th May

Somewhere in a Field in North Dorset

I am writing this by torchlight inside a tent, in a field, somewhere on the way to Bath. Yes – in a tent! It's been a really strange day and I don't know if I have the energy or the brain power to even start to think about it. It's not very late and I can still see some light outside, but I'm really tired. I hope I sleep.

So I'm here and Adam's in the van. I'm not sure about being in a tent but I guess it's ok, as long as there aren't any wild animals or angry dogs about. At least I have some privacy here and can write in this book. I'm thinking that it's not going to be so easy to carry on with this now and to keep it private. I hate the thought of anyone reading my diary. It's silly, I know, and they would probably find it incredibly boring, or really childish. I can imagine old Miss Butterwood (Agnes was her first name, or Agonies, as Nic called her. The boys called her Whoopsie or Fartypants – that's boys for you), when she used to teach English waving this to the class and saying "Filipa Thomas, is this English you are writing, or badly-punctuated gibberish?" and she would hand it back to me covered in red ink corrections and exclamation marks.

Maybe I should consign it to a bonfire. That way the angels can read it but no-one else will be able to get their hands on it. But there again, maybe I should keep it so that in the future – if we survive that long – I'll be able to remind myself what life was like when everything was normal. And if there's no-one else in the world but Adam and me, we can laugh and cry at all the silly things we used to worry about, before V Day.

He's a good guy Adam. I know he's trying to look after me – I think I got lucky there.

Chapter Twenty-Five

To Travel in Hope

Sunday 5th May, Morning

It was a bright morning and the dew on the grass told Adam that, as he thought, it had been a chilly night. There was no sign of life from the tent, so he decided he would put his boots on and stretch his legs around the wet field with the dogs. As he strode off along the side of the field, his thoughts turned to Gerry. He was someone he saw even less often than Sam and yet they too had remained quite close, tied with the bond of student comradeship, which they celebrated frequently with too much of the falling-down water. In addition to the partying, they had a shared love of the outdoor life. One fine Autumn day, sat on the top of a Lakeland fell at dusk, they were watching the low sun light the tops of the neighbouring crags in shades of red and gold. Gerry had produced a hip flask from his rucksack and they were toasting their futures after graduation.

"Adam, mate," he said leaning into him. "remember, whatever happens, wherever we both end up, we are going to meet at the Red Lion in Bond Street at six o'clock on the...whatever the date was that year when we're both sixty."

"2011, New Year's Eve."

"Yes, New Year's Eve, 2011, that's it. Make sure it's always in your diary."

"How can I forget? The Red Lion, I'll be there," Adam had said. "Mind you, it'll probably be a car park by then, I'll be old and deaf, and you'll be blind and most likely drunk, so what are the chances?"

"It won't matter, mate. We'll be there. With or without our nurses, we'll be there!"

He had wondered at the time if either of them could possibly live that long and yet, why not? But now, that memory mocked him. Could Gerry have survived? Would anyone be left alive in 2011?

He shook off this depressing thought and marched back along the top of the field to their camp. When he got there, he realised that what he hadn't given thought to last night was toileting arrangements. Pip had been content to disappear into the darkness before she went to bed. But in the bright light of day, she would have to go for a bit of a walk to find some privacy for herself. Oh well, he thought, that's just the way it is. At least she was in no danger of a stranger coming upon her at an unfortunate moment. It was another hour before there were signs of movement inside the tent, during which time Adam drank his coffee, studied the road map, looked at his 'shopping list' and generally gave thought to the plan for the next few days. He had agreed to go to Bath and see if they could find Nic's home, though he wasn't entirely happy about this idea. He did not think for a minute that this would have a good outcome for Pip.

Eventually there were stirrings inside the tent and a sleepy face poked out through the flap, looking decidedly un-awake.

“Oh, good morning!” he said. “Did you sleep well?”

“I think so,” said the face. “What time is it?”

“Just gone 9.00.”

“Oh. Sorry if I’m late up,” said the face.

“You’re alright. It’s Sunday, it’s allowed. I expect you needed the sleep.”

The head nodded and a hand emerged to stifle a yawn.

“Well take your time. Would you like some tea? I thought so. I’ll rustle one up for you.”

Adam put the water on to boil again and after a while Pip emerged with a wash bag in her hand and a small towel and looked around at the large field.

“You’re optimistic!” Adam laughed. “The loo is behind the van or, if you want a walk, down by the road, behind the hedge. And the wash basin...” Adam cast around the site with the hand shading his eyes, as if looking for distant ships. “Sorry, I can’t see one.”

“Oh, OK. But do you think I could have a bit of water so I can wet a flannel?”

“Of course. I’ll sort something out for when you get back.”

He watched her walking down the field to the gateway, the dogs in tow. With only her thin pumps on in the wet grass, she was going to have very wet feet, he thought.

When she returned, he put some water in a plastic bowl and set it up on a crate on the private side of the van and left her to do her ablutions. Afterwards she sat on the sill of the van cradling her cup of tea.

"Do you want something to eat?" he asked her. She shook her head.

"We can stop somewhere later on and have some brunch, perhaps. How is your arm, by the way?"

"It's OK. A bit sore," she said

"Maybe we should have a look at it later, make sure it's not got infected. When you've had your tea, we'll pack up the tent and get going, shall we?"

Half an hour later they were driving back down the hill to the main road. Pip remained quiet, looking out of the window. After a while, Adam decided to broach the subject of Nic:

"Pip, I was wondering: do you really want to go to Nic's house? You know that the chances of finding her alive..."

"Aren't good. I do *know* that," Pip said. "But if I don't find out for sure..."

"You'll always be wondering. Yes, I know."

They were quiet for a while and then she said,

"Nic was the only real friend I ever had. She was more important to me than anyone, other than mum and Thommo. I know it sounds silly but sometimes I think she loved me more than they did. A lot more than mum ever did." She fell silent again and Adam decided not to press her.

"There is something I need you to do for me..."

Adam thought he could guess what was coming. "You want me to go into the house for you?"

Pip nodded.

"Of course."

***

The road to Shepton Mallet was straight and free from obstruction. Pip's mood seemed to lift and as they were driving along, she said: "What about Whiskers?"

Adam looked puzzled.

"For the collie – he's got grey whiskers."

"Mm, I'm not sure about that one. Sounds like the name for a cat or a rabbit. What about Fidelio?" offered Adam. "Faithful?"

"Or Lucky. I mean he sought you out and found your house. Otherwise, he probably would have starved to death."

"Seeker?"

"Seeker..?" said Pip. "Seek, for short."

They tossed other names into the air, but none seemed to stick to the old dog, who lay peacefully asleep in the back, oblivious to the discussion of his new moniker.

"It's a pity he didn't have a name tag on him," Pip said.

The conversation lapsed again until they got close to Shepton Mallet. Without prompting, Pip picked up the Yellow Pages and looked for the address of the caravan centre.

"I don't think this place is actually in Shepton Mallet. It's in this village called Ash Hill."

"Oh, I thought it said Bath Road," Adam said.

"It is. Bath Road, Ash Hill."

"Wonder where that is. Can you find it on the map for me?"

"I'll have a go. Can't say geography was my favourite subject though," she said, ruefully.

"Ah, here it is. It's a tiny place. Looks like it's on our route anyway."

Their road would bypass Shepton Mallet, but Adam decided that the town merited a closer inspection. He drove around for a while but never found a definitive centre.

"Look!" Pip said suddenly, "Up that street. What's that big old bus shelter thing?"

Adam looked, and smiled when he saw what she was looking at, a mediaeval pentagonal building with arched, open sides and a spire on top.

"That's a butter cross, or market cross. Bus shelter!" he laughed. "It was a kind of shelter, though for market stalls, not bus passengers."

It was indeed, a very impressive market cross. But, in Shepton Mallett, living humans were there none. They drove out again, back to the main road and followed it north. The Bath Road forked off to the right a bit further on and Adam spotted a sign that said 'Ash Hill, half a mile'. When they got there, they did not need to go into the village itself as there, on the main road, was the caravan centre. That is to say there was a sign for it, and an empty building that looked like it had once been a garage and filling station. There was a chain link fence and behind it an empty concrete compound. Somerset Caravan Centre was no more, it seemed. Adam slowed to a crawl, but saw no point in stopping.

"Well, the best in the west, was clearly not good enough," he said. "That's a pity. We'll have to look elsewhere."

They drove on for several miles until eventually they passed a sign saying 'Bath, 5 miles'.

"Not far now," he said: "Do you know how to find your friend's house?"

"I've been there several times, but I'm not quite sure how to get there from here."

"That's not a huge amount of help," said Adam.

"It's in Larkhill, or something like that. The address is just Summerhill Rise, Bath. It's not too far from the centre and it's up quite a steep hill."

Adam laughed. "Most of Bath is up a steep hill. Or down one."

"I'll probably remember the way when we get into the town centre."

"Well, that's OK – we'll just stop and ask someone."

"That's not very funny," Pip said. And Adam thought: no, it really isn't, is it?

When they got into the outskirts Adam pulled over and looked at the map again. "There's no Larkhill, but Lark *Hall* is over the other side of Bath from here. Do you think that's it?"

"Yes, Lark Hall, that's it," she said.

"OK. Well it's off the London Road so I think we need to go towards the centre then look for signs for London and the M4."

The road took them through the suburbs then steeply down to the River Avon, following signs for the town centre. They went over the river and suddenly found themselves right in the centre of the city. "I think you need to go down here," Pip said, pointing to the right, but I'm not sure..." It was too late. They were quickly lost in a maze of small shopping streets. The centre of Bath looked like a scene from a disaster movie. There were cars everywhere, abandoned at crazy angles in the road, some completely burnt out; some shop fronts had been smashed in and here and there were bodies dotted about. Some of the pub doors were open and there was broken glass everywhere.

"Wow, this is crazy!" said Adam, as he weaved the van around all the cars and debris. "It's like there was a riot here. Everyone went on a giant bender."

"God!" said Pip. "Do you think some people here didn't get ill?"

"I don't know. Maybe they didn't get ill straightaway and then when they realised what was going on elsewhere, they... just went crazy."

"I guess they thought the world was ending and decided to have a party."

"Is that what they did in Weymouth?" Adam asked. "I haven't seen this anywhere else."

"No, it just went very quiet, and then very dark. I didn't hear a lot of noise, except for the Friday night, but that was only a few blokes rolling about, like any Friday night."

"Well, it certainly kicked off here one night. I wonder if anybody survived ..."

They drove slowly around the town centre and everywhere it was the same story. Several times Adam had to turn round in the road and find a different route and it took a good half an hour of driving round in circles before they finally extricated themselves from the carnage.

"This looks familiar." Pip said. "I think it's down this way. This is the way the bus goes. This is the London Road. We walked down here if we missed the bus. I used to love going into Bath but that was a real mess. Nic would be so upset."

As they got away from the centre, there was less damage evident, fewer cars strewn about and no bodies to be seen. After a short distance Pip shouted, "Turn left here, it's up here." Adam turned the van into a narrow road which went off at a tangent up a long, straight hill. "Keep going," Pip said, "it's at the top." Adam followed the road, past cottages and villas of Bath stone, small shops, a pub, a church. "Left here," said Pip, and they took a side road, still going up, past old terraces of small houses. At the top the road turned to the right and here there were larger houses, some three floors high, Edwardian or later, he guessed.

"Stop," Pip said, "it's just along here."

Adam stopped the van and looked at Pip. She sat there, not moving. The engine ticked over. The dogs sensed something was happening and got restless. He waited for the girl to move or say something. When she spoke, it was in a very quiet voice:

"It's number 15, just up there on the left. See where that high hedge is."

Adam took the keys out of the ignition and there was complete silence.

"OK." he said. "Give me a while." He grabbed a torch, got out of the van and walked to the back. He rummaged in the toolbox and got out a jemmy. He hunted about in the boot and then came out with a dust mask, which he put loosely round his neck. Hoping that Pip had not seen that, he set off up the lane towards the house with the high hedge.

He had a thought: how would he know what this girl looked like? There might be five sisters in there, for all he knew. He walked back to the van and saw Pip looking questioningly at him.

"Pip, I need you to tell me what your friend looks like, how tall she is, what colour hair."

"There won't be any other girl there, she's an only child, like me," Pip answered. "

But OK, she has bright red curly hair, quite long, down to here," she said, pointing below her shoulder blades, "and she always wears jeans, like mine."

Adam smiled to himself, imagining the pair of them together, thick as thieves.

The wrought iron gate had number 15 on it, as did the front door. There was no side access to any of these houses so the only way in was the front door, or a window. He thought he would try the door first. After he had rattled the knocker and waited a moment or two, he gave it a tentative prod with his boot, but it seemed shut tight. He then stepped back and kicked the door hard with the heel of his boot near the handle, but it didn't yield. He tried twice more, and then gave up. It would have to be the window. He realised that he should have done that straight off as it only took a bit of leverage with the jemmy on the sash window and he had it up in no time. The curtains were closed so he pulled them apart tentatively and peered in, but it was hard to make much out in the gloom.

He put his mask on tightly and lifted his leg over the windowsill, ducked under the top sash and was in. He pulled the curtains back to let in the light. The room was empty and the door closed. He opened the door gingerly and looked out into the hall. It was dark but he could see a door to the right and opened this to find himself in a large, high-ceilinged kitchen. There was a door to the garden at the other end of the room, but no other exits. He turned around and went out, trying the door on the right. This opened into another room, which looked like it doubled as a dining room and TV room. It was empty.

The stairs next. Adam took them slowly, looking up at the landing where he could see that all the doors were closed except for the one straight ahead, which opened into the bathroom. He took a deep breath and tried the door on the left. The curtains were half-drawn and the sunlight streamed in. Adam did not draw breath, but could almost feel the smell assaulting him. In the large double bed was a woman, lying on her side. Adam nearly jumped, as she seemed to be looking right at him. He started to believe she might be alive but when he shone his torch he could see straight away that she had been dead for several days. She seemed to be alone, but Adam could not see the other side of the bed. He went out of the room and took three deep breaths and then went in again. He walked over to the window and saw a pair of feet sticking out beyond the bed. He took three steps around and saw the body of a man, in striped pyjamas, lying face down on the floor. The bedside table had toppled on top of him, the lamp smashed beside it.

Adam retreated from the room and shut the door. He tried the door on the other side of the landing. The curtains were pulled back and the room was bathed in sunlight. It was clearly an office, with a desk and a filing cabinet in the corner. The room was unoccupied. He checked the bathroom... it was empty, but in some disarray. There were no other doors from the landing, so he went quickly up the stairs to the top floor. He could hear flies buzzing from the only room that he could see up there. The door was open, as were the curtains and the window. He could hear birdsong filtering in from the garden below. Adam steeled himself and stepped into the room. It was obviously a teenage girl's bedroom – the pictures of male pop stars, the Athena art poster, the teddy bears, the ornaments. And lying face down across the rich blue bed cover was the body of a girl, not tall, but with a mane of bright red hair. Her hand was stretched out towards him, as if reaching for him, or something, or someone.

Adam felt suddenly faint, a thickening in his throat. He had seen the bodies of his in-laws and his cousin, but now he felt a weight of grief he hadn't experienced before. This was a young life, a girl like Pip on the threshold of adulthood, a life to look forward to, love to find and a whole bright world to discover. But instead, her life had stopped right here, alone, in pain and confusion, and without her closest friend to hold her hand. The poster on the wall, Adam spotted, was 'The Death of Ophelia'.

He retreated down the stairs. He went through the kitchen and into the back garden. He sat on an old wrought-iron seat under a tree and breathed deeply and slowly, trying to quell the nausea and the sobs that were threatening to overtake him.

She read his expression as he walked towards the van, and he didn't need to spell it out to her. He stood at her side of the van.

"I'm so sorry, Pip."

Pip gave a little gasp and covered her face with her hands. A sob shook her and she gave a little moan. "Was she... OK? You know what I mean."

"She was lying on her bed," Adam said, "she looked quite peaceful."

"I knew that she probably...I just thought...." The sobbing overtook her.

Adam said again, "I'm sorry."

Pip sat there, saying nothing, tears filling her eyes.

He put the tools away in the back of the van and got back behind the wheel. He started the engine.

"Shall we go?" he asked gently.

Pip nodded and turned away to look out of the window.

Chapter Twenty-Six

The Old Soldier

Sunday 5th May, Late Morning

Half an hour later they were travelling north on the motorway. Pip had not spoken since they left her friend's house and Adam had left her to her thoughts. He was back in their bedroom, last Sunday, lying on the bed holding Jo as she slipped away for ever.

It had been grey all morning but now the sun was breaking through and Adam thought that maybe a hot drink and a stretch of legs might lift their moods. There was a turning coming up in half a mile and Adam thought they could pull off and find a field for the dogs to run in.

"What do you say to a hot drink and a snack?" he said, glancing over at the girl. Pip turned towards him and gave a weak smile. "Yes, OK."

Half an hour later, after a rudimentary brunch, they were sitting on the door sill sipping their drinks.

"So we are going north then?" Pip asked. "I've been following the road signs."

"Yes, that's the plan. I thought we would go into Cheltenham and see if we can find a camper van place there. Then we can carry on up to Worcester, have a look around there, then head on up to the Midlands, where my cousin and my friend are. After that we can come back through Birmingham."

"Can we go through Bournville then, where I grew up?"

"Yes, of course. We can go anywhere. We need to look for survivors and there's a greater chance of finding them in bigger cities."

When they were back on the motorway, Pip said: "So we're looking for a bigger camper van?"

"Yes. Now there are two of us we need something bigger than this. We need better facilities. We want a van that has a separate sleeping area, more cupboards and storage space. Maybe a bathroom."

Pip frowned, "A bathroom?"

"Yes. Some of the bigger vans have a basin and a toilet. You know people drive them all over the country for weeks on end and they like their comfort and mod cons. There's no reason why we can't have the best."

"I suppose not."

They took the turning into Cheltenham and stopped at the first phone box. Adam waited while Pip grabbed the directory, then drove slowly towards the town centre. They came into a long, wide avenue of regency houses set back behind walls and gardens. In the shadow of the trees the windows were dark and seemed to be watching them. Just when he thought this road was going to go on for ever, a park opened out on the left-hand side. He decided to pull up there while they looked at the directory.

"This place reminds me of Bath." Pip said.

"Similar. It's a Regency spa town. Like Bath, but with more old ladies and less students. I came here once on a conference. Have you found a camper van place yet?"

Pip passed him the phone directory, open at the yellow pages for caravans and camper vans. "There's one in Cheltenham, or near anyway," she said pointing to a box advertisement for 'Cotswold Touring Vans'. "It mentions camper vans as well as caravans. There are others elsewhere, but I don't know where the places are."

Adam took the book and looked through the entries in that section. The one Pip had pointed out was out near the Race-course, but he saw some other promising ones advertising, one near Worcester and another back the other side of Gloucester.

"OK, that one's not too far away, let's drive around the town centre a bit and then go out and have a look." He went to pass the book back to Pip but saw that she was looking intently out of the passenger window.

"Look!" she said, "I think there's someone over there." She was peering out across the park. "An old lady in a grey coat. Do you see her?" Adam tried to see where Pip was looking.

"On that bench, by the main path, under the tree."

He scanned along the path and saw a figure on a bench. She seemed to be motionless.

"Oh yes," he said. "I haven't seen her move."

"No, no. I'm sure I saw her move. There! Look, her head moved."

Again, it seemed to Adam that the woman had remained motionless.

"I think she's spotted us, but doesn't want us to see her," Pip said. "That's how I felt when I first saw you. That's why I hid from you. She can't hide so she is sitting very still. Look, her head moved again!"

"I think your eyesight is better than mine, because I didn't see anything."

"I'm sure I'm right. Adam, let's go and see her. We have to go and check."

"Well, OK," said Adam.

"It's what we've come here for isn't it? To look for survivors?"

"Yes, you're right. Let's go, but we'll leave the dogs in the van." Adam got out of the van with the wheel brace in his hand.

"You can't take that – you'll frighten the life out of her!" Pip said. "She'll think you are going to attack her... It seems safe enough here, doesn't it? She must think it is."

"Alright then. But keep your eyes peeled."

They shut the van and walked along the pavement to the park gate. Adam looked around them, along the road, at the terrace of three-storey villas on the other side, across the park. There was no sign of movement, apart from birds feeding on the lawns and flitting between the trees. They walked across the grass towards the figure in grey and as they drew close, he could see that it was indeed an elderly woman and that she was watching them approach.

"Let me go ahead and talk to her," Pip said. "We might look a bit scary."

Adam hung back while Pip walked over to the woman. She was in her eighties he guessed, with her grey hair pulled into a bun. She had long, elegant fingers like a pianist and before age had shrunk her, she was probably quite tall. With her erect posture and her way of peering over her tortoiseshell glasses, she reminded Adam of one of his primary school teachers.

She stood up as the girl drew near and huddled a bag close to her. Adam could see some wariness in her expression.

"It's alright," Pip said, "You don't need to be afraid. I'm Pip and that's Adam. We‘ve driven up from Dorset to look for survivors."

The woman looked at Pip and then at Adam, trying to size them up.

"From Dorset? But you're not from there originally, I think. I don't detect the Dorset twang," she said. Her voice was bright and clear and belying the strict frown was the hint of a twinkle in her eye.

"Well, I'm from Weymouth, but Adam comes from Reading. We bumped into each other in Weymouth." The woman remained silent, taking this in. "It was just two days ago," Pip went on, "and neither of us had found anyone else alive. And now we've found you!"

"It seems you have," the woman said slowly. "I didn't think that I could be the only person left alive, although it might have been better if I were. But there we go."

She paused and looked at them both in turn, as if making further checks on their veracity and trustworthiness, then softened somewhat.

"My name is Gwendoline Maitland, and I live not far from here. How do you do?"

"How d'you do?" responded Adam, just as Pip said "Well, we're ok thank you."

"You are taking care of this young lady then, are you?" she asked, peering over her spectacles at Adam. "That's quite a responsibility you have there."

Adam laughed. "I do my best. We have to look after each other. But what about you – are you on your own?"

"Oh, yes quite alone. The couple downstairs died on the Saturday, I think. I didn't hear anything of them after that. My friend in Park Street, she has not answered her door. As for the neighbours or anyone else in our street... nothing," she said, with a shrugging gesture.

"And how have you managed, without water and power?" Adam asked.

"I heard a car on the street outside on the Sunday afternoon, but after that, not a thing," the woman said, and then "I'm sorry, what did you ask me?"

Adam repeated the question.

"I am quite resourceful, you know. I have a stock of food and I always keep a supply of bottled water. Not that it has been very comfortable, these last few days. But I survived the war and I haven't forgotten that."

"But what will you do when the food runs out?" Adam asked her.

"When the food runs out, what does anyone do? Curl up and die."

"Oh you mustn't think like that," Pip said. "You've got to hope that there are other people about and that... well, that something will happen."

"I'm happy that you think that way, my dear. But you are the first people I have seen in over a week, and at that rate I am not going to see many more before there is nothing left to live on. Or live for. I am eighty-six and I have had my time. I cannot seriously hope to live much longer now and who knows what will happen next? If there are other people around, in any number, they may well succumb to a second wave of this... this illness, or whatever it was. Would you mind if I sat down?" she asked, and proceeded to settle herself back onto the bench. "I come over here twice a day to watch the birds and the squirrels. I came at first to see if I could see or hear anyone, but I have given up expecting that now, and I just come to enjoy the sunshine and this lovely park." And at this she indicated their surroundings with a sweep of the hand. "I must admit I was rather surprised when I heard your van thing come up the road. But what about you? Tell me what has been going on."

After this little speech, she sat back and looked at Adam expectantly.

"Do you mind if we join you?" he asked, and in answer, the woman waved to the vacant space. Adam sat on the bench beside her, and Pip sat on the other side.

He went on to tell her how he had left Reading to search for his brother and other relatives. "I came to Dorset to see a farm my family used to stay at when we were boys. It was when I was passing through Weymouth on Friday that I met Pip.

"I suppose it is like this wherever you've been?" the woman asked.

"Yes, just the same. Not a soul about. Pip will tell you what Weymouth was like," said Adam, passing the baton to Pip. Before she could pick it up, the woman said to her "What's your name? Pip was it? That's not an Indian name, is it? I am assuming you come from the subcontinent originally, though your accent is very definitely Black Country?"

Pip was a bit taken aback."

"Well... I was born in Goa, but I was adopted by an English couple in Birmingham – that's where I get my accent. They called me Pip. My name is actually Fil*i*pa, the Portugese way."

"Ah ha!" the woman cried, "Fil*i*pa – I can imagine they struggle with that. Philippa or Pip, much easier. When I joined the ATS in the war – you probably don't know what that was – the women's army really – I had a friend called Philippa She was a Pip. Gave us all the pip sometimes. Pip? Hmm – suits you, I suppose. So what's your story?"

"Well, I lived in a guest house with my parents – my adoptive parents. Just the three of us. They got ill on the Friday, like everyone else. Then I just sort of stayed put until I met Adam on the beach."

"It must have been so hard for you, when your parents died. You poor thing. Meeting this man sounds like a very lucky encounter."

"Yes, it was lucky because I wasn't going to go that way, that day, but then I heard the van. And Adam has taken good care of me since then."

The woman smiled, for the first time. "Well, my dears, I wish you the very best of luck in your journey and I hope you find some other people before too long."

At this she sat back with a certain finality that seemed to be a prompt for them to move on. There was a pause and then Adam turned to her and said:

"We hope we do. There must be other survivors out there. My idea is to find enough people to form a settlement, a sort of community. We were thinking of a farm, or somewhere else productive, where we could pool our knowledge and skills to grow food, fix machinery, generate electricity. I don't see how else we can survive. It would be great if you would join us?"

Gwendoline smiled at Adam, a touch condescendingly, Adam thought. "That's a wonderful idea, but very optimistic, if you don't mind me saying so. I really hope it works out the way you envisage it. But, no thank you – I won't be joining you."

"But why not?" said Adam. "You survived the war. With all your experience, you must have so much to offer."

"Well, that's kind of you to put it that way. But another way to look at it is to see that I am too old to be much use now. I am certainly too old to be living in a van with two strangers and to go travelling about the country. I like my bed too much."

"We are going to get a bigger van today," said Pip, "And it's going to be much more comfortable. Adam and I – well we can sleep in tents with the dogs."

"Oh, you have dogs too, do you?"

"Yes, but they're very well-behaved."

Gwendoline laughed at this. "I am sure they are," she said. "It's not the dogs that bother me."

"But we would look after you," said Pip, "you'd be alright with us."

"My dear, I am sure you are very kind people, but at my age I have certain needs and, shall we say, issues. That makes it rather difficult for me to live with other people – you will just have to take my word for it. I am afraid the answer is still no. Thank you, but no. I am quite happy here and here I am going to stay ."

Pip was about to add another line to the argument, but Adam waved her quiet.

"That's OK Pip," he said, "I'm sure Gwendoline has her reasons.

Gwendoline – is it OK to call you that? – can I ask that you think about what we are proposing? We are going north now, but we will be coming back down this way in a few days or so.

Can we come and see you and see if you have changed your mind? Please think about that. We can find a way of getting you to the new homestead in comfort and you can have your own space there." Adam looked at the woman, but she did not offer any encouragement.

"Well, think about it. But before we go today, perhaps we can help you get in some more supplies. There must be lots of things that you need and will want over the next few weeks, and we can help you find those and get them back to your house."

"Thank you, Mr..?"

"Fisher, but please call me Adam."

"Well, thank you Adam, I *will* think about it. But in the meantime, I have everything I need, I assure you. Enough to keep me going until you come by again, I'm sure. You must go and do what you need to do and if and when you come back here, I will give you my answer. So farewell and best of luck to the pair of you. I have to be getting home now."

Gwendoline sat back and folded her arms and then, seeing that neither of the travellers looked like they were going to get up and leave, she started to busy herself in her bag.

Adam stood up, thought for a moment, and then said:

"Gwendoline it's been great talking to you. Perhaps we can walk with you to your house?"

"Yes," said Pip, "please. You could tell us a bit about your life, you know, in the war."

Gwendoline laughed almost scornfully at this. "You don't want to hear about all that, I am quite sure!" she said. "That's ancient history now and you would find it quite boring."

"No, that's not true at all. I would be interested."

Gwendoline got up slowly, then smiled more gently at the young girl. "Very well, you can walk me back to my home. It's not very far and I will tell you a little about how I came to Cheltenham."

"Thank you, that would be good," said Pip, and she held out her arm tentatively for the old lady to take, but she shrugged it away.

"I'm not an invalid yet!"

Gwendoline led them across the park to a gate further down the road and, as promised, she talked to Pip about how, during her time at Bletchley Park in 1943, she had met a dashing army officer called Roger, and had fallen in love. After the war he had been posted to the new headquarters in Cheltenham and Gwendoline, now discharged from duty, found a job here to be with him. They got engaged and were due to be married in the autumn, but one day in August he crashed his sports car on a bend in a country road and was killed on the spot.

"God, that's awful," said Pip when she got to this point in her story.

"I was absolutely heartbroken, as you can imagine," the old lady said. "But you know, I got over it, after a time. They took me on at GCHQ and I had a really interesting job. I had friends and played sports, and I just got on with it."

"Did you find someone else?"

"Never wanted to really. I had loved Roger, and we had our time together. I was grateful for that and never really wanted anyone else."

They got to the corner of her road, and the old lady said that she would be fine from there. Adam insisted they went to her door – he wanted to make sure he knew where to find her. "Very well," she said.

At that moment a rangy looking lurcher appeared from behind a parked car and started barking and whining. "This poor animal is half-starved. I give it something now and then, normally something that's going off. But I can't look after it. I don't suppose you would like another dog?"

"No, we wouldn't," Adam interjected, before Pip could speak. I have already adopted two and we don't have the space for another one."

"I don't want a dog in the house, but I don't want to see him starve. But if I took him in, what would he do when I go? I can't take him with me."

"Where are you going?" said Pip, anxiously.

"Well sometimes I wish I knew," she said, with the hint of a smile. "But it's not up to me. I'll let you know when I get there."

Pip look puzzled at this, but Adam just smiled.

The dog followed them as they walked slowly down the road. They got to a large semi-detached villa with a wide, imposing door under a decorative plaster arch. The large brass plate said 42.

"Well, here we are," said the old lady. "You can leave me here now. Thank you for escorting me home and thank you for your company. Once again, goodbye."

"Goodbye and thank you. I hope you'll tell us more the next time we see you," Pip said.

"We'll see, we'll see." And with that the old lady pushed open the outer door, rummaged in her bag and found a key for the door inside, and disappeared into her flat. The lurcher sat down outside and looked forlornly at the closed door.

Adam and Pip looked at each other and shrugged. "Well!" Adam said.

"She was a funny old thing," said Pip, as they walked back down the road to where the van was parked. "She reminded me of our old music teacher – very posh, quite strict and scary at first, but quite tame when you got to know her."

"Yes, I can imagine. I don't think she was posh, just very old-school. She comes from a different time. Interesting that she worked at Bletchley Park – I wonder if she did anything with Alan Turing."

"I remember reading something about Bletchley Park and the code-breaking machine. I bet that was exciting."

"Not necessarily. Most of the people who worked there had no idea what they were working on."

"It's a pity she didn't want to come with us," said Pip when they got back to the van. "I quite liked her, and it would be good to have someone else to talk to. I mean, not that you're not interesting but... oh, you know what I mean."

Adam smiled: "I know what you mean, but we couldn't expect her to come with us in this thing. We'll come back, though, and see whether we can change her mind."

"We have to – we promised."

"I'm not optimistic though Pip. I think she is a very determined person and I think she is determined that she does not want to go on living."

"I guess that's what she meant about going somewhere, but not knowing where?"

"Yes, I think so. She thinks her time is over."

"That's...that's sad," Pip said

"It is," said Adam, "and just when we've found someone else alive. But there'll be others, I'm sure."

Chapter Twenty-Seven

The Drifter

Sunday 5th May, Afternoon

When they left the park they spent an hour driving all around the centre of the town, round Montpellier, through the shopping area, by the college, doubling back on themselves more than once. Pip seemed impressed with the elegance of the town, but Adam was more interested to see the contrast with Bath. There was no sign of any rioting or the wholesale vandalism that they saw there. There were some bodies here and there, in doorways, on benches, but generally it looked as it did in other places, as if people had just gone home to die. From the town centre Adam drove out into some of the surrounding residential estates, but they found no trace of current human activity there either. It seemed as if Gwendoline Maitland could be Cheltenham's only surviving inhabitant.

Pip navigated them out of town towards the racecourse and not very far down the road from there she spotted a sign for 'Cotswold Touring Vans'. They took the turning and within a quarter of a mile came to the site. Adam pulled up outside the showroom. Parked in front, and in a large compound down the side, were dozens of caravans and camper vans.

"I've never seen so many camper vans." Pip said. "There are loads of them."

"The only trouble is, most of them are the other side of that fence." said Adam, looking at the padlocks on the gates."

"But you can get in there, can't you? You're our master burglar."

"Well, we shall see. First let's tackle the showroom."

They got out of the van and Adam had a quick look around before he let the dogs out. He inspected the showroom doors. They were double doors and he reckoned if he could get a crowbar in between them he could probably force them open. He fetched a crowbar and a smaller jemmy and managed to get them both in between the doors, but forcing them open was not so easy. The top bolt of the right-hand door came away from the frame but the bottom one was stubbornly rooted in the concrete threshold and there was nothing he could do to shift it. He stood back, red-faced and panting while Pip looked on, concerned.

He was trying to think of a different approach, when Pip said: "Couldn't we use the van. It's got a towing thingy at the back. Couldn't you sort of back that into the glass?"

"Yes! Thank you, Pip, I had forgotten about the tow ball. But I think I have a better idea."

He took some rope from the van and lashed it around the centre of the big crowbar. Then he turned the van round and reversed it close to the showroom entrance and secured the rope, which he had doubled up for extra strength, around the tow ball and placed the crowbar through the handles of the two doors.

"*If* we're lucky, the handles won't come off the door when we pull on the rope," he said. "Fingers crossed."

He jumped into the van, put it in gear and let the clutch out slowly as he revved the engine. The rear wheels spun momentarily as the rope strained and then, with a great crash and shattering of glass, the doors burst open, the right-hand one coming right away from the doorframe.

"Well that's done it alright!" said Adam as he got out of the cab.

Pip was looking at the dogs: "Poor Bonzo, he jumped up and ran off like a shot when that door came off. And the old one isn't looking very happy either."

When they got inside the showroom, Pip walked straight over to the largest camper van and promptly disappeared inside. Adam wandered over and got into the driver's door. Pip was in the back, looking in all the cupboards, opening the doors and flaps. "It's incredible what they squash in here. It's got a huge bed that slides out, there's a loo, a big table... and how does this open?"

"You'll need the power on to get some of the things working," Adam said, "but do you think you could drive this bus?"

"You've got to be joking."

"Well, it's a nice little home on wheels, that's for sure. But there are others here to look at too. Why don't you check them out while I go into the office?"

"OK," she said. The busier, the better, he thought.

Adam found what he guessed was the key safe, but unlike the one in Reading, this one had not been left conveniently open. This would need the crowbars on it. He felt around the doors. It was not like a money safe and he could tell that the metal was thin. Back to the van then. He came back with his tools and looked at the safe door. A lump hammer and a cold chisel made short work of puncturing the thin steel plate; it only took a few heaves on the long crowbar to force the door open and Bingo! – there were rows of keys, all neatly labelled with the model names and numbers. "Now we're in business," he said to Pip, who had wandered in to see what he was doing.

"I never realised that you were a house breaker as well as an engineer. I think you've done this before."

"Yes, a week ago," Adam laughed. "I'm getting the hang of it now."

They spent a half hour matching the keys to the vans they could find in the showroom and Pip reconnoitred the interior facilities while Adam looked under the bonnets. The rest of the keys, Adam assumed, were for vehicles parked in the compound and he didn't see much point in investigating them. Pip was very taken with the first one she saw but Adam had reservations, mainly about its size and general unwieldiness.

"There are a few things we need to think about here – how we can get it around country lanes and crowded city streets, how easy it is to maintain and how accessible the engine is."

"Are you a mechanic as well then?" asked Pip. "I mean if it goes wrong, don't we just go and find another van?"

"Hmm. OK, we break down in the middle of the countryside, miles from the nearest town. Are you telling me that you are happy to walk for hours on end until you find a replacement?"

Pip put on a mock thoughtful face, as if pondering deeply this question.

"I think not," Adam continued. "But that's alright. We will just call the dealer and tell them it's still under warranty, come and get us."

"Ok, OK. I get it."

"I'm sorry," he said, trying not to smirk.

"But seriously though, I think my choice is the one in the corner. It has everything we need for living in, plus an engine with plenty of space around it so I can get to it if I need to."

"Is that the one with the hideous tartan upholstery?

"I didn't notice. But we can live with that. I'm talking about the blue and grey one." He pointed to the van in the corner. "It's called Drifter, which seems sort of appropriate for two people who don't really know where they're going. Another big plus is it runs on diesel, which means that we can get fuel from farm tanks without having to siphon it out of other vehicles."

"I certainly wouldn't have thought of that. OK, you win. But," said Pip, "have you noticed that it is the farthest from the doors?"

"Of course, that was another factor in its favour. We can have a bit of fun moving the other vans outside. You could even drive one."

"No thanks. I shall sit in our van and watch you. See how you get on."

"Oh well. But maybe you can give me a hand opening the sliding doors and then perhaps you would like to start getting stuff packed up, ready to move across."

Adam found the keys to the door locks and they managed to open the doors as far back as they would go. He then set about moving the vans about until he could get the Drifter onto the forecourt. He noticed that it had less than a quarter of a tank of fuel in the tank, so he then got another diesel van out next to it, so he could siphon fuel across. Pip wandered over with the dogs to watch the siphoning process.

"Don't get too close," Adam said, "this is really smelly stuff and you don't want it on your clothes." He managed to get the gauge up to nearly half-way, which he thought would see them through till they got up to Birmingham. It was mid-afternoon by the time they finally had everything stowed in the new van and ready for departure, by which time they were both hungry and ready for a sit down.

"Shall we try out our new kitchen?" said Adam. The new van was considerably larger than the old one. In addition to having a lot more storage, in cupboards and overhead lockers, it had a table with bench seats either side of it that could seat four. Behind that was a tiny bathroom cubicle and at the rear two bench seats that converted to make a pair of beds, or one double. The kitchen facilities, on the other side from the table, offered not only a sink and a hob, but even an oven. In camper van terms, this vehicle was at the luxury end.

Adam got the gas bottle working and they used the hob to get a hot meal together of tinned beef, tinned vegetables and instant mashed potato. Cordon bleu it most definitely was not, but it was filling and they both tucked in. The dogs, who had been curious about all the to-ing and fro-ing, had come in to check out the new home and were looking longingly at the meal. While they ate, Pip pointed out all the features that Adam had not yet had the time to appreciate.

"I can see that you're quite sold on life in a campervan," said Adam.

"Well, it seems that this is going to be my home for a while now," she replied, "so might as well make it comfortable."

"How do you like the nomadic life? Do you like being a gypsy, a wanderer?"

"I don't know yet, this is only my second day, but I think *you* are getting well-used to it. You are *definitely* a nomad."

"Well, if I am then it's because I have had to be. But I am also looking forward to settling somewhere again one day, making a long-term home. Hopefully, that will be well before the summer is over."

"Changing the subject, I've been up in the sleeping compartment, and I think it is too small for you," Pip said, with a little smile.

"You think so?"

"Definitely," she said, "*far* too small."

Adam got up from the table and walked forward to the sleeping area that was housed in the overhang above the bonnet. He patted the mattress. "It's rather cosy, isn't it? I think I could be quite comfortable here. No but you're right, it would be a bit cramped. That's alright, I'm happy in a tent. You can stay in the van, but you might have the dogs for company. And you will have to be up early in the mornings. I need my coffee shot first thing"

Once they had cleared the things away and got the dogs in, Adam fired up the engine. He then immediately turned it off again and got out of the cab.

"Last minute checks." He said, by way of explanation to Pip. He walked over to the old van and carefully went through the interior and the boot, checking that they had left nothing behind. He had already checked that his tools were all safely stowed in the locker in the new vehicle. He then took the keys out and locked the doors, walked around the van once and patted it affectionately on the bonnet. "Goodbye old girl, you've done me proud."

Then he stood back and saluted, before getting back into the Drifter and starting it up.

"What was all that about?" Pip said.

"Well, I've spent a lot of time in that van over the last week – all of my time. I shall miss the old girl."

"This one sounds like an old lorry compared to that one"

"That's the diesel engine. I prefer to think of it as sounding like a greyhound bus, rather than an old lorry. It only has 155 miles on the clock, so it is certainly not old. She's still bedding in."

"What do you think Bonzo?" she said to the terrier who was on her lap looking out of the window. "You think it's OK, don't you? What about you Boyo?" This was directed at the old dog, who was still deciding whether to get in his bed or not.

"Boyo?" said Adam, "is that what you call him?"

"Not until just then. Thommo used to say it; it's like a Welsh way of saying 'boy'. And you call them 'boys', don't you?" They looked at each other. "It sort of goes with Bonzo, doesn't it?" Pip continued. She looked at the dog, who was now settled down in his bed. "He makes me think of Thommo – sort of reliable and reassuring."

"Boyo? Boyo. Yes, I like it. Sorted – Boyo it is, then."

Adam got back to the road by the racecourse and followed it north towards Evesham. The van was a bit heavy on the steering when manoeuvring, and it wallowed a bit on tight bends, but once it was up and running on the straight it was quite easy to drive. He noticed after a while that Pip had her eyes closed and Bonzo was snoozing on her lap. He could not resist trying the radio. A hiss of static came out in stereo from the overhead speakers and nothing changed when he turned the tuning dial, except the pitch of the hiss and the volume of the crackle. The sound system was quite good, he thought. Not as good as the one he had in the Audi, but not bad. It had a cassette player as well as a radio – what a shame he didn't have some music to play on it, and he made a mental note to add that to the shopping list.

After a cursory exploration of Evesham, Adam took the road to Worcester. It was getting into early evening and Adam was thinking that they would do a tour of Worcester and then find somewhere to pitch camp for the night on the road north. They had got to Evesham without any issues, but for some reason the road to Worcester had more than its fair share of wandering beasts. There was a small herd of cows, which took an age to get past, as they insisted on running ahead of the van rather than moving onto the verge. A bit further on, on the outskirts of Pershore, a group of dogs got very excited when they drove up and surrounded the van, jumping up and barking, which got Bonzo and Boyo quite agitated, and Pip rather alarmed. The other side of the village they encountered a group of horses who seemed very frisky and were blocking the road. It took ten minutes to ease past them.

They came into the outskirts of Worcester, through some prosperous-looking residential areas. Adam took several detours around the side roads to see if there was any sign of life or recent activity, but they all looked as deserted as the roads in every other town he had driven through. In the town centre area there were more vehicles abandoned and occasionally they saw bins overturned and one or two shop windows that had been smashed. Whether that was by looters who exploited the chaos of the first weekend before the illness took them down, or by people like them, survivors, seeking things they needed, he couldn't be sure. There were one or two bodies, on benches and in doorways and he glanced at Pip from time to time to check her reactions. He was glad to get out of the town and it seemed that Pip felt the same.

"One more town and then we should call it a day, I think." Adam said, as he studied the road map. They had pulled up at a roundabout where there was a choice of routes.

"I think we will go through Droitwich and then after that we can look for somewhere to camp for the night. Is that alright with you, Pip?"

"I think I have had enough of towns today. It would be nice to be right away from them."

"We're never far from towns in this part of the world, but I am sure we can find a quiet field somewhere."

Droitwich was somehow less threatening than Worcester. With its old half-timbered houses it was more genteel and reminded Adam of Stratford. The housing estates were much the same as anywhere else, though, and they dutifully toured the back streets until Adam felt that they had done enough for one day.

"Pip can you look at the map and see if there is anywhere near here that looks like it might be a nice spot to spend the night."

"I'll do my best."

"At the moment we are just going over the river and heading to somewhere called Westlands."

"This is making me feel sick, can you stop a minute."

Adam pulled up and Pip studied the map. River...Westlands...oh, here we are. There's a house with a big lake just down the road. Might be a bit like that place in Dorset. Shall we give it a try?"

"Yes, why not? Adam said" They took the next left and then saw a sign saying *Oakwood House*.

"We need to turn here," said Pip, indicating a small lane branching off on the right. "It should take us by the lake. Then there's Oakwood house."

Adam turned into the driveway, which took them through a small wood and then opened out into a wide expanse of parkland, with a lake to the side. Ahead of them, down the drive, was an old gatehouse straddling the driveway with an arch, and beyond that a magnificent red-brick mansion.

"I think this is just about perfect. Beautiful views and perfect ground for pitching a tent. I think you've found our lodgings for the night."

He drove slowly down the long drive and then pulled up a little way onto the grass. It looked quite short, like it had been grazed recently, but there were no signs of any sheep or other livestock around now. He switched off the engine and they both got out and stretched. Adam took in the view – the lake, the woods and across the pasture, the great house. The sun was low in the sky and the house cast a long shadow, but they would be in sunshine until it set behind the distant trees.

"I think this place tops the house in Combe Bredy. Look at that house, it's huge. I think I'd be happy just with the gatehouse."

"I think I'll be quite happy with this little house for tonight," Pip said.

"That's alright then. But as I am being downgraded to the annex, which I will have to erect first, I think you should cook the supper in your new kitchen."

"You haven't tried my cooking."

"Well, there's always the first time."

"No, you really don't want to try my cooking. But I can be your sous chef, or whatever. Not that I'm very hungry."

"Nor am I, come to think of it. I suppose we had quite a big lunch. You're off the hook tonight then – a snack will have to do. Shall we get the sleeping accommodation sorted then?"

Adam put up the tent and inflated the air bed. When it was up, he tried lying on it and could feel straight away that it was going to be more comfortable for him than the little foam mattress in the old van. The flapping of the canvas, the rubbery odour of the sleep mat and the orange roof of the tent making every morning seem sunny, just within touching distance – it all took him back to the early years of his life. A tent in the back garden with his primary school friend – Neville, was it? Or a reluctantly sharing a tent with his little brother on a family holiday in Devon. When was the last time he went camping, real camping in a tent - 1974 in the Lakes with Gerry? That was their last boys trip together, he thought. They used to have such a laugh, hiking up the fells, going to the pub every night and falling back into their tents after everyone else had turned in. Since those days their get-togethers were more occasional and generally included Jo and Annie. Thinking about it, those were some great times too.

When he went back into the Drifter, he could see that Pip had busied herself making the sleeping compartment cosy. She had moved one of her cases in there and unpacked a few items to have by her bed. Although it was really not a big space – just about the size of a double mattress – a small person like Pip could fit in there quite comfortably, he thought.

"What do you think?" she asked as she came down the little ladder.

"It looks you have made yourself a nice little den there, that's great."

"I think I prefer it up here to being in a tent."

"Where's you sense of adventure? I don't know why people don't like camping ... Careful!" he said. Pip caught her arm coming down the ladder and was now clutching it.

"Is that your bad arm? Is it painful?" he asked.

"It's been hurting a bit," she said, "and then I went and bashed it."

"I think we should have a look at that, see if it's healing up ok. Is it OK if I take the bandage off?"

Pip rolled up her sleeve and held her arm out to Adam to inspect. He undid the bandage and peeled if off carefully. The wound looked red and sore.

"Mm, that's not good. I think we should put some more cream and a fresh dressing on. We will have to keep an eye on that."

"I was hoping I might have a shower." Pip said, "I've been dreaming about having a shower for a week now."

"I know how you feel. I'm sorry but you will have to dream a bit longer yet. This is a brand-new van and they have only put a little bit of water in the tank, just enough for demonstration purposes. I had a look earlier. It's one of the things I was going to do tomorrow – look for a water supply."

He put some more ointment on the wound and found a fresh dressing. "Sorry," he said, as she winced when he tied it off.

"Oh well, I guess another day of being dirty won't hurt." Pip said, looking like it might hurt quite a bit.

"You smell just fine to me."

"Well that's not very reassuring, given that you can't smell much at all."

"In the morning we'll drive down to the big house and see if we can find a tap. They might have a supply somewhere."

After a snack supper they sat and watched the sun go down into the trees away in the distance. They had not spoken for a while, when Adam said:

"You know I feel bad that I didn't put those other vans back inside the showroom."

"Why?" said Pip, "I can't think anyone will be passing there for a very long time."

"I know, but..."

"What does it matter? Whoever they belonged to is almost certainly dead and anyway, they don't have any value anymore."

"What do you mean? This van is very valuable to us," Adam said

"Yes, but if no-one else ever comes by there then they don't have any value, do they? I mean, no-one is going to pay for them. What was the price on this one – ten thousand pounds, or was it a hundred thousand? – who will have the money to pay for it? There are no banks so you can't write a cheque, and unless you have an awful lot of cash stuffed in your mattress, you wouldn't have the money."

Adam smiled at her reasoning. "No, you're right. And yet it still seems wrong to me, to treat things with so little respect."

"I take it you won't be breaking any more shop doors down then?" said the girl, without any trace of a smile.

"OK, I give in," Adam laughed, and then, sensing her mood, more seriously, "but tell me – what will have value in this new world?"

"Food, water, fuel," Pip responded, without hesitation, "friendship, love, loyalty. These will be the really important things."

"Yes, you're right. You are in a very philosophical mood tonight, aren't you?"

"No, not really. But I've been thinking..." she paused a while and Adam waited patiently for her to start again.

"I've been thinking about how you found Nic in her bedroom this morning. She was my best friend in the world and although I sort of expected that she would be dead it didn't really come home to me until I was sitting outside her house. When I saw you walking back to the van, on your own, it really hit me then." Tears were welling in the girl's eyes and she turned away from him. "Right now, the only person I've got to take care of me is you, and that scares me."

"Because I'm a stranger? Because you think I might abandon you?"

"No, I don't think you'd do that. And I don't see you as a stranger. I feel as if I've known you a long time already. But it's like..." she searched for the words.

"Like we're the only ones in the world for each other? But we're not. There are others, maybe lots and lots of people... we just haven't met them yet. I mean we found Gwendoline today and that's only on the second day of our journey."

"That's only two people in a week that you've found. What if there aren't any others?"

"I'm sure there will be. I'm quite certain of it." He gave a little shiver. "I'm getting a bit chilly now. I think I'll turn in soon, get an early night. I'm looking forward to stretching out on that mattress."

Chapter Twenty-Eight

Road Music

Monday 6th May, Morning

Monday arrived with the sound of rain pattering on Adam's tent. He turned over and tried to shut it out, but eventually he realised he was not going to get back to sleep. He wasn't looking forward to having to pack the tent away in the rain. When he poked his head out of the flap, though, the rain was not as bad as it sounded inside the tent. He stood up to finish pulling up his jeans and stretched his back out. He looked up and for a moment was surprised to find a shiny, large vehicle in front of him. He had been sad to leave behind the old van, which had been his constant companion, along with the dogs, for six days – this one was going to take a bit of getting used to yet.

He opened the side door and the dogs rushed to greet him as if they hadn't seen him for a month rather than just one night. But then for six nights they had not been separated, so they were probably wondering where their master had been. He said hello to them and reflected how a week ago, when he woke up to the cold, quiet Monday morning, the dogs had not entered his consciousness. But then, nor had a lot of things. The curtains to the sleeping compartment were firmly closed but Adam decided he wasn't going to creep around in the mornings and he got some water boiling for his coffee.

Sometime later he was finishing his coffee when a drowsy sounding "Morning" greeted him from the front of the van. He turned round to see Pip's very sleepy face peering out from between the curtains.

"Good morning. I hope I didn't wake you?"

"No, s'alright. Those two woke me up an hour ago with their whining. What time is it?"

"Coffee time." said Adam.

"Mmm, so I see. A cup of tea would be nice."

"A cup of coffee would be so much nicer. And if you have it black then it doesn't taste of UHT milk."

"No thanks. But you could make me some with milk in, not too strong."

A little while later Pip clambered down from the bedroom in pyjama bottoms and a T-shirt, and reminded Adam about driving over to the house to find a water tap.

"Yes, I hadn't forgotten. We'll do it after coffee."

"I'll stay in my pyjamas then. Then I can have a shower later."

"Why not," Adam said, smiling. "I don't suppose anyone's going to be watching you."

After coffee Adam drove down the long drive, through the gateway and into the courtyard in front of the house. He followed it round to what he assumed were stables at the rear of the house and pulled up there. They got out and looked around at the grand old house and its equally grand stables and outbuildings, all built in the same brick. As expected, there was a tap at one end of the yard, with a hose attached. How convenient, Adam thought, too good to be true. And indeed it was, as when he turned the tap on nothing came out of the hose but a dribble.

"There's no water here; that's a shame. Sorry Pip no shower this morning. We've got a bit of water in the bottles, enough for a wash if you want."

"Oh alright, I suppose."

"I'll get some ready for you," he said, and they went back towards the van.

Half an hour later they were on the road, heading north into Shropshire

Pip was looking out of the window, absently twiddling a coil of hair around her fingers, when she turned to Adam and said, "Where do you think we might find some water, you know, for the tank?"

"It will be have to be a farm or some remote house, like the one we looked at in Dorset. Somewhere off the beaten track."

"Wasn't that place off the beaten track? It seemed miles from anywhere."

"Yes it was and they probably had a private supply. But maybe it needed to be pumped from a well and without electricity..."

"Oh, yes. So where do we go now?" They had arrived at a crossroads and Pip was looking at the road signs.

"We are going up here towards Kidderminster," said Adam, turning right on to a main road, "and then we are going to head to Shrewsbury, where my old buddy lives – or lived – and after that to Telford to see if we can find my cousin.

"Do you think you might find them alive?" Pip asked later.

"I doubt it," Adam said, "but I have to find out, like you with Nic."

"Did you see them very often?"

"I haven't seen Gerry for a few years now, but we keep in touch. He and I go back a long way. I can't remember when I last saw him. I think it might have been when we met up in London about four years ago. As for my cousin, Susan, I haven't seen her or her brother for many years now. The last time was at a family wedding. But they're family and I feel I should look them up. I know genetics probably has nothing to do with why we're still here, but..."

"And if they're not alive, your cousins?"

Adam shrugged. "Then, I still won't know why we didn't get sick when everyone else did; or if we'll get sick in the future, either sooner or later."

"And the fact that you and I were both in hospital last year?"

"Yes." Adam said. "We should have asked Gwendoline about that. But I'd love to see Gerry again and as it happens he lives quite near my cousin. It sort of makes sense. And on the way back we can visit Bournville and see if there are any of your old friends still with us."

"I'd like that. I don't suppose there's much point, but it would be good to have a look around, just in case."

"Well, let's see what happens after we have been to Telford. By the way – are you planning to stay in your pyjamas all day?" he asked her, smiling.

"No, I suppose I'd better put on some clothes, just in case."

A drizzle was falling as they wended their way through the dreary countryside. Adam found the Drifter heavy on the steering and not as enjoyable to drive as the old VW van. Pip turned the radio on and started turning the dial, looking for a station.

"You won't find anything to listen to there, just different types of static," Adam said.

"You never know," said Pip, "somebody might be broadcasting somewhere, even if not in this country."

"Then you need to try long-wave if you want signals from Europe."

"The police use short wave, don't they? And truck drivers. It's worth trying all the bands." She scrolled through the three bands on the radio, but came up with nothing but static, as Adam had predicted.

"Well, it was worth a go. In fact we should try every day, maybe twice a day. Somebody might be off air now, but on again later. You know a radio ham – someone somewhere might be trying to make contact at different times of day. It's got to be worth a try, surely?"

"Yes, you're right," Adam said. "I hadn't really considered it before."

"Hey, I've just remembered!" cried Pip suddenly. "I've got some cassette tapes up in my cabin. Do you fancy some music?"

She clambered up the ladder and came back with a handful of cassettes. "I've got Queen, UB40, Led Zeppelin, Cyndi Lauper, Kate Bush or Wham!"

"My, that's an interesting collection. Was this a committee selection?"

"What do you mean?" Pip said.

Adam laughed. "I can't imagine how any one person could like such a completely varied selection of artists. I don't mind – you choose."

"Well, you're boring! Variety is the spice of life. And they all have their reasons. For a start, two of them are Black Country groups."

"Yes, that makes sense. And Wham?"

"They're just there because of George Michael."

"Oh, that's unfortunate."

"Why?" Pip asked, looking quite serious.

"Because he's a bit gay." Adam laughed.

"How do you know?"

"I don't. But you know..."

"Hmm! What do you know? And he's got an amazing voice. Anyway, Freddie Mercury's gay too, but I don't care. I'm putting Queen on."

The tape crackled and then the first track boomed out. It was not long before Adam found himself drumming on the steering wheel to the music and at one point he looked over and saw

Pip singing along with the band. They drove through Kidderminster with the music blasting out in stereo and by the time they were out on the road to Bridgenorth, Adam was singing along too. At one point they both looked at each other at the same time and burst out laughing. The sun came out and Adam wound down his window and let the world hear the music, and the world, which at that point comprised a straggle of pigeons on the road, promptly flew off in alarm. Bonzo barked in the back. "That's got the dogs up," Pip shouted over the music.

***

They got to the outskirts of Shrewsbury about midday and Adam pulled up to check the address of his friend's house. It was in the address book as 86 Queens Drive, Shrewsbury, but not having been there, he had no clue as to where it might be in the town. The only thing that stuck in his mind was that Gerry had mentioned going to watch the cricket matches at the ground just round the corner.

"Pip we need to look for signs for the cricket ground." She turned down the music (they had got to UB40 by this point) so she could hear him better. "The what?"

"The cricket ground. I think the road we are looking for, Queens Drive, is near there."

"OK. Cricket ground and Queens Drive."

They drove down the Wenlock Road towards the town centre, but saw no sign of a cricket ground. What would have been a busy road into town was empty of traffic and devoid of any human life, but not animal life. A trio of dogs trotted down the middle of the road, love-struck pigeons chased each other around, a fox trotted along the pavement, unseen by a pair of ducks and their young who were making their way across the tarmac further down the hill. Adam spotted a cat sitting on a bench in a bus shelter. "She'll be waiting a long time for that bus," he said

Ahead of them was a tall column with a figure on top. As they went around the column Pip said, "Cricket ground! It's up that way," pointing to a road to the right. It was a wide road with trees on the left and large, detached turn-of-the-century houses on the right. Further on, the land opened out on the left-hand side, and on the right the houses were now post-war.

"There's the cricket ground," Adam said, pointing to a large open space on the right. "Now we have to look for Queens Drive."

They were driving past houses built very recently and then, there on the right, was Queens Drive. Adam turned into the road, which formed the spine of a large housing estate. It was very similar to the one he had lived in in Reading, with detached houses in the latest style, set back behind open lawns. They counted down the numbers and soon got to number 86. Adam pulled up, stopped the engine and turned the music off. "Well this is it," he said. "Let's just listen a minute."

He wound down his window and they listened. The sound was the same as they heard everywhere they went, not silence, but what you might think at first was silence, until you listened harder and realised that the air was full of sounds: all the sounds of nature, but none made by man.

Adam opened his door.

"I'll wait here with the boys," Pip said.

He walked up the path to the front door, opened the letter flap and peered in. He could see a hallway, a staircase on the left, straight ahead the open door into the kitchen. He listened and he could hear the sounds of flies. That's not promising, he thought. To the side of the garage was a passageway to the back garden. It was locked, but he put his boot to the latch and the gate flew open with a splintering of softwood. The back garden was mainly lawn with some shrubs and a tree at the end. He looked in through the window to a dining room. There was no-one in there, nor in the kitchen next to that. He looked up and saw that the curtains were closed upstairs.

He went back to the front door, opened the letter flap and called out, "Gerry, It's Adam – are you there? Can you hear me? Gerry?" Silence.

He knew the scenario. Gerry wasn't alive and he and his family were probably lying dead in their beds upstairs. Should he go and check? He ought to make sure. He went back into the garden at the rear and stopped before he got to the kitchen door. The garden looked remarkably tidy and well-stocked and the grass edges were neatly cut, though the grass had grown over the last two weeks or so. There was no sign of wear from Gerry's boisterous 10-year-old twin boys, no footballs, or goal posts, no rope swings in the tree. This was not the garden that the Gerry he knew would cultivate. There would be a vegetable patch, bird feeders everywhere, maybe even chickens. But a perfect lawn – not a chance! No this was the domain of a genteel suburbanite, maybe even retired. Would Gerry really live in a house like this? More likely he'd find a dilapidated old vicarage to do up.

He went back round to the front. There was no car on the drive and maybe it was in the garage. But didn't Gerry mention he had bought a new a caravan, or a camper van, which they all went round Europe in a couple of years back? And Annie, she had a car surely? No this was not Gerry's house.

He walked back to the van. Pip was making a fuss of Bonzo, who had jumped on her lap and was now watching Adam return.

"We've got the wrong address," he said as he got back in the cab. "This is definitely not Gerry's house. Let's go."

"Well whose house...where does he live then?" Pip said

He shrugged, "No idea, but it's not here. I must have got it wrong."

"Do you think it might be number 36 instead? Or 56?"

"Or 186? Or King's drive, or Queen's Close. Who knows?" said Adam, blowing out his cheeks.

"That's a shame, and we've come all this way. I'm sorry."

"Yeah well. What were the chances of finding him alive anyway?"

"On the other hand at least there's a chance he might not be dead."

"Like Sam? I suppose so. Well," he sighed, "let's see if we can find my cousin." Pip was right, of course, but he couldn't help feeling disappointed. He would like to know, one way or the other.

Adam took them back up the London Road and then turned left on to the A5 towards Telford. The sky had darkened again and raindrops started peppering the windscreen.

"I have no idea where my cousin lives, but the address is in Wellington. I looked on the map and that's on the north side of Telford. How we find her road when we get there, I don't know."

"What's your cousin's name?" Pip asked

"Susan. She's the youngest. I met her twice, once when I was little and then again at a wedding. When she was young she had a very annoying giggle.

"You weren't impressed then?"

"You could say that. She was a lot younger than me so when she came to stay with us, with her mum, she was far too young to be of interest to an eleven-year-old boy, or whatever I was. But by the time we met at the wedding she had grown into a really interesting woman and I really enjoyed chatting with her. We promised to keep in touch but – you know how it goes. Pip, can you just check for me in that address book there and look for... Susan Rogers, I think it is. It might be under F for Fisher. Tell me the name of the road – I think it had something to do with the West Country."

Pip looked through the book. "Here we are, Susan, in brackets Rogers: 22 Tavistock Road, Wellington, Telford. Oh, this is making me feel sick."

"Tavistock, I knew it was in Devon. My guess is that it will be on a housing estate and the other roads will have names of towns too."

"How do you work that out?"

"It's what they do, the builders and developers. They will have a theme – trees, flowers, counties, capital cities, port towns, poets. I bet this one is places in Devon or the West Country."

"So how does that help us?"

"Well, if we look at the names of roads going into housing estates and see any that look like West Country towns, or market towns, then it's worth checking out the other roads around them."

"That's a good idea. I hadn't thought of that... In Bournville I had a friend who lived in Brambling Close and that was off Fieldfare Drive. I think there was a Swallow Crescent too. The builder must have been a bird fancier then."

"Aren't all builders, bird fanciers?" Adam said, smiling.

"Are they?" said Pip, looking puzzled.

"Well, they're always whistling at the birds round our way."

"Adam! That's terrible!"

"Yes, it is, isn't it. Sorry. I'm showing my age now."

"Put some more music on," he said, as they drove along the dual carriageway. He was feeling quite *up* at the moment, and Pip seemed in a good mood. They were bopping with the music as they bowled along the A5 and before they knew it they were taking the turning off to Wellington and driving into the outskirts of the town.

But an hour later they were still driving around without finding the road, or any other roads with related names. Adam was starting to get tired of driving up and down road after road of identical 70s bungalows, or 80s semis.

"It seems my theory on builders' road names doesn't hold water. I think we should call it a day, don't you?" he said.

"I think we should do another quarter of an hour before we give up. I mean we've come all this way, and if you don't find your cousin's house you will always be wondering about it. How about we try down this road?"

Adam turned into yet another new estate, this one so new it was still being built and they saw signs to the show house. The road to the right was Gordon Avenue, and was fully occupied, but looking like it had only been completed in the last year. Off there they passed Euston Close.

"I can't quite make out the theme of the names here," Adam said, "They don't seem to bear any relation to each other."

"No," said Pip, looking out of the side window, "that one's Fitzroy."

"Fitzroy? Aha! Fitzroy, Gordon, Euston – they are all squares in London, near Euston Station. Tavistock is another one – it must be on this estate somewhere."

Sure enough, a little further up the road they came to Tavistock Road on the left. This road comprised smaller, semi-detached houses, each brick built and featureless except for a bay window with mock leaded lights on the ground floor and a small porch with a tiled gable.

"There! Number twenty-two, on the right," Pip said.

Adam pulled the van up in front of the house. A black cat ran off into the back garden, looking alarmed. There was a new Ford Fiesta parked in front of the house and a not-so-new Vauxhall. The curtains were drawn closed on all the windows.

"Can I let the dogs out?" Pip called, as Adam walked up to the house. He looked around at the empty street: "I don't see why not."

He peered through the letter box but could not make anything out in the dimly lit hallway apart from the stairs. He hammered loudly on the front door and looked again through the letter box in case there was any movement from within. As before at Gerry's house, he hollered his cousin's name, but there was no response. There was no side gate and just posts and wire separating the back garden from the neighbours'. The curtains were open at the back. There was a small breakfast room which led into the kitchen. He could see nothing in either room. He went up to the back door and hammered hard on it. There was no response from inside. He tried the handle, the door opened and the minute he stepped inside the smell assaulted him. He could hear the drone of buzzing flies somewhere beyond the kitchen. There was no need to go further and he stepped quickly outside into the fresh air.

He went back to the van, giving Pip the thumbs down. She had got out and was watching the dogs, who were busy sniffing around.

"That's it then," he said when they were all back in the Drifter, "mission complete, target not found, team dismissed. That's my genetics theory disproved."

"Oh well, don't be too down about it. I mean you weren't very hopeful of finding them in the first place."

"No, I wasn't. It just means now that I'm not very hopeful about finding Sam either. Shall we go?"

Chapter Twenty-Nine

Reflections in the Rain

Monday 6th May, Afternoon

"Where do we go now?" Pip asked.

Adam glanced at the clock on the dashboard. "It's well after lunchtime, which is a shame because I was going to suggest finding a nice pub for a hearty cooked lunch. But we could find a layby or a field somewhere and tickle our taste buds with such delicious delicacies as packet soup and slightly stale crackers."

"Or cold beans and sliced processed cheese," Pip chipped in, "I had that last week – tasty!"

"So here is what I thought. I was looking at the road atlas earlier and I thought we could make our way to Bournville via Bridgenorth and Stourbridge and when we find a suitable shop, we might be able to top up our larder."

"And get some water for the tank. Don't forget that."

"No, I hadn't forgotten. But en route I thought we could go to Ironbridge and park up there for a lunch-stop. Have you ever been there?"

"I think so, once, a long time ago. Pip said, with a frown of concentration. "I think we had a school trip there, but all I can remember is going round this big old Victorian factory and dropping my lunch on the floor."

Adam laughed. "Sounds like a typical school trip. That might have been the old tile factory you went to. But the most interesting thing to me is the Iron Bridge itself, which was the first bridge made of iron ever constructed, over two hundred years ago."

"Oh, OK that's interesting?" said Pip, one eyebrow raised.

"It is to an engineering student. But you'll appreciate it when you get there. It straddles this beautiful gorge on the River Severn. And it's on our route."

"And," he added, "you can navigate me there."

"If I must," she replied

"I am sure we will see signs to it. We just need to go back to the A5."

A little later the Drifter was coming down the road into the gorge, with the Iron Bridge dominating the view ahead of them.

"Is that it?" Pip said, flatly.

"Come on, how can you not love that sweeping arch and the delicate tracery ironwork? It epitomises the spirit of the Industrial Revolution – pioneering engineering, experimental materials, practicality and elegance – don't you just love it?"

"Are you having me on? It's a bridge!"

"Well, yes. But you've got to admit, it's impressive."

"Whatever."

They drove up the road towards the bridge, the River Severn down below them on the right and little 19th Century cottages and shops on their left. Adam parked near the bridge and they all got out. Adam remembered the dog leashes and the wheel brace. They walked onto the bridge and looked down at the river rushing through the gorge below and then they looked over the other side, downstream. After that they followed the road back down the hill to the riverside, peering into the dark windowed shops as they went. At the bottom they sat on a bench near the water's edge while the dogs ran around and explored. They watched the water pouring along the narrow gorge, the ducks riding the current like surfers, the swallows racing above the surface looking for insects. Pip was staring at her feet.

"What's up Pip?"

"It's nothing," she mumbled.

"Tell me."

"I don't know, I can't really explain. Just looking at this bridge, something made by some very clever people a hundred or so years ago, and it's still here now. But who is ever going to make something like this now? Do you know what I mean?"

Adam nodded.

"And we drive about in this really expensive camper van and we're laughing and joking and listening to music; we help ourselves to things from shops, and live on tinned food, but what will we do when it all runs out? And we look in these shop windows and we know that no-one will ever go in them again to buy a present or a nick-nack. One person's hard work, all gone to waste. And all these houses up on the hill, cold and empty with dead bodies rotting away – they will start falling down and this pavement will all get overgrown and one day all of this will have disappeared. And there's just us now, maybe no-one else, and why should we be allowed to be here? Do you know?"

Adam was going to respond, but checked himself. Pip had turned away and was staring into the distance. He didn't have any useful words to add to what she said: everything she said was true.

The rain had turned to a fine drizzle and they were quickly getting wet.

"Come on," he said, "let's go and make a hot drink before we get completely soaked."

He got up, calling the dogs, and walked back up the hill, Pip following slowly behind.

Once back, they sat in the van and drank tea, nibbled at biscuits and looked at the rain sweeping down the gorge in waves of net curtains, while the dogs licked the rainwater off their coats and flopped out on the floor, with sighs of resignation – this was not weather for being outside.

Adam put his cup down and said "You know, Pip, it's not going to be easy, surviving in this new world. And however many people we find, we *will* all be just surviving. I mean, unless whole populations are existing somewhere else in the world and they come and find us, it will be years before we have even the most basic technologies of modern life working for us properly. We probably won't see any new bridges, churches or monuments built in our lifetime. So we will have no choice but to use what we have left here. And yes, it will start falling down, but one day our successors can rebuild it."

"I don't know," Pip replied. "I just don't see how we *are* going to survive. And what if there's just us and maybe a few others we find – how are we going to be able grow food, find fuel and stuff? And what use am I going to be? I don't know anything about all these things."

"You're a bright girl, Pip and you can learn to do lots of things. You didn't give up last week, when you were all on your own. Don't give up now. We have to keep going.

"But we've got to have enough of us for this to work," Pip said, "and the way things are going we're never going to find enough other people alive, however many housing estates we drive around."

Adam said nothing and swilled his tea round the cup. Tea drinking was almost a novelty for him. After a while his mind started to clear.

"You know, what you said about trying the radio bands is a really good idea. But what we should do is find a proper ham radio set – the transmitter, the aerial, the whole works. Then in addition to searching for broadcasters we can broadcast as well."

"But how would we put it all together. And how would we power it?"

"That's the easy part. I'm used to assembling machinery, and electrical items don't frighten me; I am sure I can work it out.

As for power, this van is a perfect power source. And we'll get a generator set up as well when we have a base. We drive to the top of the highest hill and we can transmit for thousands of miles."

"So where do we find one of these ham radios?" Pip asked.

"We're heading into a large city, there's bound to be one there. And you can do your stuff with good old Yellow Pages."

"Do you want to go there tonight?"

"No point tonight. It's coming on for five – the shops will all be closing soon."

Pip went to answer, and then just gave him a look.

"No, I was thinking we would go tomorrow. We could go into Wolverhampton and see if we can locate a shop somewhere. And when we've found what we want, we can go down to Bournville. This afternoon, or what's left of it, I thought we should concentrate on getting our water tank filled up."

They set off across the farmland of east Shropshire and on into Staffordshire, following the minor roads that Adam had picked out on the road map. Pip did her best to navigate. Whenever they saw a farm sign, they would investigate, Adam squeezing the van up narrow lanes and farm tracks. They tried several without success; either there were no taps that they could access, or there were taps but they were dry. Over the tops of the hedges and through gates Adam could sometimes see cattle lying on their sides, evidently dead or in the last stages of life. He hoped that Pip was not looking too hard at these. Cows massed at the gates when they heard the van approaching, pushing to get out of their fields. Elsewhere gates had been flattened and cattle were seen wandering all over the farms and the lanes. All this made for slow travelling, but Adam could not think of a better place to look for water.

After an hour and more zigzagging slowly across the landscape, they were coming very slowly down a narrow lane behind some cows, when Pip spotted a cottage which had an outside tap. Adam let her get out and try it, and there it was, running water!

"Result!" said Adam to himself, as he got out of the van. And as she came back towards him, "Put it here!" as he raised his hand for a high-five.

They managed to fill the tank using a watering can and it took about fifteen trips to the tap before it was full.

They resumed their journey, and a mile along the road they came to a village which had a good size village store. Adam applied his breaking and entering skills and they hunted around for the things they needed. They took torches and their home-made face-masks, but Pip could not stand to stay more than a few minutes in the shop. In the end, all that Adam could find for them was more tins, drinking water, long-life juice and long-life milk and some fruit. Everything else that had been fresh was quietly rotting and the area with the fridges and freezers was a no-go area because of the smell. He got his bags of booty out of the shop and took some deep draughts of fresh, damp, spring air.

"At least there were no bodies in there, that's something," he said, as he passed the haul across to Pip. She got busy putting things away while he took their rubbish out and put it in the litter bin outside the shop. He remembered that they needed some more batteries for the lamps and torches and went back into the shop. As he did so, he noticed the papers in the rack by the door. Their headlines shouted: "Unknown Virus Sweeps Far East – Major Summons Cabinet to No 10." The date on the top of the page: Friday twenty-sixth of April, 1991. The last day of the world? He picked one up, as a memento.

Adam drove on down the same road and a little later came to a large gate and a sign announcing Rashley Hall, Hotel & Golf Course.

"Shall we go there and check out a camping spot?."

"OK," said Pip, not appearing much to care.

They followed the long driveway around a lake and came up to the hotel. What had once been a modest country pile was now a golfing hotel with modern extensions. The lawns were mainly now part of the golf course, along with the surrounding fields. Adam drove off the driveway onto the grass and away from the buildings. He followed a fairway down between a stand of tall trees and out onto a wide area of mown grass with a rough either side and a lake ahead.

"What do you think Pip? Stop here for the night? Lots of lovely flat grass, ideal for pitching a tent. Boys, what do you think?" The boys in the back thought they would like to explore further and seemed keen to get out. "Come on then!" he said, opening the side door.

"It looks nice, "Pip said, "A bit like where we were yesterday."

"Yes, it is a bit. It's stopped raining now. That must be a sign. I'm going to do a recce. Do you want to come?"

"No, you go," she said, "I'll stay here and sort this place out a bit, put things away, you know."

"OK, if you're sure."

And with that, brace in hand, he strode off across the grass back towards the hotel, the dogs running along ahead of him. He was glad of the chance to stretch his legs and give the dogs a good run. It was a great place for a dog walk, for dogs and their keepers: Fairways and putting greens, sand bunkers and water traps, stands of great ornamental trees and all surrounded with lakes. The grass was wet and his shoes soon sodden, but he didn't care – it was good to be out of the van and on his own for bit. In the four days since he had met Pip, he had hardly had any time to himself, it seemed – even less time than he would have had being with the family.

That evening, before Pip had her shower, Adam took off her dressing and checked the wound. It was still a bit red, but it did not look too serious. Pip tried out the shower while Adam unbundled the wet tent and put it up. He tactfully stayed out of the van until she had finished and was back down from her boudoir in clean joggers and a towel wrapped around her head. After he had put a clean dressing on her arm, they sat down to a cooked supper, with paper napkins and a glass of wine. Pip put on some music and after supper they played some cards and chatted about life before V Day. It was a mellow evening and Pip seemed happier in herself, Adam thought.

Lying in his damp tent later that night, listening to the soft patter of fine rain on the canvas, he thought about what Pip had said earlier that day. They had to have enough people to make a community, but what if they didn't have enough? How long could he and a young teenage girl survive living on their own? This is why they had to set up a radio that could scan the airwaves across the country. It was so obvious, why hadn't he thought of it before? After meeting Pip, he assumed that there would be many other survivors around, and finding Gwendoline reinforced that assumption. But today they had driven along dozens of streets, past hundreds of houses and not seen a living soul. If there were more survivors, they might be well scattered across the country and if they drove round the country for weeks they might still never find them. Even with the radio, how many could Pip and he discover? Unless these people had the skills and the initiative to broadcast or receive, how would they ever be found?

Adam went round and round this puzzle in his mind, tossing and turning in his sleeping bag until eventually he slid into a fitful sleep. His dreams were jumbled, full of driving down dead-end roads, dogs snarling behind every wall and corner, and empty houses with their doors gaping open. At one point he even woke himself up and said "Enough!" out loud – or so he remembered in the morning. Then Sam appeared from a broken doorway. He was larking about and laughing and then, seeing Adam's concern, he came over and put his arm round him in that disarmingly caring way he could suddenly assume and said, "Hey, don't worry, it's going to be OK. You'll be alright." And after that Adam slept heavily through till the birdsong roused him in the morning.

Chapter Thirty

Metal Micky

Tuesday 7th May, Morning

The next morning, after a wake-up coffee and tea and biscuits for Pip, and when he had rolled up the wet tent for the second day running, they drove slowly back across the grass to the hotel and away down the drive.

"That was alright that place, wasn't it?" said Pip.

"Yes, Adam agreed, "beautiful grounds and probably a nice golf course too. But the breakfast was a bit disappointing."

"Oh, was that breakfast?" said Pip. "I thought that came later in the morning usually."

"Maybe, if we are lucky. Now then, miss navigator, we need to make our way into Wolverhampton and look for a radio shop. I am in your hands."

"OK. Let me look at the map. What was this place called? Oh, yes, Rashley Hall." She was looking closely at the road map and Adam slowed so he could lean across and see. "It's OK, I can do it," she said, pulling the map away out of his eye line. "Right, we need to go back to the road we were on and then turn right, no, hold on, I mean left." She turned the map upside down and looked at it that way.

It was only a few miles to the outskirts of Wolverhampton and Adam pulled up when he saw the first telephone box so Pip could grab the phone book. She started thumbing through the yellow pages to look for radio shops as Adam pulled away.

"You'll have to drive slowly if you want me to look at this without being sick all over the seat," she said. Adam stopped the van again and let her look at the index.

"They've got radio and tv sales and repairs – that's not what we want is it? Radio and hi-fi equipment? Radios – short wave, CB radio? They don't have ham radio."

"It could be either of those two other ones – radio equipment or CB radio. They sound like the sort of shops we are after."

Pip found the pages and looked at the listings and the advertisements. "There's this one in Wallsall, looks a possibility."

"That's a bit out of our way from here." Adam said. Is there nothing in Wolverhampton?"

"There's one in Perry Bar. Or this one in Handsworth – that's not far from the centre of Birmingham, I think. Have a look." She pointed to a box advertisement for the shop in Handsworth.

"Can you navigate me to that, do you think?" Adam asked.

"I can try." Pip studied the map. "I think we should get to the town centre and then follow signs for Birmingham. It shouldn't be too far off that road."

"OK. Let's give it a go." And Adam pulled away and drove towards the town centre. They were coming through a suburb, a residential area of inter-war houses, and then a long tree-lined road took them close to the centre where there were more shops and older, early 1900s buildings. There seemed to be a lot of dogs around, trotting along or just sitting in the road, and when they heard the van, some ran off, some started barking at them and some just seemed to take no notice.

"I wonder why there are so many dogs about in this place," Pip said, "I wouldn't want to get out here."

Just at that moment, a car came up behind them, sounding its horn and flashing its lights. It was the first moving vehicle Adam had seen since he first left his house over a week ago and it gave him a start. He slowed to a stop and the car pulled up alongside them. A young man, quite short, in his late twenties perhaps, jumped out, waving excitedly, and came over to Adam's door. He was wearing jeans, a bomber jacket and had a small medallion hanging over his sweater. His hair was brown with a hint of ginger, worn long at the back in the latest style. He had a cigarette in his hand. Adam wound the window down but did not open the door.

"Hello, hello! How you doing? Well, well, well. Where are you headed? Where have you come from?" the young man said, all in a rush. "I'm Michael Wheeler, but everyone knows me as Micky. Come on out and let's be saying hello properly." He spoke in a flat London accent, his words rattling out as if they had a deadline to meet.

Adam opened the door and got out. The young man thrust out his hand and Adam took it.

"Well hello. I'm Adam and this is Pip," he said, indicating across the cab.

"Hello Adam. it's good to see you, my friend. And hello Pip, nice to meet you too. So where have you good people come from?"

"Well, we have come from Shropshire today where we were looking for my relatives."

"And did you find them – alive that is? No, I thought not. There ain't many of us about." And where was you from before that?"

"We have come up from the south. Yesterday we were in Cheltenham, where we found an elderly woman living on her own."

"Did you, did you now? But you left her there?"

"For the moment yes," said Adam, "she didn't want to come with us."

"I'm from the south, as you can probably tell, from North London. I don't talk all funny like they do here." He said, putting on a Black Country accent. "But I ain't seen more than a handful of people since everything went pear-shaped and shut down, if you know what I mean. And one or two of them was on their last legs." He was looking at Pip, scrutinising her closely. "So, are you two related, friends...?" he said, looking doubtful of this suggestion, "...or did you meet up somewhere?"

Adam laughed, more at Micky's puzzled expression than the question: "No, we are not related. We found each other on the sea-front in Weymouth, last week. I was just passing through, so it was really very lucky that we spotted each other. Since Saturday we've been travelling together, looking for people, friends and relatives and so on."

"Have you now? Mmm." The young man said, continuing to look at Pip while he weighed this information. "But no luck so far – apart from the old dear in Cheltenham? Bit posh that place innit? Went there once with a job. So this is your home then?" he said, finally taking his eyes off the girl and waving his hand at the Drifter. "Nice bit of kit innit? Very nice."

"So where are you living at the moment – not in North London, I guess?" Adam asked, turning the focus back on Micky.

"No, no. My girl Tracy comes from these parts and we've been living in a flat in Brum, in the jewellery quarter. I've been working up this way for a while and we sort of got together."

"Is she still...?"

"Alive? I don't know, to be honest," and Micky gave a slightly embarrassed laugh. "We had a row last Thursday week and she stormed out and never came back." Adam's eyebrows raised, involuntarily. "Yeah, I know, you wouldn't believe it. She went the day before all the shit happened, pardon my French. I went to her mum's on the Saturday, when she still hadn't come back, but she wasn't there. Her mum hadn't seen her, she said. But the old lady was in a real bad way by then, so I didn't hang around. I didn't want what she'd got, if you know what I mean. I didn't know where else to look. Trace has got a friend in Wolverhampton somewhere, but I don't know her address. I've been up here few times, but haven't seen her, or her friend."

"I'm sorry to hear that," Adam said. "Have you got family somewhere?"

"Yeah, back in Edmonton. My mum was there. My old man moved on a few years back. My brother's out in Essex and my sister – she got married to a Canadian, so she's out there. Mum died early on, I think. All on her own, poor dear. I found her in her bed, so I suppose at least she was comfortable, you know. I went over to my brother's place, but there was no sign of life there." He gave a long sigh and blew out through his teeth. "It's all a bit shit, isn't it?"

"You could say that."

"Hey, you know, it would be good to put our heads together and hear your thoughts. I've got a few ideas, of course. I'd invite you back to my pad, but it's a bit grotty, to be honest. Be nice to have a look around this van of yours though."

"Absolutely," said Adam. "Come on in and let's have a coffee and a chat. Get out of the rain."

Adam opened the side door of the van and Micky climbed in. Adam could see his eyes flitting around, quickly taking everything in and looking like he was making mental notes.

"So you've got gas cooking, electric shower and a heater too, very nice," he said, indicating a vent above the table that Adam had not even spotted before.

"Sofa beds at the back, I see, and a sleeping platform above the cab. May I?" Without waiting for an answer, he was up the ladder and peering in between the curtains. "This must be your quarters young lady, by the looks of it."

Pip, who had stepped into the living quarters, looked uncomfortable and said nothing. Adam threw her glance, and raised his eyes heavenwards. The young man was now behind the wheel looking at the dials.

"So what's this then, two and half litre turbo diesel?"

"Yes, that's right."

"Plenty of torque there, I expect. But why diesel – didn't fancy a petrol engine then?"

"Well, the range available was not comprehensive..." Adam said, with a slight sardonic smile.

"No, I know what you mean mate. Still very nice, very nice. I could do with one of these maybe."

"You like the Quattro, then?" Adam asked.

"Yeah, very smooth it is. Picked her up yesterday, in Cradley Heath. I was using a Beamer before that, but I always wanted one of those."

"OK," said Adam, keen to get off the subject, "what's it going to be then – tea or coffee?"

"You got milk? Great – I'll have tea, a couple of sugars too if you've got some." Pip took the cups out of the cupboard and made it clear she wanted to do the domestics and leave Adam with the cocky cockney.

"You've brought your pets with too, I see, that's nice. You've got plenty of food in, by the looks of it."

"Yes, we've been getting by OK. But tell us about you, Michael, and what you have been doing since V Day."

"V Day? Is that what you call it? V for virus, I suppose. That's good! Listen, call me Micky – no-one calls me Michael, except for my mum, and she won't be doing that anymore, will she? Well, as I said I've been up here a couple of times looking for Tracey and I went down to London last... what was it now? Tuesday, I think. I didn't like it down there. Real nasty feel about the place."

Adam found this interesting and asked: "Why? What was going on there?"

"I don't know mate, it was more what *had* been going on, I think. I drove down into town proper to see what was happening, so to speak. I only got as far as Archway and the road was blocked. Someone had parked a couple of ten-tonners across the road. There was no-one about, but they hadn't got there by accident. I tried going round another way, taking the side streets, but there were cars all over the road and I couldn't get through. I gave up then. There was something fishy going on and I didn't like the feel of it. Edmonton was alright, just like around here really, – dead, completely dead. Not that that's good, but you know what I mean. It was like everywhere else, but down in town... something wasn't right."

"That's very strange isn't it? It sounds as if there are some people alive down there who don't want anyone else coming into their territory. You don't think it was military then?"

The young man shook his head, slowly. "Nah, don't think so. But who knows who might be there? I wouldn't be surprised if some of those posh Tory bastards haven't got an antidote to this virus, or whatever it is, and they're sitting in their offices in Whitehall feeling smug."

"I expect there are some politicians and civil servants alive down there, somewhere. But this was Archway, you say? That's a long way from Westminster."

"Yeah, that's what I thought. How about you – what's it been like where you've been?"

Adam gave a brief account of the towns they had visited and their experience in Bath town centre, then turned the subject back to Micky, who seemed happy to pick it up.

"Well, that's interesting. There was a bit of a racket coming from near the Bull Ring and that area on the Friday night and when I drove through a few days later I could see burned out cars and stuff – it was a bit of a mess. But it was all quiet round the Jewellery Quarter, like everyone had just curled up and died on the Friday night. But I *have* met a few people over the last week."

At this, Micky leaned forward over the table in a confidential manner.

"There was these two blokes, driving around in a top-o'-the-range four-by-four with the windows blacked out like they was the FBI or something, know what I mean? The driver was this big geezer. I say big and I mean, he was BIG! The other guy was dark, short, but really stocky, in a suit and dark glasses – yeah a suit! Would you believe it? They was really pally at first. The suited bloke – looked like he was the boss – shook my hand and said how wonderful it was to meet me and all that.

We sat in the back of his motor and he had a little drinks cabinet in there and he was offering me a whisky or something, but I don't drink and he seemed a bit off about that.

"So they asked me about what I'd been doing since V-day, as you call it. They gave it another name which I won't repeat here, in front of young and tender ears. I told them about my warehouse. Let me explain: before all this happened I was working on this big commercial contract, re-wiring this distribution warehouse out of town. It's huge this place. It's all temperature-controlled – they've got cold storage, frozen storage, dry goods, chemicals – you name it, they store it and ship it out all over the place to shops and supermarkets. And – listen to this – they've got all these big diesel generators that kick in if there's a power outage. Well, I got most of them shut off, but I kept a couple of them running, the one that operates the cold storage and the one that runs the freezers. So I have a nice little supply of fresh and frozen food for whenever I want it.

"Anyway they told me about this grand plan they had, to find lots of people and make this new *society* – yeah, that's what he called it – this new society and it would be great for me if I joined them. I would be really useful to them with my electrician's skills and all that and they would make me one of the *council*, you know like the people that would oversee everyone else. And he painted this rosy picture of life in their new society and how good it would be for me and why didn't I come with them, right now? And if I didn't, I was bound to regret it later. But the way he said that seemed to me that it wasn't so much that I would feel I had missed out, but that they would make sure my life was not going to be a bed of roses if I didn't join them – you know what I'm saying?"

Micky paused here to draw breath and he looked at them in turn, to see what effect this story was having. "Well, there was something about this geezer I did *not* like. Clearly what he was after was control of this distribution centre. He wasn't saying anything like that, but I could see his mind whirring. If he had that, then he would have a lot of leverage over people, wouldn't he? And muggins here had told him all about it. I'm wishing now that I hadn't. But I didn't tell them where it actually was. Something made me wary, so I said it was over near Fort Dunlop and when they probed, I gave them the address of a tyre centre down there, and I saw him making a note in his head like.

"Anyway, I made some excuses about things I had to do, find my sister, etc., but then as soon as I'd done that, I would come over to their place in Smallheath. They told me exactly where they were, and it would be good if I was there by seven that evening so I could meet some of the others. Well, I can tell you, I didn't go, oh no. I could see where that was going and I didn't like it, did not like it at all."

"So do you think they really have got a group of people together? It's only just over a week since the virus struck."

"Well I don't know. I mean, I ain't met anyone else and I've been driving all over the place. Probably all talk, you know what these types are like. But I wasn't about to go and find out, you know what I mean?"

Pip had made the drinks and put them on the table where the two men were sitting. She took hers over to the sofa seat at the back of the van.

"You not joining us dahlin'," Micky said to her, sounding genuinely hurt. "You've been very quiet. Yeah, I know – I don't stop talking. But I'm harmless really." And he laughed, a big, wide-open grin. "I haven't had anyone to prattle on to now for over a week. I've never been this quiet for so long, not since I had that lurgy last year."

Adam's eyes met Pips briefly, then, with a concerned face, he asked Micky, "Were you ill last year then?"

"Was I ill? Is the pope not a catholic? Oh, I was ill alright. They rushed me into the Queen Elizabeth and put loads of drips in me. It started with a sore throat and before I knew it I couldn't swallow and was having trouble breathing. Trace had called the ambulance, she was really scared, poor girl. They didn't know what was wrong with me at first, thought it was a type of virus, something they had never seen before. I only heard this afterwards, of course. I was completely out of it, in a coma. Yeah, I was in hospital for a couple of weeks, and off work for six. Cost me some money, that did. But I got over it in the end, with these drugs they gave me. Feel right as rain now, touch wood - just can't smell or taste anything much. Ironical isn't? – I've got a warehouse full of different foods, and they all taste the same to me."

"I was very ill last year too," said Pip.

"Was you? Really ill? But you're over it now then?" Pip nodded. Adam said nothing, and Micky carried on as before.

"Anyway, where was I?"

"You were telling us about your plans, what you were going to do, no?" said Adam.

"Was I? Well, I'm not quite sure. I was hoping I would find Trace, make it up with her, and then look for a house, not too far from the warehouse; somewhere I could rig up a generator and power some heat and light. We could make ourselves cosy there, have a nice little garden, a patio to have our drinks on in the summer – coke for me of course, but Trace likes her cocktails. Yeah, I know how it sounds. It's all a bit..." he searched for the word, "*superficial*, is that what I mean? But then what are we going to do, us survivors – go down the allotment and grow vegetables? Chop wood so we can sit round warming our hands on a campfire? Or be in Shorty's little empire, doing what he says he wants us to do. No, that's not me really. But I don't know... I don't suppose I'll ever find Trace now. But I might find another young lady somewhere, you never know. Ha, listen to me! I'm rambling again. So what's your grand plan then Adam, mate?"

Adam outlined briefly his idea of a community based on a farm, with sustainable long-term sources of food and fuel and water. How they would use the radio to connect with other people across the country, link up and maybe join them, or get them to join their community. He told Micky how they had come into town to look for the equipment.

"That's a good idea you have there, a very good idea. I know the place you need. I can take you there, if you like, and I can help you set it up. I had a mate in London that used to be into that stuff. He built himself a nice little set-up and we would tune into stations all over the world, talk to radio buffs in Japan, California... I helped him with some of the wiring. Yeah, I could help you with that."

"That would be really helpful," Adam said, "I'm ok with electrics, but not with wiring up radio systems. I'm more of an engineer."

"Engineer eh? What sort of engineering?"

Adam told him his background and how he was now more in management and a bit rusty on the practical side.

"Yes, but you *understand* engineering, that's a real talent. You know, you and me could make a really good team. Between us we could fix most things."

"I'm not sure about that," Adam laughed, "We can't fix bodies that get ill or don't work – that would be a more useful skill in the future, I suspect."

"Yeah, that's true mate, that's very true. Well, we'd better find ourselves a doctor then!"

The two men carried on talking about what people could usefully contribute in a small community, while Pip watched on and said nothing. Eventually the conversation came back to the here and now.

"You've got your eye on this farm in Dorset then," said Micky, "and you're going to go back there and move in with whoever you've managed to pick up on your travels. Mmm, can't say I fancy that. But you don't want to take any notice of me. I'm a towny, through and through, so the idea of living on a farm, surrounded by animals, and pig shit, does *not* appeal. I realise my food supply won't last forever. But it's going to take a good few years before I eat my way through that freezer, I can tell you." Micky chortled, "especially with my appetite!"

"I think you're wrong," said Pip suddenly. "That's a really selfish attitude, and very short-sighted." She blushed as the two men stared at her in surprise, as if they had forgotten she was there.

"Oh hello – you got a voice then?" Micky said. Then his manner softened. "Yeah, I know it sounds selfish, but I just don't see your way, Adam, I don't see your way working. You know how people argue and bicker and have different ways of doing things – it wouldn't work, or not for long anyway. At least I have the means to take care of myself and then if someone wants to work with me, welcome aboard!"

Pip sat back with her arms folded. It seemed that she hadn't taken to Micky.

"But how long will your diesel tank last?" Adam asked, "and what if your "Shorty" friend decides to muscle in on you? He won't be happy you sent him to the wrong place, will he? I think we *have* to think about the long term. We have survived this thing, this virus, and though there may not be many of us, there will be a few. We have a duty to keep mankind going. If we don't work together, then in a few years there won't be a human race anymore. No-one will be able to survive on his own for long in this world. What about the animals? Have you noticed the numbers of dogs running around?"

"The dogs? They don't bother me. I've had a few come at me but I keep them away with pepper spray. A blast of that in their eyes and they can't see, and they run off howling. I can give you a couple of cans if you like – they have them in the warehouse. But don't spray at these two – they won't be happy! As for the house, I've already planned that: put a high fence round the place, wire it up to the mains – that will keep the dogs out. Shorty and his bouncer mate, too."

"It sounds like a lonely life to me, like living in a prison," Pip said quietly. "It's not the life I would want."

"Well yeah, sure. I wouldn't want to live on my own, but Trace and me – we'd be alright there. Nice and cosy."

Adam stood up and stretched his back out, as if to emphasise what he was going to say next. "I have got to say, Micky, that I'm with Pip on this. Two people on their own against the world, I think that's doomed to failure. But I understand what you're saying as well. It won't be easy to get a group of people working together, it never is. I have been managing teams for a while and I know how frustrating it can be. There will be disagreements about the direction of the group, lots of discussion before decisions are made. But two people will be so vulnerable – if one gets sick or injured, or a baby comes along, then it becomes so hard for the other to cope. You said earlier, Micky, that you and I, with our complementary skills, would make a good team, and that's true. And with other people with other skills, we'll be an even better team. Why don't you come with us and give it a try for a while?"

Micky laughed, with a big grin on his face: "Yeah, good one mate! I can tell you have practised that little speech a few times in your job. It's nice and positive and it sounds like a good idea. The thing is though," and he paused here and scratched his chin theatrically, "that's all you have at the moment – an idea. Yes, OK, you've got a camper van with a small fridge, a farm you've seen that you want to live in, and a dream. I have all that, plus a warehouse full of food that I can run for years. And I know how to use a radio. It seems to me, old pal, that you need me more than I need you." And with that he leaned back in his seat and looked up at Adam with a look of *what do you say to that*?

Adam smiled and answered slowly, "I don't think it is a matter of who needs the other most. We two need you and you need us. But I take your point that at present we haven't established a base and we don't have other people on board."

"Hey, don't get me wrong mate. I know it's not a competition. I was just making a point. I think you are a couple of lovely people and I would really like to work with you. But why don't you stay here? I can tell that you're from somewhere not far from here. Am I right?" he addressed this to Pip. She nodded. "There you go then, this is your home country. You can find somewhere on the edge of the city where you can do what you are planning. I can help, I can get involved. But before that you need to find more people, and then I can help you set up your community. But do it up here – not down in Dorset."

For a moment the three of them were quiet, waiting for the other to speak next. Adam walked up and down the van while Micky sat back in his seat. After a minute or two, Adam spoke:

"OK, here's what I think. Firstly, you help us get these radios set up so we and you can keep in communication. Then we will continue our travels to find other people and to find a home, while you search for Tracy. We'll keep talking over the air waves and then you can decide later whether you want to come in with us and we can think about whether we want to be up here, or somewhere else. What do think, Micky, Pip?"

Micky sucked his cheeks and then gave a big sigh. "OK, Adam mate. I think that is a plan. That's a good plan." He looked at Adam deeply, as if musing over something bigger that he couldn't quite put his finger on. Then he got up out of his seat, looked over at Pip and said, "What do you think dahlin'? Is this a good plan?"

"I think it's a very good plan. There's so few of us around that we can't afford to not to work together."

"Exactly! Absolutely. Except for those two in the Range Rover, Shorty and his mate. I trust them as far as I can throw a piano, as my old mum used to say. OK, I'll take you to the radio shop, we shouldn't have any trouble getting in there, and then we can get this communication link set up. And on the way, you can come and see my warehouse – it's not far from here, and you can stock yourselves up with all sorts of goodies."

Chapter Thirty-One

Wholesale and Retail

Tuesday 7th May, Afternoon

Micky led the way to the warehouse in Wednesbury, his gleaming silver Audi weaving round parked cars, wandering dogs and blowing rubbish like a slalom racer. He would zoom ahead and then have to stop and wait for the camper van, which Adam was not able, or willing, to throw around with the same dexterity. He took them around the industrial estates until he pulled up outside a huge grey warehouse. Outside was a line of white trucks with the logo of Ransom Distribution emblazoned on their sides.

"I thought that said Random Distribution, for a moment," said Pip as they pulled up next to Micky's motor. "I think that's what our postman does."

Micky bounced over to the van and with a sweeping gesture announced, "Here we are – welcome to Micky's, the store that has everything you need, as long as you like it by the gross. Come on in. Better lock your van though – you never know who might come sniffing around, and I don't just mean dogs. He pulled a ring of keys from his pocket and opened the door to the office, which lay to one side of the building, and led them inside. "We need a torch in this area," he said, picking one up from inside the doorway and handing it to Adam. He pulled another one out of his pocket which he flicked on and shone into what was quite a large office. He locked the door behind them and then led them through and into the warehouse, via another door which he unlocked.

"It's like Fort Knox this place," said Adam.

"Well since I met our friends in the Range Rover I have decided to be a lot more careful. Follow me over to the grocery section." And with that he led them down long aisles of high steel shelving stacked high with boxes of soap powder, detergents, bathroom cleaners or soaps, shampoos and bath salts. There was enough stock here to fill several supermarkets, Adam thought. At the far side of the warehouse was the grocery section, shelves of tins, packets, jars and bottles, cling-wrapped or boxed in cardboard. And then there was the cold store, with its entrance shielded by heavy plastic curtaining, and next to that the frozen store. There was light here coming from a couple of floodlights which Micky had evidently rigged up. Adam heard the steady chug of a generator somewhere nearby.

"This is my little secret," Micky said proudly. "You can't get round the back of this building and that's where the generator is. You don't hear it at the front and you don't see any light coming out. No-one knows there's anybody in here. Come in and have a look." He parted the curtain and pointed the torch inside. The other two followed and stood just inside what looked like a vast cave, full of pallets of cold foods – butter, spread, yogurt, cold meat in packets, cheese – everything you would find in a fridge. "But this stuff won't keep forever in here, will it?" said Adam

"No, no, you're quite right there mate, it won't. But I thought about that already. What I am doing, bit by bit, is moving the stuff that I want out of here and into the freezer, where it will keep for a couple of years or more. So there it is, Micky's Cave. Have a look around and if there is anything you need, help yourself."

"Thank you," Adam said. "I don't think we're sure what we might need at the moment. What do you think Pip, is there anything you can think of that we need?"

Pip shook her head. "No, I don't think so. Except maybe some chocolates."

"Is that it?" said Micky, with a look of disappointed surprise, and then rubbing his hands like an excited shop salesman. "I bet there is something here we can tempt you with. You ought to have a look at the stuff they keep here: beer, wine, spirits, fags – they've got it all. Come and have a look."

"Well, if you've got some wine, I could always use a nice bottle and maybe some beer," Adam said. "The thing is Micky we don't have a lot of space in the van and we stocked up earlier today. But when we have established a base somewhere I am sure there will be things that we would need."

Adam helped himself to a case of a German lager that he liked and an expensive-looking bottle of wine while Pip found some luxury Belgian chocolates that her mum used to buy for a treat. Micky insisted on adding three more bottles of the wine and another box of chocolates and put them with the beer on a pallet.

"Don't carry it mate. Just stay there a mo." He walked off briskly and came back shortly driving a forklift truck. He scooped up the pallet, waved them to follow him and he took it down the warehouse to the large steel, roller-shutter door at the front.

"You can tell he's done that before," Adam said.

"He just wants to show off," Pip responded, "he loves showing off."

Micky walked back to meet them. "No point in straining yourself mate, let the machines do the lifting. Right, we'll go to the door and check the coast is clear and you can bring your van over to the door." Adam started to protest that he could carry the beer, but Micky waved him away. They followed him back across the office to the door they came in through. Micky unlocked it and peeped out:

"Aye, aye – the wolves are here. Don't go out, just wait there a minute." He disappeared back into the warehouse and came back a few minutes later with an armful of canisters and gave them to Pip.

"Here darling you take these will you? They're for you." He pulled another canister out of his pocket, leaned through the gap in the slightly opened door and sprayed outside. There was a howl of pain and a yelping noise. Micky stepped outside.

"You want some too?" they heard him say, and then there was more yelping.

"OK, you can come out now – the coast is clear."

Adam stepped outside and saw a pair of dogs running off down the yard, tails between their legs. "Were they going to attack you?" Adam asked.

"I wasn't going to wait to find out. The other day there were six of them, all barking and snarling at me. Hopefully those two will tell their mates not to bother."

"Right, bring your van over and I'll get the beer out to you," he said breezily and walked back into the building.

"Look at all this pepper spray," Pip said, "We'll never need all that."

"That's alright, "said Adam, "it will make him happy. And we can give some to anyone else we meet."

Micky rolled up the shutter and came outside with the beer. "Right, so where are you two going to head for now then?"

"The radio shop...?"

"Oh struth yes! I had forgotten for a moment. Right, let me lock this place up and I'll take you down to the radio shack. It's right in town – Brum that is – and it's down the back streets so keep your eyes peeled. If you see anyone dodgy, best not to stop."

Adam turned the van around and they waited for Micky to come out.

"He's so proud of his Aladdin's Cave, isn't he? Like a big kid," Pip said.

"Like you in the camper van place...?"

"Well, that's different. I *am* a kid. It's just that I'm a small one. And did you see how he chucked that can out of his window when we were driving here?"

"I know you don't like him much, but he would be a useful person to have on board. He's clever with his hands."

"Yes, but he is such a..." Pip groped for the word, "such a dork!"

Adam laughed. "He is a bit! But you know, I think he's alright underneath."

A little later they were driving through West Bromwich and over the motorway, following Micky's Audi, the throaty roar of its engine drowning out the music blasting from the windows every time it accelerated. When they passed the West Bromwich Albion football ground Pip suddenly exclaimed, "I've been there! Thommo took me to see a game there when I was a little girl. I think it was a cup game or something."

"That must have been exciting for you."

"I think I was a bit scared at first. But Thommo was with his mates and they made a fuss of me and gave me lots of sweets, and that's about all I remember, that and the noise of the crowd."

As they got into the centre of Birmingham there were a lot more obstacles to be negotiated in the roads, and a couple of times they had to squeeze through narrow gaps between cars and bollards or other vehicles. Once or twice Micky turned off down a side street and later seemed to be doubling back on himself. Adam guessed he was avoiding some known blockages in the road. They went right through the city centre, past the Bullring and the rail station. There were noticeably more dogs about here, and burned-out cars, as Micky had said. He also saw bodies, or at least he guessed that's what they were – Adam did not want to think what sort of state they would be in by now, with animals at them as well. They came into Digbeth and Adam saw the Audi turn off down a side street and then pull up in front of a double-fronted shop in a tall red-brick building. The sign over the shop proclaimed "Radio Shack, The Midlands Premier Communication Equipment Supplier". Adam noted that the windows were covered with steel mesh and the door looked well secured.

Micky jumped out of his car, and flicked a cigarette butt across the road, where it lay smouldering. Adam saw Pip give a look of distaste, and he smiled.

"This place has everything we'll need," said Micky. "Do you reckon you can get us in there?"

"I'll give it a go." Adam said and he went to get his tools.

"You might want to use these," said Micky, getting a pair of heavy-duty bolt cutters out of his car. "Lets' not bother with the door," he said, "much easier through the window." Between them they quickly had the mesh off one of the windows and the window glass out. Micky climbed in, picking his way through the display radios that were now sprinkled with glass. Adam followed him and shone his torch around the gloomy shop and he saw that it was absolutely full of equipment, stacked on shelves, piled on the floor, boxes, wire, aerials. "I don't think I would know where to start looking here."

"There's loads of kit here alright," said Micky, "but I know what I'm looking for to get us started. Right then," and he began looking through the boxes, quickly turning them over, checking the models and moving through the stock. Adam followed him as he picked his way through a bewildering array of gadgets.

After a while Micky had assembled a small collection of boxes near the window, in two piles.

"OK, Adam mate, this is what you need. I've put together a nice little starter kit which you should be able to assemble. Of course, normally you'd learn about all this stuff through a club and talking to old hands, but you're going to have to teach yourself. There are some books and magazines over by the counter, so we will find you some reading material in a minute. But this is the kit you'll need to do what you want."

Micky proceeded to talk him through what he had assembled – transceiver, amplifier, AC/DC power supply, microphone, headset, antenna and various cables. He had given him a static transceiver but suggested he use the portable one to start with, while they were still travelling. Then he went to the counter, rifled through the publications and fished out a beginner's guidebook and a couple of magazines.

"If you're going to teach yourself how to be a radio operator, these books will help. But you're a smart guy and you'll soon pick it up. When you have got it all set up, just spend some time tuning into different frequencies to start with and listen and see what you can pick up. Make a note of any you find, so you can pull them up again."

"So where will I find you, so we can keep in touch?" asked Adam.

"OK, make a note of this. I will broadcast every night at, let's say, 20.00 hours on this frequency. I'll use the handle "Metal Micky". It's what they used to call me at work cos I always wore metal-capped work boots. I'd seen a few toes get crushed and I wanted to keep all my pinkies intact, know what I mean? Let's think of a name for you. Now... how about Adam's Apple, or what was your surname? Oh yes, Fisher. You could be Fisherman's Friend. Or maybe not, people might think you was the coastguard or something." Micky chortled away at this.

"How about Adamantine?" Pip called across the shop, having just clambered in to see what they were doing. "Adamantine is a really hard metal."

"Yeah," said Micky, "I like that. *Adamantine*. Really hard eh?"

They got the gear out of the shop and into their respective vehicles, and the two men stood together in the road facing each other as if preparing for a farewell speech.

"Thanks for what you did there Micky, that was a big help, it really was."

"You're welcome, Adam mate. So where are you heading off to now then?"

"We're going to go back south, but first we are going to visit Bournville. There are some people there that Pip wants to look for."

"Bournville, I don't know that part. Oh, wait a minute. That's where the chocolate factory is right? When did you leave there dahlin'?"

"About four years ago. My parents bought a guest house in Weymouth."

"Well Weymouth's a nice spot to live. But I suppose you left some friends behind."

"Yes, a few," Pip said.

"So, where are you going now Micky?" Adam asked.

"I'm off to Leicester. There's a bird there I used to know, just a friend like. I thought I'd just see if she made it through, but I'm not hopeful. Got to keep looking though, haven't we? So listen you two, you look after yourselves now and keep your eyes open. I hope you find some people down your way and you get your place together. You'll be able to tell me all about it when we link up on the radio." Micky stepped forward and grabbed Adam by the arms and said, "And you look after that young lady, alright?"

"I'll try." said Adam

"And you, young Pip," Micky said, bowing low, "you take care of yourself now dahlin'."

Pip smiled shyly and mumbled something to the effect that she would. Then Micky jumped into his car and was away down the road, music blaring.

Adam and Pip looked at each other and Adam said, "Well, that was interesting, wasn't it? Adamantine eh – where did that one come from? Shall we go?"

The dogs were very pleased when they got back in the van, Bonzo jumped up on Pip's lap and was looking out of the open window to see if they were finally going somewhere that a dog might find interesting.

"I think these two might need a walk before long," Pip said.

"OK. We'll see if we can find a park somewhere on our way to Bournville. This is your home turf Pip, so you can navigate."

"The last time Nic & I went from the town centre to Bournville, we went on the number 63 bus. I don't know how to do it by car."

"Well you have the road atlas," said Adam, smiling at her, teacher-like.

Pip poked her tongue out at him. "OK, but don't blame me if we end up in Solihull or somewhere."

Chapter Thirty-Two

Dark Chocolate

Tuesday 7th May, Afternoon

"Well?" said Adam as they got back to the high street, "which way are we turning?"

Pip had her head in the road atlas. "According to the map it looks like we go down the A38, but on the bus we used to go through Edgbaston. Maybe we should go back to the Bullring and follow the signs."

"I think we are smarter than that. That way takes us south and I'm sure we can get to Edgbaston that way."

"OK, who did you say was navigating?" she said, and threw the map book on the floor.

"Alright," said Adam laughing, "you are quite right. So we turn round and go back to the Bullring then?"

"No, actually, I think you're right. Keep going."

"Sure?"

"Yes, but I reserve the right to change my mind."

"Absolutely! You have every right. And I have every right to be smug if I turn out to be right."

"I think the bus does come this way," said Pip, a bit further down the road when they came to a major junction. "And I think there's a park just down here on the left."

And there was. Adam pulled up by a gateway and turned the engine off. "Well boys, do you a fancy a walk?" Bonzo was ready to jump straight out of the open window and the old dog was sitting up looking at the door, waiting for it to open.

Pip waved her can of pepper spray. "I've got *my* wheel brace," she said.

Adam grabbed a couple of apples from the cupboard and they ate them as they walked across the grass and the dogs chased each other around.

"Do you think Micky would ever come and join us if we set up a community somewhere?" Pip asked.

"I think he might want to be involved, but only on his terms," Adam said. "He would probably dip in and out. I think he's the restless sort. You didn't like him, did you?"

"No, not really. I think he's too cocky and full of himself. He's too interested in *him* to want to help make something together with other people."

"Do you think so? I think he might surprise us. Give him time."

Pip picked up the stick that Bonzo had dropped at her feet and threw it into the bushes. He raced off into the shrubbery to look for it. "I think he likes being a wheeler-dealer," she said.

"Maybe. But once he gets tired of being on his own and realises that there is no market for him to play, he might see that what we are proposing makes sense."

Bonzo came back with a different stick and dropped it at Pip's feet again.

"Your turn."

Adam took the stick and hurled it high. It came down some distance away by a large rhododendron bush. Bonzo chased it down and then stopped. His hackles went up and he started barking.

"Looks like he's found something," Adam said, when the dog carried on barking insistently. "Shall we go and see what he's got?"

They walked over to where the dog was and Pip said, "Ugh, what's that? Is that someone's leg?"

A limb was sticking out from the bush. Adam indicated to Pip to stay there while he walked over to have a closer look. He could see that attached to the limb, under the foliage, was a naked torso and that the limb was, in fact, an arm, but without a hand. He looked from the other side and could make out that the other arm was attached, but that the legs were missing completely, as was the head. Where the neck had been severed he could see that there was congealed blood. The torso was otherwise unmarked and it seemed to him that the body had not been there that long.

Adam grabbed Bonzo by the collar and hauled him away. "Come on, let's go," he said.

"What was that?" Pip said, looking rather pale.

"It was a body, a man. Looks like he met a nasty end, and in the last couple of days, I'd say."

"Oh, God. Do you think he was murdered?"

"Well it wasn't dogs that did that to him, that's for sure. Someone didn't like him, and not only that... they didn't want anyone to know who the man was."

"You mean... he wasn't all there?"

"You don't really want to know Pip."

"But why would someone want to chop a body up and hide it?"

"I don't know. It doesn't make any sense at all."

"So, someone has survived the virus and then, for some reason, needed to kill one of the very few other people who survived."

"It looks like it. Micky had a bad feeling about the pair in the Range Rover – maybe it's something to do with them. I guess we will get to find out that not all the people who survived V Day are the sort of people we want to get to know."

"That is so sad. Actually, that's a horrible thought."

"But you know Pip, I don't think there'll be many like that. I am sure that most people will be like us. They'll want and need human company. But we always need to be on our guard."

***

Back in the van they talked about Pip's life in Bournville. "Was it good, growing up there?" Adam asked.

"I think so, most of the time. I remember it was a shock when I realised that mum and Thommo were not my real parents."

"How old were you then?"

"I can't remember exactly. I just remember waking up in the night once and thinking: '*I have a real mum and dad somewhere, far away in India*'. I remember crying a lot about that time. I am sure they broke it to me gently and maybe it was much later that it really sank in. But I got over it and got used to the idea that I was a different colour to them. It didn't matter when I was little because there were lots of Asian kids in the school. But when I got to the last year of primary school some of the kids picked up on the fact that my parents were white and they could be quite horrible about it."

"How about the Asian kids – did they give you a hard time too?"

"No, not really, maybe one or two. When I was younger, I never thought about my colour really. My best friend was Nic, and it didn't seem to bother her at all."

"Pip, you aren't pinning your hopes on finding an old friend alive in Bourneville, are you?"

"No. I know that's pretty unlikely," she said, "but as we're in Birmingham I would just like to drive around the area again, just to remind myself. I'll probably never come back up here again."

"Where do you want to go first then?" asked Adam when they came to the Bournbrook Inn.

"Take the next right. That'll take us past the chocolate factory and then I'll show you where I grew up. They drove past the factory, and further down the road there were playing fields and on one side an ornate brick building with high gables in a mock Tudor style.

"Is that a...?"

"Yes, that's the cricket pavilion," said Pip. "But you'd never have guessed. Nic's cousin Jeff used to play cricket on that pitch. Her dad took us to watch him play once."

"Wow. A bit better than our school sports changing rooms. It's very grand."

They got to the end of the road and Pip said, "Turn left here. It's just down here a way."

Adam drove slowly along the road and when they came up to a turning on the right she pointed: "Go there." And as they pulled into the road, "Stop! That was where we lived, above that café." Adam stopped the van and looked at where Pip was pointing. There was a row of small shops in a pre-war brick building, all single-fronted with plate glass windows and the door to the side, and above the shop, a single bay window. In one was a small café called Ronnie's. Adam could see tables and a counter at the back.

"It was called St Agnes Café, when we had it, same as the road. I think Ronnie might be the guy that bought it from us. Thommo used to run the café and mum worked in the chocolate factory, in the office. We lived above. That was their room at the front and I had the little one at the back. It seems like a long time ago now."

"It was only a few years ago you left, I thought?" said Adam.

"Yes, but it seems like a long time to me. Look at it now – it could do with a coat of paint. It was lovely when we had it. Thommo loved the business, all the friends he made there, you know, all the regulars. There was a Welshman who taught at the secondary school and he and Thommo would talk for hours about life in the valleys. The local vicar came in quite often, I remember. I used to like helping out when I wasn't at school. I probably just got in the way, but Thommo didn't mind. Some of the men who came in from the factory would make a fuss of me and sometimes they gave me chocolates."

"Ah. So you've been missing the chocolates have you? That's why you got some from Micky!"

"Well the lady loves..." she said, grinning.

"Why did your parents move to Weymouth if they were so happy here?"

"They didn't own the shop or the flat and I think the lease was coming up for renewal or something. Mum wanted somewhere bigger and to be near the sea, so they found this guest-house business for sale."

"Did your mum help out at all in the café?"

"Not often. She was quite shy really. She would put a flower in the little vases on the tables and she made some tablecloths, but she wouldn't help in the café if she could help it. She'd say to Thommo, *I've got my job, this is yours. I don't ask you to help me do my job.*"

"Was it the same at the guesthouse?"

"She'd help change the beds and she would do the books, but she hated having guests in the house. I don't think she ever forgave Thommo for taking her there. I felt the same about it for a while, but I never blamed Thommo like she did."

"But I thought it was your mum's idea to move by the sea?"

"Yes, it was. But that's what she was like. She would want something and when it didn't turn out as expected she would blame everyone else. I think she liked the idea of this grand three-story house by the seaside and thought that maybe she would be able to cope with having guests. But when it came to it, she found she hated it."

"But at least you have nice memories of your time here?"

"Yes, mostly. It is strange to see it now, with no-one about."

She went quiet so after a minute Adam said, "shall we go? Do you want to see anywhere else?"

"Let's go down to the end and I can show your where Nic lived, and my schools."

They drove down to the end of St Agnes Road, where they turned left. There was a park opposite. The next road on the left was where Nic had lived, and Adam stopped the van. Pip was looking down the road.

"See where that blue van is parked – that was their house there. Their garden almost backed onto ours."

"Do you want to go down there?" Adam asked. Pip shook her head. "No, it's alright. I just wanted to see the road really." Adam carried on driving and Pip indicated where they had gone to the local primary school. "It was a Catholic school, which was funny cos my folks were methodists. And down here is the girls' secondary school where I went for a year before we moved to Weymouth."

Adam carried on slowly down the road. "Where next?"

"I don't know," Pip said, "but I don't think I want to stay around here. There's no-one here and it just seems sad."

Adam let the van come to a stop and picked up the road atlas. "Shall we head south then? Find somewhere to stop for the night and then we can make our plans."

"Sounds good. What's on the menu tonight? All we had was an apple, and I threw mine away after I saw that body."

Chapter Thirty-Three

The Fisherman

Tuesday 7th May, Evening

Adam followed the road they were on and when they got to Kings Norton, he looked at the map again. "I thought we could go into the Cotswolds and find somewhere to stop there. I want to try and put the radio together. Then tomorrow perhaps go back to Cheltenham and pay a visit to Gwendoline. I think we can get across to that road, do you see, the A435?" he said, indicating to Pip where they were. "That will take us to Redditch and Alcester and from there we can drive south to Cheltenham."

"OK. Do you want me to navigate then?" Pip said.

"Yes please, just until you start to want to throw up."

"Hmmm. I'll make sure it comes your way if I do. Right, I think you need to carry on down past the station to the park and then if we go..." Pip checked her hands, "left, that road should take us across to Hollywood. Always wanted to see the big stars."

"So is that east or west then?"

"Er... east, I think. Yes, east."

They drove down through Kings Norton and as the road crossed what appeared to be a bridge, Pip suddenly shouted, "Stop! I've just seen someone. Look, behind us, over there."

Adam turned to look and sure enough there was a small boy with a fishing rod in his hand. He was waving his other arm and running towards the van. Adam stopped the van and Pip immediately jumped out and went to meet the boy. As he came close, she squatted down in the road and Adam was amazed to see the boy drop his rod and run straight into her arms. She hugged him close and stroked his head and he clung to her, his arms around her neck. Adam got out of the van and walked slowly over but kept his distance. Somehow, he felt that he should not disturb them. Pip and the boy remained like that for a full three minutes and Adam saw the boy's shoulders shaking with sobs. Adam felt a wave of emotion come over him too, tears welling in his own eyes.

After a while Pip pulled back from the boy enough to look in his face.

"Hello. I'm Pip. What's your name?" The boy just looked blankly and then buried himself in her arms again. Eventually Pip managed to stand up, holding the boy's hand. Adam saw his face, red with crying and smudged with dirt. His jumper was grubby and torn, he had a hole in the knee of his trousers and his trainers were filthy. His face looked gaunt and he seemed to have a deep frown, almost a scowl. Adam guessed he was about seven or eight, but it was hard to be sure.

"What's your name?" Pip asked again, gently.

The boy sniffed and said, in a tiny voice, "My name is Matthew Simm and I live at number 28 Prestcott Road."

"And where's that then?" Pip asked. The boy pointed back down the road.

"My name is Pip and this man is called Adam. We come from Weymouth."

"My mum's dead," said the boy, through his sobs. "so's my dad and my brother and my sisters."

"That's very sad," said Pip. "My mum and dad are dead too."

"And my aunty Shelly. And I think our dog is dead too."

"I'm really sorry. You must have been very lonely on your own. What have you been doing then?"

"I've been fishing. In the canal. I'm not supposed to go there, but Mum don't know."

"And did you catch anything?"

"No. But I caught a fish the other day and I tried to make a fire in the barbecue to cook it on but I couldn't get the fire to light properly and I was so hungry I ate a bit of the fish and then I was sick, so I threw the fish away."

"Oh, you poor thing said Pip." She gave him another hug and he started crying again.

"Hey Matthew, would you like a biscuit?" Adam asked.

The boy did not look up, but nodded his head.

"And a glass of milk?"

More nodding.

"Ok then. I'll go and get that sorted. Perhaps Pip can bring you into our nice van. What do you think Pip?"

"That's a very good idea, isn't it Matthew. Are you coming?" The boy nodded again and Pip led him gently over to the van, where Adam had already opened the side door. He let Pip take the boy in and he followed. The boy smelled strongly of dirt, sweat and urine. It was quite overpowering, but somehow Pip was able to ignore it. The dogs were very interested in the boy and spent a long time sniffing him all over. He did not seem afraid and he stroked their heads.

"You sit down there Matthew," Pip said, steering him into the seat at the table.

"You can call me Matty," the boy said, "everyone calls me that."

"Right, Matty then. That's a nice name."

"It's my grandad's name. Can I have my milk now?"

"Of course, "said Adam, who already had it poured, and he passed the cup to the boy. He took it and drank it down in one draught. "Would you like some more?" The boy nodded, and it went the same way.

"Can I have that biscuit now?" the boy asked, looking at Adam for the first time.

Adam gave him some biscuits and he ate them hungrily and then looked around for something to wash them down. Adam filled up his mug for the third time.

"You need to take that steady Matty, or you will make yourself sick." The boy looked up at him and then took a big gulp, but did not drink it all. Pip went to offer him a banana, but Adam waved her back.

"I think he needs to take it slowly. I don't expect his stomach is used to a lot of food." He stood leaning against the cupboard and looking over at the young lad, who was clearly traumatised and physically in a bad way.

"Matty, have you been living in your house since your family died?" Adam asked

The lad looked down at the table, unsure of what his answer ought to be. "I've been living in the shed," he said quietly.

"That can't have been very comfortable"

"I went there cos it wasn't very nice in the house."

"No, I'm sure it wasn't."

"I was scared," the boy said"I never saw a dead person before." He started sobbing again and Pip reached over and held his hand.

"It must have been very frightening for you. But wasn't it frightening in the shed too?"

"Yes," the boy said between sobs.

"And a bit dark?"

"I had a torch. And there was an oil lamp of my grandad's I lit that every night. It ran out two nights ago."

"That was clever of you. What did you do when it ran out?"

"It was dark everywhere and I sort of got used to it. Tiggy used to come in and curl up next to me."

"Who's Tiggy?" Pip asked

"Mrs Tompkin's cat, from next door."

"Oh, that was nice for you."

"Yes, cos I could hear owls and I don't like them, but I knew that Tiggy would chase them off."

"Why don't you like owls then?"

"Cos they have them in scary movies and they're bad, aren't they? I don't like animals, 'cept for Tiggy and Thor."

"Who was Thor – your dog?"

Matty nodded. "He stayed with me and then one day I found him lying on the ground. He had been sick. I think he was poisoned."

"Oh, that's really sad. You poor thing."

"What have you been eating then Matty?" Adam asked. "Did you have any water?"

"No. The water stopped working when the lights went out. I drank pop and milk but the milk went bad. I ate things from the fridge, and it started to smell in there. So I got some tins and took them out to the shed. Beans and meat and stuff. When they ran out I went into Mrs Tompkins kitchen and got some food from her kitchen, but I stopped going in there because of the smell. I've been into some other houses and got stuff but then I got too scared to do that."

"When did you last eat something?"

"I think it was the day before yesterday, I can't remember. Can I have that banana now?"

"Of course," Adam said and passed one over to the boy, who wolfed it down.

"Matty, would you like to stay with us tonight?"

The boy carried on eating and looked down at the table.

"Or would you rather go back to your shed?" he said, at which the boy shook his head vigorously. "You can stay with us if you want to."

The boy looked up, but not at Adam. He looked around the van slowly and then said, "It's a nice van. Do you live in it?"

"Yes, we do," Pip answered. "We have been living in it while we drive around the country looking for people."

"Have you found anybody?"

"Yes, we found a lovely old lady and today we met a man called Micky. He was driving a car in Wolverhampton."

The boy looked blankly at Pip for a moment and then said, "I heard a car go down this road one day. I was in the shed. I ran down our road but when I got there it had gone. Then one night I thought I heard a helicopter going over."

"When was that Matty?" Adam chipped in.

"I don't know," the boy said quietly, looking at his hands. "It was Saturday, I think."

"Last Saturday, or the one before?"

"I don't know. I can't remember. I think I heard it." The lad looked uncomfortable.

"Don't worry, it doesn't matter when it was," Pip said, putting her hand on his arm.

Adam came to the table and squatted down next to the boy. "I have a suggestion. Why don't you have a shower in our little bathroom and we'll find you some clean clothes? Pip will help you. Then I can make us all a nice meal and you can have dinner with us. How does that sound?"

Matty thought hard about this and then asked, "Will the water be hot?"

"Yes," said Pip, "It's lovely and hot. You will really like it. I'll show you how to work it. Adam, are we going to stop here?"

"I think it would be better if we go down the road a little way, get out of the town a bit."

"Isn't that a good idea Matty? You can sit in the front with me."

"OK," said the boy.

Adam drove them down the road for half a mile and then took a right into a lane which led them away from the houses and into the countryside. He pulled up by a gateway into a grassy field where there were no animals. They all got out of the van and the dogs ran off into the field.

"What are the dogs' names?" Matty asked as he watched the dogs racing around. Pip told him.

"They're funny names," he said.

"Are they? I have heard stranger names than that," Pip said, "and now I think we should get you ready for your shower."

They got things ready and Adam said quietly to Pip over the boy's head,

"Do you think you might have some clothes he could wear? Mine would be far too large."

Pip thought for a moment. "I'll have to see what I've got. I have some jogging pants, I think and a t-shirt."

"I'm not wearing girl's pants," the boy said suddenly. "Why can't I wear my own clothes?"

Adam and Pip looked at each other, then Pip answered: "your clothes are all torn and dirty. We don't have a washing machine, so we are going to find you some other clothes. But don't worry, no-one's going to see you in them."

Matty let Pip help him out of his clothes, which she put outside the shower room door. Adam heard the shower running and then he heard the boy ask Pip if she would help him. He heard them talking together and wondered if she had ever had to bathe a child before – she did not have a sibling. Matty seemed to be happy to let Pip wash him and he heard them laughing about something. After a while the shower stopped and she brought him out, wrapped in a towel, and sat him on the sofa bed while she went up the ladder to find him something to wear. Adam looked at the boy's skinny arms and legs and saw some sores.

"We will have to put some cream on those," he said.

The boy shrank away from him and didn't look happy at the prospect.

"Pip can help you," Adam went on. "If we don't treat them, you will get very sick, and you don't want that, do you?"

Matty shook his head. Pip came back with some clothes and said to Adam,

"I might need some help with that. I'm a bit squeamish."

In the end Matty let Adam apply the cream and some plasters, while Pip held him and tried to distract him with stories of all dogs they had seen. When his sores were all treated and covered up, Pip helped him into the clothes she had brought down for him. She put him in pyjama bottoms and a t-shirt, which she thought he could sleep in comfortably as well, and although they had to roll up the legs of the pyjamas, he didn't look totally out of place in her things. He sat quietly on the sofa, patting Bonzo, who was glad of the attention, and watching Adam and Pip prepare a meal.

"Where is he going to sleep?" Pip asked Adam.

"He looks like he might drop off at any minute, right there on the sofa. I was thinking we could make him up a bed there with the spare blankets and he would have the dogs for company."

"And he can have their whining in the morning to wake him up, like I get every day."

"Is that what they do?" said Adam.

"Yes, every morning. It's Bonzo – he wants Boyo to play with him and Boyo wants to sleep, like me."

"That's why I like the tent!" said Adam, laughing.

They sat down to their supper at the table and Adam and Pip tucked in hungrily, but, as suspected, Matty only ate a little before he started to nod off. He picked the boy up and laid him down on the sofa at the back of the van and covered him with a thick blanket. Matty was sound asleep as soon as his head went down.

"Poor lad. He probably has not had a proper night's sleep since it all started."

"He must have been so scared," said Pip. "Can you imagine, at that age, what it must have been like?"

"Yes. Well, no, I can't really. It will take a long time to wipe those memories from his mind. Will you be alright with him here tonight, or do you want me to sleep in the van as well?"

"I think we'll be alright. I'll leave a light on for him."

"Good idea. But use a torch, can't risk flattening the battery. We don't want to get stranded here."

After supper Adam put the tent up and got his bed ready. The grass was still very damp from the rain, but the sky had cleared, and it was getting chilly. He took the dogs for a last walk and then sat in the van with Pip, drinking a can of beer from Micky's pack. She was reading a novel and picking at the chocolates while he read through the radio instruction manual. He had already decided he would leave setting it up until tomorrow but tonight he could get an understanding of the components and the basics of radio broadcasting.

It wasn't long before he started to feel drowsy and he stood up to go to bed. Matty was snoring quietly on the sofa, and Pip was reading by torchlight.

"Tomorrow, we need to check your arm." Adam said, "You haven't mentioned your arm hurting, has it been OK?"

"I haven't noticed it actually."

"Well we need to have a look in the morning and maybe we can remove the dressing. I think we need to get some more first-aid stuff, and antibiotics and antihistamines. We need to find a pharmacy."

"I am sure we will find one on our journey," said Pip.

"And," said Adam, "we need to fill up with diesel."

"It will be a busy day tomorrow, by the sounds of it."

"So better get some rest then," Adam said. "I'll see you in the morning, co-driver. Goodnight boys – there are three of you now."

Chapter Thirty-Four

The Road to Broadway

Wednesday 8th May, Morning

Adam woke feeling cold and stiff. In the night his sleep mat felt too thin and the cold and damp seemed to seep up from the ground. He became aware of noises in the van: Bonzo whining and barking and the sound of a young boy's voice. That brought back a memory of Oscar running up and down the stairs very early one morning. Adam could hear him counting the stairs as he ran up and down. "Oscar!" he had called out, "What are you doing, it's only six o'clock?" Oscar came into the room, put his hands on his hips as if to say *Do I have to spell it out for you?* "Daddy, I'm practising for my running race."

He reached for his watch – it said six-thirty. He groaned to himself and tried turning over and putting his head under the pillow. He hoped Pip was awake, but he knew that it was unfair to expect her to deal with Matty. At that moment he heard the van door opening and then the dogs snuffling at his tent flap.

"OK, OK. Hello boys. Yes, I am awake now." He looked out of the tent and saw Matty jump down from the van and relieve himself on the grass. Adam got dressed and clambered out of the tent. Matty was running after the dogs but he stopped when he saw Adam.

"Hello Matty, how are you today?"

Matty said nothing.

"I don't bite, you know," Adam said. "Are you hungry?"

Matty nodded.

"Well let's go and see what we can find, then. Would you like some milk?" The boy nodded again. "You could say, yes please."

"Yes please." The boy said, obediently.

They went into the van and Adam saw that Pip's curtains were closed.

"Let's be very quiet because I think Pip might be asleep."

A voice came from aloft: "I wish I was."

"Oh well, we are all awake now," Adam said. "Matty, did you sleep well last night? I expect you were tired." Matty looked at him blankly and Adam wondered whether that might be a question he didn't get asked very often.

Pip came down the ladder in her pyjamas looking tired and grumpy and went into the shower room. She poked her head out and said, "Can I have a shower?" And when Adam said there might not be enough hot water, she made her disappointment quite clear. Adam poured the boy a glass of milk, which he drank down in great gulps and banged his glass down on the table.

"Can I have a banana?" he asked.

"Well we were going to have some breakfast a bit later, but if you are hungry now, you can have one. Are you?"

The boy nodded.

"Is that '*yes please*'?"

More nodding. Adam laughed and gave him a banana. The boy wolfed it down and asked for another. He made a big bowl of cereal and put that in front of him. Matty got stuck in and munched away happily.

Adam made himself a strong coffee and sat down opposite Matty at the table. When Pip had been upstairs and come down again, now dressed, Adam said, with a slightly arched eye-brow, "Bad night?"

"You could say that!" she said. "This one was crying in the night and he had wet the bed."

"I thought I could smell something, but I assumed it was the dogs. What did you do?"

"I came down and cleaned him up, as best I could, and I turned the mattress upside-down. I didn't know what else to do at two in the morning."

"I'm sorry you had to deal with that. If I had known, I would have come and helped."

"And then he asked if he could sleep in my bed and he looked so sorry for himself, I couldn't say no. So he spent the rest of the night with me, wriggling and snoring."

"I didn't mean to snore. I can't help it," said the boy, starting to cry.

"Hey, I'm sorry Matty," said Pip, going over to him and giving him a hug. "It's alright. Everyone snores. I snore. Adam snores like a bull elephant on heat, as Thommo would say."

The boy stopped crying and looked at her curiously.

"Like an elephant?"

"Yes. Like this," And Pip made an impression of an elephant's trumpet and Adam laughed. Matty looked over at Adam, then back to Pip and then, as if checking it was OK to, he laughed as well. It was a strange laugh, a bit like someone who had never heard a laugh before, trying to copy the sound.

Pip made some tea for herself and sat down at the table next to the boy.

"Can I have some?" he said.

"Some tea?" Matty nodded. "OK then." And she poured some of her tea into another cup and added extra milk. Matty blew on it and sipped it carefully.

"It's not very hot," he said.

"You shouldn't have it very hot, it's not good for you."

"When my dad makes it, it's really hot. He spilled some on me one day and I got burned."

"Really. That's bad. Were you alright?"

"I had to go to the doctor and he put special cream on it."

"Oh, poor you. I expect your father was upset."

"He was really angry. I think that's why he spilled the tea on me."

Pip and Adam shared a glance and Adam cut in:

"Matty, how would you like to go and see a really old village that looks like something out of the olden days?"

"Alright," the boy said, looking down at his tea. "What's olding days?"

Adam thought for a moment. "Have you ever seen Robin Hood on the television?" The boy looked blank. "Or Oliver Twist?" "The Three Musketeers?" There was still no hint of recognition from the boy, but he could see Pip stifling a giggle.

"OK. It's a little town with these lovely big old houses, and quaint cottages and it's very pretty. You'll like it."

"Well *I'm* intrigued," said Pip, "where is this olding place?"

"It's called Broadway."

"Broadway? Yesterday it was Hollywood and today it's Broadway. Wow – West End tomorrow?"

Adam laughed, "Yes, very good."

"Is it like going to the fair?" said the boy, and Pip smiled.

"I tell you what," Adam said, resignedly, "why don't we go there and you can decide for yourselves what it is and whether you like it. Alright?"

"Alright. Anything you say," said Pip.

Half an hour later they were on their way out of town.

"Are you sad to be leaving your old hometown?" Adam asked her.

"No, not at all. It was sad seeing it yesterday. A big city without any people in it – well it's not a city anymore."

"But then, I guess, Weymouth is not Weymouth anymore either," said Adam.

"No, it's not. Nowhere is the same. Even the countryside is not the same. But in a way, it's not quite so different."

"Yes, somehow it doesn't seem so bad out in the country. I wanted to get out of Reading. I thought it was because I wanted to get away from memories of Jo and the children. But whenever I have driven through towns, I am always happier when I leave them behind."

Pip said nothing and Adam was lost in his own thoughts. A while later he said: "It's very quiet in the back – is he alright?"

Pip turned round to see what the boy was doing. He had gone into the back of the van and had been playing with Bonzo, but now he was curled up asleep on the floor next to him.

"He's sound asleep. I could nod off myself. I'd really like to go back to bed."

"Why don't you? I'll be alright."

"OK then," said Pip, yawning, "if you're sure?"

***

When they got to the turn-off for Evesham, Adam decided to head into the town and look for somewhere to get some medical supplies. He soon found himself driving down a long high street with a variety of small-town shops and stores. There was a pharmacy on the left side of the street and he pulled up. He got out of the van and wandered over to the shop. He didn't think it would be too difficult to get the door open and he went back to the van for his tools. With a bit of heft on the crowbar he was in. He had made a mess of the woodwork and there was no way that door would close properly again. He needed to work on his breaking and entering techniques he thought – he didn't like leaving such a mess behind. The shop was quite gloomy, so he went back for the torch. The two dogs were wandering around the street hunting out new scents and the boy was peeing in the gutter. He smiled and thought of Oscar.

"Hello Matty, did you have a nice rest?" he asked.

Matty ran over to the shop. "What are you doing?"

"I'm looking for some medical supplies. We need some more bandages and some medicine."

"Did you break the door?" the boy asked.

Adam pondered what to say to this, and decided honesty was simplest:

"Yes, I had to. I don't think the shop keeper is going to be coming back now."

"Is he dead?"

"I don't know, but I expect so. Lots and lots of people have died and that's why there is nobody about and no cars on the road."

"Are we going to die too?"

"We are going to try not to." Adam said and seeing Matty's puzzled look, said, "No. No, we're not going to die."

The boy thought about this for a moment and then ran off after the dogs. Pip emerged from the van and wandered over.

"Where are we?"

"In Evesham. Could you grab a torch? I can't see too well in here."

Pip came back with a torch and found Adam in the shop. "I need some things too." she said and started to look over the shelves. Adam found the first aid items he was looking for and then took the torch and went into the storeroom and began looking through the boxes of drugs. They seemed to be arranged alphabetically and Adam was looking along the shelves trying hard to find the names of any drugs he or the children had in the past. Pip came to see what he was hunting for.

"Can you remember the names of any antibiotics? I never need them normally."

Pip helped him look through the boxes and eventually they found some that they were sure were antibiotics and not anything else. Finally they filled a bag with all the tablets, ointments and dressings they thought they might need and went back out onto the street. It was very quiet out there, and of Matty and the dogs there was no sign. Adam put the bag in the van and looked around. All of a sudden there was an almighty uproar of barking from down a side street. Adam grabbed the wheel brace from the driver's door and set off towards the noise, shouting to Pip, "Grab the pepper spray."

He turned the corner to see a stand-off between Matty and the two dogs and three strays. The strays were snarling and growling and trying to get at the boy, who was screaming and crying. Boyo and Bonzo were bravely holding the attackers off. Adam waded in with the wheel brace and sent one dog reeling. The other two jumped at him and one got hold of his sleeve, hanging on grimly as he tried to wield the wheel brace. Meanwhile the other had his teeth around his foot. The first dog was coming back at him now and was trying to get his other leg and Adam was spinning and kicking, trying to get the animals off him. Just then Pip arrived, with a can of pepper spray. She got the cap off and sprayed it towards the dogs. Instantly the dogs backed off, whining, and at the same time Bonzo and Boyo howled and backed away, shaking their heads with the pain in their eyes and noses. Pip was about to go after the retreating strays with the spray, but Adam said, "No, that's enough. Let's go."

He grabbed the boy and hauled him back to the van, pushing him in the door and indicating to Pip to follow. He went back to fetch the two dogs and, grabbing both by their collars, dragged them reluctantly away and back to join the others.

Once inside, with the doors closed, Adam sat down. Pip was squatting, consoling the frightened boy. All of them had red eyes and tears running down their cheeks. The dogs were quite distressed and were pawing at their eyes. Adam's were stinging and he felt a bit nauseous.

"Pip, take Matty into the closet and wash his eyes with water, you too." He took a bottle of water from the fridge and splashed it over his face and into his mouth. He then filled up the dog's water bowl and both animals lapped greedily. He tried to pour some water onto their eyes too, but the dogs shook their heads away.

When the youngsters emerged, Matty's crying had subsided into occasional sobs. Pip's eyes were red and raw.

"Well, that stuff works alright! Now we know, we'll be a bit cleverer next time and make sure we are not in the firing line," Adam said.

"I had no idea it was that strong," said Pip. "I think the wind blew it back in our faces."

"We'll have to remember to just use a short blast and make sure our faces are covered or at least turned away. But well-done Pip, you saved the day. Those dogs were not going to let me go."

"Are you badly bitten?"

"I don't think so," said Adam pushing off his sneaker, "one just got my sleeve and I think my shoe took the brunt of the other. There's a nice set of teeth holes in the leather, but my foot's OK, just a few red marks."

The boy was still hanging onto Pip. She held him away from her and looked him over. "Did the dogs bite you at all Matty?" she asked him.

He shook his head, and pointing to his two defenders, said, "*They* protected me."

"What heroes they are, they're good dogs. Well done boys, that deserves a treat later I think, don't you Adam?"

"Definitely. I think we all do."

"My throat hurts," said Matty, "can I have a drink?" Adam passed him a cup of water and the boy sipped at it. "Can't I have milk?" he asked.

"Just have water now, it will be better. Right now, I need to find some fuel for the van and then we can stop later and have a drink with some biscuits. How does that sound?"

As they pulled away down the high street from the pharmacy, Adam glanced down the side street to see if the strays were still there, but there was no sign of them. In the town square the van disturbed a huge flock of small birds that rose up in a cloud and Adam spotted some other animals – foxes or cats, he couldn't see – running for cover, no doubt surprised by their arrival. Here and there in the town were dogs rooting about for scraps of food and some would look up and start to follow the van.

As they drove out of the town Adam spotted a truck by the side of the road that he was able to siphon some diesel from. When he got back in the van he noticed, to his annoyance, that some fuel had got on his jeans. Matty, who was in the front of the van with Pip, said "What's that smell?"

"Phewee. Even I can smell that," Pip said

"Sorry," said Adam, "couldn't help it. But at least we have a full tank now. Broadway next, then Cheltenham and pay a visit to Gwendoline. Perhaps she might like some lunch with us."

When they got to the outskirts of Broadway they were driving past 20th century houses and a 20th century filling station. Pip did not seem impressed: "So what's so special about this place? Doesn't look like Robin Hood country to me."

"Be patient," Adam said, "You'll see."

When they eventually got into the broad avenue at the centre of the village, she seemed a little more interested.

"Look at this old village, Matty" Pip said to the boy, who was busy playing with Bonzo. He looked up and said, "What village?" and carried on playing.

Pip laughed, "Looks like we are missing something here. What's the big draw?"

"It's beautiful. The Americans love it here. You have to admit, it is rather a lovely place," Adam said.

"It is alright, I suppose, but give me Weymouth any day."

"Well give it a chance, let's see the whole village first."

"Have you been here before?"

"I came here many years ago when I was working in Stratford. It was a Sunday in summer and the place was just so packed with tourists that you couldn't even walk on the pavements. But everyone told me how pretty it was I said to myself I must come back another time when it was not so crowded."

"I don't suppose it has ever been as empty as this before."

"No, that's true."

At the top of the village Adam turned the van around and they drove slowly back through the high street. He was busy looking at an old building on his right when Pip shouted, "Adam, stop!"

He hit the brakes and everyone lurched forwards. Ahead of him, in the road, but stepping back smartly onto the pavement, was a woman. She was younger than him, early thirties he thought, attractive in a neat-and-tidy sort of way and smartly dressed in a skirt and top, with flat shoes. For some reason that Adam could never quite figure out, but never forgot, his first thought was: Sunday school teacher. He turned off the engine and for a moment everyone was quiet, just struck dumb by the sight of an ordinary woman standing by the side of a village street.

Chapter Thirty-Five

Lunch at the Office

Wednesday 8th May, Late Morning

"There's a miss," Matty said. Adam was just registering this when he saw Pip get out of the van. A *miss*? Yes, of course, a schoolteacher *Miss*. Pip walked up to meet the woman as she came toward the van and Adam saw them introduce themselves. The woman leaned forward and took both Pip's hands in hers. Adam got out and walked over as Pip was saying "... and this is Adam." She held out her hand and in a quiet voice said, "Hello Adam, I'm Yvonne."

Adam took her hand and held it gently, but firmly.

"Hello, Yvonne, it's really good to meet you."

"For me too," she said. She was well-spoken but her voice trembled with emotion. "I was starting to think I would never see another human being ever again."

"We have not met many, in several days travelling. Pip and I bumped into each other last Friday and young Matty there, we found yesterday."

"And their families – dead?"

"Yes, and mine."

"It's so terrible. I lost my son, a toddler, and my husband. You can't imagine how wonderful it is for me to know that there are other people still alive." The woman brushed away the tears from her eyes. "Where have you come from then and where are you going?"

"We have driven down from Birmingham today and are on our way to Cheltenham," Pip said. "Before that Adam and I came up from Dorset."

"Really?" said the woman.

"There's a bit more to it than that," Adam said, "why don't you come in and meet the boys"

"The boys?" Yvonne queried.

Pip laughed. "You'll see."

The woman came over to the van and Adam opened the side door. Matty was playing on the floor with Bonzo.

"Boys, this is Yvonne. Matty, come and say hello," said Adam.

Bonzo came over and greeted the stranger in his usual enthusiastic way, though the compliment was not returned. Matty looked at his feet and said, "Hello."

"Come on in," Adam said. "We can offer you tea and coffee, with milk and sugar, or wine, beer and even – ta-dah! long-life orange juice."

Yvonne spotted the cafetiere on the side and said, "I'd love a cup of coffee."

Pip invited her to sit down at the table and she sat, hands neatly in front of her on the tabletop, looking around the van, and then down at her hands. She smiled at Pip and then looked away quickly and the two women said nothing, as if both were unsure how to start a conversation.

Yvonne was fairly tall, with light brown hair, not long but tied back in a tight ponytail. She was quite attractive with a small sharp nose and a pretty little chin. She made Adam think of a bird, a heron perhaps. He glanced over as he was making the coffee, and it seemed to him that the woman was quite overcome. He also noticed that when Bonzo came over to her, she recoiled slightly as if she was not comfortable with animals. Matty broke the ice. He had been staring at her quite intently and now he said:

"Is you someone's mum?"

Yvonne gave a quick smile and then said,

"Yes, I was someone's mummy. My little boy, Ralphy, was three years old."

"Is he dead?" Matty asked

"Yes, yes he is."

"My mum's dead, and my brother."

"Oh, I'm sorry."

"And my sisters and my dad, I think."

"And how old are you, Matty?"

"Seven. Are you coming to live with us?"

The woman smiled.

"No," she said, "I have only just met you and I don't know anything about you yet."

"It's nice here. They make hot food. And there's a bathroom and an upstairs. It's a lot better than the shed."

"I am sure it is," she said, "and you are very lucky that these nice people found you. So what are you all going to do now?"

"We are going to Cheltenham to call on an elderly lady we met on Sunday," Adam said. "We are hoping to persuade her to join us in setting up a new community in Dorset."

"So, another survivor. There are a few of us around then?"

"It seems so, though few and far between. Yesterday we met a young guy in Wolverhampton, Micky. He's not keen on moving to Dorset, but we hope to keep in touch by radio. Our plan is to try and find as many people as we can. Without the numbers, we can't survive, let alone grow."

"No, indeed," Yvonne said. "I started to think that maybe I was the only one alive."

"So did I," interjected Pip, "I think we all did."

Adam brought the coffee to the table and a milk carton. "I'm afraid we didn't bring the china tea set with the milk jug."

The woman smiled and took her cup and added some milk.

"Yvonne, tell us your story. Where have you been living?"

"I have been living right there in that office," she said, pointing to an elegant, double fronted building with a polished black door and gold lettering on the windows pronouncing *Applewhite, Thorney – Solicitors, Notaries and Commissioners for Oaths*.

"I work there, or did, of course. I lived on the edge of the village, but after my husband and son died on that dreadful weekend, I knew I couldn't stay in the house, so I moved into the office – I had the keys. I made a bed on a couch in the front office, brought the camping stove over so I could make hot drinks and soup and I have been living there for the past week. I have driven around the local area a few times, but I have not seen a soul." She paused to collect herself. "It's not been easy."

"No, I am sure it hasn't," Adam said. "I couldn't stay in my house and I wanted to try and find my brother, so I started driving around the country. But how did you keep yourself together?"

"Well, some of the time I haven't, I'm afraid. I am not always as strong as I want to be. But I read, and I try to find uplifting and encouraging things to keep my spirits up. I did a lot of cleaning and tidying and organising in the office, trying to make a home there, and to keep myself busy. Sometimes I go over to the church and just sit there and pray. At first, I would walk around the village, just listening to the quietness – and the birdsong of course. But recently there are more animals about and they are becoming a nuisance. I suppose they are hungry."

"Do you have any family around here?" Pip asked.

"My parents live in Stow on the Wold. I drove down there on the second day after the event, maybe the Tuesday. They were dead. My brother is in New Zealand with his family. I often think about them and wonder if it is just the same there."

"Have you driven far since – you know, any other towns or villages"

"Not really. I drove to the next village to see if I could friend a friend but I find it hard, with all these animals everywhere."

They sat and talked about what had happened and what was going to happen, telling the stories, about Pip's parents, about Adam's family. Matty came and snuggled up against Pip and watched the grown-ups for a while until he got restless. Pip suggested that she could take him out with the dogs, just up and down the street, being very careful and going armed with the spray can. Adam was reluctant to agree to that, so Yvonne suggested that they could all go for a stroll while the sun was out, and then they could see inside the offices where she was living.

The four of them and the two dogs went for a walk through Broadway. The broad high street, with its elegant houses set back, their honey-coloured Cotswold stone golden in the sunlight, and the trees full of bird song, was indeed very attractive. Adam sensed that the young woman was more relaxed out of the van and was enjoying showing them around her beautiful village. She was showing it off and at the same time lamenting the life that had gone out of it, the friends and neighbours who were no more.

"It's a lovely village," Pip said, "have you lived here all your life?"

"No, I came to work for the solicitors and then I met my husband here."

"What was his name?"

"His name was Peter. Ralph was getting ready to go to school at the end of the summer."

They walked back up the street and put the dogs back in the van and then the woman took them into the offices and up to the rooms she had made her home. There was a large office at the front on the first floor, with a bay window and a view of the high street. It had a huge mahogany desk and matching chair, a smaller table with three chairs round it, filing cabinets and bookshelves filled with law books. On the walls were old watercolours of Cotswold towns. Under the window was a leather couch, on one end of which some bedding was neatly folded.

"This is my home now," she said. "There's a kitchenette next door and a cloakroom, of course. With my stove I can make meals if I feel hungry, though very often I don't. I have an oil lamp and torches, so I can read at night, when I can't sleep."

"Is that often?" Adam asked, "that you can't sleep?"

"Yes. I don't sleep well." she said, with a weary note in her voice. "Sometimes I find it easier to sleep in the afternoons, when it gets very warm in here. At night the building creaks and groans and seems to be alive." She gave a little laugh, as if to say how silly that was.

"I think it would be rather scary staying in this place at night," Pip said.

"Matty, who had been half-listening, while spinning the globe on the desk round and round said, "Is there ghosts in this house?" and then, "Where's your bedroom?"

"Here," Yvonne replied, smiling at the boy, "right here in this room. This isn't a house, it is an office."

"An office? Like the headteacher's office?"

"Well, I suppose so," she laughed, "have you been in there Matty?"

"Only once. When I was in trouble. It wasn't big like this office."

"Do you have any water in your cloakroom, or the kitchen?" Adam asked.

"Yes. There is a tank in the loft here, I believe, but I don't know how much it holds. I have been using it very sparingly. Luckily the village shop was left open, so I've been able to get drinking water and other supplies from there. There's an awful smell in there now and I have to wear a scarf sprinkled with perfume when I go in. I have enough tins and packets to keep me going for a long time, but of course there are no fresh fruit or vegetables and my small supply of apples and oranges is getting near the end now."

She paused and then looked Adam straight in the eye. "Adam, do you think you really will be able to find enough people to make a community that can survive – feed itself, keep warm and, well, keep alive?"

"I think so," Adam replied. "If we can get together a group of ten or more people, then yes, why not? Think of the skills and knowledge that could be pooled. If we don't believe that we can do that, then what's the point of carrying on?"

"Yes, I suppose you're right. But what if you can't find ten people? There were times in the last week when I didn't even think I *wanted* to carry on."

"So what would you do – put an end to it all?"

"Oh, I couldn't do that," the woman said, "for a start I was brought up a Christian and to us suicide is a sin. But I don't think I would have the courage to kill myself. I don't know what I thought. I suppose I was just leaving myself in God's hands."

"If there is a god," Pip came in, "don't you think he would want you try and survive and look for other people?"

"Yes, you're right, I am sure that's what God would want me to do. But if he brought this... this plague to end the world, then maybe he doesn't want any of us to live."

"And yet here we are," said Adam. "Tell me Yvonne, have you ever been very ill before?"

"Well, I had mumps quite badly as a child, but until last year I had always been well."

"And what happened last year?"

"I came down with this really bad flu – or that's what they thought it was – in the spring. I was in hospital: quite ill I was. It took them some time to work out how to treat it."

Pip could not contain herself: "That's what happened to me, and Adam. Isn't it strange? And Micky – he said that he was rushed to hospital. Did you lose your sense of smell?"

"Well only for a week or two, while I was ill. Though I did lose my appetite and even now things don't taste like they used to. My hearing was affected as well. I had really painful ears when I was ill and since then I have been slightly deaf. When I heard your van drive past earlier, I was not sure if I was dreaming it or hearing the wind."

"Don't you think it's a strange coincidence though..." Pip resumed her line of thought, "that we were all three of us very ill in hospital last year and that nobody knew what it was that made us ill – and all three of us, four counting Micky, have survived? There's got to be a connection."

"It does seem odd, doesn't it? And what month did it happen to you? You said summer?"

"Yes, early summer, June, I think. Or end of May – I remember it was hot at the time."

"It was May when I got ill, late Spring. The weather was very warm for the Whit Monday holiday, I remember," said Yvonne.

"I was taken into hospital in June," Adam chipped in, "but I think I had been ill for a while before it became too bad. Pip is convinced it is why we are still here now. I wasn't sure at first, but you have to admit that it is a very strange coincidence."

Matty, who had been doing some drawing at the desk with some paper Yvonne had found for him, suddenly piped up: "I went to hospital. My mum had to take me."

"When was that Matty?" Pip asked.

The boy looked blank, "Dunno. They sent me home from school cos I was really ill. I couldn't do sports day."

"That sounds like summer term," Pip said.

"As you say, it does seem a very big coincidence. Do you think it has given us immunity?" Yvonne said.

"You could be right," said Adam. "Maybe what we had last year was the same or a similar virus and that's what's given us immunity this year. But it doesn't explain what this disease, this virus, is and where it came from so suddenly and how it spread so rapidly,"

Yvonne stood up from the edge of the window ledge where she had been perching and walked across the room. Clearly, she felt that the conversation had run out of wind.

"Can I make you all some lunch, before you go?" she asked. "I made some flat bread this morning. It's quite tasty just warmed up over a low gas and we could have soup with it."

"That sounds great," Adam said, "can I help?"

"Oh no, that won't be necessary. It will only take a moment – we can sit in the kitchen."

Yvonne went out of the room and Adam and Pip looked at each other.

Pip nodded towards the door and whispered, "Apple white or thorny - what do you reckon?"

Adam smiled and said, "Not sure. Not quite apple white, I don't think."

"Do you think she will want to come and join us?"

"Mm, I don't know. Maybe you might be able to persuade her."

"Me?"

"Yes, you. I think she is a bit wary of me, but with you and Matty I think she will feel a bit safer. Give her time."

Pip went to look at what Matty had been drawing. "Look at this Adam. This is very good Matty, is that your dog?"

"Yes, that's Thor."

"He looks very fierce," Adam said. It was surprisingly good for a seven-year-old, he thought.

"Are we going now?" the boy said, hopefully.

"We are going to have some lunch with the nice lady first, and then we'll be going." Pip answered.

"Is the miss coming with us?"

"We don't know Matty. Why don't you ask her in a minute?"

Yvonne called them into the little staff kitchen area along the passageway. She had set a table with plates, and bowls which she filled with soup hot from the little hob. In the middle was a plate full of warm, home-made flat breads.

"This looks tasty," said Pip, "How did you make the flat bread?"

Yvonne told them about her grandmother's recipe and how she cooked them in a frying pan.

Over lunch Yvonne asked Pip about her parents, her school life, where they had lived before, why she called her father "Thommo". Adam felt that she was wanting to ask Pip about her Indian heritage but could not quite bring herself to.

Later, Yvonne made coffee and while they drank it Adam brought the conversation back to their plans – would she consider joining them? She bit her lip and seemed uncomfortable with the question.

"You know Adam," she said, looking first down at her cup and then into Adam's eyes, "I think if God has allowed us to survive – or maybe I should use the word "chosen" – if God has chosen us to survive, then it must be because he has some purpose for us. I don't know what that is, but I think I *will* know, it will become clear."

Yvonne stopped, as if that was her answer, but Adam looked back at her, waiting for her to continue.

"The thing is, I don't know that I will be up for whatever he might want me to do." The woman looked down at her hand and fiddled nervously with her coffee cup. "You know, I'm not very... strong. I don't think I'm a very good person and I'm not sure I'm worthy to accept the responsibility. I don't suppose you can understand that."

Adam said nothing but continued to look at her. She was trembling slightly, and seemed a bit agitated. He wondered whether he intimidated her somehow.

Pip broke the silence. "I don't think any of us think we are... *worthy*," she said. "But if there's a reason why we're here, whatever it is, don't *we* have a reason to try and carry on? It's sort of something we have to do. Isn't it?"

"You may be right, I don't know," Yvonne said. "I think I need some time to think about it. I'm sorry it's just that... it's just rather difficult for me."

Adam put his cup down and sat back in the chair. "You know Yvonne, that's quite understandable. I get how you feel. I have a suggestion: why don't you come down with us to Cheltenham to meet Gwendoline? I think you'll like her. You can drive your car and maybe Pip could ride with you. We can talk together, all of us, about our ideas, how we think they will work out and what is best to do and maybe, if you still feel unsure, you could stay with us for one night. Then tomorrow, if you don't want to come with us, you can drive back here."

"Yes," Pip said, "why don't you do that? That will give you more time to think and to talk to Gwendoline too. Please come."

Yvonne continued to look at her hands. "I don't know. I'm sorry I'm being so... It sounds like a sensible plan and I do appreciate what you are trying to do here, to help me, to... take me under your wing, it's just..."

Matty, who had been looking at the woman for the last few minutes, suddenly said, "Miss, are you going to come with us? You can sit in the back with me."

Yvonne looked at him, a look of surprise crossing her face, and then she gave a little laugh: "You're a love! That's so nice of you to ask. You know Matty, I would love to come in the back of your campervan with you. But I think Adam's right. I'll drive down to Cheltenham with you and then decide what to do. Thank you, Adam, thank you Pip. You probably think I'm very silly but what has happened has been so... difficult and now, meeting you today, when I had almost given up hope – it's all a bit overwhelming." She reached for another tissue from the box and blew her nose loudly, composed herself, sat up straight in her chair and said, "You're right, it's what I'll do, come with you. But you'll need to give me some time to get ready. I need to think about what to bring. Oh, I don't think I have much petrol."

"Don't worry, take your time," said Adam. "Give me your car keys and tell me where your car is and I will fill up the tank for you. Matty can come with me and Pip can stay here and help you, if you like – unless you'd like Matty to stay?"

Yvonne smiled, "I think Matty would rather be with you, wouldn't you Matty?" Matty nodded. "But how will you get petrol? Or maybe I shouldn't ask. Thank you. The car is right outside the office and there are the keys. I hope it starts alright."

After half an hour Adam and Matty stood in the road outside the solicitor's office, with the two dogs researching the tell-tale signs of the local wildlife nearby. Adam had the car full of petrol, oil levels and tyres all checked, while Matty was carefully polishing the headlights with a cloth that Adam had provided. The boy clearly had an appreciation of the motor car. Pip came to join them, carrying a small suitcase.

"She's on her way, just locking the place up."

Shortly after, Yvonne emerged through the large oak door with a large case and a bag. She locked the heavy door and checked it was secure, then walked over to her car. She saw Adam smiling at the cases.

"If I do decide to come tomorrow, then I think I have everything here that I want to bring," she said. "And if I don't, well, I can bring it back again."

"Good idea," said Adam. "Pip, are you happy to go with Yvonne? Can you remember where Gwen's house is?"

I think so," said Pip, "but it might be best if you lead the way."

"OK, Matty and I'll go ahead. We'll take it nice and slow and keep you in sight all the way. Shall we go?"

Chapter Thirty-Six

Tea at Number 42

Wednesday 8th May, Afternoon

At two-thirty they set off in convoy, Adam and Matty leading the way and the two women following in Yvonne's car. Adam drove slowly, but even then he felt he was going too fast for Yvonne and had to keep slowing down. They met a herd of sheep on the road as they neared Winchcombe and Adam was willing Yvonne to keep close behind the van as he forced a way through, but instead she seemed to hang back which allowed the animals to fill the space between them and block her path. He began to wonder how long it might take them to get back to Dorset at that rate. He decided there was no point in trying to drive any faster so he rested his arm on the open window ledge and enjoyed the views across the Cotswold countryside. When they eventually started getting into the northern outskirts of Cheltenham he pulled up and checked the road atlas. Yvonne pulled up behind the Drifter

Pip came up to his window and said, "Need your navigator?"

Adam smiled and said, "No, I think I can work out the route thanks. How's it going in there?"

Pip pulled a face. "She is so...uptight. I think she's worried that an animal might go under the car."

"You need to try and persuade her to keep closer behind me. I keep thinking I'm going to lose you."

"I'll try," the girl said and walked back to the car.

Adam found his way round the town centre and it was not long before they were driving down the side of Montpellier Gardens. Adam stopped and Yvonne pulled up behind. He walked over to Yvonne's window.

"The woman we're hoping to visit, Gwendoline, lives just the other side of this park. She won't be expecting us, of course, and she may not even be there. But we can park outside her house and wait and see if she turns up. It was number forty-two, wasn't it Pip?"

"Yes, that's right. I was just looking to see if she was in the park, but I can't see her."

They drove along the west side of the park and then turned along the south side. There was no sign of Gwendoline or anyone else. Adam turned into her road and then pulled up in the middle, opposite number forty-two. The car pulled up behind and Pip got out. Matty immediately ran to her to tell her all about the sheep in the road and had she seen them.

"I saw them," she said. "Weren't they silly, getting in the road like that! Are you going to knock on the door Adam?"

"I thought she might have heard the engine." Adam looked up at the window. "Let's give her a minute or two."

When no-one appeared at the door, or the window upstairs, Adam walked over and banged loudly on the large blue door. He waited by the door while Pip stood in the road. Adam knocked again and waited. Then he heard Pip shout "Hello, Mrs Maitland, it's us again," and she waved up at the window. Adam stepped back into the road as the window opened and the old lady looked out, looking surprised and a tiny bit annoyed. "Oh, it's you. Just wait a minute. Just wait. I'll be down in a while," she said.

Adam smiled to Pip. "She doesn't look very happy to see us," he said.

"I expect she was having an afternoon nap."

Adam walked over to Yvonne, who had remained in the car. "Are you going to come and say hello to Gwendoline?"

"I thought I might wait here until you have spoken to her. I expect we have given her a bit of a shock," she said.

"Yes, you might be right. But I'm sure she'd like to meet you."

At this moment the door opened and Gwendoline stepped out.

"Well, well, this is a surprise," she said, as if it wasn't altogether a pleasant one. "I see that you have added to your number. I did not really think you would come back this way, and certainly not so soon."

"We said that we would come back and see you," said Adam, "and today we were passing this way. Let me introduce you to Yvonne. Yvonne this is Mrs Maitland, Gwendoline."

"How do you do, Gwendoline. I am so pleased to meet you," said Yvonne, stepping forward and offering her hand.

"How do you do, Yvonne...?"

"Haskins. Well my maiden name was King and that's the name I prefer to use. But... "

Gwendoline waited a moment for her to finish what she was going to say and then said, "Well, it's a pleasure to meet you, Yvonne. So how did you get to meet our traveller friends?"

"They were driving through Broadway, where I live. They saw me and stopped."

"I suppose you have been on your own?"

"Yes. My son and my husband died on the Saturday."

"Oh, dear. That must be very hard for you."

"It's hard for everyone, isn't it? These children here lost their parents."

"Children? Ah I see we have another one. What's this little fellow's name?"

Pip put her arm around Matty and steered him towards the old lady. "Hello Mrs Maitland. This is Matty. We found him on the road in Kings Norton. Matty say hello to Mrs Maitland." Matty mumbled and shrunk back behind Pip. "Matty! Don't be shy now."

The old lady gave almost a laugh. "I expect I look a bit frightening to him. I'll get him talking in a minute. Well now you are here, I suppose I ought to be hospitable and invite you in. I have to tell you, I wasn't expecting company and I'm not very well equipped for entertaining. But I can offer you tea and I expect I can find a biscuit."

"Tea would be great, wouldn't it Adam?" Pip said.

"Yes please, Gwendoline. I'd like to see your apartment."

"Hah! It's nothing special," Gwendoline said, "though I'm very happy here. Come on up."

Adam rounded the dogs up and put them back in the van, while the others followed Gwendoline slowly up the stairs to the top flat. He caught them up before they were inside. She led them down the passage to the large sitting room at the front, which had three sash windows overlooking the street and the houses opposite.

"Make yourselves comfortable, I have plenty of chairs."

"What a lovely room this is, Gwendoline. You have some beautiful things," Yvonne said, looking around her.

"Yes, wow," Adam said, taking in the decorative plasterwork, the oil paintings and watercolours, the antique vases and the furniture. It looked like a room in a National Trust property. He did not know anything about antiques, but he imagined that they were all collectables.

"Yes, well, I have picked up some things over the years. I used to go to auctions when I was younger. I was lucky enough to have had a bit of money come to me from my late father. And I always worked, of course."

Pip sat down on the small two-seater and pulled Matty down next to her. She was a bit worried about what he might break if she let him go, but he sat very quietly, clearly overawed by the elderly lady and her drawing room. Or maybe by the number of adults all around him. Yvonne looked uncertain as to where to sit so Adam opted for the leather armchair and left the large sofa for Yvonne, where she could sit next to the old lady. She hesitated a moment and sat down, very neat and upright, at the far end, and Gwendoline sat at the other.

She told them about the state of the flat when she first came here in the fifties and how she had slowly brought it back up to its former glory.

"This street was a bit run down then. Nobody had much money after the war and of course there was bomb damage here and there. But now these properties are quite sought after it seems. Now, does everyone want tea? Not this young fellow, I expect."

"Can I help you?" Yvonne asked.

"There's no need, but yes, why not? We can have a little chat."

Yvonne got up and went with Gwendoline to the rear of the apartment. Adam looked across at Pip. "Are you alright? How was the journey?"

"It was OK. She didn't say much at first. I think she was concentrating so hard on the driving. I've never seen someone so nervous before, but I don't know if it was me, or the animals. She was petrified that she was going to run something over."

"I know what that can feel like," Adam said, "but did she ask you any questions?"

"Loads. She wanted to know all about me and all about you, what I thought of you, was I ever worried about you, you know, doing something to me."

"Really?" Adam said and then laughed. "I hope you told her that you weren't."

"I said I wasn't worried cos I kept a knife by my bed," said Pip, with a smirk.

Adam laughed loudly, then quickly suppressed it.

"I told her that you had taken good care of me, when there was just the two of us, and that I was sure you would look after her, and Matty, just as well."

"I did think she was wary of me, but I don't know why. She had a husband, and there would have been men in the office."

"Maybe that's why," Pip said, "I don't think her husband was very nice to her."

"Did she tell you that?"

"No, but every time she mentioned him, even though she said how terrible it was losing him, she looked like she had a nasty taste in her mouth, do you know what I mean?"

"Who had something in her mouth?" asked Matty all of a sudden. "Who are you talking about?"

"Oh, it's nobody you know," Pip said, "just someone that Adam and I met."

"Are you talking about the miss?" The boy had a sly look on his face.

"Doesn't miss a trick that one. We'll have to mind our Ps and Qs." Adam said.

Matty looked at him for a moment, as if trying to puzzle out what was really going on. Then he jumped up from the sofa and said, "Can I go and play with the dogs?"

"We're just going to have tea with Mrs Maitland." said Pip.

"I don't want tea. I want to go and play."

"Matty we're not going to be here very long. When we have had tea, then perhaps we can take the dogs for a walk in the park and you can throw sticks for them."

"Thor didn't fetch sticks. But Ryan's dog did. He was funny."

"If I find some paper, do you think you could draw a picture of Ryan's dog?" Adam asked.

"Dunno. I'm not very good at drawing animals," the boy said.

"Yes you are. You drew a really good picture of Thor earlier. Or you could draw your house, with your mum and your brother and sister – we'd like to see that, wouldn't we Pip?"

Adam found Gwendoline in the kitchen, talking to Yvonne. They stopped when he walked in, so he asked the old lady for some paper and a pencil and left them to it. He set Matty up on the floor and then for a while the boy was quite absorbed with his drawing. The women came back with the tea things and some chocolate biscuits, which Matty spotted straightaway. Yvonne poured the tea and they sat around a low table. The old lady opened the conversation about their plans.

"Yvonne tells me that you have asked her to join you in going back to Dorset. She has some reservations, just as I did, and I can understand why. For a start, assuming you have the skills to get some sort of power supply working in this house you have seen, how long will it take you to get it up and running and fit for civilised human habitation, if you know what I mean?"

"From what I saw, I don't think it will take very long to set up home, either in one of the cottages or even in the farmhouse," said Adam. "The cottages looked like holiday rentals and look as if they have not long been refurbished. We have power in our van and a good supply of diesel fuel on the farm. There is a water supply, probably piped into the houses. For the first few days we have the van and a tent as alternative sleeping accommodation. If you're worried about comfort, Yvonne – well there'll be everything there that we need to start with, and what we don't have we will... procure locally."

"I don't think it's just comfort that Yvonne is worried about," Gwendoline said.

Adam looked puzzled, but it seemed Pip knew what she was getting at.

"If you're worried about Adam," she said, "I can tell you that he has looked after me very well and I'm not worried about him. If three... women cannot hold our own against one middle-aged man..." Pip was smiling as she said this but Adam raised his eyebrows, "...well, maybe not middle-aged. But anyway, without him we would not be sitting here together."

"I wasn't implying that Adam was anything other than a model of discretion," Gwendoline said, "but ladies need their privacy and their comforts, don't they my dear?"

Yvonne looked embarrassed but said, "Yes, we do, I'm afraid."

"It's OK, I understand," Adam said. "There are plenty of options at the place that I have in mind: two cottages, the farmhouse and the house up the lane. In time they could all be made very comfortable. And as for me – and them," he said indicating Pip and Matty, "well you will have to take us as you find us. But I have to say that survival long-term will depend on a lot of hard work and we will need to draw on all our resources. Our first job is survival and comfort may come later. No-one will survive on their own, but several people together – then there's a chance."

Yvonne coughed. She looked like she wanted to speak but was not quite sure how to start.

"Adam, I think Gwendoline may have misunderstood me slightly," she said, hesitantly, "This isn't about you – it's about me. I'm used to being a very... private sort of person. Even with my husband, maybe especially with my husband, sometimes I found it difficult to... let go. I'm not very good with groups of people and I struggled when it came to entertaining clients. I need to know people for a long time before I feel comfortable with them. Your plans sound really good. I just don't know whether I would be able to fit in, whether I would let you down or... let myself down."

There was an awkward silence, as no-one knew what to say next. Matty saved the day by looking up from his drawing and saying:

"Do you want to see my new picture of Thor? It's better than the first one I did."

"Oh yes," said Pip quickly. "Why don't you come and show us all your picture?" The picture was passed around and duly admired.

"Can you draw your friend's dog? You know, the funny one, who chases sticks?"

"Dunno," Matty said, frowning.

"Well, have a go and see how you get on."

"I could draw Bonzo and Boyo."

"That's a splendid idea," Gwendoline said, clapping her hands. "And don't come back until you have drawn both of them. Now Adam, where were you going next today – back to Wiltshire, or somewhere else first?"

"My plan was that we would set off to Dorset tomorrow, hopefully with you and Yvonne. You could travel with Yvonne and we could be there by lunch time. That would give us plenty of time to settle in and get everything organised."

"Oh, I see. And tonight?"

"I thought we could spend the night here. Yvonne could stay with you perhaps and we could stop in the van, outside or down by the park. But if you really don't want to come with us, Gwendoline, then maybe we could help stock up your pantry and your coal store to keep you going for a few more weeks."

"Well that would be helpful, I suppose. Thank you. That's quite a good plan. Now Yvonne, what do you think of that? It would give you some more time to consider your options, so to speak. As for me, I still don't think I'm ready to make that journey, so I *won't* be going with you tomorrow. But you have your car and if you decide not to go, or you go and decide you don't like it, you can always come back and visit me here. But I warn you, I'm not always very good company."

Yvonne gave a timid laugh: "I don't suppose I am either, very often. I *would* like some more time to think about things, and I would like to spend some more time talking to you. Perhaps I could help you cook a meal for everyone while Adam goes to get supplies?"

Gwendoline agreed to that, and they decided that after tea she would look at her larder and make a list of things she needed. They continued to talk together, over their tea, about what had happened, how many survivors there might be across the country and whether it was the same all over the world. The old lady remained mostly quiet during this conversation but listened attentively. Eventually she spoke:

"Adam... given the challenges you will be facing, technical and logistical, do you not think this is going to be too much for your small group to undertake? For a start you will need manpower to do some of the things that will need doing, and as far as I can see you only have one man. Don't you think it might be better to spend some more time reconnoitring the towns and cities to find more survivors so you can build your community?"

"As for the manpower," Adam said, "you're right, there will be some heavy work to do when we start cultivation, but there are machines in the farm we can use for that."

"Only for as long as you have fuel."

"We'll have fuel. There'll be an awful lot of diesel fuel sitting in tanks around the local farms, enough to keep us ploughing and sowing for a good while. We'll do some more reconnaissance trips, but it is not the most efficient way to find other people like us. We've driven many miles and only found three people."

"But how else will you find them?"

"Ah," said Adam, "that's where the radio comes in," and he explained his idea about using the radio they had acquired to scan the airwaves for any broadcasts they could find, across Britain and beyond.

"I think that's a really good idea," said Yvonne.

"Yes, I hadn't thought of that, which is odd really, given I was a radio operator for a while," Gwendoline said. "But, of course, you will only find those people who have access to a radio and the ability to use it, and they will be few and far between."

"Yes, that's true," said Adam, "but if the idea came to me, it could easily come to others too. And if there are other groups of people forming, they will come to this thought eventually."

"Yes, you're probably right. But what about those lone individuals who have not found anyone else – like Yvonne here, or Pippa?"

"Pip, you mean? My thinking is that once we have contact with others in different areas, we can encourage them to scout the area around them. And one would expect that intelligent and resourceful people will already be driving around and scouring their neighbourhoods. But there is nothing stopping us using a second radio and broadcasting from the van while we reconnoitre different places. Actually, I was hoping to set it up tonight and try it out."

"I would be interested to look at that. Why don't you do it on the dining table, after we've had supper?"

"Yes, alright, that would be good, thank you. I'll be happy to show you – you might be able to help me operate it."

"Yes, if I can remember. But this modern equipment will be quite different from what we had, of course."

"I'm sure the principles are the same," Adam said and then, after a pause:

"Gwendoline, I wanted to ask you a question: were you ill at any point last year? Seriously ill?"

The old lady looked at Adam and frowned: "Well, that's a curious question. Yes, as a matter of fact I was. It was late spring, well after the Festival, of course. In fact, it was after the Race Night in May. I was invited to go to that with some friends, but I didn't think I could manage it anymore. I used to love to go to the Race Night. Yes, it was a few weeks after that, end of the month I think, that I started to get quite unwell. I had a neighbour who looked in on me and brought me her old magazines. She found me in bed, almost unconscious. I don't remember a thing about it. She called me an ambulance and they took me into the General."

"Did they know what it was? How were you ill?"

"I was having trouble breathing, a bit like an asthma attack I believe, but I wouldn't know as I've never had asthma. It started with a cold and it just got worse. It was lucky that Hilda had a key and decided to look in on me. I don't think the doctors knew what it was. But eventually they told me that they had been in touch with colleagues at Bristol and they had found a drug that sorted it out. Apparently, there were other people ill elsewhere at the same time. Quite strange it was. But why do you ask?"

"Because I was very ill at the same time, as were Pip and Yvonne. Micky, who we met in Wolverhampton, told us he was in hospital last year and we think probably Matty had been ill too. And all of us have survived this virus."

The old lady sat back in her chair and looked hard at Adam.

"Well, that is interesting," she said, "Ha! So five people have an illness, a serious illness, in late spring last year, and a year later we find that we are unscathed when the rest of the world has succumbed to a deadly virus."

"Yes."

"Did you lose your sense of taste and smell," Pip asked.

"I didn't have much of a sense of smell anyway and for years things had tasted dull, but, yes, what little I had has gone and I can only really taste sweet things. I'm afraid I live mainly on sweet foods now – I've given up healthy eating. But then at my age, I think, what does it matter?"

"I think I'm the same," said Pip, "I love biscuits and cakes but savoury things don't taste as nice anymore."

"Well, you need to eat properly, my girl. You can't just live on sweet things. You're still growing."

Pip was just about to reply to that, but Adam cut in.

"I don't enjoy food like I used to, and after my recovery my wife would try and make me eat healthy, balanced meals. Now I just try and bring back memories of the tastes I used to enjoy so much."

"And Adam makes really tasty food, with lots of vegetables, so that's alright."

"Do you indeed?" the old lady said, looking at Adam with a twinkle in her eye.

"The young men I knew wouldn't have known which way up to boil a chicken or roast an egg."

Pip laughed . Adam smiled and said,

"I'm glad Pip likes my food, but I suspect that after a week of eating cold tinned food, anything hot would taste delicious. Talking of food, perhaps you can tell us where you do your shopping: do you have a local grocery or supermarket that keeps the things you want?"

"I can get most of what I need from the little supermarket down the road. But I used to have my coal delivered. Its smoke-less fuel, of course, not that dirty old house coal that we used to burn. The coal yard is out of town aways, but I think Mr Singh in the mini-market kept some and I believe that the filling station on the Gloucester road has some. Once upon a time everything was delivered, including my wine, but now I have to fetch them myself. When we have got a list of things I need, I can tell you where to find them."

"Do you want to come with me Matty?" Adam said.

"I want to play with the dogs. You said we could take them to the park."

"Did I? OK, we'll take the dogs down to the park for a run and then we will come back and go and find supplies for Mrs Maitland. How does that sound?"

"Are you coming as well?" Matty asked, looked plaintively at Pip.

Pip looked across to Adam for approval.

"Why not?" Adam said. "And then we will come back and pick up the shopping list."

The three of them went out to the van and let the dogs out. They walked down to the park and the boy went racing off after the dogs, chasing them around the grass.

"He's got some energy to burn, that boy," Adam said.

Once they had done the full circuit, they rounded up the dogs and walked back to the van. Matty wanted to stay in the van with the dogs and did not seem so keen to go back into the old lady's house. He was protesting this, when he suddenly said,

"Look, there's another dog!" and pointed at the house. Sure enough, in the lobby was the lurcher they had seen on their last visit. Matty ran up and went to stroke the dog, who gave a warning growl. "I think he wants to go in," Matty said.

"Well, we can't let him in Matty. He lives outdoors."

The young boy held out his hand slowly and the lurcher sniffed it, then let the boy stroke him. "I have a feeling I know what's coming next," Adam said.

"Why does he live outdoors? That's not very nice. He could come with us."

"I told you," Adam said to Pip. "I'm sorry Matty, but he can't come with us. He has to stay here and take care of Mrs Maitland."

"What's his name?"

"I don't know if he has one. You'll have to ask Mrs Maitland."

"Is that the old lady or the miss?"

Pip laughed. "Mrs Maitland is the elderly woman. The other lady is called Yvonne."

The boy considered this for a moment and then said, "Can I stay outside with the dog?"

"No," said Adam, "because you have to help me go and find the groceries."

"What's that?"

"Groceries? You know, the shopping."

They went back upstairs and Gwendoline presented Adam with a shopping list and details of where he could find everything. "Yvonne tells me that you know how to get into buildings and houses, so presumably you will be alright getting into the shop. Burglary is not normally something I would condone but we live in strange times, and I'm sure we did worse things in the War. You're taking the boy with you?"

"Yes. He has to learn the tricks of the trade," Adam said, with a wink. "Come on Matty, you're coming with me. Are you coming Pip?"

"She can stay with us," the old lady said, "she and I can learn some cooking skills from Yvonne."

Pip shrugged, as if to say, *well, it seems not.*

Matty followed Adam back to the van, where Adam held the passenger door for him. Matty wanted to go in the back with the dogs, but Adam explained they needed a rest after their walk, which was quite true as both dogs were sprawled out on their beds. The boy sat quietly in the front seat as Adam drove to the mini-market that Gwendoline had directed them to. He was still shy with Adam, but seemed happy enough to help him get the tools out of the back of the van and to watch while he went to work on the front door of the shop. When the door sprung open with a crack Matty laughed and said, "Cor! That was a big bang!"

Adam gave him the torch to hold while he looked along the shelves.

"It smells in here," the boy said, "I don't like it. Can I go outside?"

"Just hold your nose like this," Adam said, demonstrating on his own nose, "and you'll be alright." He found various items, put them in a bag and told Matty to put them by the van. "Don't let the dogs out, though," he called to him.

When he came out with another bag full, he found Matty trying to put his bag into the van whilst keeping Bonzo inside. "I said put the basket by the van, not in it!"

Adam got the shopping into the van, hauled Bonzo back and told Matty to climb into his seat.

As they drove down the road, looking for the filling station, Adam said, "Matty you have to do as I say, especially with the dogs. It may not be safe out there."

The boy was very quiet for the rest of the trip and stayed in the van while Adam loaded up with small sacks of coal which they found on the forecourt of the filling station. They were making their way back across town to number 42 when Matty said

"Sorry Adam."

He pronounced it A-*dam* and Adam had to keep himself from laughing.

"That's OK Matty."

They got the groceries and the coal up to the flat, Matty helping with the small bags. The women were busy in the kitchen and, having checked through the supplies, the Gwendoline dismissed the boys. Back in the sitting room Adam found that she had dug out some old games from her cupboard and Adam showed Matty how to play draughts.

That evening they sat down to a three-course meal. It was the first proper meal that any of them had had for a long time, and it really was very impressive, the more so as it had been cooked on a makeshift hob over an open coal fire. Gwendoline made it clear that Yvonne had directed operations and she and Pip had merely acted as sous-chefs. She found a very good bottle of claret in her wine rack and was keen to assure them that this was the first wine she had drunk for many a month. Adam was not sure that their jaded palates could do a fine claret any justice, but he enjoyed it none the less and was quite happy that the other three declined a second glass and left him to finish off the bottle.

After dinner, Adam fetched the radio equipment in from the van and began to assemble it on the dining table. Gwendoline directed the washing up operations in the kitchen, then came to see how Adam was getting on. She brought him an oil lamp, which she lit and placed near him to throw some light on the equipment.

"It looks very different from the wireless equipment we had at Bletchley," she said. "That was so big, all the valves and the huge speakers. These modern radios are tiny."

"We are going to need to make an aerial in here," said Adam, unrolling a reel of wire.

"I suggest you run it along the curtain rail and down the walls either side of the window. That's what I did in my flat in St Marks, after the war. I am afraid you probably won't get a very good signal here. We are quite low down and surrounded by houses. You need an aerial on the roof really. But what are you going to do for power?"

"This one runs on batteries or mains."

Gwendoline watched him putting it all together.

"I remember I used to tune into all the European stations and see how many words I could understand. I learned lots of words from different languages during the war. Couldn't speak any of them, but I could make sense of quite a few."

She left him to it and went back to join the others in the sitting room. Adam could hear the hum of their conversation, punctuated by occasional cries of triumph or despair from Matty, who was playing draughts with Pip. After some time spent fiddling with the tuning, and moving the aerial wire in different positions, Adam was at last able to start scanning the wave bands. He was following the instructions in the manual he had picked up, learning which frequencies were used most often, but all he could find were fifty different types of static. After a while he gave it a rest and went to join the others, who were drinking coffee that Gwendoline had served up in fine, small china coffee cups. Matty had curled up next to Pip on the sofa and had fallen asleep. Adam sat down with his coffee on the large leather armchair which had been left for him, as 'man of the house", as Gwendoline informed him. The candles in the candelabra that she had brought in cast flickering shadows on the walls.

"Any joy?" said Gwendoline brightly.

"No, not really. Just lots of static."

"Yes, well, that's to be expected, isn't it? In normal times you would be hearing a cacophony of music and chatter, so much so that it could be quite overwhelming. You would have to tune very finely to the frequency you wanted. But now? Will there be anyone broadcasting?"

"Didn't Micky say he was going to broadcast every evening?" Pip asked.

"Yes, he did, at twenty hundred hours, eight o'clock. We've missed that for tonight."

"Have you tried transmitting yet?" the old lady asked him.

"No, not yet."

"Well why don't you transmit on that frequency your Micky chap was using? Just put a message out there a few times and see if anyone comes back."

Adam looked a little uncertain, so the old lady continued:

"Just say your name and that you are broadcasting from Cheltenham, England. There is a group of three adults and two children." she said, and seeing Pip's frown, "I'm sorry my dear, technically you are still a child. A group of five who have survived and are fit and well."

"Yes, come on Adam. You can use your new handle: *this is Adamantine calling, over,*" Pip said, in a mock aircraft air traffic controller's voice.

"Alright. I'll give it a try in a minute. Or you could do it, if you like. Why not?"

When they finished their coffee they all went into the dining room and Adam tuned to the frequency. He and Pip took turns speaking into the microphone and then pausing to see if there was any response. After five minutes they tried again on another frequency, Adam noting down the ones they had used. After an hour, nothing had come back and they decided to give it up for the night.

"Don't forget, without proper lighting, anybody alive will most probably have given up by now and gone to bed. In Europe it will have got dark two hours ago."

"Talking of which," Adam said, "we ought to get going and get this lad to bed. And I need to put up my tent."

"In the dark?" asked Yvonne.

"Yes. Well by the light of the headlights. That's not a problem."

"I suppose you will go to the gardens, will you?" asked the old lady.

"The park, where we met you? Yes."

"I'm sorry that I don't have any more beds to offer you. I can't even offer you a lawn to put your tent on."

Adam assured her that they would manage just fine and that they would come back in the morning at ten o'clock. He picked Matty up from the sofa, and Gwendoline found a blanket to put over the sleeping boy. Then they made their way down to the van and got Matty onto the sofa at the back. "What's going on?" he asked sleepily, and then went back to sleep.

Chapter Thirty-Seven

Southward Bound

Thursday 9th May, Morning

Adam had a restless night. Matty had woken up crying in the early hours and he had to comfort him. Then he wanted to go "wee-wee", so Adam had to help with that and then get him back to sleep. By the time he had done that and got back into his sleeping bag, sleep had fled and he tossed and turned, thinking about the day just gone and what was to come: how Yvonne would fit in with them, how she would cope. There was something troubled about her that she kept squashed down inside and maybe that was what kept her so buttoned-up – she didn't dare let the monster out. But she did seem quite practical, and she hadn't fallen apart after she was left on her own. She had made a new home and was cooking meals for herself. Perhaps she was stronger than she looked.

When Adam did eventually drop off again, he had strangely mournful dreams, about driving down a long road, and when he looked back he could see this beautiful town that was his home, but he was going into a dark forest. Though he wanted to turn the car around, he was unable to, it kept on running straight along the road, taking him further into the woods. He woke himself and then slipped into another dream in which Sophie was dressed in her fairy outfit and she was dancing in front of him on the grass, laughing her lovely cheeky laugh and smiling and he was laughing too. She was holding out her hands to him to come and dance with her. "Dance with me Daddy, dance with me," she was calling, over and over again, but as Adam went to get up she ran away with a naughty grin on her face. He could not get up from his seat, his legs just would not respond. Eventually she ran off into the woods and Adam found that he was quite alone, and an unbearable sadness welled up inside him. When he woke up, he found he was weeping into his pillow.

He came to, slowly, and became aware of rain hammering on the roof. He felt in no hurry to get up and it seemed that everybody else was still sleeping, including the dogs. He lay there for a while, lingering on the image of Sophie dancing on the grass. Sophie, Daddy's darling little girl, spinning around on the sitting room rug and then collapsing in dizzy giggles onto the sofa. Sophie calling him from her bedroom: "Look Daddy, come and look at what I've made!" Sleepy little Sophie, snuggling up for a bedtime story. Sophie, dancing away into the darkness, never to grow old, never to grow up, never to throw her arms around her Daddy's neck ever again.

A small voice called out to him: "A-*dam* – was you crying?" Adam rolled over on to his back and saw Matty standing next to his bed, looking down at him.

"Hello Matty. I was just thinking of my little girl. I was missing her."

"What's her name?"

"Sophie. She was two a few weeks ago."

Matty looked at him for a moment and then said, "Can we get up now?"

Adam smiled to himself. His watch said six-thirty. He yawned. "Alright then. But be quiet now because Pip is still asleep."

Matty sat on the floor and played with Bonzo, who participated half-heartedly until he'd had enough and gave the boy a warning growl. Adam closed his eyes and hoped the boy would leave him alone for a while but no such luck. A small voice said, "A-*dam*."

"Yes Matty."

"Have I got to wear these clothes again? I want to wear jeans, like you."

Adam looked over at the boy, who was standing there in Pip's knickers, holding the rest of his clothes that were borrowed from the girl. They really would have to find him some new clothes, he thought.

"Hmm. We will find somewhere to get you some new clothes. Alright? But for the moment you will have to put those on again."

"Can we get me some new clothes today?"

"We'll see what we can do. In a minute we need to look at your sores."

After he had checked the boy over and applied cream Adam found the boy a banana and sat him down opposite him at the table. They would need to find him some toys, he thought, something to keep him occupied.

"Do you like reading Matty?"

The boy had a mouthful of banana and shook his head.

"What about adventure stories?"

"My sister reads them to me," the boy said. "I'm no good at reading. But I know my letters."

"That's good. Reading is so important. What *do* you like doing?"

"Well," the boy frowned and took another mouthful of banana as he thought about it, "I like fishing and football and cars and... drawing and... Have you got my fishing rod?"

"No," Adam said, remembering that the boy had been clutching one as he ran towards Pip two days ago, "I think you dropped it. We will have to find you another one."

"Today?"

"Well maybe not today. We'll see. Where we are going there is a pond and you could fish in there."

"Brill!"

They sat there for nearly half an hour while Adam drank his coffee and the boy seemed quite happy to chatter away. Adam learned about his family, his two older brothers – the oldest one seemed to have left home – and his big sister. It seems that Matty was the baby brother and Adam guessed that they made a fuss of him. He talked about his mum and how she went out to work as a cleaner. His father did not seem to appear much in the conversation. The boy seemed quite bright, though he could not read or write, and Adam wondered what went on at home that kept an intelligent child from acquiring the rudiments of primary education. Did he even go to school most of the time?

In due course Pip emerged from the loft and made herself a cup of tea. She plonked herself down on the seat next to Matty and gave him a glass of milk.

"You still got your 'jamas on," Matty observed, "Why?"

"Because some people get up too early and make lots of noise when I am still sleeping."

"You're not sleeping now."

"No, that is very true. But I would like to be."

Adam laughed. "Bit early for you, is it? I'm sorry about that. This one was up early. Anyway, you can get some sleep on the journey."

"Hmm. Not so sure about that. She's very...edgy."

"I have been thinking about Yvonne. If she does decide to come today, I am going to suggest that she rides in the van. She can leave her car here for now, and we can always find her another one in Dorset."

"You might have trouble persuading her."

"I'll find a way. Otherwise, if we go at her speed we won't get there this week."

When they had finished their drinks and Adam was thinking that it was a reasonable time to be knocking on Gwendoline's door, there was a tap on the window and there was Yvonne, sheltering under an umbrella. Adam opened the door and let her in.

"I thought I would come down and see how you were getting on," Yvonne said, looking around at the strewed bedding and the wet dogs licking themselves on their beds. "It all looks very cosy in here. Hello Matty, hello dogs. Gwendoline says to tell you that she would like to make you some breakfast before you set off and we can have a chat."

"That would be very civilised," Adam said. "We were going to come down shortly, but we didn't want to arrive too early."

"Gwendoline has been up since six. I don't think she's a big sleeper."

"How was your bed? Did you sleep well?" Pip asked.

"Yes, thank you, quite well. It was very comfortable. Well, I'll go back and tell her you are on your way."

"We can give you a lift," said Adam, but Yvonne was already stepping back out into the rain.

Upstairs at number forty-two they ate toast from bread Adam had found partly defrosted in a freezer in the mini-market. Gwendoline had an old toasting fork and they used that in front of the fire, which she had resurrected from last night's embers. The old lady was holding court.

"Now as you know, I am not going to come with you today, but I will be most interested to hear how you have been getting on, should you come back this way another day."

"Oh, we'll definitely do that, won't we Adam?" Pip said.

"Well, we shall see," the old lady continued, "As for Yvonne here, I have persuaded her that she should go with you. There is no future for her here on her own, or even with me, and I think she has lots to offer."

Yvonne gave a nervous laugh. "I wasn't sure about it, but Gwendoline has pointed out that if it doesn't work out, I can always come back. What's more she's said that I could always stay here. But I had a long think about it last night, after you had gone. I listened to what you said yesterday Adam and you're quite right. I know you're right. We have to work together, find other survivors and bring them on board. If God intended us to survive this... plague, then it is our duty to live, and not to cower away and wait for death to take us."

"That's great," said Pip, "we're really glad, aren't we Adam? I'm sure you won't regret it."

"Yes, that's good news Yvonne, welcome to our club. We look forward to having you with us."

"Thank you," Yvonne said, reddening and smiling.

"Is you coming with us, Miss?" Matty asked, with a mouth full of toast.

"Yes, Matty, I am."

"But what about you Gwendoline?" Adam said. "What if you later decide you would like to join us, which we really hope you will? We don't know when we might come up this way again and we have no way of keeping in touch with you."

"That's not strictly true, is it?" the old lady responded. "I can't get in touch with you, but you can keep in touch with me. If you broadcast at that frequency, I will be able to tune into it on my radio. Although the reception is not wonderful here, I can pick up small European stations and the police and coastguard chatter, and I have heard amateur enthusiasts too. I don't do it often now, but I used to like eavesdropping on other broadcasters. I will make a point of tuning into that frequency after supper each night and see if I can pick you up."

"I didn't think of that," said Adam, "that's a very good idea. And if we are coming up this way, or anywhere near, we'll be sure to drop by and I will transmit a message over the nights leading up to our visit. Of course, I won't know whether you will have picked the message up or not, but hopefully you will."

"And we can give you updates on how things are going with us, what the property is like, "said Pip. We can do up a room for you and you will be so curious to see it you won't be able to resist coming down."

The old lady laughed. "Steady on there, young lady. It will take a lot more than a soft bed and pretty wallpaper to get me to come. I shall be more interested in the plumbing and the power supply – and the fuel of course. Winter will be coming round quicker than you know it. But of course, you must tell me everything you are doing. Tell it to the world, if they are listening."

They got ready to depart and Adam broached the subject of the car with Yvonne. When he said that he thought it would be safer for Yvonne to travel in the van, she agreed without hesitation. They said their farewells to Gwendoline, and Yvonne let the others go to the van while she had a private word with the old lady. When she got in the cab she said to Adam, "I am so glad that I met Gwendoline, she's a wonderful woman. She has been a big help to me, really encouraging. Thank you for bringing me here to meet her."

"Not at all. I'm glad you got on so well with her. I think she took to you better than she did to us, at first meeting, at any rate."

Yvonne was very quiet as they drove out of Cheltenham and onto the motorway and Adam could sense the tension in her. She had her left hand on the door handle and Adam wondered whether she was wanting to hold on, or to get out. Pip, who was sat just behind Adam at the table, was trying to get Matty to sit down with her and not stand between the driver and the passenger seat.

"Are we going back the same way?" she asked.

"I was looking at the map earlier. I think it would be better if we stayed on the motorway all the way down to Taunton and then cut across into Dorset from there."

"That's good. I don't think I want to go near Bath again."

"Was it very bad there?" Yvonne asked.

"It was chaos in the town centre," Adam said. "It looked as if there had been a crowd there, intent on wrecking the place the evening the virus struck. It was quite strange."

"It was horrible," Pip added.

"Pip's best friend lived in Bath. We went to see if we could find her, but sadly..."

"She was...? Oh I'm so sorry. You poor girl, losing your best friend. That's very sad."

"Thank you," Pip said.

"We've all lost people, and that is why we have to find others. But it is not easy, I know."

They all fell quiet again. Even Matty, who was looking out of the side window, was lost in his own thoughts. Adam picked up speed on the motorway and, after seeming a bit agitated for a while, Yvonne asked him to slow down.

"I am worried what you would do if an animal runs out in front of you," she said.

"Yes, you're right," said Adam, letting the van slow again, "It has happened before. It's very easy to let this thing run away with you, she purrs along so nicely."

"It is a lovely vehicle. It has everything you need when you are travelling, I suppose. I take it you took it from somewhere?"

Adam told her the story of his first van and then, after meeting Pip, the need to get something bigger and how well the Drifter had served their needs so far.

"I have to say though, that after a week of sleeping on the floor and in a tent, I am looking forward to lying in a proper bed again one day. My back is feeling it a bit now."

Yvonne asked about the farm that Adam was taking them to. She wanted to know all about it, what was there and how Adam thought they could make it a viable homestead and base for the community he hoped to build. He was quite surprised by the depth of her questioning. Clearly, she had been thinking about what Adam had told them last night and she had lots of questions about technical issues and the problems they might face. It seemed that in the days since her husband and son died, she had focused on the practical aspects of her long-term survival, partly as a way of taking her mind off her grief. But now she wanted to know what Adam's plans were.

"You know, Yvonne, I have these ideas in my mind but until we get there and start to get established, I don't really know how things are going to work in practice. I can see us setting up generators, get machinery working, ensuring we have clean water, heat or power for cooking, but beyond that it is very vague. I have no knowledge of horticulture or farming. I don't know what we should try and grow and how to go about doing it. I don't know anything about slaughtering or butchering meat. All I know is that we cannot live indefinitely on tinned food raided from grocery stores and that we will need to harness the knowledge and experience of as many people as we can gather together."

"You're right, it won't be easy to do all the things that will need doing with this little group of three, especially as we have a youngster to take care of. We're all going to have to learn new skills. I do wonder whether we should put our energies into finding more people while they are still managing to stay alive before we start undertaking all these difficult tasks."

Adam explained that his idea was to find a base where they could stay safely, set up the radio so they could scan for other broadcasters and send out their own regular broadcasts. Yvonne probed this plan and picked holes, but in the end she seemed satisfied that Adam had thought things through and that maybe it could work. Pip had evidently been listening to their conversation whilst keeping Matty amused and now she chipped in.

"Before I met Adam, I didn't have a clue what was going to happen to me or how I could survive. I wasn't entirely sure that I wanted to... you know, keep going at all. I was really scared. Then when I did think about it, I realised that I had no real idea about how to look after myself. But since I've been with Adam, I see that we can all do things we didn't know we could, and I think he knows what he is talking about. I think it's a really good plan. I know I was really lucky to have spotted him that day and that he came back the next day to look for me."

"Yes, you were very lucky to have found him dear. It must have been very frightening for you, being on your own there. And I'm very grateful that you decided to drive through my village yesterday, else we would never have met. But Adam can't do everything. And you know, Gwendoline was telling me last night all the things that the women had to do in the war. Many of them had known nothing before but domestic duties, but they learned and they did what they had to. We can do our bit too."

"And Matty too," Pip said, "You'll help, won't you?"

"Yes," the boy said. "What I got to help with?"

"Oh, there will be lots of things you can do, you'll see."

"Can I have some new clothes first? I don't like these things."

They all laughed and Pip reassured him that he wouldn't have to go on wearing her clothes for ever.

Driving down the motorway was straightforward, as it had been three days earlier and apart from a herd of sheep grazing the bank of wildflowers at the side of a cutting, nothing had changed. They were soon heading south on the west side of Bristol. They had just passed the docks at Avonmouth and were on the flyover crossing the Avon when Matty said "I can see smoke."

"Oh, where's that Matty?"

"Yes, I can see it too," Pip said. "Look Adam, over there, on Yvonne's side."

Adam slowed and looked across to the left. Sure enough, a spire of dark grey smoke was reaching up into the sky above Bristol.

"It looks as if it's coming from behind that hill," Yvonne said.

Adam stopped the van and got out of the cab to have a better look. The smoke was coming from far beyond the hill and judging from its slow progress upwards, it was some way off. Yvonne had her window wound down and they were all looking out at the smoke.

"I reckon that's coming from the centre of Bristol," Adam said, getting back into the van and wiping the raindrops from his face.

"There's no smoke without fire," Pip added, helpfully.

"And that looks like a very big fire to me. I think we should go and investigate. What do you think Yvonne?"

"Well, it could have just started naturally, perhaps."

"But what could have started it?"

"I think Pip's right," Adam said, "without electricity or gas, it's very unlikely that it has started spontaneously. There's not even any sun today."

"It will give us a chance to see if there is anyone about," Pip said, "Bristol is a big city so if we are going to find anyone alive, this would be a good place to look. Don't you think, Yvonne?"

Yvonne did not look entirely comfortable about the idea of driving into the city, but she stayed quiet.

Chapter Thirty-Eight

Old Flames

Thursday 9th May, Late Morning

Adam turned the van round, drove back to the last interchange and took the road into Bristol. They followed the old west road down into the Avon Gorge, where Adam pointed out to Matty the Suspension Bridge soaring over the road. He was suitably impressed. "Wow!" he said, "can we go over it?"

"It reminds me of Ironbridge," Pip said, "you know, the river and the bridge high above it."

As they came out of the Avon Gorge towards the old part of Bristol they could see the smoke again, now a tower of swirling greys and blacks rising high into the grey sky above the town. It was coming right from the heart of the city centre and Adam turned off the main road down towards the river. Either side of the road were tall nineteenth century buildings with shops, banks and restaurants fronting the road. At the end of the street a pall of smoke filled the road, blocking their route, and Adam stopped the van. The smoke seemed to be coming from somewhere on the left. He got out and turned to say, "Don't let the dogs out."

Pip said to Adam "I'm coming too," and asked Yvonne if she would keep an eye on Matty. As they got nearer, the wind changed direction and the smoke cleared from the road and when they got to the junction they could see the source. Along the road to the left a large old building was well ablaze with fire and smoke pouring from its windows. As they walked closer, they could feel the heat and they stopped some fifty metres from the fire.

"It looks like an old hotel, doesn't it?" Pip said.

"That was the Grand," Adam said. "I had a drink in the bar there once on a pub crawl. It was a lovely old place, as I remember."

"You won't be able to do that again," Pip said.

"No. That's doubly true now."

"I wonder how it started. It's really blazing."

At that moment there was a loud crash and a jet of flame shot up from the upper floor and clouds of smoke poured out."

"Looks like the roof has gone," Adam said. "Time to retreat." The smoke was spiralling down into the street and starting to come towards them. They turned and walked quickly back to the junction just in time to see Matty running towards them, followed by the two dogs. Yvonne was following.

"I tried to keep them in, but Matty insisted on coming to see the fire," she called out.

Adam called the dogs and he and Pip managed to grab them. They all stood and watched the fire consuming the building, Matty with eyes like saucers. The frontage started to come down and every time a new piece fell the boy said "Cor! Look at that!" or "Wow!" Meanwhile Yvonne watched with a look of horror on her face.

"At least we know there won't be anyone alive in there," Pip said.

"But it's so sad," Yvonne said," I hate to see a building burning. It's a terrible thing, fire."

"If it was someone that started the fire, let's hope they got out in time," Adam said. "I'm going to take these boys back to the van. Come on boys, Bonzo, Boyo. Heel!"

The dogs followed him, obediently and Adam was quietly chuffed. Pip and Yvonne came after, with Matty and they were soon back in the van, the dogs shaking the rain off them all over Matty, who thought it was hilarious.

"I'm going to drive around the centre a bit and see if we can see anybody. Everyone OK with that?"

There were no dissenters, so Adam took them on a small tour of the city centre, criss-crossing the streets of restaurants, old houses, modern shops and offices. After about twenty minutes of to-ing and fro-ing they were driving along the side of Castle Park when Adam spotted a figure, a woman, walking away across the grass. Adam sounded the horn and the woman stopped, turned and stared. Then she shouted at a figure further away, a man. He stopped, turned and looked back, swaying slightly. She shouted again and beckoned for him to come. She waved at the van, to indicate that she had seen them, and then walked briskly back to the man. She took him by the arm, grabbed one of the two bags he was carrying and steered him, like a shopping trolley with a wonky wheel, towards the van. Adam turned off the engine and got out. The couple came towards him, seeming oblivious of the rain, which looked like it had already soaked them. They looked grubby and dishevelled and wore an odd assortment of clothing, but some items looked almost new. They looked like they had been sleeping rough for a while.

"Well hello. I'm Babs," the woman said and, waving her arm at her companion, "and this is Snarky. Say hello, Snarky. I apologise for this shambles of a man. He was a bit upset and had a bit too much to drink. Look what we have here Snarky, some people in a camper van. Come and say hello."

"Hello," said the man, unsteadily, "I'm John."

"Hello John, I'm Adam. It's a bit wet to be out and about – are you on your way home?"

Babs gave a hoarse, dismissive laugh. "We were at home. Nice place it was too, but then it burned down."

"My God, Adam said, "were you in the Grand?"

Babs gave another, mirthless laugh: "We'd been there about a week, and very cosy we were too. But then somebody, some drunken arse – mind my language –burned the place down."

"Oh dear, that's sad. That was a fine old place," Adam said, glancing towards the van, where Yvonne and Pip looked on. Clearly, they did not wish to venture out into the rain to greet this forlorn looking pair. "Look, you'd better come into the van for a bit and dry off. We can offer you tea or coffee."

"Eh, Snarky, what do you say to that? A hot drink would be very welcome, very welcome indeed. Thank you."

Adam showed them into the back of the van and introduced them to the others. Yvonne, who had stayed put in the passenger seat, turned and said hello, rather coolly. Pip stood up, introduced herself and ushered them to the sofa at the back of the van, where they sat down, their bags arranged around them. Matty just stared, while the dogs sniffed them suspiciously and then decided that they were harmless.

Babs was a broad, sturdy woman, in her forties, perhaps, with untidy, shoulder-length strawberry blonde hair spilling across her face. She wore a long, green patterned skirt over scuffed mid-calf leather boots, a baggy pink mohair jumper and a short fur coat. A sagging, damp red felt fedora was perched on the back of her head. Her eyes were hollowed out from her sallow face and they flitted around, quickly taking in the surroundings. Her hands were large, and blemished with prominent veins and blotches, as of a much older woman, and the varnish on her fingernails was chipped. She coughed continuously, a raspy, nagging sound which punctuated her sentences at random.

John, or Snarky, was a man in his late forties with long thin, lank greying hair pulled across his balding scalp and tied in a ponytail. He wore an expensive-looking tan leather jacket over a check shirt and a yellow waistcoat, with new-looking brown corduroy trousers and brown shoes, and a red scarf around his neck. His shirt and jacket were stained and covered in sooty black marks and his trousers were covered in wet patches. His right hand was wrapped in a makeshift, white cotton bandage. He slumped down on the sofa and looked around at the van and these new, strange people with his mouth open and a surprised look on his face.

"Would you like tea or coffee?" Pip asked, trying to sound friendly.

"Oh tea for me darling," Babs replied, looking the young girl up and down. She spoke loudly in a rasping Bristol accent. "And he'll have the same. Won't you Snarky? No more drink for you today, you old sot. So what did you say your name was – Pip, was it? Is this your family then?" The woman looked across at Yvonne as she said this, assessing the possible relationships here.

Adam took the lead: "No, we're not related, any of us, but we are a sort of family now I suppose. I met Pip in Dorset and then we found Matty in Birmingham and Yvonne in Broadway."

"Birmingham, eh? I was up there recently. You sound like a Brummie too, darling. What were you doing in Dorset?"

"We moved there from Bournville – my parents ran a guest-house."

"Oh, a guesthouse. Very nice. And what about you? What are you doing with these people?" Babs asked, looking at Yvonne who looked even more uncomfortable with this question.

"I was living on my own after my family died and Adam and Pip suggested that I joined them in setting up a base in Dorset."

"A base, you say. What sort of base?"

Adam gave a brief explanation of their plans and then, turning to the man, asked what their history was.

"I come from London. Worked for the Inland Revenue," he mumbled, "and then when I met Babs, I came down here to Bristol."

"You never worked in your life, you old toss-pot," Babs cried, "I worked for the Revenue – leastways, they used to take all my wages in taxes! I was a landlady and that's where I first met this reprobate, for my sins. He was a right smoothie then. But then much later we got together and then – and it's a long story – we fell on hard times."

"And that's how you ended up at the Grand then?" Adam asked.

"We've been living there since all the shit happened. Found it was open, so we moved in. Not exactly paying guests, though." Babs chuckled, and then seeing Yvonne's displeasure at this remark, she added: "And I bet you didn't pay for this lovely mobile home either, did you?"

As if in answer, Matty suddenly spoke up: "It's not her van, it's Adam's. It's a *camper* van and it's got beds and a bathroom and a kitchen."

"Is that right? Well luvvie, as I say, it's a very nice van."

"Your clothes are all wet and they smell funny," the boy added.

"Matty, that's not a nice thing to say," said Pip. "This lady got a bit wet in the rain."

"That's alright darling, he's only a kiddy. You look like a bright boy, Matty. Where's your mummy then?"

"She's dead," the boy said and looked down at his feet.

"I'm sorry to hear that, darling. You are lucky that these nice people found you then."

"It seems you were lucky to get out of the hotel in time," Adam said, "the fire was really raging when we got here. How did it start exactly?"

The woman laughed. "That's what I've been wanting to find out. How did it start Snarky? Do tell everyone."

The man looked uncomfortable and shifted in his seat. "I told you, Babs, you know full well."

"Well tell me again – they all want to hear."

John glared at her, but she indicated she wasn't going to take no for an answer. "I fell asleep on the bed and when I woke up the curtains were on fire. I didn't have any water to throw on them so I had to get out of the room and then..."

"And how did the fire start Snarky?"

"I was smoking," the man mumbled.

"Yes, that's right – you were *smoking*," she said, pointing her finger at him. "You were lying on the bed with a bottle of Glenlivet in one hand, a magazine in the other and a fag in your gob, oh yes – and a candle on a saucer by the bed – and then you dropped off." She was getting into the swing of the story now, "As did the fag – onto the magazine. And when that caught fire and burned your hand you dropped the whisky and whoomph! You were smoking alright – you were lucky you didn't go up in flames, the amount of alcohol in your body. You could have been burned alive, you silly sod. Mind you, that's no less than what you deserved."

"Alright, alright. Don't go on. They've heard the story now."

"See the problem was," said Babs turning back to Adam now, "it was very comfortable in the hotel, a bit too comfortable. I mean for someone who likes a drink *now and then,*" looking back at the man, "a bar full of spirits – well actually two bars – that was a bit too much of a temptation. I should have been keeping an eye on him, I suppose, but God, I'm not his nurse-maid."

The woman caught sight of Yvonne's raised eyebrows: "Yes, well, you can tut-tut over there, but this silly old sod saved my life once, so I can't walk away from him. Can I?" she asked, turning back to the man, "even though you're a drunken old tosspot. I tell you, it's like having a child to look after."

Matty, who had been listening closely to this strange woman, laughed out loud at this.

"So, when did you first know about the fire?" Adam asked.

"I was downstairs in the lounge when I heard him screaming and shouting for me up on the first floor. When I got up there his room was full of smoke and I could see that the fire was already out of control. He had been trying to put it out by beating it down with his coat but the curtains caught and then the smoke got too thick. I had to drag him out. There was nothing we could do to stop the fire. I found a fire extinguisher and tried to use it but I couldn't get it to work. The corridor filled up with smoke and well, we just had to get out of there. By the time we got outside we could see that the fire was spreading through the first floor. It was scary just how fast it went up. We watched it from across the road for a bit but when the windows started blowing out, we decided to move on."

"By the time *we* got there the roof was already starting to collapse, so you wouldn't have had long," Adam said. "Where were you living before you went to the hotel?"

"We were living rough. We'd been moving around for a while. After we were in hospital last year – that's where we met up again actually – they moved us into a house and we were there for a couple of months. But after that it was a question of staying where we could, really – squats, hostels – wherever there was a bed and some food. Because we didn't have an address or any I.D. we couldn't get any work and nor could we claim any proper benefits. That meant we couldn't find a permanent place to live. So it was doss house here, a homeless hostel there and sometimes just a bench in the park. They kept moving us on. Not long ago we'd been sleeping rough up on the Downs."

"That's awful!" said Pip

"Well, darling it weren't a barrel of laughs, but – you know. I'd done it before. It was up there that I took some bad stuff – you know what I mean. I passed out and it was Snarky here that went to get help and they got an ambulance to take me into the Infirmary. I would have been a goner. It was this old fool that saved my life, bless him."

"Is your name Snarky?" Matty said, laughing. "That's a funny name!"

"Yes, where *did* you get that from? Was it from work?" said Babs, "Or is it because you're a bit snarky and snidey sometimes?"

"Snarky and Spidey? – that's funny," Matty said and he carried on chuckling.

The man coughed and said "It was my Mum used to call me 'The Snark'. I never came back for tea in time, so she said I was like the Snark, the mythical creature in that poem. You know, never gets found."

"Oh yeah, I remember: The Hunting of the Snark" said Pip, who was in the process of handing out the mugs of tea, "That's about a crew of people, all beginning with B, who go hunting the Snark."

"That's it," the man said, "and the name sort of stuck."

They drank their tea and talked about what had been happening since the virus struck. Babs and Snarky had been living in a squat with some people they knew, but they all died within a couple of days. They wandered around the town to see if there was anyone else alive, but they found no-one. They had seen a couple of military Land Rovers driving away along the road from where they were walking but it appeared whoever was driving had not seen them or did not want to stop. That was the only occasion Babs saw or heard any sign of life, though Snarky claimed he had heard vehicles driving around one day. They did not know why they had managed to survive the virus, and Babs had not made the connection with their stay in hospital last year. Adam asked them what their plans were now they were homeless again.

"Well we were heading for another hotel where we know the back door is always open. Not as nice as the Grand, but better than a park bench. Course the problem now is finding food that's still fit to eat. Can't eat out of tins for ever." Babs sat back in her seat and looked over at Adam. "But you know, your plan makes a lot o' sense, a lot o' sense. The more I think about it the more I see that we got to do something. We can't just stay here dossing about for ever. If we joined up with you we could play a part in the community you talk about. Yeah, yeah, I know what you're thinking," this with a glance at Yvonne, "but we can clean ourselves up, get ourselves together. We've got some talents between us, we have. I used to run pubs and do the cooking lot of the time. And old Snarky, when he worked for the Revenue, he was in charge of the catering at their London office. He was quite a chef, in his day. Yes, we could make ourselves very useful."

This little speech was greeted with an embarrassed silence as Adam, Yvonne and Pip all looked at each other, but the woman did not wait for them to come up with a response.

"Well I can see that suggestion went down like a lead balloon." she laughed. "What do we want with a couple of dossers who've just set the Grand on fire, you're asking? Yes, I can see how it looks. But you don't know what we are capable of. And what are these two going to bring to the party?" condemning the other two women with a withering glance. "It takes all sorts to make a community and there's no telling who's going to pull their weight when it comes to the graft. And what you're talking about – there's going to be a lot of hard graft needed."

"You are absolutely right," Adam said, "it's going to take a lot of hard work and I have no doubt that you're both very capable people, or could be. The reason I hesitated, and I expect it was the same for Pip and Yvonne, is that I was thinking how you would travel with us. We really don't have enough room in this van to take you with us."

"That's a bit of a poor man's excuse," Babs said. "Be honest, you don't want us to come along."

"No, that's not true," Pip said, "anyone should be able to join in. We all have to help each other. I think that you need our help now, but later one of us might need help too, in a different way."

Yvonne decided it was time that she contributed to the argument.

"Adam's right, there isn't enough room in this van. And, I have to add, that even if there was, I don't think I would want to travel with you in your present state." She had started uncertainly, her voice wavering, but now she spoke with increasing confidence. "I know there probably aren't many of us left and we have to make room for everybody but...frankly he's a liability."

"Well that's nice, isn't it?" Babs said

"I'm sorry but I mean: look at him, John, or Snark or whatever his name is: he's so drunk he can barely stand up. I've managed to survive this plague, thanks to God's good grace, and I don't want to die in a fire because of someone else's irresponsible behaviour. I mean, really – he doesn't deserve to have survived. I'm sorry to have to say this, but it had to be said." Yvonne sat back in her seat, shaking and red in the face.

"Well it's quite clear what you think of us, miss hoity-toity, butter-wouldn't-melt-in-your-mouth. I'd like to see how you got on without these people to look after you." Babs hauled herself up out of her seat and advanced, finger jabbing, towards the front of the van where Yvonne was sitting... "You can act all holier-than-thou in your pleated skirt and head-girl sensible shoes, but how do you think you're going to look when you've been digging out some mangy, worm-eaten spuds from a muddy potato patch? You look at us and think we are a pair of smelly street rats, but you might not smell too good yourself in a month or two."

"Well!" Yvonne gasped, a look of indignation raising her eyebrows even higher than usual. "That's not what I am like, at all. You know nothing about me. I'm a damn sight tougher than you think, but at least I have some pride in my appearance!"

"Pride!" Babs scoffed." Pride won't get you anywhere in this world, my lover and nor will talking posh and looking down your nose at everyone."

Matty had been watching this argument with eyes and mouth wide open, but now he closed his eyes and covered his ears.

"This man, my very good friend, John – he has an illness and it's called alcoholism. That's not something you can get over without help." Babs was standing, hands-on-hips, then waving theatrically, "He's sick, he has a sickness. But he can recover, with help and I have seen it done. I know I weren't there when he got himself on the bottle in that hotel – I shoulda been and I weren't. But he saved my life once, and I am going to help him save his own life now. If we were to go somewhere right away from the temptation of easy liquor, he could get himself back on the wagon. But we don't need your help Miss prim-and-proper, thank you very much – we can do it on our own. So I will say, thank you little darling for the tea and thank you Adam for your hospitality, I wish you all the best with your plans. As for you... they are welcome to you. Come on Snarky, we're going."

The raised voices seemed to have brought the man out of his stupor and now he wanted to speak. He stood up, a little uncertainly, then pulled himself up to his full height and smoothed down his shirt and trousers.

"Hold on a minute Babs, just wait a minute. I would like to say something." Babs went to speak but he waved her to be quiet, and carried on in a slow, deliberate fashion: "I think you're being a bit hasty there. This woman is quite right, I *am* a liability. I'm ashamed of what I did. I let myself go and I have disappointed myself. I know I can do better than that."

"Oh, stop your wittering man, we are going NOW!" the woman cried. She went to grab his arm, but he swayed back out of reach.

"No!" he spoke softly, but firmly. "Just for once, let me speak. These people don't want us in this state and they're quite right to think that way. I mean, look at us – we don't deserve to have survived that, that plague or whatever it was. We need to get ourselves together, prove to ourselves – and not anyone else – that we can look after ourselves and be responsible. No, let me speak!" Babs stood, mouth open as if to say something, but now she sat back down on her chair. The man went on:

"I can beat this thing. I know I can. It's not going to be easy, but I have done it before and I could do it again. I want to be rid of it. I really do." He looked round at the woman who was looking at him with a look of condescension.

"I got a fright today. I could have been a goner, just like *you* were nearly a goner that day up on the Downs. But sitting here and listening to what Yvonne there was saying, I say she's right – I need to pull myself together, we need to clean ourselves up. I am ashamed of myself. I'd like us to do that and then perhaps we can go down to wherever they are setting up camp and maybe then they will let us join them. I can drive there, I can find us a car – we can show them that we can play a part in their new community. That's what we have to do Babs."

"Oh Christ, I've heard it all now. Give me strength!" said Babs, getting up and wrapping her fur coat around her. "Get the bloody violins out. You're all mouth and trousers you are. Give it half an hour and you'll be smashing an off-licence window to get at a bottle. I'm going, you come or stay, I don't care. I need a smoke!" And with that she picked up her bag, stormed out of the door and strode off across the park.

They watched her go and nobody spoke, except Matty, who looked up at Adam and said "Has the bad woman gone now? I didn't like her".

John stood where he was, swayed a little, and looked at them all in turn.

"I'm sorry about that everyone. Babs can be a little hot-headed at times. She'll simmer down in a while. And, Yvonne, I do apologise for all those things she said to you. That was very... very unkind of her."

Adam had watched the whole drama unfold without saying a word, but he now got up from the table. "Well, that was interesting. Phewee." He blew through his teeth and shook his head. "That's one hell of a woman you've got there John. I hope you can get things straightened out between you and I really hope you can kick the alcohol habit. As you say, it won't be easy." He paused, thinking carefully what to say next. "Look, I'll tell you where we are going and if you are able, come down and see where we are and how we are getting on. I'm sure we can make a place for you somewhere. And Babs, though I think we'll need to be convinced that she could fit in, and I'm not sure that she would want to anyway. But it's not just my decision – you'll have to convince everybody that you can work with us and not be a danger to us. Yvonne, Pip – are you happy for me to tell John where we are going?"

They both said yes, Pip with a smile, Yvonne not so enthusiastically. Adam found some paper and wrote down what he thought was the address of Whitehouse farm, along with some directions and the road number which he found on the atlas. John took it with a thank you, or three, and shook Adam's hand firmly. He said thank you and gave a little bow to Pip and then Yvonne, did up his coat, picked up their other bags and stepped out into the rain.

"He's going to get soaked again," Pip said

"Well let's hope he can dry out later – in more ways than one," said Adam.

They watched John make his way across the park, his step a little more certain than it had been an hour earlier when the woman had dragged him over to the van.

"I feel sorry for him," Pip said, "having to hang around with that woman. If he's Snarky then she is definitely *Sarcky*. Do you think he *will* stop drinking?"

"In my experience once you are an alcoholic, you're always one. I was married to one," Yvonne said.

"That must have been difficult," Adam said, as he started up the van.

"Yes, it was, though perhaps not the worst thing. He wasn't like that man. I think John has lost his dignity and knows it. My husband never realised what he had become."

"I thought Babs was quite funny at first, but then she was so awful, the things she was saying to him and about him – it wasn't very nice," said Pip.

"Well I'm very glad they are not coming with us, either of them and to be honest I hope that we never see them again."

"Do you think they will ever find their way to that farm Adam?"

"I would be surprised," Adam said, "but you never know. And we need to get there today if we can, so shall we go?"

Chapter Thirty-Nine

Out of Hours

Thursday 9th May, Late Afternoon

Pip and Yvonne said that they could do with something to keep them going, so as soon as they were out of the town Adam found a place where they could let the dogs out. The rain had eased now, so Pip and Adam took Matty around a large field with the dogs, leaving Yvonne, who had volunteered to make them a snack, in the van.

When they got back to the van Yvonne had made them a snack and coffee and tea.

"How do you like our kitchen then?" Adam asked her.

"Well, it has everything you need, except an oven. It is so clever how they squeeze everything into such a small space."

After they had eaten and were finishing off their hot drinks, Yvonne brought the subject round to Babs:

"I hope you don't think I spoke out of turn when I said I did not want those two with us. I know God has a place for everyone, but that woman was so uncouth and he, he was... I don't know how best to say it... a waster, a wreck. He would have been a big problem for us. I probably shouldn't have said what I did, but... well I just had to say it."

"Babs was a bit of a hothead, as John said, and very opinionated," said Adam, "I am sure she could be very annoying, but underneath it all I think she was OK. I think that in this new world, when there are so few of us around, we have to be more tolerant. That's not something I've always been very good at, I know. Perhaps you were a bit too hasty to condemn her."

"I don't understand how you can be so... so accepting. She was a monster of a woman. Her language, her attitude. It was awful. The way she spoke to me. And the way she treated that man."

"Actually, I think in her own way she cared for John quite a lot. It's her manner to be sarcastic and loud – probably comes from years in the pub trade. She could be quite funny – she made me laugh, some of the things she said. I can see that you two rubbed each other up the wrong way, but I'm sure, given time, you could iron out your differences."

Yvonne gave a sceptical humph but did not respond.

"Pip and I were talking about them and I think it was wrong of us to drive off and leave them. I am wondering now whether we should go back and try and find them."

Yvonne turned on him sharply: "If you're going to do that then I am not coming with you. You can take me back to Cheltenham and leave me with Gwen."

Adam laughed momentarily, then bit his tongue. "Pip, what do you think?"

"Don't ask Pip," Yvonne said, "she's just a girl. *You* need to make a decision Adam."

"I am not *just* an anything," Pip said. "I might be young, but I am not a child. I think we should stop arguing. I think we should carry on to Dorset, as we planned, and then maybe later, when we go looking for other people we can come back to Bristol and see if we can find them. That's if they have not come and found us first."

"I think you're right, Pip," Adam said, "we shouldn't let those two come between us and derail our plans. Hopefully they will pull themselves together. Yvonne, you and I should bury our differences here and let's carry on. What do you think?"

Yvonne, sniffed, straightened herself up and looked as if she was having to accept a humiliating defeat. "Yes, I suppose so."

"OK, that's agreed then," said Adam. "I propose we head for Dorset, but en-route we need to look for some clothes for Matty and some other things. There are one or two things I could do with and I expect you might too, Pip?" Pip nodded. "I was thinking that Taunton might be a good place to find clothes shops and other things. We should have looked in Bristol, but Taunton will do just as well, as we are going past. What do you think Yvonne?"

"Yes, that's probably a good idea. Perhaps we should draw up a list of what we need. See what food we have in stock."

"Matty could do with some drawing paper and pens. He likes drawing, don't you Matty?" said Pip.

The boy nodded and then said, "Do you think I could have a car to play with?"

"I am sure we can find you something. You can have a look when we find a toy shop." Matty's face lit up.

"There's a big department store in Taunton, I believe," Yvonne said, "I can't remember what it's called, but they would probably have toys as well as clothes."

An hour later they were driving along the high street in Taunton. Halfway down on the left was Hatchers Department Store, with its broad frontage and plate glass windows, some with mannequins modelling clothes and others with displays of household and furnishings items. Adam pulled up near the double doors of the entrance and went to get his tools. The others got out and Adam had to tell Matty sharply not to let the dogs follow. Pip waved her can of pepper spray to let Adam know she had it. Adam went to the boot, but didn't open it. He was looking at the shop doors.

"I don't think I'll need my tools," he said, "someone's already been in here."

Sure enough, one door was unlocked, and had clearly been forced.

"That's quite a neat job," he said, "someone knew what they were doing. Pip can you grab the torches?" She went back into the van to get them, and they all went into the shop.

Adam went ahead and checked that there were no sounds coming from inside the shop.

"It's rather spooky, isn't it?" Yvonne said as they walked away from the doorway into the darkness.

"I don't like it in here," Matty said. He was clutching Pip's hand.

"There's nothing to be afraid of. You can help choose some clothes when we get to that section," she said.

Adam was pointing his torch at a store guide sign. "It's on the first floor. Need to go up the escalator." He had been casting around in the darkness with his torch but so far could see no signs of anything being disturbed. He wondered what the intruders had come in for.

They filed up the escalator and into the complete darkness of the first floor. Eventually they found the children's clothes and though it was not easy by torchlight, they managed to find some jeans and other clothes that would fit an eight-year-old. Matty wanted to put them on there and then, but Pip explained that they did not have time. Once they had fitted him out with a new wardrobe the girls went to find things in the ladies' section while Adam took Matty over to Menswear.

They reassembled with arms full of clothing, which they took over to the cash desk to find some bags to put it all in.

"It doesn't seem right, not paying," Yvonne said.

"You can pay if you want to," Pip laughed, "but I didn't bring my purse."

Adam suggested that the women wait there while he took Matty up to the toy department. When he came back down with two bags of stuff, with Matty, who was looking very excited, carrying a bag of toys, Yvonne said,

"I'm glad you're back. I don't feel safe in here. I keep thinking that there might be someone else here. Or some bodies."

"I've been looking around, but I don't see any sign of anyone. Whatever they broke into the shop for, they came and went without leaving any traces. As for bodies – you'd smell them long before you got to them. I expect the staff locked up and went home on the Friday evening and never came in again."

They went down to the ground floor and out of the shop. They were all relieved to be outside in daylight again. Adam thought how they would have to get used to that darkness, especially come the winter.

After the blackness in the shop and with the clouds now lifting, the light seemed incredibly bright and it seemed to lift all their moods. They got their bags into the van and packed them into the little space that was left in the sitting area at the back, and Adam said, "Now this van is definitely, completely full. We are not putting anything else in here as there is nowhere left to put it!"

Matty could not understand why he couldn't put his new clothes on and play with his toys all at once. In the end they persuaded him to put on some jeans and a t-shirt before they let him unpack his toys.

"Are you going to navigate us to Dorset, Pip?" Adam said.

"I thought I was going to be in the back with Matty?"

"Can't you do both?"

"No, I cannot! Not unless you want me sick all down your back."

"I can do it," said Yvonne, "If you tell me where we are headed."

"Great," said Adam, "here's the road atlas. We are heading for Dorchester. Take us there!"

She reminded Adam that they were going to stop for supplies first so on the way back out of town they stopped at a small supermarket. Once Adam had got the door open he and Yvonne found the things they needed. He made her tie a scarf tightly around her face, but even then she had trouble stopping herself from retching, so in the end Adam took the list and the torch and sent her back outside. He did three forays into the shop, coming out for air each time, and managed to get almost everything on the list. He was getting quite practised at holding his breath while he dashed around the shop.

Back in the van, shopping stowed, Yvonne apologised to him, "I'm sorry, I wasn't much help to you in there. It was quite claustrophobic in the dark and I'm afraid I just couldn't cope with the smell."

"That's OK," said Adam, "I've had a bit of practice this last week or so. You can make up for it by navigating us to Whitehouse Farm."

"Thank you, Adam. Now I'll need my glasses for this." As they drove back out of the town she said, "Peter used to ask me to navigate if we went somewhere new and then he would shout at me if I got it wrong, so I hope you won't do that." She peered at the map, flicking over the page and back again. "Now there is a direct route, but it seems to take the B roads. Or we can keep to the A roads, but it's a bit further."

"I think the A roads would be best – probably not so many small villages to get stuck in. And I won't shout at you if you get it wrong."

"Well, that's a relief," Yvonne said.

"But," he said slowly, "if you do get it wrong, you will have to sit in the back and play snap with Matty."

"Right!" said Yvonne, very seriously, "I won't get it wrong then."

She got them onto their route. It was a good road and in normal times Adam would have put his foot down along here, but with the ever-present threat of a collision with a deer or any number of other creatures wandering on the road, and with Yvonne sitting in the passenger seat, he took it slowly. Even though she was now a little warmer with him, he could sense that as soon as she was in the vehicle she was on edge, as if very apprehensive about something as yet unseen.

The late afternoon sun lit up the water drops on the roadside trees and hedges so they sparkled like tiny fairy lights. The countryside was flat here and not especially pretty, but it was a pleasant drive and Adam felt quite upbeat. It felt good to be heading south again, towards Dorset, to their new home. It was a little like coming home after a being away on a work trip, or perhaps, like driving to a favourite holiday destination – there was the warm anticipation of going to something familiar and at the same time feeling a little excited about something new.

Matty was happily playing a game with Pip in the back – he appeared to have bonded with the girl really well, Adam thought. Yvonne had been very quiet on the journey to Taunton but she seemed to have thawed a little after the shopping expedition and Adam thought it might be an opportune time to find out more about her former life. Evidently it was in her nature to be shy and reserved but Adam hoped that her defensiveness and prickliness would mellow as she got to know and trust them better. If not, then living and working with her was going to be hard work. He decided to plunge straight in:

"Yvonne, I get the impression that your husband could be a difficult man – is that right?" He glanced over to see how she reacted to this question.

She looked a little surprised, took a deep breath and said, "Well...actually, the man was a bully."

Adam had not really been expecting that. "I'm sorry, is this something you would rather not talk about?"

"No, it's fine," she said, hesitantly. "Um, well...alright then. When I first met Peter, I thought he was a real find. He came from a good family, was doing very well in his career; he seemed popular with his work colleagues and had lots of friends; my parents liked him and he ticked all their boxes – the ideal husband for their daughter. He was good-looking and he treated me like a lady and, frankly, I fell head-over-heels in love with him."

There was a pause, so Adam said "But?"

"But once we were married my eyes were opened. No, that's not quite fair. For a while after the wedding, we were happy, at least I thought he was happy too. He wanted a family, lots of children – he was one of seven – and it became apparent quite quickly that he saw my role as being the traditional wife: the mother of his children, hostess for his business entertaining and his general helper and, well frankly, his servant."

"I guess that was not the life you had hoped for?"

"Well not exactly. I had my job, not a high-flying career, but I enjoyed my work. I was always organised, neat, perhaps fastidious even, at school, and working in the law suited my personality. I was quite shy as a girl and doing important work behind the scenes was just perfect for me. I didn't ever think that I would have to give that up."

"But why did you need to? These days, with child-minders and crèches and the like?"

"That's what I thought, but Peter had different ideas." She paused a moment and then carried on. "He was doing well and earning good money. He had some very well-heeled clients and he expected me to play my part in wining and dining them, oiling the wheels of business, if you like. He made it clear that he did not want me to work at all, not even part-time."

"How did you feel about that?"

"I wasn't happy, but I realised that this was what everyone was expecting me to do: my parents, because that was the way of the world to them, and his friends and colleagues, because they all had stay-at-home wives. My friend Sally told me I should put my foot down and refuse to give up my job, but I was an old-fashioned girl and I had promised, in front of God, to honour and obey my husband. You might find that strange, as a "modern" man, but I took my vows in church, and I was going to be true to them."

Adam felt he did not have any useful comment he could make there, so he waited for Yvonne to carry on.

"It was only later I realised that Peter expected me to obey him in everything he demanded of me and some of those things were... well not what I was used to doing, let's put it that way."

Adam's mind wandered briefly over the many types of things that Yvonne might not be used to doing but quickly came to the conclusion that it was probably something that he shouldn't probe too deeply.

"I was twenty-four when we got married, which was quite young really, especially as I was a bit of a late developer. Peter was a few years older than me and was impatient to start making a family. Unfortunately, hard as we tried, a baby did not materialise and after a while I could see Peter getting concerned about this. I started to feel like one of Henry the Eighth's wives – produce me an heir, or else."

"Hopefully you didn't think you were going to lose your head?"

"Not exactly, but I did start to get anxious. I knew just how important it was to him."

"And that anxiety is not a good recipe for having a lovechild," said Adam, "But were you ever in... danger?"

"I don't want to talk about that here," Yvonne said in a low voice and when Adam looked across, he saw Yvonne indicate the rear of the van. Matty was chattering away to Pip, so he did not imagine that Pip had heard anything, but clearly Yvonne was not wanting younger ears to hear.

She carried on, quietly: "Eventually I managed to get pregnant – I was twenty-eight by then – but then I lost the baby." She paused and looked away.

"Oh, I'm sorry," Adam said.

"Fortunately, Ralphy came along a couple of years later and Peter was much more content for a while. Ralphy's a lovely boy, very quiet-natured – a bit like me, I suppose. As he grew up, so Peter became more disappointed in him. It seems he was not the boy that Peter had been hoping for. I... I'm sorry."

"That's OK," said Adam, gently. "We don't have to talk about it."

Yvonne took a deep breath and blew out slowly. "I think perhaps I shouldn't say any more, not here."

"I think I get the picture. It wasn't the happiest of marriages, was it? I'm sorry."

They fell silent for a while and Adam tuned into the chatter coming from the table, where Pip was playing a game with Matty. After a while Yvonne spoke again:

"So what about you Adam – was your marriage happy?"

"Yes, we were very happy. Jo and I got together nearly ten years ago now and got married in eighty-three. Just over a year later, Oscar came along and then Sophie two years ago. We were very lucky. We had good jobs, two lovely children – it was just perfect really. Too good to last, as it turned out."

"You mean – things went wrong?"

"No, not at all. I was talking about the virus."

"Yes, of course. I see. It was the worst thing in my life when Ralphy died, I…" She couldn't continue. After a while she composed herself and turned to Adam and asked:

"Adam, it must have been just as terrible for you too. Yet you seem to be so cheerful and positive. How is that?"

Adam laughed. "Am I? I think I do it for Pip, and Matty. At night, then it's not so easy. In the days after V Day, when I was on my own, I began to wonder what the point was in carrying on in this world."

"I know what you mean," Yvonne said, quietly. "But you don't believe in another world, do you?"

"I don't know about that. I am living in this world at the moment and that's the one that counts. I just tell myself that we have to have hope, we have to believe. And now that we have a few of us, our little team or family, we have to believe in ourselves and each other."

"Yes, you're right."

"And look," said Adam, defiantly and loudly, "the rain has stopped, the sun is shining, it's May! There is so much still to live for."

"Amen to that," Yvonne said, and behind her Pip sniggered, and Matty copied her.

After Crewkerne the road to Dorchester wound its way through several villages before getting up onto higher ground, where it ran straight as a die, and they had open views on either side. It was a fine evening and Yvonne seemed happy to enjoy the ride. In the back it had gone very quiet and when Adam tilted his rearview mirror, he saw that Matty had gone to the back of the van and was, as often it seemed, curled up on the floor with the dogs.

After a while Pip popped up between the two front seats to see where they were.

"I see you've worn Matty out," Adam said, "has he worn you out too?"

"Well, I'm glad of the break," Pip said, "but we've been having a nice time actually, doing drawings and playing ludo. He's quite competitive – he doesn't like losing. How long before we get to the farm now Adam, do you think?"

"Once we get round Dorchester, it's not too far. Maybe another half an hour."

"I'm quite looking forward to seeing the place again, though I can't remember it very clearly."

"You had your mind on other things that morning, didn't you?"

"I'm very interested to see the place," Yvonne said. "I have a sort of picture in my mind from what you were telling us, but I suspect it will turn out to be quite different. What are the plans for this evening when we get there?"

"If we can find the keys for all the places, it would be good to look them over. Hopefully there will be some comfortable beds and some nice clean linen, so that some of us might sleep in comfort tonight. But we will have to use the van for cooking and eating, and we will need to get Matty settled for the night."

They talked about the things they would need to do this evening before it got dark, and what their priorities would be tomorrow. Yvonne got quite involved with this discussion and showed that she had a very practical mind. In his "team" Adam was repositioning her from "critical and negative" to "observant and questioning". He could see that he would need to involve her in the decision-making process at all stages and he wondered whether she felt the need to assert her opinion now because of her experiences in her marriage.

Chapter Forty

Whitehouse Farm

Thursday 9th May, Evening

It was coming on for six in the evening by the time Adam turned off the main road and started up Hangman's Hill. He followed the lane past the two farmsteads and up to the top of the hill, where wide views of the Dorset coast opened out, a broad plain of green and, beyond, glimpses of the bright blue of Weymouth Bay glinting in the evening sunshine.

"I can see the sea!" Pip cried.

"That's a beautiful view," Yvonne said. "Is that the farm down there?"

Ahead of them the lane dropped down and there was the white house on the left and, beyond that, nestling in the trees, the farm. He drove slowly past the house and down to the farmyard. It all looked exactly as it had a week ago. "Welcome to Holmwood," he said.

"So this is the farmhouse and the cottages you were telling us about. And was that the White House back there?" Yvonne asked.

"Yes, that's right," said Adam. "That gives us more options, but I think these places might be better to start with. We can look at all the possibilities and see what will work the best."

They all got out of the van and the dogs raced off to explore. Matty, who had woken up as they came down from Hangman's Hill, climbed out and looked around at the new surroundings.

"Is this where we're going to live?" he asked Pip.

"Yes," she said, "hopefully."

"Which house will we be in?"

"We don't know yet. I expect we'll be sleeping in the van tonight."

"Why?"

"The thing is Matty," said Adam, "we have to sort some things out first. If you could keep an eye on the dogs, that would be really helpful."

"Alright," the boy said, and he ran off after the dogs, trying to round them up, but they would have none of it. Yvonne was looking through the windows of the farmhouse. Adam was stretching his back out by the van thinking what to do first. Pip came up and stood next to him.

"Thank you for keeping Matty entertained," Adam said, "I hope he wasn't too tiresome."

"No, he was fine. Thank you for driving – again. I heard some of what Yvonne was telling you. I think I'm starting to understand why she is the way she is."

"Are you? I guess she has had a tough time of it. Don't let on that you heard though – she thought you couldn't hear us."

"I won't," said Pip.

"OK, so what are we going to do first now then?"

"Well," said Pip, "how about we look at the farmhouse and see if we can find the keys to the other places."

Adam walked up to the front door and gave it a try. It was locked. The windows were closed and he did not want to break one unless he had to. He walked across to try the door of the stables, which adjoined the farmhouse on the left-hand side, but this too was locked, as he expected.

"Hmm," he said, "going to have to try the back. You coming?"

They walked back up to the lane and round to the back gate, which gave on to a gravelled parking area behind the two properties. Again there were no doors or windows open.

"How are we going to get in?" Pip asked.

"By a window – that would be easiest. But I need to think about which one would be best to break. I am going to get some tools." He walked quickly back to the van and Pip followed at her own pace. When he got there Yvonne was standing by the front door of the newer house on the right side of the farmhouse.

"This one's open," she called out. Adam walked over and joined her in front of the door, which now stood wide open.

"Well! That's a surprise. Well spotted Yvonne." He realised now that this property was actually a new construction. It was rather plain and featureless, with a central entrance door and windows symmetrically placed either side. He stepped into the hallway and discovered straightaway why Yvonne had stayed outside: the smell was overpowering. He stepped outside, took a deep breath and went back in, holding his nose. The hallway had doors issuing into the rooms at the front of the house, whilst at the back, beyond the staircase, he could see through to a large, modern kitchen. He glanced into the front rooms and then had a look into the kitchen. The body of a large dog lay across the floor. That would account for some of the smell, he thought. He walked back to the front door to get out into the fresh air when he noticed a large key box on the wall to the right of the door. Inside were several hooks with keys on, door keys of various sorts and vehicle keys. He grabbed all the keys except the vehicle ones and lurched outside. Yvonne and Pip were waiting, a few paces away.

"That's a bit high in there!" Adam said, after he had taken a few deep breaths. "But I think I have found the keys we need."

They quickly identified the keys for the farmhouse and the stables. They went to the farmhouse first. Adam turned the key in the lock and walked into the hallway. This house that he was calling the farmhouse was actually smaller than the more modern house where he got the keys. It seemed to be newly decorated in pastel colours and smelled fresh. A peep into the sitting room at the front told him that this was not a lived-in home, but a holiday rental. He let the others know that it was safe to enter, and went through into the back room, which was a modern, open-plan kitchen-diner. The back door gave out onto a little garden and the yard they had walked round to just before.

Adam went over to the sink and turned on the taps, and water came out. Pip and Yvonne came in and he said "Good news – we have water! From both taps. I'm going to have a quick look upstairs and see if I can find the tank."

He left them looking around the kitchen while he went up the steep staircase to the bedrooms. There were three rooms, all nicely decorated, all with beds made up. There was a small bathroom, again with water in the taps. On the landing there was a locked door. With some trial and error, he found the key and opened it. He had not brought his torch, but he could see by the light coming through the bedroom window that there was a hot water cylinder which was fed from a pipe from above. He guessed that was the cold-water tank and when he ran the hot tap for a while, he could hear the tank filling up. There was water and it was flowing. Where from, he would investigate later.

The other two had come up to see the bedrooms, so he told them about the water tank. They went back down to the hall and just at that moment the two dogs came in, closely pursued by Matty. All three had muddy feet and Adam just managed to head them off before they could get any further into the house.

"Whoa! You're not coming in here like that, and you Matty – you're covered in mud!"

Pip asked. "Matty, what *have* you been doing?"

"The dogs found a pond and went in to chase the ducks. I tried to stop them and I got my feet wet."

"I'll say!" said Adam, "Come on you lot, outside. Matty you need to find some clean dry grass to clean your shoes. And don't come in here or the other house until you have got cleaned up."

Matty looked sheepish, then trudged back outside with the dogs.

"That's the hazard of being on a farm," Yvonne said, "It's a very nice cottage though. Shall we look at the other one?"

They went to the small dwelling next door, which had a sign outside saying 'The Stables'. This was a smaller house, single storey with a bedroom in the attic and a small bedroom and bathroom on the ground floor. It was open plan, with a large kitchen dining room, which had a sitting area at one end. The taps had water. Like the farmhouse, The Stables was modern, clean and bright and ready for holiday guests. Pip came back down from the attic room and announced, "This will do me nicely."

"The bedroom, you mean?" said Yvonne.

"No, the whole place," Pip said, quite straight-faced.

"Well, I think that would be a bit selfish... oh, I see." Yvonne gave a half-smile. Adam was admiring the kitchen area.

"They have done these places up very nicely, I must say. It looks like they had bookings imminently, maybe even for the virus weekend."

"Like we had at Serendipity," Pip said.

"OK. It's just gone six," Adam said, as they stepped outside. "We've got another couple of hours of daylight to get some food organised, get the sleeping arrangements sorted and get Matty settled somewhere for the night. We also need to think about how many lamps we have. *And* I want to get the radio set up and see if we can make contact with Micky. I don't know if anyone else is hungry yet but I am and I expect Matty is too, so I think we should aim to eat fairly soon and then we can talk over dinner. What do you say?"

"I could eat something soon," Pip said

"And me," said Yvonne. "I don't mind putting something together while you get on and get the radio set up. Did you have anything in mind?"

"No, not really," Adam said. "You'll have to improvise with what's there. And whatever it is we can wash it down with a bottle of wine – toast our first night at Whitehouse Farm. Or is it Holmwood? I'm not sure now."

"We can call it whatever we like now, can't we?" said Pip, "New start, new owners, new name?"

"I don't think we can call ourselves the owners," Yvonne said.

"I don't see why not. But maybe new tenants would be better."

They went back to the farmhouse and helped Yvonne go through the larder until she found some ingredients they could use to put together a meal. Adam left them to decide the sleeping arrangements for the night and they decided that they would sleep in the farmhouse, and Pip said, magnanimously, that as Yvonne was older, she should have the large front room and she would take the small room with the single bed. It was agreed that, for tonight, Matty should sleep in the over-cab compartment and Adam would make a bed up in the van with the dogs. He felt it was only fair that, as Pip had taken responsibility for looking after Matty in the daytime, Adam should take care of him at night and let Pip get some sleep.

Once that was agreed, Pip helped Adam move the girls' cases into their respective rooms. When they were up in the large front bedroom, Adam asked Pip if she was happy with what had been agreed.

"I'm OK with that," the girl answered, "I mean it's not as if I can't change my mind later, is it? But how about you? Why don't you and Matty sleep in the stables?"

"Maybe tomorrow we might. It would be nice to be able to stretch out in a real bed again. But I think it's best if we don't change his routine too much all at once. He doesn't like being on his own at night. And this way, one of us at least can get a good night's sleep."

"Well, if you're sure... but we could swap another night. I quite liked my tiny bedroom in the van. Well, except for the sun coming in early in the morning, and the lack of privacy."

"There you are then. You can have your own private bedroom in the house with no interruptions."

Back in the kitchen they found a rather muddy-looking Matty playing with his new cars on the table. Two weary-looking dogs were sitting on the floor by the kitchen area keeping a very close eye on Yvonne who was going back and forth to the campervan to attend to the culinary operations.

"I've told him he needs to put his cars away now as we are going to have supper soon," Yvonne said.

"Come on then Matty, do as Yvonne said," Pip said. "Oh, look at the state of you – you're covered in mud! And look at what you've done to your new jeans and trainers. We're going to have to get you cleaned up."

Matty looked at his clothes and, with a look of surprise, saw the mud.

"Sorry Pip," he said, with what looked like genuine remorse. "I was only playing with the dogs."

"It's no use apologising to me. It's your own clothes you have ruined."

"They're only a little bit muddy. Can't you wash them?"

"No, I can't, actually," Pip said indignantly. You need to get them off and get in the shower."

"Do I have to? I don't like the shower."

"You liked it well-enough the other day. Come on."

"I wants to have a shower on my own. My mum lets me, and I don't want to take my clothes off in front of her."

"Who's *Her*?" Adam asked.

"Miss."

"*Her* does have a name, you know. It's Yvonne," said Yvonne, in a schoolmistressy voice.

"Sorry miss, I mean Vonne."

"It's ***Y***vonne. And I'm no longer a miss as I am married."

"Yes miss, I mean, E-vonne."

"That's alright Matty," Yvonne said, laughing. Go and have your shower now."

Adam left Pip to sort Matty out while he fed the dogs. Then he set about getting the radio wired up. He ran the aerial out through a window and up along the wall, hoping it would give a good signal. The farm was in open country, but they were near some very large metal buildings here and Adam was not sure what effect they might have. It didn't take him long to get the radio working, and he scanned through the wave bands, trying to pick an intelligible sound amidst all the static. At one wavelength he could hear what sounded like music, but it was very distorted and it could just have been noise. Somewhere else he thought he heard a snatch of human voice but though he hovered around that frequency for fifteen minutes, he did not hear it again. When Yvonne announced that dinner was ready, he tuned into Micky's frequency and left it on so they could all hear if he came on air.

Yvonne had managed to create a casserole out of a medley of ingredients and they all fell to it hungrily. Adam had opened one of the special bottles of wine he had got from Micky's warehouse.

"A toast to the new home!" he said, and they all echoed it.

"To the team!" Pip offered, and that was endorsed.

"And to our driver," said Yvonne, smiling at Adam, and clinking his glass.

They all praised Yvonne on her casserole and Matty joined in with "to E-vonne!"

As they set to their supper, they talked about the day's events. Then Pip related some of her earlier adventures with Adam and had them all laughing with her account of the acquisition of the Drifter and the tedious driving around Wellington trying to find a road with a name that might have some connection with Tavistock, where Adam's cousin lived.

"Tavistock – what would you think of? Towns in the West Country? Market towns of southern England? Oh no, nothing obvious like that. Brainbox here spies Fitzroy Close and says, all matter-of-fact, '*Here we are then, it will be on this estate*' and I'm thinking, how does he work that out? You'd never guess the connection, Yvonne."

"Mm, no, I can't' think of one," Yvonne said

"Well next we saw Euston Drive."

"Oh, yes, I see. Fitzroy Square, Euston Square, Tavistock Square."

Pip looked at her and rolled her eyes.

"Another brainbox, I might have guessed," she said, tossing her head back. "I don't know any of those places. Where I come from, we have the Bullring and New Street; Euston is a station, and Fitzroy is certainly too posh for the likes of us. I thought Adam was a genius, but I guess it's just that I'm a stupid Brummie." And with that she pulled a dopey-looking face.

Matty who found this ever-so funny laughed loudly, which made the others laugh too. The conversation stayed light, as they chatted about other silly things they had done since V Day, and it seemed that everyone was happy, for the moment, to put aside thoughts of the future, or the painful events of the Virus weekend.

Adam noticed that he was getting through most of the bottle of wine on his own, but, what the hell! They had got to the farm and taken the first steps to establish a home – wasn't that a good reason to relax and celebrate, just a little? Looking at the others smiling and chatting, he felt a warmth, a camaraderie with this small band of companions that he had known for such a short period of time. He wasn't sure how Yvonne might fit into the picture yet, but he definitely felt that in Pip and Matty he had acquired a new family, not that they could ever replace the family he had lost. There were big challenges ahead, but now was the time to make bonds and enjoy the small pleasures.

After they had finished supper they got everything cleared away and washed up. Matty was reluctant to go to bed, so Pip and Yvonne went off to the farmhouse to get unpacked and settled in their new rooms. Yvonne came back to have a shower and Adam warned her that there was not a lot of hot water. He was concerned about how much juice there was in the battery so, just in case, he started up the van to keep it charged, which meant he then had to explain to Matty, who thought they might be going somewhere else.

The boy then said, "Will you read me a story?"

"I don't think we have any story books in the van, Matty. I'm sorry."

"Can you tell me a story like you did the other night. I liked that one."

Though surprised, Adam was quietly chuffed. "Alright," he said, "now where had we got to?"

"Tell me about the frog who turned into a man."

"Oh yes, well there was a big flash and the frog was gone, but in his place stood a tall, handsome, prince."

"Was he very rich?" the boy asked, very seriously.

"Oh yes, of course. He was the son of the king – remember?."

"Was his dad the king?"

"Yes, that's right."

"Was his dad nice to him?"

"Hmm, no, I don't think he was very nice. But that was because he was ill and that's why the prince had to find a wife. You see, once he had a wife he could take over as king and rule the kingdom." Adam went on to weave an impromptu and improbable story about the prince and his golden camper-van, his pet dogs and a monkey called Pippin. Matty sat in his bed, rapt, as Adam talked. He was reminded of Oscar, who used to love a bedtime story. When he saw the boy's eyes starting to droop, he wound up the story and brought it to a conclusion, closing the imaginary book in his hands. Matty looked at him and then said sleepily, but very earnestly

"A-dam, is you my dad now?"

Adam almost laughed, but stopped himself. "Would you like me to be your dad, Matty?"

"Yes."

"Well then, that's settled. I'll be your new dad. What do you think?"

The boy didn't respond. He had got the answer he wanted and he snuggled down under his covers and immediately fell asleep.

The radio was still hissing with static but there had been no call from Micky and it was after eight now, so Adam turned it off. The sun was low in the sky behind the barns and he could see a pink tinge on the small white clouds overhead. He decided to go out for a walk and catch the sunset. He found his boots, put his sweatshirt around his shoulders and headed outside. He poked his head into the farmhouse and told Pip that Matty was asleep and that he was taking the dogs for a walk. He took the track he had taken last Saturday, up towards the spring, and then carried on up the hill behind. At the top of the hill was a tumulus surrounded by an open expanse of grassland commanding a fine view in all directions.

He looked back down the path to their farm and was surprised to see just how many buildings there were on the site. Mostly they were agricultural buildings, but there were also some ruined cottages or stores, built of stone. Behind the farm, a little way off, he could see a large house with some other buildings clustered around it. He couldn't see how the place was accessed, though there seemed to be a farm drive coming down from the north. He would have to investigate that tomorrow, he thought. To the south there was a line of green hills and, beyond, he caught glimpses of the sea, where small pink clouds seemed to bob along the horizon. It was very quiet as he sat on the grass at the top of the hill and the dogs were content to sit down beside him, survey the view and sniff the breeze. The air was cool up here, and he hugged his sweatshirt around his shoulders as he watched the shadows creeping up the hill opposite.

It was a fortnight now, he reflected, since he had got home that Friday to find his family ill and Jo struggling to cope with tending the little ones. A fortnight only, yet it was hard now, as he sat here looking over the darkening Dorset countryside, to think of himself back in Reading, to remember how life used to be before the world changed for ever. He started thinking about Jo, the last time they properly had together, the last evening before the virus came. He remembered that they had sat on the sofa in the sitting room and Jo wanted to talk. She wasn't happy at work, she felt frustrated and unfulfilled but didn't know what to do about it. But there was more, he remembered now. That conversation had petered out when, out of the blue, she asked him how he would cope if she wasn't around. "What do you mean?" he asked, but when he pressed her on what she was talking about, she just laughed it off and changed the subject. He was tired and hadn't thought much of it at the time but later, as he was drifting off to sleep, he wondered whether there was something more. And then the next day the virus came, his world changed for ever and he forgot all about it.

Thinking about it now, two weeks later, was she talking about dying? She had had some blood tests a while before but had told him they were all clear. Did she know something that she hadn't shared with him? Had she had a premonition of her death? He would never know the answer to that but in hindsight the conversation was strangely prescient. She had indeed gone away, and so had the children, so had the rest of the world. Now here he was, in this place with these total strangers - to try and make a new life?

The events of that terrible weekend were etched deep into his memory and yet they lay below the surface. Everything that had happened since, everything that had brought them to the farm – this was the new life. His former existence with Jo and the children, the world before V Day – that was a different life. It was as if, in that awful, cataclysmic event, he had died and been reincarnated as a new Adam, in a completely new world. Tomorrow he would have to put his mind to the future, but for now, as the evening slowly darkened into that strange in-between period of twilight, he just wanted to pause in this moment, this small space between lives.

He turned his gaze back towards the setting sun and saw there was a wall of dark cloud rolling in from the West. It looked like a weather front was coming in and there would be no lingering sunset glow this evening. A breeze got up and he shivered. At that moment everything that he had envisaged for the new life they would create at the farm seemed far off. The vision for the future which he had been peddling to Pip and Yvonne, and everyone else they had met, seemed clouded and obscured. How could he ever contemplate that these four people, this little nuclear family, could survive, let alone thrive, in this new world? How long would they have fuel? How long would they have enough food to eat? How long before an illness struck which they could not battle? Now that they had finally got to the promised land, what exactly was it promising? Hard labour, suffering, loneliness, desperation? If he really looked into the future, that was all he could see. Was survival ever a serious option? The very task of living started to look daunting to him now.

At that moment Bonzo suddenly took off back down the path and Adam turned to see Pip walking up to join him.

"Hey you!" she said, breathless as she came close. "You could have waited for me. I was just about to give up trying to find you and go back before it got too dark."

"Sorry. I felt I just had to get out and get a feel for the place before I turned in."

Pip sat down beside him, hands around her knees, looking at the view. The dogs settled either side of them, like bookends.

"You know," said Pip, "I have good feeling about this place. I think you've chosen well."

Adam turned his gaze back from the advancing gloom and said, "Thank you, that's good to hear. I was just starting to wonder if I've been kidding myself with this whole farm community idea. I mean, can we really do this, you know – this little family?"

"Hey, don't go all wobbly on me now. You got us all here, didn't you? And you saved my life, and Matty's and probably Yvonne's too."

"Well, that's a bit of an exaggeration..."

"No, you did, you really did," Pip said. "Adam, we can do this thing, you know we can. We can do anything!"

"I hope you're right," he sighed, looking away into the distance. Then he turned and smiled at the small, dark girl he had spent so much time with this last week and gave her a squeeze.

"You know what, Pip, you *are* right. I think we probably can."

The End

About the author

Alan Michael Butler

Alan grew up in Dorset and Hampshire before going to Aberystwyth to study English Literature. He moved to Oxford, where he broadened his education working in the theatre and the wine trade. Latterly he has worked in finance and education.

Alan has a deep love of the countryside and is a keen walker and photographer. Two years ago he completed a walk the length of England, which he documented in a series of photo journals, *From Bournemouth to Berwick*. He lives now in Wiltshire, where he can easily access beautiful countryside both in Cotswolds and on the Wiltshire Downs.

Alan writes poetry and short stories. *Quiet World* is his first full-length novel, the idea for which grew out of the eerie peacefulness of the first Covid lockdown where nature carried on as normal while our lives were so altered.

The sequel to this book, *In the Heat of Summer*, will be coming out in 2026

Printed in Dunstable, United Kingdom

75132864R00282